GREEN-EYED DEMON

Jaye Wells

www.orbitbooks.net

ORBIT

First published in Great Britain in 2011 by Orbit

A CIP catalogue record for this book
is available from the British Library.

ISBN 978-1-84149-758-7

Printed in the UK by CPI Mackays, Chatham, ME5 8TD

Papers used by Orbit are natural, renewable and recyclable
products sourced from well-managed forests and certified
in accordance with the rules of the Forest Stewardship Council.

Mixed Sources
Product group from well-managed
forests and other controlled sources
www.fsc.org Cert no. SGS-COC-004081
© 1996 Forest Stewardship Council

FSC

Orbit
An imprint of
Little, Brown Book Group
100 Victoria Embankment
London EC4Y 0DY

An Hachette UK Company
www.hachette.co.uk

www.orbitbooks.net

Dedicated in memory of two of the best
storytellers I've known:

Charlotte Hughes, one of my first uppity-woman
role models, who also taught me about
strength and forgiveness.

Jay Migues, my favorite Cajun and the embodiment
of laissez les bons temps rouler.

Graves at my command
Have waked their sleepers, oped, and let 'em forth
By my so potent art.
But this rough magic
I here abjure.
— William Shakespeare, *The Tempest*

*O*n my extensive list of enemies, the top two spots belonged to Lavinia Kane and time. One I planned to kill as soon as possible. That is, if I didn't run out of the other one first.

The dashboard clock flipped to 10:01. The ones mocked me like two extended middle fingers. Impatience was my third enemy.

I'd already been sitting in the white van parked on a windy stretch of road near Pacific Palisades for twenty minutes. The hood of the van stood open, but the engine idled in preparation for the ambush.

"Giguhl, any visual on the car yet?"

"Negative." His voice crackled through the earpiece, but his body was perched in a tree just outside the Dominae compound.

I sighed. "Okay, thanks."

"Don't you mean 'roger'?" he responded.

"Whatever," I said. "Let me know the minute the gates open."

"Hey, Sabina?"

"Yeah?" I said a tad more impatiently than I intended.

"Why can't I have a gun again?"

I rolled my eyes. "I might be crazy, but I'm not stupid, G. Now focus."

"I live to serve," he grumbled.

I settled back into the seat. Outside the van, the landscape offered little distraction from my impatience. Scrub brush, low stone walls, and roadkill speed bumps. Light from the City of Angels rose above the shadowed hilltops like a dusty halo.

Los Fucking Angeles.

Whoever said you couldn't go home again was full of shit. The truth is you *shouldn't* go home again. And when I'd left California, I'd promised myself that I wouldn't return. Ever. But Fate—that fickle bitch—made a liar out of me. Again.

Three days earlier, my twin sister, Maisie, had been kidnapped from a mage estate in New York. Three weeks before that I hadn't even known she'd existed. The long-story–short version is our vampire mother died in childbirth a few months after our mage father was murdered. Because mating between the races was forbidden, Maisie and I were separated at birth by our vampire and mage grandmothers to keep the peace. Maisie was raised by the mage side of the family in New York, and I got the short straw—a vampire upbringing in Los Angeles. The desire to meet my long-lost twin was one of the reasons I'd left Los Angeles.

The fact our vampire grandmother, Lavinia Kane, wanted me dead was the other.

But now the tables had turned. Lavinia had kidnapped

Maisie in an effort to hurt me. So now I would do a little kidnapping of my own.

Giguhl's voice bounced off my eardrum, making me jump. "Big Black is on the move. Should be on your tail in T minus sixty seconds."

A sudden rush of blood. My hands tightened on the wheel. Showtime.

"Be ready when I summon you," I replied in a calm tone.

"Ten-four."

In my previous life as an assassin, I'd disposed of problem vampires for the Dominae. Therefore, despite the personal stakes and the adrenaline surge, my body had kicked instinctively into mission mode.

I shifted the car into drive. The sweat on my palm meant it took two tries to manage.

"Hey, Red?" This from Adam Lazarus—hottie mage and the third member of our little team. We used to have a fourth—a Vanity demon—but she'd been kicked off the team twenty-four hours earlier after an unfortunate incident involving a vampire strip club, a large explosion, and a lover's quarrel with Giguhl.

"Yeah?"

"Are *you* ready?" The mage always had a frustrating knack for breaking through the insulating layers I'd built around my feelings. Damn him.

Two pinpoints of light turned onto the road several blocks back. I took a deep breath and willed my heart to slow. "Are you kidding?" I snorted. "Totally."

He knew me too well to buy that. "We'll get her back, Sabina." His tone had a hint of unwelcome pity.

I ignored the spark of fear that flared at his words. "Of

course we will." Not getting Maisie back was not an option. "Okay, everyone, switching to radio silence. Let's do this."

My hands contracted on the steering wheel, my knuckles pale in the dim light. I tried not to focus on the only glitch in our plan: We were about to kidnap the wrong Domina.

In a perfect world, the vampire in that Mercedes would be my grandmother. When she'd taken Maisie, she'd sealed her fate with me. Although, to be honest, she was pretty much at the top of my "must-kill list" for a host of other reasons that included manipulation, lying, kidnapping, attempted murder, and the destruction of my prized Ducati.

Yeah, I know. We make the Manson Family look like the Brady Bunch.

Anyway, Lavinia wasn't an option for the kidnapping plan, because she rarely left the Dominae compound. But Persephone left the grounds each Tuesday to host a mass for the plebian vamps at a temple located in Santa Monica. And with the war between vampires and mages looming, the Dominae needed to spread anti-mage propaganda to strengthen support for the war. Where better to do that than at a religious service?

Besides, of the three Dominae who ruled the vampire race, Persephone was the weakest. *Weak* is relative when discussing ancient female vampires, of course. But Persephone tended to be more interested in preserving history and promoting spiritualism among the vampire bourgeoisie than in crushing opposition or amassing obscene fortunes like the other two Dominae. That meant she'd be far easier to manipulate than Lavinia or Tanith—the Beta

Domina, who controlled their business interests. The plan was to nab Persephone and deliver her to the faery and mage leaders for interrogation and a possible hostage exchange. Simple.

If we survived.

The Mercedes was about two blocks back now. A few car lengths behind that, I spied the headlights of the beater pickup we'd boosted. Adam held the truck back at a conservative distance as he waited for my signal.

"Wait for it," I said, my eyes glued to the mirror. When the target was a block back, I tensed my foot over the gas pedal. "Nothing to see here." With each turn of the sedan's wheels, my heart picked up speed. "Just a broken-down van."

Almost there.

The Mercedes' dark-as-midnight windows prevented me from counting heads. Looked like we were going to have to do this the hard way, as usual.

"Now!"

I punched the accelerator. The tires spun for a moment on gravel before jumping out onto the road. Squealing brakes and a blaring horn. Every muscle rigid as I braced for impact. The scream of crunching metal. Vertigo and pain as the van tipped and slid several hundred feet. The seat belt dug into my skin but kept me from being tossed around like loose change in a dryer. When the world stilled again, ominous silence reigned. Scratch that, not silence exactly. The van's radiator hissed, and someone was groaning.

Oh, right. That was me.

"Now, Giguhl!" I grunted. With a punch of the button, my seat belt spat me at the passenger's door.

A burst of light flashed outside the van, signaling Giguhl's arrival. Shouting and gunfire commenced on the road. I crawled into the van's cargo area. The cooler I'd stashed earlier lay near the door. I wrenched it open and grabbed a bag of blood. My fangs made quick work of the silicone casing. For once, the chemical taste of the blood didn't bother me as I gulped down the vampire version of a healing potion and energy drink in one.

The van's back doors wrenched open. I tumbled out and landed at Giguhl's hooves. He didn't waste time asking if I was okay. Instead, he hooked his claws under my arms and lifted. When my feet hit pavement and I swayed, he steadied me. Nodding my thanks, I pulled a gun from my waistband.

I turned to survey the scene. The Mercedes was trapped between the van and the pickup, which now sported an accordion for a fender. Just beyond, Adam approached the Mercedes from the rear.

"Go," I said to Giguhl. He moved so fast I could barely track his movement. The next thing I knew, he was crouched next to the Mercedes. I aimed my gun at the driver's side and pulled off two rounds. Only instead of shattering the windshield, the bullets left spiderwebs on the bulletproof glass.

The Mercedes' engine roared and the van lurched a few inches forward. The car's wheels spun, kicking up a plume of smoke and gravel. "Adam?" I called.

"I'm on it!" The hair on the back of my neck prickled as he cast a spell over the lurching car. The engine emitted a loud death rattle before finally dying.

"Look alive, that's probably one-way gla—"

A bullet exploded from the passenger's side of the

windshield. I ducked and rolled, coming up in a crouch near the intersection of the Mercedes and the van's undercarriage. "Now, G!"

With a predatory smile, the demon punched a hole through the driver's window. Crucial design flaw of bulletproof glass? It can't keep out a determined demon. Using one massive claw, Giguhl reached in like a cat into a fish tank and pulled out the wriggling vamp from behind the wheel.

"Giguhl! Catch!" Adam yelled. He tossed an applewood stake at the demon, who caught it with his free claw. Two seconds later, the vamp ignited as his soul escaped and his ashes scattered to the wind.

"There's a metal partition. I can't get to them this way," Giguhl yelled as he reached in for the passenger.

"Got it!" I sidestepped my way toward the back door. Adam approached the one on the other side. A couple more bullets zinged at us through the glass but went wide. That's the problem with one-way glass. Bullets can get through from the inside, but the layered glass makes anything but point-blank range inaccurate.

At least that's what I thought until Adam yelped and his head dropped out of sight behind the car.

"Shit! Adam?" My heart thudded in my chest like a piston. It's one thing to shoot at me, but it was something else to hurt the mage.

"I'm okay. Just missed me."

My pulse slowed from panicked to pissed.

More shots exploded out from the rear windows. I ducked next to a quarter panel, trusting the car's armored walls to protect me.

"Giguhl!"

"Got my hands full," he grunted. I looked over and saw him crouching under the busted window. Two bullets zinged over his horns. While the driver had been taken by surprise, the passenger was using Giguhl for target practice.

Time to end this shit. I banged a fist on the hood. "Come out with your hands up and no one else gets hurt."

Two shots exploded from the back window. I cursed under my breath. Looked like we had ourselves a regular Mexican standoff until someone ran out of bullets.

"Sabina?" I barely heard Giguhl over the constant barrage of gunfire.

"What?"

"If I create a distraction, can you take this guy out?"

I nodded. "Be careful."

His black lips spread into a grin. "Yes, ma'am."

He held up a claw. He counted down from three with his talons. On one, he leapt up onto the roof of the car and began rocking it side to side. I jumped toward the open window. The vamp's attention was on the ceiling of the car as he held on for dear life.

"Hey!" I yelled. His head turned, and his eyes widened a nanosecond before I delivered a bullet into the center of his forehead. His body ignited, making a mess of the Corinthian leather.

"Nice!" Giguhl said, pumping a fist as he jumped off the roof.

I wiped a hand across my brow. "Too early to start celebrating, G."

As if to support my claim, a new volley of gunfire came from the back of the car. Giguhl and I squatted down and duckwalked toward the front bumper. I met the mage's eyes over the hood. "Any ideas?"

"None that don't involve one of us gaining an extra orifice."

Toward the end, his voice sounded unnaturally loud. That's when I realized the gunfire had ceased. The sudden silence jarred me into stillness. I narrowed my eyes and watched the back door. The car started rocking again, but this time from inside. Something was going down in the back seat.

I scooted along the side of the car toward the back, careful to stay out of sight. Muffled shouts leaked from bullet holes in the window. Two voices—one male, one female—argued with increasing volume. The car continued to shake until, suddenly, a single gunshot cut off the male's shout. Little wisps of copper-scented smoke leaked from the holes.

"You okay, mancy?" I whisper-shouted at Adam in the unnatural silence that followed.

"All clear," he replied. "But I wouldn't mind someone telling me what the fuck is going on."

That made two of us.

Two seconds later we got our answer when the door next to my head flew open. The panel knocked me on my ass. The gun slicked against my palm. My breath came out in pants as I raised my aim up the height of the door.

A mop of kinky mahogany curls cleared the top of the door. And below, a foot clad in a low-heeled black pump stepped onto the blacktop, followed by its twin. Next, a slender, milky hand with bloodied cuticles grasped the doorframe.

When the face came into view, my stomach dipped with dread. Persephone's classically beautiful face didn't feature a Roman nose, two beady black eyes, or a butt-cleft chin. No, only one Domina was cursed with such mannish features.

Tanith.

I suddenly wanted to vomit all over those sensible but unattractive shoes. Besides being the ugliest of the three, she was also the smartest and a mistress of the bitchly arts. In other words, she was a complication I didn't need. With a shaky hand, I kept the gun's unblinking eye trained on the Domina. "Tanith? What. The. Fuck?"

The businesslike smile accentuated Tanith's unfortunate features.

"Sabina," she said. "Forgive my presumption in killing the final guard. But time is money and the wait was growing tiresome."

I blinked in surprise. Giguhl came up behind my back. His claws hooked under my arms and lifted. My feet hit the ground without my aim ever straying from its target. Adam skidded around the trunk to take up position behind one of the most powerful vampires alive.

"Why did you kill your own guard?"

She scowled and crossed her arms. "Your ambush was an unwelcome surprise at first, but as I sat there waiting for my guards to dispose of you I had a sudden flash of inspiration." She shrugged. "Killing that last guard was the most expedient course of action."

"What did this flash of inspiration entail exactly?" Adam asked.

The Domina barely spared the mage a scornful glance. With her eyes on me, she said, "Before we discuss that, perhaps you should enact the escape portion of your plan before the backup those guards called arrives." She paused and narrowed her eyes at us. If she'd been wearing spectacles, she would have lowered them down her nose. "You do have an escape plan, don't you?"

Even with my gun, a demon, and a mage surrounding her, she stared us down like we were incompetent underlings.

"Of course we have an escape plan. But I'm seriously considering aborting this mission altogether unless you explain yourself. Why did you help us?"

She tilted her head like something I said didn't compute. "I'm helping myself. Or rather, you will be helping me. I assume your plan is to trade me for your sister?"

I squinted at her, neither confirming nor denying. But her unmitigated gall left me speechless. Like I'd ever help a Domina again after everything they'd put me through.

"Do you honestly believe Lavinia will agree to a trade?" Tanith snorted. "Of course you do. You get that naiveté from your mage side."

I took a long cleansing breath through my nose. "How about you spend a little less time insulting me and a lot more time explaining why you think I'd ever help you."

"Because I know where Maisie is. And I have a plan that not only helps you save her, but also ensures this distasteful war business is taken off the table forever."

"Where is she?" I demanded.

"She's not in Los Angeles. That's all I'm willing to tell you until I have certain assurances from both the Hekate Council and Queen Maeve."

"Now who's being naive? Or are you forgetting the army you sent a few days ago to kill off most of the mages in New York?"

She held up a finger. "Correction. Lavinia sent that army. It wasn't until after the attack that she told Persephone and me that she's formed an alliance with the Caste of Nod."

The Caste of Nod is a mysterious sect made up of members of all the dark races. As far as I could tell, their goal was to cause me a lot of fucking problems. In New York, they'd orchestrated several attempts on my life because they thought I was destined to unite all the dark races. That's the last thing they wanted, because only an all-out war between the races would bring on the second coming of Lilith. In other words, they were total wackos. And homicidal ones, at that.

"Assuming I believe Lavinia acted without your knowledge, why haven't you confronted her?"

She laughed—an awkward, insincere sound. "Surely you haven't been away long enough to forget how things work here. Confronting the Alpha Dominae is a death sentence."

I frowned. "But law dictates the three of you share power equally."

"Despite what the laws state, your grandmother has been the de facto leader of the vampire race for centuries. Persephone and I assist her in running things, of course, but she holds all the real power. At best, she could have the Under Council strip us of our titles. At worst, well…" She trailed off, knowing she didn't need to finish the thought. After all, I used to make my living being the worst-case scenario for vamps who pissed off the Dominae.

"What about Persephone?"

Worry lines creased her normally smooth forehead. "Unfortunately, Persephone remains loyal to Lavinia. She's too weak to be a real threat anyway. As for why I'm here, well, it's simple." She adjusted the French cuffs on her white shirt. "I'm double-crossing your grandmother." She paused to let the concussion from that bombshell sink in. "I'm going to help you find Maisie in return for the Hekate Council and the Queen's support in my plans."

"What plans?" I crossed my arms. This ought to be good.

"My plan to become the sole ruler of the Lilim, of course." Tanith's lips lifted, flashing a little fang. "In order to take control of the vampire race, I need Lavinia dead and an alliance with the Council and Queen Maeve in my pocket."

In the stunned silence that followed that announcement, I literally had no idea what to say to her. Instead, I glanced at Adam and waved my gun to indicate I needed a moment of his time. "Giguhl, watch her. She moves an inch, rip off her fucking head."

The Mischief demon cracked the knuckles of his claws and waggled his scraggly black brows at the ancient vampire. Tanith tapped her toe on the asphalt but otherwise remained unimpressed. With one last parting glare at the Domina, I went to join Adam for a private confab.

"What the fuck?" he asked, crossing his arms.

"That pretty much sums it up for me, too."

He nodded absently.

I continued, "I don't suppose we could just kill her now and save ourselves a lot of trouble."

He gave me one of his Sabina-be-reasonable looks. "Red, I know it's a curveball, but our goal was to kidnap a Domina, right?"

"Yeah, but—"

"The way I see it, we have two choices." He counted the options off on his fingers. "We can stand here all night questioning her motives and risk becoming bull's-eyes for more of her guards. Or we can continue with the plan and get her to a place filled with heavily armed guards of our own and let the leaders sort it out."

Twenty feet beyond Adam, Giguhl called. "I vote for C) Stop yapping and get the hell out of Dodge."

"I concur," Tanith added.

So much for talking in private.

Nosy demons and vampire leaders aside, I didn't like this one bit. But I wasn't any more interested in becoming target practice than he was. "Everyone circle up."

Tanith's impatient nod indicated her displeasure over further delays. I nodded to Giguhl. He grabbed the ancient vampire's arms and led her to the side of the road so Adam could work his magic.

A split second before Adam's whispered incantations dematerialized our bodies, a gun exploded from the tree line. Giguhl yelped, "Not again!" Then, just as suddenly, darkness and a rush of cold wind swept us away to the Seelie Court.

I'd never been to the Seelie Court before, but I knew it was located somewhere in North Carolina's Blue Ridge Mountains. So when we materialized in a dank cave instead of on a forested mountainside, I was a tad surprised.

A wet roar echoed off the damp stone walls and low ceiling. Turning, I realized the sound came from the curtain of water covering the cave's entrance. "Where are we exactly?" I shouted to Adam over the waterfall's racket.

"The middle of nowhere." He shot a meaningful look toward Tanith.

The Domina stood nearby, suffering Giguhl's restraining claw with dignity. At Adam's comment, a small smile quirked her lips.

I nodded, understanding he didn't want the Domina to be able to find this place on her own later. "So where's the court?"

He smiled and pointed to the wet, craggy wall on the far end of the cave. "Through there."

I blinked at the solid stone. "Why not just flash us in there directly?"

"The walls are warded to prevent unexpected guests. Which means we have to wait for someone inside to open the portal."

I relaxed a fraction. When we called Orpheus with the plan of kidnapping a Domina, he'd been pretty resistant at first. Said he didn't want to risk losing us *and* Maisie. But in the end, Adam and I convinced him that bold action was our only hope. It didn't hurt that he liked the idea of one-upping Lavinia, too. Once he'd given us a green light, we'd coordinated watches and plans so that once we arrived with our quarry, things would go smoothly.

"Is this gonna take long?" Giguhl said.

I frowned at the demon. "Why—you got somewhere else to be?"

He shot me a bitch-please look. "No but I'd like the record to state that getting shot in the ass still isn't fun." He shifted around to show me his left ass cheek where his black sweatpants now featured a perfectly round bullet hole. I couldn't see any blood in the dim light, but I could smell it.

"Sheesh, G, again?" Adam said.

"Yes, Mr. Perfect, again. Lucky for you bitches I'm a fast healer."

I was saved from having to respond to that when a tingle of magic rippled through the cave. The wall Adam pointed to earlier began to pulse and shimmer with flecks of light. The hair on my neck prickled, and the low thrum of magic made my stomach contract. One second the rock sparkled like fool's gold, and the next it disappeared altogether. On the other side of the portal, the silhouette of a female appeared.

"Who seeks entrance to the realm of Queen Maeve, leader of the Truatha de Danan?"

Adam stepped forward. His relaxed posture hinted at familiarity with this ritual. Not a surprise, since he'd spent time there a few weeks ago to broker an alliance with the Queen on behalf of the Hekate Council. "Adam Lazarus, Pythian Guard for the ancient and venerable Hekate Council, and my companions Sabina Kane, High Priestess of the Blood Moon and granddaughter of the Hekatian oracle Ameritat Graecus—goddess protect her soul—and Alpha Domina Lavinia Kane; Tanith Severinus, Beta Domina and prisoner of the Hekate Council, and Giguhl, fifth-level Mischief demon from the Gizal region of Irkalla."

I looked over my shoulder at Giguhl and rolled my eyes. But the faery on the other side of the portal followed the tongue-twisting protocol just fine.

"Knight Lazarus, you and your companions are expected. I, Calyx, keeper of the portal, on behalf of Queen Maeve, grant you entrance to the faery realm."

The sheet of magic wavered and disappeared with a pop. All formalities gone, Calyx waved us through with frantic movements. "Quickly."

Adam and I fell back so Giguhl and Tanith could go through first. By silent agreement, we both felt it important to get the Domina safely inside. Neither of us put it past the vamp to spring a last-minute trick on us.

Just beyond the opening, all I could see was darkness. Not a surprise, given it was nighttime, but I didn't like the idea of just strolling through a magical portal without knowing what waited on the other side. But Adam's firm hand on my back urged me through.

The second we'd cleared the plane separating the two

worlds, the gateway snapped shut. I took a moment to survey my surroundings. On this side, the entrance was hidden in a sheer rock wall climbing hundreds of feet in the air. I was looking up the rock face when Giguhl nudged me on the back. "Red, check it out."

I turned and stilled with my mouth hanging open. Looming ahead of us was a building that could only be described as the largest, most elaborate tree house in the history of ever. An engineering marvel made of glass and wood, the structure rose high above the forest floor.

Given its overwhelming size, I could only register flashes of details. Like how the moonlight glinted off hundreds of round windows. How the wooden bridges spanned between towers like spider silk. And how the carved balconies seemed to float on air.

As my eyes lowered, I finally noticed the line of fae guards forming a crescent behind Calyx. Two came forward immediately to take custody of Tanith. The ancient vampiress endured the exchange before saying, "I demand to see Queen Maeve this instant."

While her imperious tone was not a surprise, her impatience was ironic, given the complexity and length of most vampire protocol. Vampire Sabbath alone took four hours. And don't get me started on the red tape and time wasting at the Dominae's Under Council meetings. They made the IRS look efficient.

Anyway, half the guards turned and ushered Tanith away before I had a chance to argue. Although I wasn't really in a position to do so anyway. Our job had been to get the kidnapped Domina there. I didn't have much say in what the Hekate Council and the Queen did with her. Unfortunately.

I originally had assumed the other guards hung around to protect us. Until one came to stand next to me and another beside Giguhl. They didn't touch us, but it was apparent they weren't just being friendly. I opened my mouth to demand an explanation when Adam cleared his throat.

I shot him a glare.

"Keep it together, Red," Adam said. "The Queen isn't as flexible or forgiving as Orpheus."

I sighed and forced my shoulders to relax. Orpheus— or rather, High Councilman Orpheus of the Ancient and Venerable Hekate Council—was not what I would consider a flexible male. Sure, he'd been like a father to Maisie and had eventually warmed to me, but he also tended to be a tad impatient about my tendency to question any and all authority. And judging from Adam's comment, the Queen—who already wasn't my biggest fan—wouldn't find my smart mouth or rebellious ways charming, either. Gods save me from touchy leaders with their demands for "respect."

"Hurry," Calyx said. "We must not keep the Queen waiting."

I sucked in a breath and pasted a smile on my face. "Lead the way!"

Adam shot me a look that indicated I'd overdone it with the false cheer. Whatever. I just wanted to get inside and find out how to get my sister back. If that meant enduring persnickety regents and courtly etiquette, I'd deal.

Ten minutes and eleventy thousand steps later, we emerged from the spiral staircase hidden inside the massive tree that led from the forest floor up to the fortress. I guess the faeries decided if all their other security measures didn't work, they'd exhaust their enemies before they made it inside.

From the tree staircase, we emerged into a great hall. Tall convex windows curved up to a blond wood ceiling carved with elaborate Celtic designs. The effect was like standing in a bubble balanced in the tree canopy. Braziers set into the support posts around the room glowed warmly from some light source I couldn't name. Not fire, obviously, given the extremely flammable nature of the structure. But something else, some kind of faery magic.

Hundreds of faeries in all shapes and sizes representing the many species of fae filled the space. Despite the cultural variations in costume, they all wore jewel tones— the deep, saturated colors of rubies, amethysts, sapphires, emeralds, and topaz. I dismissed the eye-pleasing but oddly coordinated color scheme and focused on the familiar faces that broke free from the crowd.

Orpheus led a small procession of what was left of the Hekate Council. If we'd been in New York and in the Council's ceremonial chambers, they'd all have worn white Greek chitons that indicated their status. But since we were in the Queen's domain, they wore outfits reflecting their status as visiting diplomats instead—black slacks and different-colored Nehru-style jackets. The overall effect was very Star Trek, but I figured no one wanted to hear *that* opinion right then.

Behind the four members of the Council, Adam's aunt Rhea—who served as my magical mentor back in New York—followed with two Pythian Guards, who were the mage version of the secret service and special ops rolled into one. The small mage contingent approached Tanith and her fae guards with grim expressions.

Terse nods were shared before a loud knocking boomed through the cavernous room. Tension rose as everyone snapped to attention. The sea of fall colors began to part, opening a wide aisle down the center of the great room.

"Bow for Her Magnificence, Queen Maeve, defender of the Fae, sovereign of the Seelie Court, and most honorable Mother of Autumn." The tall, reedy male wearing an emerald green robe looked around the room expectantly. A heavy gold chain with a medallion hung on his chest. His regalia marked him as a very important faery, but the female who appeared from a door on the side of the room commanded everyone's attention.

As one, the entire room lowered into submissive bows. I didn't like kowtowing to anyone but went along with it to avoid inviting attention. Of course, that didn't keep me from peeking beneath my hair to gawk at the regent.

I'd heard many stories about Queen Maeve—few of them complimentary—so I expected her to present an impressive figure. But I hadn't expected her to look so...old.

Gray hair—not silver like Rhea's but wool-gray like she needed a good dousing with Miss Clairol—fell around a roadmap face. Her skin was the color of fresh cream but sagged around the jaw, like gravity was winning the tug-of-war against youth. If I'd been pressed to guess her age in human years, I'd say she looked to be in her midfifties. Hard midfifties.

She wore a midnight-blue silk tunic with strands of silver woven into an elaborate Celtic design on the high tab collar and wide cuffs. A silver band etched with the same pattern circled her forehead. Once she sat, her posture was as rigid as the wood of her throne, which was carved with leafless, skeletal trees and a waning moon. A large tapestry behind the throne depicted a crest bearing a cauldron, spear, shield, and boulder.

Orpheus began to lead all of us toward the Queen, but a bejeweled hand rose to halt our progress. She waved over the steward and whispered something to him. After a moment, he straightened and called out in a high, clear voice, "The mixed-blood and the demon are not welcome."

I stiffened in surprise. "What the—"

Rhea's papery-smooth hand found mine and squeezed hard. "Quiet, child."

"But—"

Adam nudged me with his elbow. I jerked my head in his direction, upset he wasn't getting my back on this. "She's still pissed about Banethsheh," he said in an undertone. "I promise I'll tell you everything after, but you have to chill."

The urge to rebel threatened. But then the Queen's cold eyes found mine and narrowed. That's when I realized Adam hadn't been overstating. Even though I'd killed the Queen's turncoat ambassador, Hawthorne Banethsheh, in self-defense, she obviously blamed me for the entire matter. Granted, I probably could have handled it better, but blaming me for his death was ridiculous. It's not like I forced Banethsheh to try to kill me on behalf of the Caste of Nod. But the Queen obviously was in no mood to be reasonable.

I held her gaze brazenly for a moment before backing down. I hated doing it, but I also knew that my presence in the room would only complicate an already tense situation. And right now it was more important to learn Maisie's location than to salve my wounded pride. Those around me let out a collective breath, as if they had been expecting a trademark Sabina outburst. I nodded at them and fell back to join Giguhl. The demon met my eyes, his expression both impressed and empathetic.

The procession moved forward. Adam turned to shoot me a grateful look, but the fae guards standing on either side of the massive maple doors closed it in his face. Which left Giguhl and me standing in the antechamber like two assholes without invites to the party of the year.

"Well, that sucked," I said.

Giguhl bumped my shoulder. "Oh, I don't know. If you think about it, it's probably for the best."

I looked up at him. "Why?"

"Face it, Red. Even if the Queen had forgiven you for setting fire to her ambassador, how long do you think you'd have lasted in there before your big mouth had her calling for your head?"

I pursed my lips. "You have a point."

He put an arm around my shoulder. "Of course I do."

A throat cleared behind us. Calyx, the fae who'd led us in, stood by the doors. A fae guard stood behind her with a long sword resting in a sheath on his back.

"If you'll follow me," Calyx said, "I'll show you to the Autumn Garden. Your mate will join you there once he has been excused by the Queen."

I went still when she said "mate." Part of me longed to correct her. Tell her Adam wasn't my mate at all. Just a good friend. A fighting partner. But the snort from Giguhl's mouth and the knowing look in his goat-slit eyes told me it'd be best not to acknowledge the mistake.

"Yeah, okay," I said. "Let's go see this garden, I guess."

I'll give the faeries this: They know how to rock some landscaping. The Autumn Garden took my breath away, which is saying something, because I rarely notice nature. A dozen varieties of maples in brilliant yellows, crimsons, and oranges unfurled like colorful parasols against the green, blue, and gold of the conifers. Elaborate Japanese bridges spanned lily-dotted ponds. The same faery lights I'd seen in the throne room hung here from metal lanterns, which cast a golden glow on the river-rock pathways. And set on small islands in the ponds, among the splashes of jeweled koi, were elaborate pagoda-shaped birdhouses. The winged garden sprites who lived in them flitted among branches and leaves like spastic fireflies. Their high-pitched conversations sounded like birdsong as they buzzed near the edge of the pond where we sat.

Despite the idyllic setting, I was ready to storm back inside and demand entrance to the great room. My ass ached from the bench, and my cuticles were bloody and sore from my nervous chewing. And if I had to listen to one more minute of my demon's increasingly pathetic and creepy attempts to get a piece of rebound faery ass, I was going to cut a bitch.

"You ever let a demon through your portal before?" he purred to Calyx. The tip of one claw swirled lazy circles in the mossy pond water.

"Um, I don't think so," she said hesitantly, looking around like she couldn't wait to escape.

He winked at the faery. "Trust me, sweet cheeks, you'd remember having a demon in your portal."

I rolled my eyes and waved away a garden sprite who buzzed too close to my ear.

"Bitch," it squeaked.

Hoping to escape the awkward come-ons and think in peace, I went to pace on the bridge. My skin felt too tight and my head buzzed with possible outcomes to the meeting. I still couldn't believe the Queen had banned me from the proceedings. Normally I'd be pissed that no one stood up for me, but in the grand scheme of things, my pride wasn't as important as progress in finding Maisie. Still, it rankled. If it weren't for me they wouldn't have Tanith at all.

If it weren't for you, Maisie wouldn't have been kidnapped in the first place, my conscience whispered. I squinted against the memory of the message Lavinia left for me to find when she'd taken Maisie out from under my nose: a white canvas with the word "checkmate" written in blood. That round had gone to my grandmother, but I was tired of playing games. I just wanted to my sister back, and then I wanted to focus on building a new life that didn't include prophecies or politics.

Only clear heads and unemotional logic would

accomplish those goals. Sitting around mooning over how it all made me feel was a waste of time. I just wished Tanith's supposed defection hadn't thrown such a wrench in the plans. Our original strategy was elegant in its simplicity: Kidnap Persephone and trade her for Maisie.

But now we not only had the wrong Domina, but that one that suddenly claimed to be an ally. If it were up to me, I'd continue with the original plan. The problem was my goals and the goals of the Hekate Council and the Queen were not the same.

I was no stranger to the push-pull between leaders and the foot soldiers they used to carry out their plans. The minute you added political or diplomatic concerns to a mission, you were asking for complications. And I worried those complications might make saving my sister less important to the leadership than preventing war.

So, I had to admit that even though in the long run peace was preferable to this constant state of almost-war, my preference was to trade Tanith, save Maisie, and let the bullets fall where they may.

Of course, the other option was that Tanith was full of shit and she'd been sent by Lavinia to fuck us over. Either way, I didn't see anything positive about Tanith's declaration of independence from Lavinia.

A sharp pain in my hand cut my thoughts short. I looked down to realize I'd gripped the bridge's railing so tight that a shard of wood had broken off and embedded itself in my palm. Gods, I was losing it. I hadn't even realized I'd stopped pacing until that moment. I took a deep breath and removed the wood. The small wound would heal quickly, but I needed to do something about the tension knifing my shoulder blades.

Using my uninjured hand, I kneaded at the hot spot and willed myself to relax. Soon enough Adam and the others would come out to let me know the plan. I just prayed they made the right decision.

Now that I'd tuned back into my surroundings, Giguhl's deep voice reached me across the water. He and the faery Calyx were in the same spot and hadn't noticed my minor existential crisis. "Do you have a sister?" he asked Calyx.

Just then, a bright orange koi with black spots mistook Giguhl's finger for a worm. "Ouch!" His claw jumped out of the water with a splash.

The corner of my mouth twitched. I started to tease him, but movement across the garden caught my attention.

Two large doors opened and Orpheus, Rhea, and Adam appeared on the path leading into the garden. Their grim expressions formed a knot in my stomach and made my shoulders tense up again. A Pythian Guard and another faery guard lead Tanith out behind them. Orpheus said something to the mage guard, who moved to stand in front of Tanith and the fae, presumably to give us some privacy. Over his shoulder, Tanith flashed me a smug smile that cued warning bells before the mages even reached me.

"Let's walk." Orpheus was all business. It had been only a few days since we saw each other, but the lack of warmth in his greeting put me on edge.

Calyx mumbled something about being needed elsewhere. Never had a female looked so relieved to escape a come-on. Crestfallen, Giguhl watched her go.

I nodded and held out a hand for him to precede me toward the nearest bridge. Once he'd passed I looked at Adam, who held his aunt's arm like a gentleman. His expression didn't give much away. Figuring I'd find out the bad news soon enough, I smiled at Rhea. "How are you?"

She leaned forward and kissed my cheek. "Tired," she said honestly. "Come on, let's get you filled in on the... developments."

I held my tongue as she took my arm. But I wanted to ask Rhea what she was doing here. Last I'd heard, she was heading out to recruit mages from around the country to build up the army the Hekate Council would need in the war that now seemed inevitable. But given the obvious tension I'd seen so far at the faery court, it made sense Orpheus would call her back to give him counsel on this delicate matter. But I could ask Adam all about that later. Right now, I needed different answers.

Orpheus led us over the bridge to a grassy island on the other side of the pond out of hearing range of the ancient vampire and her fae guards. When he turned to face us, he didn't bother with small talk. "There's been a change of plans," he began. I swallowed the curse that bubbled up at the confirmation of my fears and nodded. He continued, "We've agreed to help Tanith if and only if her information leads to Maisie's safe return."

"And if she's lying?" I asked.

"Then we will not hesitate to execute her."

So far, that was the only part of this new plan I agreed with. "So where's Lavinia keeping Maisie?"

"New Orleans," Rhea said.

"That's random," Giguhl said. I had to agree with his verdict. I'd been expecting to hear Lavinia had my sister in some remote location in California. We never would have found out they were in Louisiana on our own.

"Why there?" I asked.

"Tanith claims it has something to do with Lavinia's connection to the Caste," Orpheus said. "Apparently Tanith and Persephone have been kept out of that end of things."

"A smart move on Lavinia's part, given how easily Tanith just rolled over on her, " said Adam.

"I don't suppose she gave you an address?" I asked.

Orpheus grimaced and shook his head.

"Not to be ungrateful about Tanith's generosity or anything," I said, my voice dripping in sarcasm, "but this sounds like a wild-goose chase. How are we supposed to find Maisie in a city that size? I've never even been to New Orleans. Have you, Adam?" He shook his head, looking as frustrated as I felt.

"Knowing your grandmother," Orpheus said, "I doubt she'll hesitate to make her presence known once you're in the city."

"That's comforting," Adam said.

"I have an old friend there who may be able to help you," Rhea said. "Her name is Zenobia Faucher. Owns a magic shop on Bourbon Street. I'll put a call in to her."

Well, that was something at least, I thought. "Okay, so what are you going to do with Tanith?"

"Queen Maeve is taking custody of her."

My eyes widened. "Why her and not you guys?"

"She's being a—" Rhea paused as if stopping herself from saying something scandalous. "Well, let's just say she's being difficult. She's got her guards watching our every move and demands to be included in all our meetings. Orpheus has his hands full trying to placate her while also trying to find a new base of operations. And I'm leaving tomorrow to pay a visit to the midwestern mage communities to try to recruit some warm bodies."

I cursed under my breath. "How do you think this is going to play out?" I nodded toward Tanith, who prowled on the other bank of the pond. Her red hair blended into scarlet leaves behind her, making it appear as if her face floated in a pool of blood.

"The Queen is quite proud of how easily *she* brought the Domina to justice." Scorn soured his tone. "But you can bet she'll be quick to place blame on our shoulders should the plan fail."

"Of course she will," Adam said.

"Regardless," Orpheus said, "We're at the mercy of the Queen's superior resources. Namely, a tower to hold Tanith in until we know whether she's telling the truth."

My fingernails carved half-moons into the palm of my free hand. "I'd like the record to reflect that I think we should just kill Tanith now. She's a liability."

"Ditto," Giguhl said. I shot him a grateful look. Sometimes it was good to have a minion.

Adam shot me an annoyed look. I ignored him. Someone had to say it. He never would, out of respect for his leader and his aunt, but I had no such qualms.

"Taken and noted," Orpheus said. "But not possible. If she's telling the truth, she could be our best chance of preventing a war we have no hope of winning at this point."

Rhea sighed. "Orpheus is right. This is all we've got right now."

"There's something else," Orpheus said. His already grave tone took on a don't-test-me-on-this edginess. "I know this is not the outcome you'd hoped for. But it is imperative Lavinia doesn't find out we have Tanith in our custody."

I opened my mouth to argue, but Orpheus cut me off.

"No. Lavinia must believe Tanith is dead. When the Dominae guards find nothing but ashes in her limo, they'll believe she perished. You will not tell Lavinia otherwise."

I clenched my jaw so hard my teeth ached. Finally, I looked him dead in the eye. "Even if telling her would save Maisie's life?"

The leader of the mage race leaned in, his height formidable and his anger palpable. "Don't you dare imply I don't care about Maisie's safety. I helped raise that child like she was my own."

My stomach cramped with guilt as I finally noticed the dark circles and tension lining his face. I'd been so wrapped up in my own challenges, I'd failed to consider that he might be as upset as me. The mages had sustained extensive loss of both life and resources when the Dominae attacked them. In addition to mourning those deaths, it had to be a major blow to Orpheus's pride to rely on the Queen's help and suffer her whims, especially since she obviously had no qualms about taking advantage of the mages' weakened power structure. And while he played political chess with the Queen, he was obviously also worried about Maisie. She was like a daughter to him, yes, but as the ceremonial head of the mage government and an oracle who helped him make decisions, she was also his friend and confidante.

Feeling like an ass, I took a deep breath. "I'm sorry. I know you're doing the best you can."

Orpheus executed a dignified nod. "Just as I know you and Adam will make sure Maisie gets home safely."

"And once you find Maisie," Rhea said, "we can figure out how to best use Tanith's defection to our advantage."

"One thing's for sure," I began, "Tanith won't have a chance in hell of taking over as long as Lavinia's alive."

"That may be true, but finding Maisie is your priority."
Orpheus looked me dead in the eyes.

"Of course it is," I said automatically.

"That said, if you get an opening, take it."

A quickening began in my midsection. It was one thing
to want to kill my grandmother. It was something else to
be ordered to kill her by the leader of the mage race. It
was like getting a green light from the universe. Then a
thought occurred to me. "The Queen is down with that
part of the plan?"

"She wants to capture Lavinia for questioning." Orpheus
winked. "But she couldn't complain if you accidentally
killed that bitch during a rescue attempt."

A slow smile spread across my lips. "Now, that's a plan
I can definitely get behind."

"We thought you'd enjoy that," Orpheus said.

Rhea shifted uneasily. "I wish we'd had more time to
train. Your skills are still too raw. Plus there are the emotional aspects of the task in front of you . . ."

Up until recently, the silver-haired mage had spent
weeks training me in the finer points of magic. We'd only
just gotten to the good stuff when all hell broke loose in
New York. The good stuff being my ability to harness the
Chthonic magic I'd inherited from my long-dead mage
father. Chthonic magic is what most humans call black
magic. The truth is, no magic is entirely black or white.
But, even on the grayscale, Chthonic magic definitely
trended toward the darker side with its emphasis on death
and fertility magic. I still didn't know enough to com-
mune with the dead—not that I was eager to do *that*—but
I did know how to torch someone from twenty paces. So
that was something.

As for the emotional aspects she mentioned—

"Don't worry," I said. "I won't let my temper get the best of me."

Four dubious expressions greeted my statement. I put my hands on my hips. "Okay, fine. We all know I'll lose my temper, but at least I'm better at channeling my anger now."

Rhea patted my arm. "Yes, you are. Just remember that Lavinia's going to try to knock you off balance. Use your head and you'll be fine."

Giguhl threw an arm around Rhea's shoulders. "Don't worry about Sabina. She's got us to back her up."

Rhea frowned at the demon. "Wait, where's Valva?"

Giguhl cringed away from Rhea with a hiss.

"Ixnay on the Alva-vay," I said under my breath. After the "incident" at Fang's strip club just after we arrived in Los Angeles a couple of days earlier, Valva had become She Whose Name We Dare Not Speak.

Rhea's expression bordered on dumbfounded. "Sorry?"

Luckily, Adam stepped in with an appropriately diplomatic response. "Let's just say she won't be joining us and leave it at that." He shot a pointed look toward the pouting demon. Rhea's mouth formed an O and she nodded.

"Understood."

"As much as I hate to interrupt this intriguing discussion, we need to get moving. The Queen wasn't happy when I told her you'd want a word with Tanith before you left."

I frowned. Normally Orpheus was the man in charge. Hearing him admit he needed the Queen's leave worried me.

Rhea nodded. "I'll just go call Zenobia now and let her know to expect you tonight." She excused herself to make the call while Orpheus, Adam, Giguhl, and I went back to where Tanith and the guards stood.

As we approached, Tanith's eyes stayed on me. I met her stare with one of my own. I didn't see any point in pretending she was anything other than my enemy until she was proven otherwise. Orpheus dismissed the guards.

"I trust everything is in order?" she asked Orpheus.

He nodded. "Yes, Sabina has agreed to the terms."

She nodded. "Including the one we discussed out of the Queen's hearing?" I knew immediately she meant the part about killing Lavinia.

"You bet your ass," I said, crossing my arms.

She pursed her lips and looked me over. "I almost wish I could be there to see that battle."

"Really," I said, my tone heavy with boredom.

"Of course. How could it not be a spectacular show?" She paused and speared me with a challenging stare. "One wonders, though, do you really think you have what it will take to best your grandmother?"

"As much as I appreciate your concern," I said, my tone heavy with sarcasm, "It's wasted on me. Killing is what I do, remember?"

"The forbidden fruit doesn't fall far from the tree, child. You inherited that bloodlust from your grandmother. You're also not the only one driven by an all-consuming need for revenge."

I didn't have to ask what my grandmother wanted avenged. After all, my own desire for vengeance was intimately connected to her own. When my vampire mother and mage father decided to ignore centuries of law forbidding relations between the dark races, they put into motion a series of events that led to this crossroad. From my parents' deaths to my betrayal of the Dominae to Maisie's kidnapping a few days ago, the past lay out behind me like a roadmap of pain. And it was now up to me to put a stop to Lavinia before she could punish Maisie and me further for a situation we did not create. Not to mention, if Lavinia had her way, she'd destroy everyone else I cared about with the senseless war she'd been trying to ignite among all the dark races.

I looked around and saw that several of the beings I cared about—Adam, Giguhl, Rhea, and Orpheus—had formed a protective circle around me. I smiled at Adam, who wore a particularly fierce expression as he stared down the Domina. Yeah, I had a lot of reasons not to lose.

I took a deep breath and looked Tanith in the eye. "As much as I appreciate your heartfelt concern, there's no reason to worry about me. I have advantages Lavinia couldn't dream of."

*F*lashing into New Orleans was like diving into a luke-warm bath. I grew up in Los Angeles, so I was no stranger to warmish Octobers, but the humidity was a new and not very welcome experience. Not only did the wet air heighten the sour scent of trash and body fluids in the alley, but my hair also instantly kinked.

In the last few days I'd done enough magical travel that the vertigo I'd originally experienced had dulled into mild nausea. Unfortunately, the same couldn't be said for Giguhl.

His hairless-feline incarnation hunched on a pile of old newspapers. The sounds coming out of him were a cross between dry heaves and hairball expulsion. In demon form he was fine, but something about mixing his cat form and interspatial travel turned him into a bile factory.

"Did you have to aim at my shoes?" Adam asked dryly.

I knelt down beside the cat and patted his disconcertingly smooth head. "You okay?"

"Gark!" His cat ears swiveled as he turned to look at me. "No, I'm not okay. Why can't we just take a plane or car like normal people?"

I squinted at my hairless cat/Mischief demon. "Normal, Giguhl? Really?"

"Whatever, trampire." He shook himself and stood, his paws sticking to the humanity stew covering the asphalt.

Dismissing the grumpy demon, I turned to Adam. "How far is this place?"

"Couple blocks maybe." He pointed to the mouth of the alley. Actually, it wasn't so much an alley as walking space between two buildings. At the end, a green wooden gate separated us from the street. "That should be Bourbon Street."

Two filthy paws landed on my jeans legs and Giguhl looked up with wide, pleading kitty eyes. "Bael's balls, can we get out of here already? This alley smells like Satan's asshole."

And with that, we set off to find Rhea's friend.

But first we had to dodge drunk coeds, puddles of vomit, and strings of beads that flew like shrapnel through the air. For a random Tuesday—or early Wednesday morning, rather—in late October, the place was hopping. Normally I would have spent more time taking in the crazy, but I'd already been in three time zones that night and had bigger issues on my plate than figuring out who was headlining at Larry Flynt's Hustler Club.

Giguhl, on the other hand, spent most of the walk with his little cat mouth hanging open and his eyes wider than saucers. "It's like heaven," he breathed when we passed a generously endowed blonde as she traded her dignity for a handful of cheap plastic beads.

A couple of blocks down, Adam stopped outside a

three-story building. A neon sign over the door advertised "Madam Zenobia's Voodoo Apothecary."

I stopped next to Adam and frowned up at the sign. "Rhea didn't mention her friend's magic shop specialized in voodoo."

Adam shrugged. "Well, it is New Orleans...."

I reached past him and pulled at the door. Considering the hour, I was surprised to find it open. A bell sounded and the scent of incense and musty, arcane things drifted over us.

"After you," I said.

He walked in, his shoulders tense. I shifted Giguhl to my other arm and performed a scan of the street for suspicious characters. But in the bacchanalia that was Bourbon Street, *suspicious* was a relative term. But I didn't see any red-headed offspring of Lilith and Cain—aka vampires—so I let myself relax.

I turned and walked through the door. Only to stop short as my retinas burned with confusion. Apparently, in addition to voodoo, Zenobia's other hobby was hoarding. Masks, large glass jars full of mysterious herbs and spices, dolls, chicken bones, bits of ribbon, and figurines with impossibly large phalluses cluttered every inch of available space. Even the speakers, which piped in drum music, were bedazzled with beads and stickers.

Near the back of the store, a set of narrow stairs led to a second floor. A curtain made from wooden, bone, and crystal beads separated the sales floor from the employees-only areas. Adam beelined to a desk near the curtain and rang the silver bell. I took the long way around to the back, scanning the store for possible exits and potential weapons. If we were staying here, I'd feel better knowing what resources I had at my disposal if Lavinia showed up.

A few moments after Adam rang the bell, the curtain parted to reveal a bald male with big brown eyes and even bigger glasses with black plastic frames. He was maybe five-foot-five, and his thin frame bordered on fragility. He wore threadbare jeans and a vintage T-shirt that accentuated the birdlike bones of his chest. The strong scent of lavender that swirled around him indicated he was some type of fae.

When he spotted Adam, he stopped in his tracks. "Where *you* at, *cher*?" he purred in a surprisingly deep baritone.

Adam shifted on his feet uneasily. "Hi, is Madam Zenobia around?"

"Might I tell her who's inquiring?"

"I'm Adam Lazarus." He gestured toward me. "This is Sabina."

I hefted the cat. "And this is Mr. Giggles." That earned me a hiss in the ear.

"That's the ugliest hairless pussy I ever did see." As the fae slapped the counter and laughed at his own joke, Giguhl dug his claws into my shoulder.

"From the looks of you, you haven't seen many pussies, period," the demon cat growled.

The male stopped laughing with a gasp. "Not that he's wrong, but... did your cat just talk smack to me?"

"He's actually a demon," I explained lamely. "And he's kind of sensitive about the hairless thing."

The fae's eyes widened. "Ooh! A demon?"

I nodded. "Do you mind if I let him change into his true form?"

The male put his chin in his hands. "This I have got to see."

I grimaced. Considering Giguhl always ended up naked when he changed forms, the fae was about to see more than an eyeful. I set the cat on the floor. "Giguhl, change forms."

When the brimstone-scented cloud dispersed, a seven-foot-tall, green-scaled, black-horned, butt-naked demon stood beside me. I kept my eyes averted, but the fae's gaze zeroed in on Giguhl's, um, little demon. "Well, hello," he drawled. "The demon's got himself a little pitchfork."

I grabbed a pair of sweatpants from my backpack and tossed them to Giguhl. Maybe it was me, but he seemed to take his sweet time pulling them on. Almost like he was enjoying the attention. I shook my head. I'll never understand demons.

"Err, anyway, Rhea sent us," Adam said, clearly bemused.

The fae male dragged his eyes from Giguhl and perked up. "Rhea's friends? Why didn't you say so? Madam Z is expecting you." He came out from behind the desk and slipped a hand around Giguhl's massive biceps. "I'm Brooks, by the way."

As he pulled the demon toward the stairs, he called back toward Adam and me, almost as an afterthought. "Y'all come on now."

Upstairs, Brooks led us down a hallway to a red door. He held up a finger to indicate we should wait there and disappeared behind the portal.

I leaned back against the wall. Adam crossed his arms and leaned next to me with a sigh.

"He's . . . friendly," Giguhl said, filling the silence.

I smiled. "I like him. But is it just me, or did anyone else notice that he's a"—I paused for dramatic effect—"faery?"

The corner of Adam's mouth quirked. "You don't say."

"Surprising he didn't freak out when we walked in with a cat." From what I knew, faeries hated cats as a rule. My old nymph roommate, Vinca—gods rest her soul— took a long time to get used to having Giguhl around. They eventually warmed up to each other, but it had been touch and go there for a while.

"Couple of species don't consider cats mortal enemies. It's too soon to know which he is, though," Adam shrugged. "But I will say he seemed to be quite a fan of Mr. Giggles."

Giguhl waved a claw over himself. "Can't blame him for digging this fine ass."

I rolled my eyes at the demon. "Anyway, something tells me this Madam Zenobia's going to be interesting. Isn't it odd for a mage to practice voodoo?"

"I've never met any who did, but who knows? The mages down here are a different breed from the ones in New York."

"Literally a different breed?" Giguhl asked. It was a fair question. Mages were created by the goddess Hekate, but that didn't mean there weren't offshoots of the original race. After all, faeries had dozens of subspecies.

Adam shook his head. "No, I just meant it wouldn't surprise me if they did things differently here. Since they're so far from the central group in New York, it would make sense they've developed their own ways of doing things."

The door opened again and Brooks stuck out his head. "Madam Zenobia is ready to receive you."

He stood aside to allow us entrance. I noticed his eyes on Adam's impressive posterior as he walked by. As I passed, Brooks smiled knowingly at me, totally unembarrassed to be caught looking. Since I'd been watching it myself, I couldn't really blame him.

I heard the shuffle of hooves behind me and stopped. Turning to Giguhl, I said, "Wait here, okay?"

"Why?" Giguhl asked.

I shot him a look that shut him up pretty quick. He just crossed him arms and leaned back against the wall. Just as I closed the door I heard him say to Brooks, "So you're into dudes, huh?"

When I heard Brooks laugh, I decided it was safe to leave those two alone for a few minutes. Shutting the door the rest of the way, I turned to look around.

Just a few candles lit the room, leaving most of the place cloaked in shadow. My vampire eyes adjusted easily to the low light, but Adam squinted around the room, trying to spot our host. I'd already seen she wasn't there, so I took the opportunity to case the place.

From the looks of things, this was a sort of receiving parlor. Except most of the parlors I'd seen in books didn't feature altars covered in skulls, candles, and chicken bones. A sitting area squatted under a floor-to-ceiling window that looked down on Bourbon Street.

Two closed doors were across the room from the windows. I assumed Zenobia must use this floor as her living area, so one of the doors probably led to another hall or possibly a kitchen and bedroom.

The door on the left opened and Madam Zenobia walked out. I'm not sure exactly what I'd been expecting a voodoo priestess to look like. Probably someone old and possibly obese. Blame it on movies, I guess. But I should have known better than to base my expectations on popular culture. After all, Hollywood had been getting vampires wrong for decades—don't get me started on the soulless undead thing...or the godsdamned sparkling. Regardless, the female who glided out of that doorway was definitely not old or fat.

Candlelight cast a golden glow on her flawless tawny complexion. Dark waves framed high cheekbones. A simple white tunic and jeans hugged her curvy frame. There was no guessing her age, but her confident posture and warm brown gaze hinted at wisdom gained from lots of life experience.

I glanced at Adam. His mouth gaped wide enough for a small bird to take residence. I nudged his arm. He closed his maw, but his eyes didn't leave her. I guess I couldn't blame him.

Okay, I totally could. Madam Zenobia was a stone-cold fox, and seeing Adam watch her with adoration normally reserved for goddesses made jealousy rear up like a green-eyed demon.

She approached with a wide, welcoming smile. "You must be Adam and Sabina. Welcome to New Orleans." She pronounced the city with a syrupy drawl—*N'Awlins.*

Zenobia held out a finely boned hand to Adam. Unlike when he met Brooks, he didn't hesitate to bow over it and deliver a gallant kiss to her knuckles. "Madam Zenobia," he said. "It's a pleasure."

Her laugh sounded like rustling velvet. "Please. Call me Zen. You're practically family anyway."

"All right." Adam flashed his dimples at her. "Zen."

Maybe I was imagining things, but I could have sworn

he added a little extra baritone to his voice. I tried not to give in to my sudden urge to kick him in the shins.

Instead, I stuck out my hand. "Hi, I'm Sabina."

She turned toward me and her smile dimmed a little. "Ah, yes, the mixed-blood. It's nice to meet you."

I ignored her mention of my heritage, which frankly was none of her godsdamned business, and focused instead on our connected hands. Normally, when I made contact with a mage I experienced a tingle of magic. Not so with this one. Hmm.

"Please sit." She motioned to the sitting area. "You'll have to forgive my appearance. I'm afraid I had already retired for the evening when Rhea called."

Adam grabbed the only chair, which meant I shared the couch with Zenobia. "We apologize for the lateness of our arrival, but our business is urgent."

"It's fine. Really." Zen waved away his apology. "Rhea said you were looking for a missing relative?"

I scooted over a bit to create some space as I faced her. "Yes, my sister—twin, actually. We have reason to believe she's being held somewhere in the city."

Zen grimaced sympathetically and patted my knee. "That's horrible. Do you know who kidnapped her?"

I nodded. "Our grandmother."

Zen's mouth fell open in shock. "Are you serious?"

Seeing my jaw tense, Adam stepped in. "It's a long story." Adam leaned forward, cutting off my retort. "But I'm sure you understand our eagerness to get started tracking them down."

"Of course. Naturally, you're welcome to stay here. Brooks and I will do whatever we can to help."

While Adam filled Zen in on the little we knew about

the situation, I eyed the female. Something was off about her. I couldn't put my finger on it, though. She was perfectly pleasant, in an annoying, gorgeous kind way, but her actions weren't what gave me pause. I thought back to the lack of tingle when we'd shook hands and decided to perform a test.

I'm not proud of what I did next, but, well, I leaned over and—as subtly as possible, mind you—sniffed her. Instead of sandalwood—a signature mage trait—I got a whiff of dirt. I frowned and scooted closer. Another sniff. Yep, definitely dirt.

But since it's impossible to be inconspicuous while smelling someone—

"Excuse me?" Zen interrupted Adam and shot me the side-eye. "Did you just smell me?"

Adam gave me an exasperated look. I ignored him and squared off with Zen. "You're human!"

She squinted at me, as if trying to figure out if I was crazy or just slow. "Right?" She drew the word out like it should have been obvious.

I pointed a finger at her and turned toward Adam. "She's human!"

Adam lifted his ass off the chair and sniffed the air in front of her. Zen drew back against the far edge of the sofa. "Brooks!"

"I'll be damned," Adam said finally. "She *is* human."

"Ha! I told you." We closed in on her, examining the voodoo priestess like an alien life-form.

The door burst open. Despite his petite frame, Brooks was all shoulders and fists when he reached us. "Back the fuck up!"

Giguhl stumbled in after Brooks. He looked to me for

direction. I shook my head. I didn't need a demon to help me handle a pissed-off human and a male faery.

Adam and I raised our hands and backed away slowly. "No harm meant," Adam said quickly as Brooks advanced. To Zenobia he said, "We just assumed you were a mage."

She narrowed her eyes. "Why would you assume that?"

"Why wouldn't we assume it?" I shot back. "Rhea said you could help us navigate the dark-races subculture down here. We had zero reason to think you're human."

"For your information," she said, raising her chin, "I'm only three-quarters human. My grandfather was a mage. My grandmother and mother were both voodoo priestesses. Rhea sent you to me because I'm connected to both the humans and dark races in New Orleans."

"Still," I said, ignoring her explanation. "I can't believe Rhea send us to a dirtnapper for help."

"Oh, I get it." She crossed her arms. "You're a dark-race supremacist."

My mouth dropped open. "That's the most ridiculous thing I've ever heard."

"Really? How many mortally challenged individuals do you count as friends?"

My chin came up. "Please. I've known lots of humans."

"Sabina, I don't think it counts if you ripped their throats out," Giguhl said.

"Hey!" I glared at my disloyal minion.

"Vampires are the worst." Zenobia screwed up her lips. "Immortalists, the lot of you."

"Excuse me, but I'm only half vampire. And you have a lot of nerve. Like humans are any better. Last time I checked, you don't exactly consider cows your equals."

Her back went up. "Are you calling me a cow?"

I raised an eyebrow. "Moo."

By this point, Zen and I were nose-to-nose. I was *this close* to flashing fang when Adam wedged himself between us. "Okay, ladies, let's simmer down."

I glared at Zen over his shoulder. "She's the one calling me an immortalist."

"Please," Giguhl said. "You totally are."

I shot a glare at my demon. "Watch yourself, G."

"I'm just sayin'. She kind of has a point."

Zen raised a told-ya-so eyebrow at me. She received double birds in return.

"Giguhl," Adam snapped. "You're not helping." He pushed Zen toward Brooks while he used his body to scoot me back.

I crossed my arms and gritted my teeth together. How dare that bitch call me out like that. And, hello? I wasn't the only one who thought Zen would be a mage. But did she call Adam names? Of course not.

Adam pulled me into the hallway, slammed the door behind us, and trapped me against a wall. "You need to apologize," he whispered.

"What! Like hell I do. She's the one—"

He put a hand over my mouth. "Shut up and listen, okay? We need her help. So you're going to swallow your pride and apologize. Got it?"

I tried to sear him with my eyes.

"Sabina, please." The pleading in his tone was what finally got me. I suddenly missed the old days when I didn't give a shit about the consequences of losing my temper. But he was right. We needed Zen's help if we wanted to save Maisie. Besides, I respected Rhea too much to be such a bitch to her friend after she'd gone out of her way to offer help.

I sucked in a long, slow breath. The inhalation brought both a measure of calm and the heady sandalwood scent of Adam. Closing my eyes, I nodded my surrender. He removed his hand, and when I opened my eyes again I was rewarded with a trademark Lazarus smile. Suddenly I felt a lot better about agreeing to supplicate myself.

I licked my lips. "Fine, I'll apologize. But I want the record to reflect that I don't like her."

"Taken and noted," he said. "But I think she's okay. We just got off to a bad start."

I didn't share his optimism about Zenobia's potential but kept that opinion to myself. See? I was already growing. Never let it be said I can't learn a lesson.

When we walked back in, bodies scattered like cockroaches in a suddenly illuminated room. Giguhl and Brooks scampered over to the altar, where they tried their damnedest to look like they hadn't just been eavesdropping.

Zenobia sat near the window like a queen waiting to receive visitors. I swallowed the flare of pride that threatened to make me renege on my promise to Adam. Instead, I called up Maisie's face in my mind's eye. I took a deep breath and reminded myself this apology was nothing more than a necessary evil en route to finding my sister. I stopped in front of the voodoo priestess and tried to look contrite. "I'm sorry I called you a cow."

She inclined her head. "And?"

I paused, trying to figure out what else I had to apologize for. "And what?"

"You forgot to say you'll be more generous in your attitude toward the mortally challenged."

Oh, for fuck's sake, I thought. Adam cleared his throat,

a subtle reminder to keep my temper in check. With great effort, I nodded. "I promise I'll *try*."

She ran a tongue over her teeth as she assessed my sincerity. "In addition, I demand that you vow not to feed on me, my employees, or my customers."

I looked up at the ceiling, praying for patience. "Not a problem." The truth was, with the exception of a slipup in New York no one knew about, I hadn't fed directly from a human in weeks. I still didn't like the taste of bagged blood, but I had to admit it saved me a lot of trouble.

Zen nodded in approval of my easy acceptance of her terms.

I continued. "Just point me in the direction of the nearest blood bank and we'll be good to go."

Zen drew back with a grimace. "I'll do no such thing. The good people of New Orleans need that blood more than you."

I sighed. "Look, lady, what do you expect me to do? Starve?"

"I didn't say that," Zen said. Her smile gave me a feeling I wouldn't like the next thing out of her mouth. "There is another perfectly acceptable solution. A butcher friend of mine would be happy to sell you all the cow's blood you'll need."

"Fine." Not that I was looking forward to sucking on farm animals or anything, but I just wanted this conversation over with already. I raised an eyebrow, challenging her to add another stipulation.

Instead, she stood up with a clap. "Excellent! And now that that's settled, why don't I show you to your rooms?"

"Wait," Adam said.

"Yes?" she said with a raised eyebrow.

"You're still going to help us?"

"Of course, *cher*. A proper southern woman never allows a simple misunderstanding to get in the way of hospitality." She chuckled and rose from her seat. She paused. "Besides, Rhea warned me about this one's"— she nodded toward me—"colorful personality."

She sauntered over to Adam and slid her arm through his. He laughed—somewhat uncomfortably, mind you— and seemed to enjoy playing the gallant gentleman as he led her from the room with Brooks and Giguhl trailing them. I glared after them but managed not to call out a *colorful* retort.

Zenobia's passive-aggressive comment had painted me in a corner. If I argued her point, it would just prove she'd been right.

Before I joined them, I cracked my neck from side to side. Breathing in a martyred sigh, I reminded my temper to behave itself. If I'd learned one thing, it was that killing people who annoyed me generally created more problems than it solved.

I mentally patted myself on the back. See? Totally growing.

Half an hour later, Adam, Giguhl, and I walked toward the halogen lights in Jackson Square. After Zen had shown us our rooms—actually an attic apartment on the third floor of her building—we'd decided to do a quick walking tour of the immediate area. I wouldn't be able to sleep without knowing exactly where I was and what lurked in the French Quarter's shadows.

We passed Pirate's Alley and entered the square in front of St. Louis Cathedral. Two young boys played large plastic buckets like drums for a crowd of tourists. Palm readers sat behind card tables scattered throughout the area. No one found it ironic to offer such a pagan service in the shadow of the looming cathedral.

With a sigh, I allowed my worries to float away down the Mississippi. My shoulders unknotted, and my breathing slowed for the first time in days. I even found myself smiling at a persistent fortune-teller who promised she could tell my future. Even if I thought she could help—which I didn't—I was content to allow myself to be in the now for the moment.

We were finally getting somewhere, and while the situation was far from ideal, I could almost feel Maisie here. Maybe it was wishful thinking, but the city pulsed with magic. A dark, earthy energy swirled beneath the streets, down in the city's swampy foundations.

But I also detected a lighter, more familiar power in the air. If this magic had a color, it was cool cobalt blue. If this magic had a scent, it was bright cedar and jasmine.

My chest swelled with hope and my pulse picked up. Maisie was here somewhere. I just knew it.

Then my gaze landed on a middle-aged woman forking a twenty over to a fortune-teller with greasy hair and a couple of missing teeth. The trust and naked hope in the customer's face gave me pause. Did my expression mirror hers?

Adam backtracked a few steps to check on me. Giguhl was perched on his shoulders, but the cat was too busy taking in the carnival of the senses to notice my distress.

"Red? You all right?" Adam asked.

I took a deep breath and dragged my eyes from the desperate woman at the table. I knew better than to put my faith in intangibles. Gut feelings, talismans, prayers to selfish gods—these things wouldn't get Maisie back. Only clear thinking and strategy would get the job done.

I nodded at Adam. "Yeah, just watching foolish mortals get suckered out of their rent money." Dismissing the scene with a wave, I pulled him away. As we walked, I pulled Giguhl onto my shoulders. For some reason, the weight and warmth of his little body helped dispel some of the lingering fog of worry.

We skirted the square containing a statue of Andrew Jackson and headed up the brick avenue toward the river. A crowd gathered at the corner, watching a living statue pose. The woman was dressed to resemble the Statue of Liberty, with her skin painted convincing verdigris. We paused at the edge of the crowd and watched her for a moment.

"Oh, my gods, what's that smell?" Giguhl hissed from my shoulder. His little pink nose went up like a periscope searching for the source by smell alone.

I sniffed the air. The muddy scent of the Mississippi melded with the seductive aroma of warm blood flowing through all those mortal veins. But I was confident neither mud nor blood were making Giguhl squirm and snort the air like it was cocaine. Instead, I took a wild stab that it might be the scents of sugary fried beignets and smoky chicory coffee coming from the other side of the street.

"Café du Monde," Adam said, pointing to the patio with its green-and-white-striped awning and the long line of mortals looking for a fix.

"Can we get some?" the demon cat hissed by my ear. "Pleeease."

I exchanged a look with Adam. The defeated kind two tired parents shared over the head of a whining toddler. Finally, the mage sighed. "You want some, too?"

I shook my head. Adam lifted the hairless cat from my shoulder and held him like an ugly football under his arm. "Come on." He shot me a long-suffering look. "We'll be right back."

While the mage jogged across the street to join the long line outside the café, I leaned against a brick wall to watch the performers. The area was humming with activity. In addition to Lady Liberty, a man in a tinfoil suit performed The Robot to music blaring from a boom box near his feet. Beyond them, artists hawked portraits of jazz greats and woven reed baskets to tourists exiting the hansom cabs parked along Decatur Street. Further downriver, a paddle-boat curtsied in the water like a young miss at a cotillion.

I was just about to carry on with my stroll when a familiar screech made my veins go arctic. I ducked out of instinct and scanned the sky. Sure enough, a white-feathered form circled the cathedral's spire. I knew without a closer look that the owl had blood-red eyes.

Stryx.

The owl had followed me for weeks—all the way from Los Angeles to San Francisco and then across the country to New York. Originally, Adam and I thought Stryx was a spy that worked for the goddess Lilith. She was stuck in Irkalla, the dark-race underworld, and it was believed Stryx served as her eyes on earth. Back then Stryx mostly stayed out of my way, so I considered him harmless.

But in New York I found out he hadn't worked for Lilith at all, but instead had been spying on me for the Caste of Nod. The owl had shared my location with them so they could orchestrate attempts on my life. During the big bat-tle at the mage compound I'd shot the winged rat, but apparently he'd recovered from his injuries.

And his presence in New Orleans meant we were on the right track.

I turned to go tell Adam, but the scent of copper hit my nose like a punch. Unlike the pleasant metallic scent of warm blood, the telltale aroma of vampire stunk like the residue of copper pennies on the skin.

My stomach dropped as I swiveled to scan the area. So many people milled around I didn't see her at first. Then, as if Moses had parted it, the crowd dispersed.

She stood as still as one of the living statues in front of

the iron fence skirting the square. Her carmine hair stood out like a wound against the funeral-ready black dress she wore like a shroud.

Lavinia.

I'm not sure if I whispered her name aloud or screamed it in my head. Either way, seeing her stand not fifty feet away made my pulse jack into hyperdrive. Cold sweat drenched my skin, and every muscle in my body tensed. I froze, waiting for her to run or attack or...something.

Instead, she merely raised an eyebrow in challenge. In typical Lavinia fashion, she was making me come to her. My sweaty palm curled into a fist. I briefly considered pulling my gun, but with so many mortal witnesses it would be too risky.

Moving slowly, I narrowed the distance between us. My mind spun through every possible scenario. Lavinia hadn't randomly chosen this spot. Despite vampires having little concern over the safety of mortals, for the most part we followed an unwritten rule that required discretion around them. As Alpha Domina, Lavinia might consider herself above that rule, but she was counting on me being very aware of our audience. Which meant she wanted to talk. And that heightened my anxiety even more. A fight I could handle, but a talk meant surprises. I'd had enough of those to last me eternity. Especially since my grandmother always knew which buttons to push—the ones that would fuck with my head.

Of course, I showed none of this unease to her. I simply stopped and tilted my head, telling her it was her move. The corner of her blood-red lips lifted, but she humored me and took several steps forward. Now only about five feet separated us.

Five feet and a chasm of bitterness so wide and deep it could never be crossed. Not without one of us dying. And I planned on living for a long time yet.

"Sabina," she purred. Behind her, Stryx came to land on the tall black gate. His red eyes didn't blink as he watched me. "You don't call. You don't write. It's enough to break a grandmother's heart."

My eyes narrowed. I wanted to punch that shit-eating grin off her face. Instead, I said, "Oh, Lavinia." Her eyes narrowed at my impertinent use of her given name. Good. "Let's not fool ourselves. We both know you don't have a heart to break." As I spoke, my hand snaked back between my waistband and leather jacket.

"You've always been such a troublesome child. Always needing to be reminded to use your head," she said, clucking her tongue and looking pointedly at my bent arm. "However will you find that sister of yours if you kill me now?"

"First of all, there's no way killing you wouldn't be the best thing that happened to me ever." The sweat-slicked surface of my palm slid across the butt of my gun. "And as for Maisie, well, you let me worry about that."

She crossed her arms and regarded me with a tilt of her head. "If I may offer another suggestion?"

I hated myself for hesitating. I should have already put a bullet between her eyes, witnesses be damned. But concern for Maisie and, frankly, plain gut-twisting fear stilled my hand. My eyes narrowed. "What?"

"Surrender."

A laugh escaped from me. A harsh, angry sound. "You're unbelievable."

"And you're naive if you think you'll emerge victorious

if this comes to a battle. Besides, do you really want your sister's death on your conscience—"

"Please. Drop the patronizing act, okay? We both know you'll kill Maisie if I surrender."

She pursed her lips so hard they turned white. "Do not interrupt me again, child. You forget to whom you speak. Do you think I achieved the rank of Alpha Domina by being nice? I have spilled a river of blood in my lifetime. One mighty enough to rival the one behind you."

I raised my chin. "I killed Tanith." If I couldn't tell her the truth, I'd use a lie to my advantage.

Her expression flickered. "So I heard. A regrettable loss. Tanith had a killer instinct for business, but she was no fighter. Do you honestly think you can best me?"

My hands trembled now. I ignored her question. No point in answering it anyway. We both understood the odds here. "If you're so confident in your victory, why not let it play out?"

"Because despite your high opinion of your significance, you're merely an inconvenience. One I'd like to dispose of quickly so I can focus on more important issues."

The jab hit home, but I didn't show it. "You mean the war."

She tipped her chin to acknowledge the truth of that statement. "Among other things."

"So the prophecy, then? If you really believe I'm destined to fuck up your war plans, why haven't you killed me yet?"

"What I believe in is inconsequential. Master Mahan has plans that happen to support my personal goals." When she said that name—"Master Mahan"—Stryx hooted softly. I ignored him because, well, I didn't like looking at him with his freaky red eyes and his creepy tendency to screech my name at odd intervals.

I'd never heard the name in my life. "Who is that?"

Lavinia tilted her head and gave me the same look one might give a slow child. "Master Mahan"—another hoot "—is the leader of the Caste…among other things. And he's eager to meet you, Sabina."

Obviously, I needed more information about that, but I knew she was trying to sidetrack me. "And what do you want?"

"To erase all mages from the planet." She smiled with anticipation that made my blood run cold. "Especially the mixed-bloods."

I didn't react to her bait. After all, it's not like she'd said anything I didn't already know. "And Master Mahan? What does he want?"

She shrugged. "He wants the mages dead, as well, but for a different reason."

"You forgot to mention he wants me dead, too. To ensure the war happens, right?"

Her eyes shot left. "You'll find out his plans for you soon enough."

I sighed. Cryptic bullshit always annoyed me. "How can I be sure Maisie's even still alive?"

She withdrew something from the pocket of her dress. Gold glinted as she held it up to the light. Recognizing the jewelry, my veins went icy.

Maisie's necklace.

The amulet symbolized her position as the High Priestess of the Chaste Moon. The moonstone matched the one around my own neck, as did the inscription on the gold setting, which read: *For she is the torchbearer, this daughter of Hekate; she will light the way.* In fact, the only difference between my necklace and Maisie's was the smear of blood across the surface of her moonstone.

My stomach cramped with fear for my twin. I reached for the amulet, but Lavinia pulled it out of range, forcing me to step forward to capture it. Finally, my hand closed around the warm golden chain and I jerked it away.

"This doesn't prove shit," I gritted through clenched teeth.

"It's the best you're getting. Surrender now and you can go see her for yourself tonight."

"Where is she?"

"Someplace most vampires wouldn't be caught dead." She chuckled as if she'd made a joke. "Now, are you going to surrender? Or are you going to force my hand and make me pick off each of your friends to make you see reason?" She jerked her head to indicate something behind me. I looked over my shoulder to see Adam crossing the street. The cat's ass jutted from inside a white paper bag in his arms. The mage's eyes scanned the crowd, obviously looking for me.

I turned back to my grandmother with a smile and crossed my arms. I opened my mouth to say something about it being too late to surrender, not that I ever really considered the option.

But before the words came out, Lavinia leaned in. Cold white hands clamped around my upper arms. "Her blood tastes like nectar."

A flash of white rage exploded in my brain. Then an image of my grandmother bent over Maisie's neck made my vision go bloody. I sprang forward with hands bent into claws and fangs snapping.

From far away, I heard Adam shout, "Sabina!"

Too late. Too late for reason. Too late for strategy or cool heads. The reel tape of Lavinia feeding from Maisie played over and over in fast-forward. And the soundtrack to that horror film was the voice in my head chanting *kill, kill, kill.*

Lavinia stumbled back, out of reach. Rage rocketed me forward. My nails sunk into the flesh of her shoulders. Slow motion. The whites of her eyes. My fangs throbbing. The descent toward her throbbing jugular. A loud *pop*. Stryx's ear-piercing screech. Flapping wings. A hot blast of magic.

My momentum thrust me forward into empty air. The spot where she'd stood only milliseconds before. Ground rushed to meet my face. Crack of bone against brick. Stinging palms. The air and all sense knocked out of me.

*A*dam skidded to a halt above me. The cat's tail jutted out of the bag in his arms.

Shaking myself, I tried to figure out what the hell just happened. "What the fuck, Adam?" I demanded.

The concern on his face morphed into confusion. "What?"

"Why did you zap her?" I demanded.

He went still. "Sabina, I didn't. Couldn't get a clear shot."

My mouth fell open. "Well, how in the hell did she just disappear, then?"

But then it hit me. She'd fed from Maisie. I squeezed my eyes shut. Beyond my horror that Lavinia had fed from her own flesh and blood, a new terror dawned. Now that my grandmother had Maisie's powerful blood in her system, she'd be harder to kill than ever. Sure, she was a powerful vampire—maybe the most powerful—but now Maisie's blood also gave her the ability to use magic.

But that wasn't the worst of it. Normally, injecting some form of the forbidden fruit into a vampire's bloodstream cancelled out their immortality and allowed them

to be killed. Yet I'd been staked twice in the heart with
applewood and lived. My mixed blood somehow protected me from the effects. That same mixed blood also
flowed in Maisie's veins. And now, Lavinia's. Which
meant my grandmother might now be unkillable by conventional means. If one considered applewood stakes or
bullets filled with cider conventional.

Before I could fill Adam in on this black news, several
humans surrounded us. Their expressions ranged from
concerned to amazed. They stared for a few tense moments
before a smattering of confused applause rippled through
the group.

A balding man with a Nikon dangling around his neck
held out his hand. A crumpled dollar bill dangled from
his grip. I stared at him, dumbfounded.

"Wow, y'all are amazing," he said. "I ain't seen magic
like that since that David Blane TV special."

"How'd your friend disappear like that?" the guy's
friend asked.

I scowled at them and took Adam's hand to stand. The
necklace lay a couple of feet away like litter in the street. I
went to grab it, but a dowdy woman in a New Orleans
Saints sweatshirt picked it up first. I ripped it from her
hands and barely managed not to hiss at her for daring to
touch Maisie's amulet. She scowled at me. "How rude!"

Dismissing her, I pushed my way through the crowd
around Adam, ignoring questions and pats on the back.
"Let's get the hell out of here."

Adam put his free hand around my arm and led me
through the throng. As we went, he mumbled excuses and
vague explanations to the crowd. But basically they all
seemed to believe we belonged to some sort of magic

troupe and that Lavinia was probably hiding in the bushes somewhere nearby. I would have found it amusing if I hadn't been so busy freaking out.

As soon as we exited the square, Giguhl came up for air. His entire head—from his whiskers to his bald bat ears—was covered in white powder. He blinked the sugar from his eyes and looked from Adam to me. "Uh-oh, what'd I miss?"

"She wanted me to surrender," I said. My legs felt wooden as we sped through the French Quarter. With so many humans around we couldn't just flash out, so we walked fast enough to cover ground quickly but not so fast to raise attention. As I walked, my brain was filled with a tangle of thoughts—none of them positive.

"Fucking dirtnappers," I ranted. "I should have just shot her and been done with it. But noooo. I had to worry about scaring the widdle humans. Stupid!"

Adam patted my arm. "Sabina, I know you're upset. You have every right to be. But try to keep it down before one of the mortals you're cursing hears you."

"To hell with them!" I yelled.

A passing trio of mortals shot me nasty looks. I hissed at them. Not the most mature of reactions, but I was pretty screwed up. After all, it's not every night a girl gets a chance to kill her nemesis and blows it.

Adam sighed. "Okay so she wanted you to surrender. What happened next?"

For some reason, I couldn't stop shaking. I rubbed my arms and tried to remember. But before I could gather my thoughts, Giguhl snorted.

"She's a real piece of work. Like you'd ever surrender."

With her threats still echoing in my ears, I had to wonder

if the possibility was really so far-fetched. After all, she'd promised to come after my friends until I surrendered. "Maybe I should have," I said. Now that it was over and the shock was wearing off, new concerns cropped up like weeds. How long until Lavinia came after Adam and Giguhl? Had my refusal to cooperate pissed her off more? Would she take it out on Maisie now? Gods, what had I done?

Adam squeezed my arm and pulled me to a stop. "Absolutely you should not have surrendered. Don't even go there."

I rounded on him. "I have to go there, Adam. She all but promised she'd pick each of you off until I gave myself up."

His chin went up. "Let her try to come after me."

I pulled my arm from his grasp and prepared to drop the next bomb. "She's fed from Maisie, Adam."

His jaw clenched and his eyes went all cold and flinty.

"That's how she flashed out earlier," I continued, determined to drive the point home. "And if she's capable of sinking fangs into her own granddaughter, do you really think she'd hesitate to take you out?"

He got in my face, his voice low. "Do you really believe I'd let you sacrifice yourself to that monster just to protect me?"

"Yeah," Giguhl said, his head jutting up between us. "Enough with the crazy talk, Sabina."

I pulled back and considered the two stubborn faces of my friends. Their loyalty meant a lot to me, but I'd do whatever I could to protect them. I also knew surrendering wasn't a real option.

I blew out a breath and willed my stiff muscles to relax.

"Okay, fine. No surrender. What now? Gods only know what she's doing to Maisie at this very minute." I felt like I was going to throw up as the possibilities paraded through my fatigued brain.

Before tonight it was easier to look at this mission as just that—a series of strategies toward a predetermined goal. But now? Now it was impossible to separate the mission from the dawning horror in my gut, the nagging worry about Maisie, the rage I felt toward my grandmother. And, knowing Lavinia, it would get worse before it got better.

If it got better.

"We need to talk to Orpheus," I said. "It's not too late to trade Tanith."

Adam's face went still. Like he was mentally maneuvering his way through a minefield. "Sabina," he began slowly, "you need to take a deep breath and think."

"I am thinking, Adam. I'm thinking that if we don't act soon, Maisie will die. We have to get her out of there."

Adam crossed his arms. "Orpheus made his stance clear. Lavinia must not know Tanith is alive. It would ruin any advantage the mages and fae have right now."

I snorted. "I'm not so sure about that anymore."

Adam grabbed my arm. "What the hell does that mean?"

"Guys," Giguhl said. "Take a deep breath. We're all on the same side here."

Ignoring Giguhl, I pushed Adam away. "It means you seem more interested in staying in Orpheus's good graces than in saving Maisie."

His eyebrows slammed down. "Really? You want to go there right now? Because you know damned well Maisie is as much family to me as Rhea. In fact, considering you've only known her for about three weeks, you have less of a connection to her than Orpheus or me. Just because we have different ideas about how to save her doesn't mean we care less."

"I just find it interesting that your ideas also happen to be exactly what Orpheus told you to do."

"For the record, my allegiance has always been to the Hekate Council," he said. "I'm a Pythian Guard, remember? I swore to uphold the decisions of the Council in all things. But that doesn't mean I don't have my own brain, Sabina. And my logic tells me that in order to save Maisie and ensure the war ends, we keep the Tanith thing under our hats as long as possible. And not to be too blunt here, but if anyone's motivations are questionable, they're yours."

Giguhl emitted a scandalized whistle.

I jerked toward Adam, forcing him to meet my glare. "Excuse me?"

"Please. You've made no secret of the fact you want Lavinia dead. Maisie getting kidnapped gives you the perfect excuse to pursue that goal with abandon."

My voice went nuclear winter. "If all I care about is killing Lavinia Kane"—I pointed behind us in the general direction of Jackson Square—"why is she still breathing? If all I care about is killing her, why am I advocating trading Tanith, which would take away the opportunity for a showdown? And if all I care about is killing my grandmother, why would I bother taking any direction from the Queen or the Council? I'm a godsdamned assassin, Adam. Do you really think I couldn't launch a covert operation to kill her on my own without the complications of partners or saving Maisie?"

When I finished speaking, Adam stood silent for a few

moments. The air between us was so cold and tense it might as well have been frozen. The paper bag crinkled as Giguhl shifted uneasily and looked between us to see who'd strike first. Finally, Adam blew out a breath. "How does it feel?"

"What?" I barked.

"Having someone accuse you of being a blind idiot who's only motivated by selfish interests." He mercilessly held my gaze. "Doesn't feel good, does it, Sabina?"

I swallowed that bitter pill with a grimace. "No."

Giguhl stuck his head up between us. "Can we stop beating each other up long enough to remember that we all want the same thing? We're a team, remember?"

Before I could answer the demon in the affirmative, Adam added, "This won't be the last or worst surprise we'll face from Lavinia." He grabbed my hand. "We can't let her screw with us. And we have to stop beating each other up every time we're scared or angry."

I squeezed his hand back. "You're absolutely right. Of course." I sucked down a deep breath, hoping to cleanse away the lingering smoke of anger and fear. Looking from Adam to the still-tense Giguhl I said, "Sorry, guys. I guess I just don't handle scared well."

The corner of Adam's mouth lifted. "Actually, you handle it better than almost anyone I've ever met."

His words made me choke on my calming breath, which released in a snort. "Riiight."

"Now let's go back and get some sleep. Tomorrow we'll get a head start before sundown with Zen's contacts. If we're lucky, we'll find Maisie before the moon is high."

I tried to feel comforted by his optimism. But the truth was, luck and I hadn't been on speaking terms for a long time.

The next evening, I woke to the dulcet sounds of a snoring demon. Groaning, I rolled over and pulled a pillow over my head. Probably I should have gone to the living room and told Giguhl to knock it off. But my body refused to move. Another volley of snorts wormed its way through the layers of goose down over my ear. Who was I kidding? Giguhl and snoring went together like mages and magic.

I tossed the pillow to the ground and stretched. When my hand hit something warm and hard, I yelped and jerked my head to the side.

"Mornin', sunshine," Adam said. He was turned away from me, which afforded me a lovely view of golden skin, broad shoulders, and rippling muscles.

"What the—" I said.

He turned toward me, and whatever I'd been about to say evaporated on my tongue. Oh, gods, the front view was even nicer. His torso drew my eyes like a magnet. I peeked lower, but the sheets covered him from the waist down. I wondered if he'd notice me pulling them back to do a commando check.

"Earth to Sabina?" he said, amusement lacing his tone.

"Hmm?" Then I blinked. My gaze snapped back up to his sleep-rumpled face. "Wait, what the hell are you doing in my bed?"

The night before, sleeping arrangements had been based on gender. That meant I got the bedroom, with its double bed, while Adam and Giguhl got the larger sleeper sofa in the living room.

He nodded toward the wall, which practically vibrated with the noise coming through it. "He's been doing that all day."

I rubbed at my eyes and yawned. "So you decided to disturb my sleep instead?"

"Sabina, I came in here three hours ago. You've been out the entire time." Adam rested his head on his biceps and smiled like he knew a secret. "You talk in your sleep."

"Do not!"

"You totally do."

My cheek flared with heat. "What did I say?" My brain scrambled to recall dreams, but I couldn't remember any.

He shrugged. "Actually, it was more like sleep mumbling. I couldn't make out any words." He raised an eyebrow. "But rest assured, I'll be paying better attention tonight."

"Good luck hearing me from the floor, mancy."

He sat up then. His hair stood in adorable little tufts all over his head. "You're joking."

I shot him a look to assure him I wasn't.

"Oh, I get it. You don't trust yourself alone with me."

I stopped halfway out of the bed. "If you mean I don't trust myself not to punch you, you'd be correct."

"Did you know physical threats are a sign of sexual interest in some cultures?"

I shook my head at him but smiled despite myself. "You're insane."

He lay back with his arms behind his head, which only served to give me a better view of the manly banquet that was Adam Lazarus. "Am I? Or am I so close to the truth it's scary?" He was smiling in a teasing way, but his words had an edge to them.

Of course, and I'd never admit this to him, he was totally right. But his teasing made panic flair in my gut. "Fine. You want to sleep in this bed?" My feet hit the floor and I marched into the bathroom before he could respond. "It's all yours."

A few minutes later, I spat out a mouthful of toothpaste and glared at my reflection. "Don't even think about having sex with Adam."

This was not the first time I'd had to have this little conversation with myself. The attraction between us had been growing steadily over the last couple of months. Many of my initial arguments against pursuing anything with him still applied, including the fact that a mixed-race union between my parents had resulted in both their deaths and a lifetime of bullshit for me. Granted, I was only half-vampire, and with each passing day I lost a little more of the bloodsucker identity I'd once wrapped around myself like a security blanket. Hell, before things had gone south in New York, I'd seriously been considering throwing caution to the wind and making a real go with Adam.

But shit *had* gone south. And the idea of cozying up with Adam made me feel pretty fucking guilty in light of the fact my sister was being held captive and drained of her blood. Not exactly the kind of concerns that fostered romance, you know?

All that should have been enough to keep me from entertaining the thought of opening that door and throwing myself at the mancy. But there was another thing—a secret—that put a nail in the coffin of any potential.

Back in New York, I'd run into an old flame, a vampire and former assassin named Slade Corbin. At first I'd kept him at arm's length, but with Adam away at the fae court and some major emotional turmoil going on, I'd turned to Slade as both a distraction and a tool of self-sabotage. No one knew of the one-night indiscretion. Not even Giguhl. But the incident proved to me that I couldn't be trusted not to hurt Adam.

I performed three resolute taps on the sink with my toothbrush. The sounds echoed behind me. I looked up and realized someone was knocking on the door.

"What?" I barked.

"Who're you talking to?"

I went still. Obviously, he'd heard me, but had he understood what I'd said? "No one."

"That's funny," he said. "I could have sworn you just told someone not to have sex with me."

My stomach dipped. I looked in the mirror again, hoping the correct response might suddenly appear on its surface. If I opened that door, he was going to force the issue. *Maybe,* I thought, *if I just ignore him, he'll give up and go away.*

I shook my head. Who was I kidding?

When I opened the door, he blocked my exit with hands on either jamb. One eyebrow lifted in challenge.

"Did anyone ever tell you eavesdropping is rude?"

He ignored my offensive tactic. Moss green eyes pulled me in like a tractor beam. Or maybe he moved. I couldn't tell, because I was too busy being relieved I'd already brushed my teeth. Then his sleepy scent hit me. Warm and spicy. Like whispered secrets between tangled sheets.

All conscious thought fled like a thief in the night. A shock of recognition as his lips brushed mine. Soft. Hesitant at first. When I didn't fight it, he sank into the kiss. But his hands still gripped the doorframe, as if he didn't trust himself to touch me fully. His chest teased my breasts through the thin fabric of my cotton tank. His scent and his kisses lulled me into a trancelike state.

"Sabina," he whispered against my lips. He pulled me in. The move made the amulets between my breasts clink together.

Oh, shit! Some sister I was. "Slow down." I placed a hand on the smooth skin of his chest. His heart thumped against my palm. "We can't do this."

He pulled back, his expression part frustration and part concern. "What's wrong?" he whispered.

I couldn't speak for a moment. The truth—the real reason I held him off—slammed through me like lightning. *Because if I let you inside, you'll see how truly broken I am and leave.*

When I didn't answer Adam right away, his face went all pinched. "Just answer one question for me."

I licked the taste of him off my lips and tried to focus on keeping the panic off my face. Inside, though, my gut felt like it was taking a ride on a tilt-a-whirl. "Shoot."

He paused, letting the tension mount. His solemn gaze met mine. "How long are you going to make me wait?"

I considered making a joke. Blowing the whole thing off like nothing had happened. But I cared about Adam too much to dismiss his genuine interest with careless sarcasm. "I don't know."

He stared at me for a few moments. Behind his eyes I could see the wheels turning. Weighing the options and eventualities. Finally, he breathed out through his nose, like expelling bad energy. "Well, I guess that's better than 'never.' "

He could have interrogated me. Forced the issue. The fact he didn't made me feel even more guilty. "I'm sorry. I just—I need time." *To figure out how to be with you without destroying us both.*

He ran a finger down my cheek. "Time is a precious commodity right now, Red. Wait too long and it might be too late."

I swallowed hard. Went still as my stomach clenched with dread. Hadn't Maisie said almost those exact same words to me in New York when she'd encouraged me to admit my feelings to Adam? "I know."

He leaned forward and placed another soft kiss on my lips. When he pulled away, he held my gaze. "Soon, Sabina."

This time his words weren't so much a threat as a promise. Of what I wasn't sure. I had a hunch he meant he'd grow tired of waiting and give up, but he could have just as easily meant soon he'd be making his big move. Either way, the message came through loud and clear. He knew I was purposefully keeping him at arm's length. He probably even thought he knew why.

But instead of coming clean, I merely inclined my head to acknowledge I'd heard him. That seemed to be enough for him, because he turned away without another word. As the door closed behind him with a click, I sagged against the doorjamb for a moment. Then I straightened myself up and went back into the bathroom for a cold shower.

*   *   *

Half an hour later, I emerged from my room ready to take
on the evening. We only had about an hour of sunlight
left, so going out now wouldn't wreak too much havoc on
my energy levels. Unlike full-blooded vamps, I could go
into the sun without dying. But it seriously taxed my system, so I tried to limit my exposure.

In the kitchen, Giguhl sat at a Formica dinette with a
mug of coffee and a plate of pastries in the center. He
looked up from the *New Orleans Dispatch* when I entered.
Over a mouthful of fried dough and powdered sugar he
said, "Brooks brought us beignets!"

I blinked. At first I hadn't noticed the fae. He leaned
against the sink, chatting up Adam. "Hey, Brooks," I said.
"Thanks."

He saluted me with his pink mug, which read, *Put on
your big-girl panties and deal with it.*

"Morning, *cher.* You sleep well?"

"Mmm-hmm," I said, keeping my tone breezy as I
went to the coffee pot.

"Adam was just telling me he didn't sleep well at all,
poor lamb."

I shot a pointed look at the demon. Giguhl raised a
scraggly black brow. "I wonder why?" He turned a page
and took his time readjusting the paper before continuing
in a singsong voice. "Could it be because someone played
musical beds in the middle of the night?"

I glared at the demon. "He moved beds because you
snore louder than a congested wildebeest."

Giguhl stage-whispered to Brooks, "Denial."

"That's enough, G," Adam said quietly.

Giguhl grabbed his coffee mug and two extra beignets

and stood. "If you need me, I'll be in the other room catching up on my stories." With that, he made a dramatic exit that gave Blanche DuBois a run for her money.

I sighed. "Gods, what a drama queen."

"Red, give him a break," Adam sighed. "He's still nursing a broken heart."

"Oh, yeah. The end of his weeklong affair with Valva must really be hurting his heart. Give me a break, Adam." I snorted. "What did he expect hooking up with a *Vanity* demon?"

Brooks let out a low whistle. "I have to say, y'all are definitely the most...entertaining guests we've ever had."

I grimaced, worried we'd worn out our welcome before we had a chance to make any headway. "I'm sorry. We're usually much better behaved," I lied. "It's just kind of a stressful time for everyone."

Brooks shrugged. "Not to worry, *cher.* As long as you don't destroy any property or eat any of our patrons, you're welcome here."

"Thanks, Brooks."

Adam cleared his throat and changed the subject. "I called Orpheus while you were in the shower. Filled him in on your little chat with Lavinia last night."

I paused on my way to the fridge for some milk. "And?"

"And," he sighed, "as expected, he wants to go ahead with the plan. We're supposed to focus on finding Maisie's location."

I gritted my teeth and continued to the fridge in the hope of buying some time before I blurted the curses jockeying for position on my tongue. Trying to find Maisie was our plan anyway, but having it reported to me like an order rankled. But I knew that was mainly my ego talking. After my argument with Adam the night before, I'd realized I needed to keep a better handle on my temper if we were going to make this work.

As I walked, my fingers found Maisie's amulet. I touched it briefly as a reminder to stay focused and calm. Swallowing my indignation, I pulled the fridge handle. Inside all I found was empty shelves, no light, and stale, warm air. I turned and shot Brooks a confused look.

"Oops, forgot to tell you the Frigidaire is broken," Brooks said. "I threw some little cups of creamer in the bag from Café du Monde, though, if you need it."

I mumbled my thanks and pulled a shot of creamer out of the white paper bag. As I poured, I finally responded to Adam. "Sounds like a plan," I said diplomatically. "Did he mention what we're supposed to do when we find her?"

Adam cringed. "Yes. We're to report our findings to him and wait for further instruction."

The second creamer tub popped in my hand, spraying me with a small geyser of milk.

Brooks, oblivious to the undercurrent of tension, said, "Zen's got a dorm fridge in her workroom downstairs if y'all need to keep anything cold."

Figuring it was best to avoid a discussion about Orpheus's instructions at present, I wiped my hand on my jeans and changed the subject.

"Is Zen around?"

Brooks set down his mug. "Actually, that's one of the reasons I stopped by. Madam Z's volunteering at church tonight, so I'll be helping you."

Adam frowned. "Church?"

"Sure. Zen's a devout Catholic."

"Isn't it kind of unusual for a voodoo priestess to be Catholic?" I asked.

"Honey, this is New Orleans. Very little is considered unusual here. You'll see."

I let my curiosity slip away. Zenobia's religious beliefs were none of my business. But the fact she wasn't around to help frustrated me. I looked at Adam. "What now?"

He opened his mouth to respond, but Brooks beat him to it. "I hope you don't mind, but I took the liberty of setting up a meeting for you."

I scrubbed my face with a hand, thinking what I really needed was a vacation. "Someone with ties to the local vamps?"

"You could say that," Brooks said. "I can take you to meet Mac now if you'd like."

"Can you just give us an address and we can go on our own?"

Brooks shook his head. "Actually, it's better if I handle the introduction. Some of the dark races down here get a tad suspicious about strangers."

"Totally understandable," Adam said.

Brooks snapped his fingers. "Oh, I almost forgot. Zen asked me to give this to you when you woke up." He handed over a piece of paper with an address on it.

"What's this?"

"The address of the butcher's shop she told you about."

I'd forgotten all about the cow's-blood thing. "Thanks," I said, glancing at the clock. It was already six p.m. "Should we go now before we meet your friend?"

"Oh, don't worry," Brooks said, waving a hand. "The shop is open all night. You can head there after." He paused and narrowed his eyes, looking at my mouth for telltale signs of fangs. "Unless you're hungry now?"

I smiled, showing lots of nonpointy teeth. "I think I can manage."

"All righty then," Brooks said, setting his mug down with a thump. "Let's head out to Lagniappe's."

I frowned. "Lawn yaps?"

"That's the name of Mac's bar. It means 'a little somethin' extra.'" Brooks chuckled like he'd made a joke.

"What's 'extra' about this place?" Adam asked.

Brooks grinned from ear to ear. "You'll see, *cher*. You'll see."

*W*hen Brooks informed us we'd be walking to the club, I was wary. On one hand, I wanted to see more of New Orleans's famous French Quarter. On the other, the more time I spent out in the open, the more chances we'd give Lavinia and her goons to make a move. Adam's shoulders were tense and his eyes alert as we headed one block over to take a left on Royal Street.

After a few minutes, though, I found myself relaxing. The streets were crowded with tourists, which made blending easy. When I asked Brooks why so many people were in town, he explained that with Halloween that weekend, lots of people came in town early to party.

"Shit, I totally forgot about Halloween." I mentally counted back and realized that it was already Wednesday. We only had three days until Halloween reached the Big Easy and complicated our lives.

"Oh, yeah, it's probably our biggest celebration outside of Mardi Gras. Parades, costumes, street parties. There's even a huge three-day music festival in City Park—Voodoo Fest.

The lineup this year is awesome so lots of folks are celebrating Halloween in the Big Easy."

Adam shot me a meaningful look. "That should make things interesting."

I nodded and nibbled on my lip. The parties and people might help conceal our presence a little longer. But it also made security an issue. Not only did it increase the risk of humans seeing something they shouldn't, but it also raised the odds of innocents getting harmed if shit went down. Plus there was the whole issue of not being able to spot enemies approaching with thousands of costumed people filling the streets. But if I had my way, we'd find Maisie long before the festivities heated up on Saturday night.

We made it down Royal without incident before Brooks took a sharp right on Toulouse. Just past Pat O'Brien's, a neon sign advertised our destination. From the outside, Lagniappe's looked like any other French Quarter bar. Inside, the decor was typical bar. In fact, the only interesting detail was a stage set across from the long bar. Given Brooks's claim that the bar offered a little something extra, I found myself disappointed.

"It's pretty empty," Adam observed as Brooks led us through the empty tables toward the back. Despite the lack of clientele, rock growled from the speakers. Something by Melissa Etheridge.

"Won't be empty for long," Brooks yelled. "The show starts at nine. By then the place will be filled to the gills."

I reserved judgment on that claim, because we'd reached a door bearing a sign that read "Private." Brooks knocked twice. I didn't hear anyone answer over the blaring music, but he opened the door and ushered us inside anyway.

A petite brunette sat behind a desk in the corner. From my vantage point she looked like another human at first. But when I sniffed the air I caught the scent of dog and relaxed. I'd been expecting a vampire, of course. But a werewolf would do. I was just relieved Brooks had brought us to someone who might be more plugged in to the dark-race underworld than Zen might be.

"Brooks!" the female called as she rose to greet us. "You brought friends."

"Hey, girl!" Brooks said, going in for a hug. When they were done, he turned and held out a hand.

"This is Sabina Kane and Adam Lazarus. They're staying at Zen's."

Mac approached with a warm smile and an extended hand. "Nice to meet you. I'm MacKenzie Romulus. You can call me Mac."

She moved to Adam just as her last name sunk in. "Wait, did you say Romulus?"

When she nodded, I continued. "You wouldn't be related to Michael Romulus, would you?"

Her eyes brightened. "He's my uncle."

My mouth fell open. Hard to imagine the straitlaced Alpha of New York weres was related to a female who owned a dive bar in New Orleans. "What a coincidence," I said. "I just saw him a few days ago."

"I've been meaning to call him since I heard about the trouble in New York. Please tell me he wasn't in the middle of all that."

I cringed. "Actually, he was. He and his pack helped the Hekate Council when they were attacked by the Dominae."

Her eyebrows knitted into a frown. "Is he okay?"

I nodded. "Your uncle's hard to kill." I didn't mention the fact I'd tried it myself and failed. Luckily, Michael and I had moved past that conflict in time to team up against the Caste's attack. "Didn't get so much as a scratch. In fact, I probably owe him a dozen favors for saving my ass. He's good people."

She smiled and motioned to some seats in front of the desk. "Well, any friend of Uncle Mike's is a friend of mine. Have a seat."

"Actually, if y'all will excuse me?" Brooks cut in. "I need to get ready for my set."

"Oh, that's right," Mac said. "Scoot."

Brooks turned to go and then stopped. "Will you two stick around to see the show?"

I blinked. "You're performing?"

Brooks smiled. "Yes, ma'am."

I glanced at Adam to make sure he was cool with hanging out. He shrugged and nodded. "We wouldn't miss it."

When Brooks was gone, we all took seats around Mac's desk. "So, Brooks said you needed some information about a missing mage?"

I nodded. "My sister. She was kidnapped by a vampire during the attack in New York."

Mac paused in the middle of distributing beers around the room. "What makes you think she's here?"

I hesitated. Mac might be Michael's niece, but as far as I was concerned, no one could be trusted. So I skipped the part about kidnapping Tanith. "Let's just say we're going on a credible tip."

Mac took a pull from her beer and sat back in her chair. "And how exactly do you think I can help?"

Mac's directness made me like her even more. "Brooks

said you had connections with the vamps here. Do you mind if I ask what exactly your connection is to them?"

She took her time answering. Pulling open a desk drawer, she withdrew a pack of American Spirits. After offering the pack to us and shrugging at our refusals, she used a pack of matches with the club's name on them to light her cigarette. I tamped down my impatience. From what I'd seen of Mac so far, she was shrewd. She knew as much about us as we knew about her, which is to say not much. Only a fool would show all his cards now.

She blew out a chain of smoke rings before answering. "Let's just say it's in my best interest to have allies among all the dark races."

"I'd imagine so, being so far away from your pack and all." I was digging. For all I knew, she could have been the Alpha of a New Orleans pack. But something about the way she carried herself told me she was too much a rebel to follow any pack.

She took another drag. "Among other things."

"We were hoping you might be able to tell us if there's been chatter lately among the local vamps."

She pursed her lips. "What kind of chatter?"

Adam leaned in. "Anything out of the ordinary. New vamps in town, changes in power structure. That kind of thing."

"Now that you mention it," Mac said. "I've been getting a feeling something's coming. Can't put my finger on it, but the vamps I know, well, lately some of them have been tense."

"What do you mean?" I asked.

She shrugged. "You have to understand, the vamps here are pretty disorganized and usually keep to small cliques.

There's turf spats every now and then, but with all the tourists there's plenty to go around for everyone. But over the last few days the vamps I know have been acting kind of on edge, like they're bracing themselves."

"Any idea why?" I asked.

"Not a clue. Although I did hear one of them talking about some weird owl."

Adam and I stilled and looked at each other. "Red eyes?" I asked.

Mac tilted her head. "Yeah. You know anything about that?"

"I might," I evaded.

"Anyway, I guess this owl's been hanging out around some of the vamps' regular feeding grounds."

"No one's mentioned a new vamp in town?" Adam asked.

She shook her head. "If you tell who or what exactly you're looking for, I could ask around."

"Here's the deal. I can't tell you specifics. The less you're directly involved, the safer you'll be. Suffice it to say, though, the vamp we're after is extremely dangerous."

"Gotcha," Mac said, her eyes meeting mine. Her expression indicated she respected the need to keep some cards close to my vest, too. "I'll ask around. See if any of my contacts have anything to say."

"We'd appreciate that." I resisted my sudden urge to pump my fist in the air.

"Of course, in return for this favor, I'd ask one in return. To be called in at a future date."

I looked at Adam. He nodded. "That sounds reasonable."

Mac clapped her hands. "Well, now that that's taken care of, why don't we go grab some seats outside? The show's starting in a few."

*   *   *

Brooks wasn't lying when he said the place would get crowded. I just hadn't expected a bar owned by a werewolf to cater to mostly mortal clientele. The place reeked of dirt and Dixie beer. Not that I minded the beer. In fact, as we waited for the show to begin I helped myself to a few chugs.

Adam and I sat with Mac toward the back of the audience.

"So what kind of show is Brooks going to do exactly? Does he sing or something?"

Mac smiled. "He didn't tell you?" When I shook my head, she laughed. "Let's just say it falls into the 'or something' category."

As if on cue, the lights dimmed and spotlights danced across the red curtain. Catcalls and hoots followed. I shrugged and took another sip of beer, feeling more relaxed. Adam and I still needed to discuss what to do next while we were waiting for Mac to come through with more info. But for the time being, I was content to sit back for a couple minutes and watch the show.

"Ladies and gents, welcome to Gender Bender night at Lagniappe's," the announcer called over the speaker. "Tonight we have a special treat for y'all. Everyone give a warm welcome to the Big Easy's newest drag sensation— Miss Pussy Willow!"

As the audience went wild, Adam turned to me and mouthed, "Pussy Willow?"

I shrugged, mystified, and turned my attention back to the stage. The curtains parted and a vision appeared onstage with a flourish of pink feather boa and attitude. She wore a full-length purple sequined gown and six-inch stilettos. The cut-to-there slit revealed legs that would make a Rockette jealous. And to top it all off, a tiara twinkled from atop a Farrah Fawcett wig.

The female looked around the audience, searching for someone. When she saw Adam and me, she waggled her fingers and winked.

My mouth fell open and I hit Adam on the arm. "Oh, my gods, is that Brooks?"

He rubbed his arm and said, "No way."

"Helloo, darlings!" Pussy Willow called. "Where y'at?"

While the audience ate up the banter, Mac leaned over. "Isn't she great?"

Now that the initial shock had passed, I had to admit Brooks was looking pretty fierce. I nodded absently, my eyes riveted on Brooks/Pussy Willow vamping across the stage.

Mac leaned over and spoke into my ear. "Excuse me for a minute."

I nodded absently, unable to pull my eyes from Brooks chatting up the audience. I felt a nudge at my elbow and looked up to see Adam staring pointedly at the front of the club. I followed his gaze and saw a redhead standing by the door. Her eyes scanned the dark place, obviously looking for someone. When she saw Mac, her expression brightened. Unlike Brooks, the new arrival wasn't tucking anything but a pair of fangs.

While we watched, the vamp leaned in for a kiss, but Mac waylaid her with a shake of her head and a glance in our direction. The vamp frowned. Her eyes found mine and narrowed. I looked away instead of engaging in a stare off. The last thing I needed was to be recognized or seen as a threat to the local vamps.

Adam kept his eyes on the pair for me. "Mac's taking her back to the office."

Mac rushed the vampiress through the club, like she was worried about them being seen together. She closed the office door behind them.

Interesting.

"Think that's her contact?" I said.

"I'd say it's a safe—" Before he completed that thought, music blared through the club. The opening strains sounded familiar. But it wasn't until Brooks lip-synched the opening lines to "I Touch Myself" that I spewed beer all over the floor.

I'd barely recovered when Brooks threaded the boa between her legs and gave her lower decks a good swabbing. She wadded the pink feathers into a ball and threw them. The boa hit Adam square in the chest before sliding into his lap. He stared down at the feathers the same way he might have if someone had thrown an actual boa constrictor at him.

"Pussy Willow's got a crush on you," I sang.

That earned me an epic glare.

He picked up the boa and took his time wrapping it around my neck. Crossed the ends and pulled it tight like an über-feminine garrote. He leaned in. His glare was gone. In its place, a mischievous glint shown in his eyes. "I wonder if there's a matching muzzle."

The crowd roared at something onstage and we both turned. The song was almost over, and the whole room tensed in anticipation of Pussy Willow's grand finale. We weren't disappointed. First, she spun in circles like a dreidel with her arms spread wide as she mouthed the refrain over and over. Just when the song reached its crescendo, Brooks dropped into a split that defied several laws of physiology and psychics.

I jumped out of my seat to join the rest of the audience in a standing ovation. Adam stood beside me with his jaw hanging down to his clavicles. "Holy shit!"

"No kidding," I said. "I don't know about you, but I need a stiff drink after that."

He paused. "You want me to get you something from the bar?"

I shook my head. "Nope. I want to go see a butcher about some blood."

9

After a quick good-bye to Brooks, we left him to enjoy his post-performance glow. The plan was to hit the butcher shop on Magazine Street before heading back to Zenobia's.

As the St. Charles streetcar rocked its way toward the Garden District, Adam and I lapsed into silence. Under different circumstances, the trolley might have been a pleasant way to see the city. But my thoughts inevitably turned to Maisie, and the nocturnal scenery only served to depress me. Spanish moss draped the trees like funeral shrouds. The old houses crouched on either side of St. Charles like mourners watching a funeral procession, their dark windows like eyes closed in grief.

Adam took my hand, his warm on my cold skin. "We'll find her."

I looked up into his eyes. I wanted to grab his words out of the air and cling to them like a buoy. But the practical side of me knew it wouldn't do any good. Hope was a mirage. And reality was a harsh mistress. "You don't know that."

He sighed, his own frustration making his shoulders tense. "You're right. I don't."

I swallowed and looked out the windows again. My hand found the two amulets—mine and Maisie's—as if the contact might somehow forge a real connection with her. Instead, the metal and stone just felt cold against my skin. Adam didn't let go of my other hand, and for once, I didn't worry about what he might think my easy acceptance of contact might mean. He was offering much-needed comfort, and I'd be a fool to refuse it out of pride.

Gears hissed under the trolley, signaling an upcoming stop. I squinted and saw we'd finally reached Washington Street. "This is us."

We exited the car and jogged across St. Charles to enter the stately neighborhoods of the Garden District. According to Brooks, if we kept going straight for a few more blocks we'd end up on Magazine Street. The street was dark and mostly mortal-free, except for the homeowners tucked away inside their mansions. I could just scent their blood in the damp air.

After growing up in the urban sprawl of Los Angeles, New Orleans was like an entirely different country. Between the antique architecture, the slower pace of life, and the spicy southern culture, I found myself liking what I'd seen of the city. Maybe once all the drama was over, I could come back to enjoy the city's delights.

Once we turned onto the shop-lined Magazine Street, the butcher's place was hard to miss. Two eight-foot tall phalluses—okay, maybe they were sausages—flanked the doors and a sign on the front door read: Cajun Sausage Fest, Home of the World's Best Boudin.

A small bell dinged as Adam I entered. The shop

boasted a long meat display case and a few bistro tables pushed together in one corner. The place was empty of customers for the moment, thank the gods. Not a surprise, given the late hour. But who knew? Maybe when the bars cleared out, hordes of drunks stumbled through the doors in search of sausage.

A portly human male burst through the horizontal plastic flaps separating the shop from the work area in back. He'd pasted his thinning brown hair across a shiny pate. The comb-over, in addition to not fooling anyone, also accentuated his jowls. His apron had a threadbare appearance that indicated religious washing and heavy use. A beige short-sleeved dress shirt and brown tie—complete with a gold tiepin—peeked over the top of the apron.

When he saw us waiting for him, he paused. His eyes widened a bit and then narrowed as if he was sizing us up. I couldn't blame him, really. I'd imagine his normal clientele didn't include leather-clad vampires and mages in dusters.

I held up my hands. "Hi there. Madam Zenobia sent us."

He visibly relaxed. "Alodius Thibodeaux at your service."

I nodded. "I'm Sabina and this is my friend Adam."

Alodius's eyes narrowed. "Where y'all from?"

"New York," I said automatically. Then I paused. Since when did I consider New York home? For the first fifty-three years of my life home was Los Angeles. Funny it only took a few weeks with the mages to change so much of my identity.

"Ah," he said. The single word came out sounding like a verdict: *Yankees*. "So you're an old friend of Madam Z's, you said?"

"She's putting us up for a few days," Adam lied. "She said you might be able to help us acquire some ... blood."

"I see." He pursed his lips and nodded. "Well, *cher,* you come to the right place. Alodius slaughters his own product, so we've got lots of fresh blood. Bovine or porcine?"

My nose crinkled at the idea of drinking pig's blood. Not that cold cow's blood sounded any better, I guess. "Cow's fine."

"An excellent choice. Most of my vamp customers prefer bovine."

His casual attitude about discussing blood preferences with a vamp surprised me. Most places I'd been, humans were blissfully unaware of the existence of vampires. But this guy seemed like he dealt with this sort of thing all the time. I leaned forward and whispered, "You know many vampires?"

"Some. Most around here prefer to eat off the hoof, but every now and again one'll find hisself here." He shrugged. "You pay Alodius twenty a pint, yeah?"

I wasn't sure what was more disturbing, his insistence on referring to himself in the third person or his prices. "I'll take two pints to start."

"Yes, ma'am. We'll ring that up for you *tout de suite.*"

He went to a cooler behind the counter. From it he retrieved a milk jug filled with red liquid. I shared a grimace with Adam. Thank the gods I didn't have to worry about food poisoning.

While he worked, he chatted away like a jaybird. "Y'all in town long?"

"Just got here yesterday," I said. "Not sure when we'll leave."

Adam shot me a look. I frowned at him. No sense being rude to the guy. Even though he was human, he seemed friendly enough.

"Well, you came to the right place. Old Alodius has the best blood in town."

Watching the cold cow's blood drip into the plastic container, I had my doubts. But I figured it couldn't be worse than the bagged blood I'd been forced to consume in New York. I had no idea how to respond, so I just made the appropriate noises. Adam was suddenly busy studying a diagram explaining different cuts of meat.

"You a mage, son?"

Adam's head swiveled slowly on his neck. "What's it to you?"

I shot Adam a look. The last thing I needed was for him to piss off my blood supplier.

"Just making conversation. Most of your kind high-tailed it outta here a few days ago. Oddest thing. One day they're going about their biddness and the next thing, poof, all gone."

"That's interesting," Adam said evenly.

"Alodius? Can I ask you a question?" I jumped in to prevent any further probing.

"Shoot."

"You're human, right?"

"No, darlin'." He chuckled from low in his belly. "Alodius ain't just human. He's Cajun."

I frowned at the odd man's insistence on referring to himself in the third person. "Okay, so how exactly does a Cajun end up serving cow's blood to vampires? Most people would freak if they knew they had a vampire in their store."

"Darlin', this is N'Awlins," he said, as if that explained everything.

"Yeah, but—"

"Y'all got to understand. People down here? We been

raised hearing stories from our *Mameres* 'bout ghosts and voodoo. So when old Alodius got older and learned the world is chockablock with vampires and other magic things?" His shrug was decidedly Gallic. "'Course it helps that selling blood and raw meat to your kind brought Big Poppa some sweet *Mameaux*." As he drawled out the words, he lazily dragged his right thumb across his fingers.

"Ah," I said.

He handed over a plastic bag filled with two plastic tubs of blood. "Speaking of, *cher*, there's more where that come from." He grabbed a magnet shaped like a kielbasa from the top of the raised counter. "This here's got Alodius's number. You call him anytime and he'll fix you up proper."

I nodded my thanks and stuck the magnet in my back pocket. "Thanks, Mr. Thibodeaux."

He waved the air like he was trying to shoo a fly. "Mr. Thibodeaux was our father. It's Alodius." He winked at me like a conspirator. "Or Big Poppa."

I squinted, trying to wade through the pronoun soup. And wondering if I dared ask why he called himself Big Poppa. He seemed nice enough, but I was beginning to wonder if this odd Cajun was a few shrimp short of gumbo.

"Okay," I said slowly. "Alodius, then."

"Y'all sure you don't want some boudin to go with that blood? Maybe Madam Z can cook y'all up some dirty rice?"

After he rung up the blood and the pound of sausage he'd talked us into, Adam threw some money at the crazy Cajun and pushed me out the door. As the bell dinged again, Alodius called out: "Y'all don't be strangers, y'hear?"

"That guy was weird," Adam said.

"I don't know," I said. "I thought he was friendly." I swung the plastic bag as we strolled. Despite the worries hanging over me, I felt optimistic for some reason. Maybe it was the beautiful night. Or the bag of blood in my hands. Or the hot mage walking beside me. Either way, I was determined to make the most of the few moments of peace I could get.

I took a deep breath and tried to enjoy the parade of Greek Revivals, Italianates, and Queen Anne Victorians on display. Up ahead, the sidewalk buckled where the roots of an ancient oak had protested being smothered with concrete. When we reached it, I stepped over. But Adam had been too busy watching for attack to notice the crack. He ended up sprawled on the pavement at my feet.

"Oops, sorry," I said, grabbing his arm. "Should have warned you."

He grimaced and dusted off his pants with as much dignity as he could muster. Before he could retort, a shriek ripped through the night. We went still. My heart ran laps around my chest. My eyes narrowed.

Fucking Stryx.

"Shit," Adam said under his breath. He ducked down as if expected the owl to dive-bomb at any moment. Which, come to think of it, wasn't out of the realm of possibility.

"Do you see him?" I said, crouching next to the mancy.

Out of nowhere, a flash of white zoomed in from the right. A blur of beak and talons flashed. Adam jerked away with a curse. A streak of blood ran down his cheek.

"That's it. I'm killing that bird right fucking now." My

eyes scanned the branches overhead for a pair of glowing red eyes or a mass of white feathers. I pointed to an upper limb. "There." I grabbed for my gun.

"Sabiiiiina!" the owl screeched. The hairs on my neck prickled. He rose like a ghost from the tree. I tracked him with the muzzle of my gun, ready to finish the job I'd started in New York. He flew in circles, taunting me. "Sabiiiiiina!"

At the last moment, Adam put a hand over mine. "Wait, maybe we should try to catch him and see if he can tell us anything about Lavinia's plans."

"Adam, he's an owl. What's he going to tell us?"

The mage shrugged. "Maybe we could use him as a bargaining tool."

I rolled my eyes. "Right, because Lavinia will totally barter the Oracle of New York for an owl. Come on, Adam."

"Look, he works for the Caste, right? Maybe he's got some value or something. We need every advantage we can get. Or has it escaped your attention that we still have no idea where Lavinia's keeping Maisie?"

I cringed inwardly. Of course it hadn't escaped my notice. I berated myself hourly for that fact. "Fine. Do your best, magic man,"

Adam slowly rose from his crouch. Stryx broke out of his circle and shot off into the night like a bullet.

"Shit! Let's go," I said, already running. Adam kept up, muttering something under his breath. A laserlike flash of magic shot through the air. The hair on my arms prickled as the shot went wide. The owl's hoot sounded suspiciously like a laugh.

Unfortunately for the bird, this only served to piss the mage off even more. Adam dug in, picking up speed even as he raised his hands and shouted, "*Zi dingir anna, kesh-ada, Stryx!*"

The owl's latest screech cut off like someone pulling a needle from a record. His white body nosedived to the ground and disappeared into a group of shrubs along the garden wall of one of the mansions. We high-fived before zooming to retrieve our feathered captive.

Adam pushed the branches aside to reveal Stryx's inert body. "Is he dead?" I whispered.

He grabbed the owl by its legs. Its head hung just a couple inches over the sidewalk. Unmoving and spookier than ever with its sightless red eyes.

"Nope. Just catatonic." Adam raised his eyebrows. "What now?"

"Hey, this was your plan. If it was up to me, we'd take that bird back to that butcher. Alodius probably thinks owls are good eatin'."

Adam's lips quirked. "Or he'd give us the name of some cousin of his that lives in the swamps who could give us a good deal on some taxidermy."

I pursed my lips as if considering it. "Now that you mention it, I wouldn't mind seeing this damn thing stuffed and mounted."

Adam shook his head at me. "Or we could take him back to Zen's, lock him up, and then figure out how to use him to find Maisie."

"Oh, all right," I said. "But you might want cover him up or something."

With that, Adam tucked the owl's body under his duster and we made our way back to Zen's.

10

By the time we finally made it back to the shop, it was pushing one in the morning. Even though I normally hit the sack at dawn, I was ready to crash the minute we walked in the door. Too bad we still had to deal with Satan's owl.

When we opened the door to the attic apartment, we found Giguhl and Brooks sitting on the couch together. Brooks was back in his male gear—jeans, T-shirt, et cetera. Giguhl sat with his arms crossed over bulging biceps. He still wore the sweatpants he had on earlier that evening when we...

Oh shit.

We'd totally forgotten Giguhl when we left. I took a step forward, ready to apologize. But Brooks held up a hand and shushed me. He patted Giguhl on the arm. "Sabina. Adam. Giguhl has something he'd like to say to you."

Giguhl's determined expression faltered. "I don't think—"

Brooks nudged him. "Go on. Tell her what you told me."

I shot a look at Adam. He shrugged and rolled his eyes.

Giguhl took a deep, bracing breath and rose from the couch. "Guys, I—" he shot a look at Brooks, who nodded encouragingly. The demon seemed to inflate a little and continued. "I felt disappointed when you left this evening without telling me. It hurt my feelings that you didn't consider me in your plans."

I felt bad about forgetting him and all, but an emotional intervention wasn't on my list of things I wanted to deal with. I set down my bag of blood with a martyred sigh.

Giguhl tossed his claws in the air. "Don't sigh at me! I've been worried sick, and your continued lack of consideration is unacceptable."

I dropped down on the couch. "Giguhl, what do you want from us? There are some places you can't go in either demon or cat form." It was a lame excuse. I'd smuggled him into lots of places, but I didn't know what else to say. The truth was I had been so wrapped up in my own drama that I'd totally forgotten about him. But admitting that would hurt his feelings even more.

"We've always figured out ways for me to come along before," he challenged. His eyes shifted back and forth between Adam and me. "I thought we were a team."

From the corner of my eye I saw Adam cringe. I couldn't meet the demon's accusing gaze, either. When we'd decided to find Maisie, we'd all agreed it would be as a team. But the whole concept of thinking about someone else's feelings went against my natural instincts to just take care of everything myself.

"Look, G, I'm sorry we didn't tell you where we were headed. But you seemed kind of out of it, so I didn't even consider you might want to come. I'm sorry. It won't happen again. Right, Adam?"

"Sorry, G. You're right. We are a team."

Giguhl tilted his chin down, accepting our apologies. "One more thing. The next time you have a chance to go to a drag show, I don't care what you have to do, but you better smuggle my ass in."

I'd totally forgotten about the faery's show earlier. "Oh, right. Great show, Brooks."

The fae winked at me. "Thanks, hon. Adam? What did you think?"

Adam looked a little pained as he struggled for a response. Finally, he settled with, "It was . . . something."

While Brooks smiled at the mage, Giguhl turned to me. "Please tell me you took pictures."

"Sorry, G. I was so entranced it didn't occur to me." Turning to Brooks, I said, "Where did you learn to do the splits like that?"

With his eyes on Adam, he said, "I'm extremely flexible."

I changed the subject. "I have a question. How do you prefer to be addressed?"

Brooks smiled. "You mean do I consider myself a 'he' or a 'she'?" When I nodded uncomfortably, Brooks continued. "I know it gets confusing. A lot of queens don't go by 'she' at all, some insist on 'she' all the time, and others only when they're in drag. Me? I'll answer to anything."

I nodded. "Good to know. I didn't know if you were sensitive—"

Brooks waved a hand. "Darlin', I tuck my unmentionables and secure them with duct tape." Giguhl hissed and Adam covered his crotch with his hand.

I laughed. "Well when you put it that way ..."

Adam dropped his protective hand and shifted uncomfortably. "Since you're in a sharing mood, I've got a question, too. Which species of fae are you exactly?"

Brooks crossed *his*—I'd decided to stick with the masculine for simplicity—arms, his expression gone from flirtatious to defensive. "Why?"

Adam shrugged. "Just wondering. Most of the fae I know try to live near green spaces or have access to other fae."

Brooks's chin went up. "I suppose I would do that, too, if I'd been raised among the fae."

I frowned. "What does that mean?"

Adam nudged me. Under his breath he said, "He's a changeling."

I looked up at Adam. "Huh?"

But Brooks stepped in. "He said I'm a changeling. My fae parents left me with humans right after I was born. I was raised as a human kid until it became obvious I wasn't like the other children. I tried to hide it for a while, but then I couldn't deny it any longer. Unfortunately, my human parents weren't too thrilled when I came out of the faery mound, so to speak. They kicked me out when I was fourteen."

My mouth dropped open. "That's terrible."

"It happens to lots of changelings, unfortunately," Adam said. To Brooks: "How did you end up with Zen?"

"She volunteered at a shelter I crashed at when I was seventeen. By then I was pretty messed up," he said vaguely. "But Zen recognized that I was fae and helped me. Got me cleaned up. Gave me a job and a place to live. Without her, I doubt I'd still be alive."

We were all silent as we listened to his story. On some level I could relate to not being accepted by your family because of something you couldn't control. But even though Lavinia was about as nurturing as a viper, at least I'd never had to live on the streets. I'd liked Brooks before, but now I respected him, too.

"Wow," Giguhl said, dispelling the solemn cloud that hung over our group. "You're just like *Pretty Woman*."

Brooks nodded solemnly. "Except I'm still waiting for my Richard Gere."

Giguhl sighed. "Aren't we all?" He looked around at each of us with a can-I-get-an-amen look.

I shot a frown at the demon. "Anyway, Brooks, I'm glad everything worked out."

Adam nodded. "Ditto."

"Thanks, guys. Now, what took you so long to get back? You left the club hours ago."

Giguhl turned to look at us with his arms crossed. "Yeah! What gives?"

"We went to get Sabina blood and ran into an old friend." He folded back the flap of his duster, revealing the unconscious owl.

Giguhl cringed with his claws up defensively. "What the hell?"

Brooks scooted back behind the demon. "Is it dead?"

"Just unconscious," I explained. "How long can he stay like that, Adam?"

The mage frowned. "Not much longer. We probably need to rig up some sort of cage for him while we sleep."

"Excuse me," Giguhl interjected. "What the hell does kidnapping Stryx accomplish?"

Adam sighed and rose, leaving the owl in the seat. "I'll

go see if Zen has anything we can use while you explain it to him, Sabina."

My lips pressed together as I glared at the mage. Just before he closed the door, I caught a ghost of a smile on his lips. Ass.

"Wait. Before you tell us, can you please cover that thing?" Giguhl said. "It's creepy as shit."

For some reason when Adam zapped the owl, its eyes stayed open. Despite Stryx being unconscious, the surface of the blood-red pupils shifted and spun like a mesmerizer. Something told me if I stared into them too long I'd end up hypnotized—or worse. I shuddered and tossed a blanket over the bird.

Ten minutes later, Giguhl and Brooks had the full story and were sitting as far away from the unconscious owl as possible.

Adam returned then, carrying a birdcage. Actually, the ornate design and massive size made it into more of a bird mansion. Zen followed him through the door. I stifled my grimace at her arrival. She might have rubbed me the wrong way when we met, but she was nice enough to put us up for free and all.

"Where'd you find that?" I asked.

Adam nodded toward the voodoo priestess, who made a beeline for the blanket-covered lump. "She had it in her shop."

Zen rushed over and removed the blanket. "Holy Loa, that's a big owl."

"Cover it back up," Giguhl said, covering his eyes lest he accidentally look into the psychedelic orbs. Zen frowned at the demon but did as he asked. I had to admit I found the demon's aversion odd, too. After all, it wasn't like Giguhl hadn't been around Stryx before. Plus, as the reigning Demon Fight Club champion of New York City's Black Light District, Giguhl wasn't exactly a wimp. But even I had to admit those freaky eyes and the owl's preternatural stillness were pretty freaking ominous.

"Thank goodness I had a cage large enough," Zen said.

I ignored her and spoke to Adam. "Sure, it's big enough. But will it hold him?"

Adam tapped the edge. "It's just bronze, but I can ward it so he can't get out and kill us in our sleep."

"Oh, that's comforting."

The mage shot me an evil grin that did little to ease my concerns. "Nah, it'll be fine for now. We can figure out something more permanent in the morning."

"I know you aren't leaving that demon bird out here with me," Giguhl said, rubbing his arms.

I rolled my eyes. "Quit being such a baby."

The petite faery patted the menacing seven-foot-tall demon's arm. "Don't worry, big guy. We won't let the owl hurt you."

Giguhl sent me a look that clearly said *At least someone cares.* To Zen he said, "You got any of them voodoo bags or whatever to protect me from him?"

Zen smiled. "A *gris gris* bag? Sure, if that'll make you feel better. Come on." She took the Mischief demon by the arm and led him out, presumably to go to her workshop. As he passed, Giguhl flicked his forked tongue out at me.

As annoyed as I was by Giguhl's easy transfer of affections to Zen, I appreciated them getting him out of there so I could concentrate. Brooks, however, stayed behind. He watched the bird with fascination.

"Is he really a demon?"

I shook my head. "Not technically. He's a spy for this

secret sect of dark races called the Caste of Nod. He also feasts on the blood of the dead."

Brooks's eyes widened. "I think I'll go check on Zen and Gigi."

I paused. "Gigi?"

Brooks blushed. "It's a nickname I came up with for Giguhl. He said he doesn't mind it."

"Hmm." I squinted my eyes at him. Considering Giguhl had rejected my own pet names for him, his easy acceptance of such a ridiculous nickname from Brooks gave me pause. "Whatever."

With the fae finally gone, I turned to Adam. "You want me to hold the cage while you stick it in?"

"Or since I'm already holding the cage, you can do the honors."

I sighed and stomped over to the owl. Keeping him wrapped in the blanket—because touching his feathers creeped me out a bit more than I wanted to admit after the ribbing I'd given Giguhl—I gingerly lifted the owl. Getting him inside the cage was a little trickier, but after some maneuvering I finally dumped him inside. After locking the little door tight, I dropped the tainted cover like a hot match and rubbed my hands on my jeans.

"Should we wake him up to make sure it holds?" My tone clearly indicated I thought that was a really freakin' bad idea.

Adam nodded and carried the cage into the kitchen and placed it in the center of the table. "You might want to stand back."

I took three big steps back and palmed my gun. "You don't have to tell me twice."

The mage whispered something under his breath. A

pop sounded, and a small plume of smoke rose from the cage. The bird came to life in an explosion of avian rage. Terrible screeching filled the space. A blizzard of white feathers blew around the room. The owl's body slammed against the bars of his prison.

When the chaos began, Adam jumped out of harm's way to join me at the doorway. "He keeps that up and the whole thing's going to tip over."

The cage already had scooted four inches toward the edge of the table. I nudged Adam's ribs. "Maybe you should put it on the floor."

"I'd prefer to keep all my fingers, thanks." He waggled the digits in question. The room tingled with magic that made the hairs on my arms prickle as the cage rose from the table. The bird's furious movements made the whole thing wobble in the air. But a few moments later, the cage safely touched down on the linoleum.

"There," Adam said, brushing his hands together.

"Sabiiiina!"

I cringed. "Oh, shit, you've angered it."

"Me? He hissed *your* name."

For some reason, a memory from that night in Jackson Square with Lavinia flashed into my head, giving me an idea. "Hold on," I said. "I want to try something." I took a step closer to the cage. Stryx flung himself against the bars. Showing no fear, I paused and looked directly at the owl. "Master Mahan."

"Hoot?" Instead of the evil hiss of before, the owl's call now sounded plaintive, a little sad.

"What the . . . ?" Adam said, looking confused.

"The other night every time Lavinia said that name Stryx did the same thing. What do you think it means?"

Adam rubbed the patch of hair on his chin. "Well, we know Stryx works for the Caste, right? Damara told us that back in New York." Damara was Rhea's magic apprentice who had been secretly working with the Caste to try and kill me. At the end, she'd sung like a canary and shared all sorts of interesting tidbits about her connection to the Caste. Except for the trying-to-get-me-killed thing, she was really not much more than a misguided, naive girl. Too bad her choices got her killed. "Maybe the truth is Stryx really belongs to Master Mahan."

Hoot.

"Like a pet, you mean?" I said, eyeing the owl dubiously.

Adam shrugged. "Maybe. I wish I knew more about this mysterious Caste leader. I mean, what kind of being would keep *that* as a pet?"

Before I could answer, Stryx hissed and rammed his head into the bars. He seemed even angrier, if possible. "The more immediate question is: Will the cage hold?"

Adam squinted at the bars. "Not sure. I can ward it so he can't get out, but maybe we should secure it just in case."

I pursed my lips and looked around the room. "What if we put the whole cage in something sturdy?" I nodded toward the far end of the kitchen.

"Sabina, don't you think that's a little cruel?"

I crossed my arms. "Adam," I said, matching his tone. "He's a godsdamned vampire owl from the depths of the underworld. Given the chance, he'd drain each of us dry and pluck out our eyes with his razorlike beak. So, no, I'm not particularly worried about stowing his cage in a broken refrigerator. Especially if it means we get a decent night's sleep."

Adam thought about it for a moment, his eyes on the fridge. While he pondered, Stryx kept up his berserker act. The cage squealed across the floor like nails down a chalkboard. Finally, the damned thing hit the edge of the cage so hard it slammed into Adam's foot. The mage yowled and jumped. I bent down to look at his foot and found a new hole in his boot leather courtesy of the aforementioned beak. The owl stilled. Then something that sounded specifically like an evil cackle rose up from the cage.

I glanced at Adam with an eyebrow raised. He scowled down at me like a judge handing down an order of execution. "Put the fucking bird in the fridge already."

The next evening, we all gathered in the shop. Giguhl catnapped on the counter. In deference to his desire to be more involved, we'd come to an agreement about him staying in cat form while in the public areas.

Zen and Brooks discussed inventory over by a display of voodoo dolls. I leaned against the counter, chugging cow's blood, and tried to shake the fog out of my head. Adam stood bleary-eyed behind the counter, nursing his coffee.

I wrinkled my nose at the cloying scent wafting up from the cat. "Giguhl, do you really need to wear that thing down here?" He wore a red chamois bag attached to his cat collar. Zen had anointed it with jasmine oil, which alone might have been okay, but mixed with sandalwood, comfrey, and gods only knew what else, the aroma was overpowering.

The cat perked open one eye. "Don't take your grumpiness out on me. It's not *my* fault the stupid owl screeched all night."

I scowled at the cat and took another swig of caffeine. My idea of sticking Stryx in the fridge the night before hadn't been so brilliant, after all. The box kept him contained, all right, but instead of dampening the incessant banging and offended screeches, the hollow box amplified the racket. It hadn't been so bad in my bedroom, since I could close the door. But the racket forced Adam and Giguhl out of the living room and into my bed. Around five a.m, they burst in and took over despite my vehement protests. I finally gave up when Adam reminded me that putting the bird on ice had been my idea. Therefore, I'd spent the majority of the day wedged in between a hot mage and a snoring demon.

Zen walked over and interrupted my grumpy woolgathering. "I take it you still haven't figured out how to communicate with the owl?"

Adam sighed and set down his mug. "No. I tried to talk to it before we came down, but he wouldn't stop hissing and scratching. You'd think he'd run out of steam at some point, but—" He shrugged and shook his head.

Zen pursed her lips. "Have you considered asking the spirits for help?"

"That's not exactly my area," Adam said. "But we're open to suggestions."

I leaned with my elbows on the counter, both eager to hear the voodooienne's ideas and resentful that we needed a human's help to find my sister. However, the sad fact was, despite my mage heritage, I knew very little about magic. Sure, I'd had some preliminary training from Rhea, but the sum total of my skills included summoning Giguhl and the ability to immolate my enemies with my eyes. While the latter option held great appeal where

Stryx was concerned, I wasn't ready to give up on the possibility he could help us find Maisie.

"I think I might have an idea," Zen said. "A few years ago one of my clients had a relative in a coma. Very sad." She paused to make sympathetic noises. "Anyway, the client asked me to summon a spirit to communicate with the unconscious girl. I was thinking we might be able to use the same idea with the owl."

Adam stood up straighter. "You mean have the spirit read Stryx's mind?"

She shrugged. "Why not? It's worth a shot, right?"

"What exactly would we need to do?" Having no practical knowledge of voodoo, I was worried the ritual might involve goat sacrifice or something.

Zen chewed her lip. "It's a bit tricky. We'd need to use the body of a recently deceased person as a medium for the spirit."

"And how exactly do you propose we get our hands on one of those?" Adam asked.

Zen smiled. "I have my ways. It's gonna have to happen tomorrow night, though, before Halloween."

I frowned. "Why not on Halloween?"

"Because then the portal to the spirit world will be wide open, and things could get unpredictable," Rhea said.

Adam looked at me with his eyebrows raised in question. I said, "This ritual doesn't involve me having to drink any potions or anything, right?"

Zen frowned and shook her head. "Of course not."

Given my past horrors with vomit-inducing potions, I had good reason to ask. But maybe it was a mage thing to make people miserable with potions. Within one week of arriving in New York for magical training, I'd had two embarrassing incidents. The first happened when Rhea's turncoat assistant, Damara, had tried to poison me with a mixture of strychnine and apple juice. My vampire genes protected me from the poison, and my mixed blood saved me from the forbidden fruit, but nothing prevented me from blowing chunks all over the Hekate Council. The second event happened during a vision-quest Rhea insisted I do to find my magical path. The hallucinogenic tea she'd given me led to a very unpleasant half hour before the freaky Chthonic visions began.

But Zen's expression held no hint of guile. And if it meant we'd get Maisie back ASAP, I could deal with a little irritable bowel syndrome again. "Done and done."

Zen nodded. "Good. I'll make preparations. The ritual is best conducted before midnight, so we should head out about ten tomorrow."

"Sounds good," Adam said. "Thanks, Zen."

She started to walk away but stopped short. "By the way, are you planning on going by Alodius's place again anytime soon?"

I frowned. "Why? Do you need something?"

She nodded. "Some chicken feet. With Halloween the day after tomorrow, the tourists have been buying charms like crazy. I'd go tonight myself, but the widow Breaux needs me to come undo a hex."

Across the store Brooks snorted. "Again? That's the third time this year."

"It's her own damn fault for stepping out with other women's men. But her checks always clear, so . . ."

"That's okay, Zen," Adam said. "We can pick up some chicken feet for you."

She smiled at the mage. "Thanks, Adam." She waved and walked off toward the office.

I swallowed my opinion of Adam's ass kissing along with my last swing of coffee. Just as I was setting down my mug, the door to the shop opened.

"Hey, Mac!" Brooks called.

"Hey, good lookin'," she called to the fae before approaching the counter. We all exchanged tense nods. "You guys got a minute?"

I frowned, wondering what had the werewolf looking so upset. "Sure."

Mac looked over her shoulder to where Brooks was dusting some chicken bones. When she glanced back at me she said under her breath, "Alone."

"Of course," I said to her. I called, "Hey, Brooks, we're going to go out back for a minute. Do you mind if Giguhl stays here?"

The cat lifted his head sleepily. "Huh?"

"No problemo," Brooks said.

"Go back to sleep, G."

The cat licked his lips and yawned before resting his head back on his paws. I held a hand out to Mac to lead the way. As Adam fell into step beside me, he shot me a concerned look. I shrugged. We'd find out soon enough what was on the were's mind.

We went out the back door into the courtyard behind Zen's shop. A small fountain bubbled along the west wall. The festive, but thankfully muted, sounds of Bourbon Street added to the soundtrack.

Once we were all seated around the table in the center of the courtyard, Mac finally spoke. "I have some news that might interest you."

She didn't mention that the contact was her girlfriend, even though from what I'd seen she clearly was, but I didn't blame her for not going there. It wasn't our business.

Until it was.

Mac pulled a piece of paper from her pocket. "Not sure if it's important, but I thought I'd pass it along. My vamp contact told me some bigwig just bought a mansion in the Garden District."

"And?" Since I'd been expecting something bigger, I tried to put a leash on my impatience.

"And several murders have occurred in the area. The police are calling them 'stabbings,' but the wounds are all in the neck. So unless someone's stabbing tourists with grilling forks..." She shrugged. "Plus all the work on this house has been done at night. During the day the place is totally dead and there are blackout curtains on all the windows."

"Hmm." Sounded like a stretch to me—until I glanced at the address. "Wait. Prytania Street?" I shot a meaningful glance at Adam. Back in New York, the mage headquarters in Manhattan was called Prytania Place.

"Does that mean something to you?" Mac asked.

"Maybe," Adam said with a shrug.

I tucked the address in my jeans pocket. "Thanks, Mac. We'll head over there in a few."

She inclined her head. "I'll let you know if I find anything else out."

"Actually, I was wondering if you might be willing to set up a meeting with your contact."

Her eyes went all suspicious. "Why?"

I leaned forward, trying to ease her sudden tension. "We appreciate your help. It's just that maybe if I could talk to this friend vampire-to-vampire, I might be able to see if there's anything she's overlooked."

Mac shook her head. "I don't think she'd agree to that."

"Why not?" Adam asked, his voice quiet.

Mac's eyes shifted left. "She doesn't want any trouble."

"Look, Mac, the fact is that if this vampire we're looking for really is in town—maybe even in this house you told us about—trouble has come to New Orleans. And sooner or later it's going to find your friend."

"You don't know that."

I leaned back and crossed my arms. "Actually, I can guarantee it. Because the vamp we're after is—" I paused and glanced at Adam. To this point I'd avoided mentioning Lavinia's name, but obviously the time had come to tell Mac so she could warn her friends. "Her name is Lavinia Kane."

Mac blinked in confusion. "And?" So much for my bombshell. I guess it wasn't surprising, since Mac was a werewolf and not a vamp.

I decided to put in terms a werewolf could understand. "She's the Alpha of the entire vampire race."

That got Mac's attention. "Holy shit."

"Exactly. Now you know why we hesitated telling you before." When Mac nodded with her mouth hanging open, I continued. "But now that this happened? Your friends need to be really careful."

Adam cut in. "In fact, you should tell your friends not to engage if they see her."

Mac's eyes narrowed. "Why?"

"Lavinia's one of the oldest vamps alive. Your average vamp won't stand a chance."

Her chin lifted. "But you're planning on taking her on, right? What makes you so tough?"

I tried not to react to the challenge in the were's eyes. "Because I have the best training for the job and the best reason to want her dead."

Mac sucked in a deep breath through her nose and pursed her lips. "Okay. I can't promise my friends will listen, but I'll try."

"In the meantime, we'll check out this address. You tell your pals to let us know if they hear anything else, okay?"

"Maybe you should give me a description of this Domina. Just so they know to avoid her if she shows up."

"She's a little taller than me. Dark, dark red hair—burgundy, I guess. But don't worry, they'll know her when they see her."

"How?"

I shrugged. "They'll have a sudden urge to genuflect before her."

"Ah. Okay, I'll tell them." She rose to leave, looking a little shell-shocked.

"I have one more question," I said, placing a hand on Adam's arm when he moved to stand, too. "Has anyone you've talked to mentioned seeing an out-of-town mage around?"

Mac frowned and shook her head. "I'm sorry. But since most of the mage residents left a few days ago, a new one would definitely be noticed."

Mac saw my expression fall and rushed ahead. "But I'm sure it doesn't mean anything. I mean, your sister's bound to turn up soon, right?"

I sighed. "You're probably right."

Unless Lavinia had already killed her.

When Zen showed us to the garage behind the shop, I was surprised to see an ancient yellow car waiting for us. Not really sure what car I'd imagined a voodoo priestess might choose, but it certainly wasn't this.

"A Gremlin?" I asked, trying to keep the judgment from my tone.

Zen patted the hood lovingly. "This here's Saint Expedite." She chuckled like she'd made a joke. I glanced at Adam, who merely shrugged in return. "Don't get to do much driving in the city, but when I need to get around this baby gets the job done."

After that, she apologized for the cluttered back seat and the heavy scent of dried herbs permeating the interior. "Won't matter too much, since the front windows won't roll up anymore."

As we'd gotten ready to leave before Zen showed us the car, I insisted Giguhl put on a little something to ward off the chill. The ensuing argument was why we were leaving Zen's an hour behind schedule. But after Zen's explanation about the windows, I shot Giguhl an I-told-you-so look. His tail swished, and he turned his back to me. The position gave me a nice view of his hairless ass sticking out from under a black sweater. The view I could have done without, but being right went a long way toward soothing my aching pupils.

A few minutes later, Zen waved us off merrily and headed out to handle her own business. As we drove out of the French Quarter toward the Garden District, Giguhl perched his little naked paws on the dashboard and looked out the windshield. He ducked and weaved to avoid getting beamed by the chicken foot—used to "kick evil back," according to Zenobia—hanging from the rearview mirror.

Our first stop was back at Alodius's butcher shop. We decided to hit there first and get it out of the way before we checked out Mac's lead. That way I'd also be able to grab some more blood before potentially rumbling with the vampires in the house on Prytania. Normally I didn't need it every day, but I guess since the blood wasn't from a human it wore off faster. I can't say how much I enjoyed having to drink double the cow's blood to stay strong.

The trip down to the Garden District was much faster this time, despite the Gremlin's questionable transmission. Adam pulled in front of the shop and left the engine sputtering and wheezing.

I reached for the handle. "Aren't you coming in? After all, you're the one who volunteered to get chicken feet for the voodoo lady."

"Careful, Red, or I'll think you're jealous." Adam smiled knowingly.

Giguhl snickered. Ass.

I looked away. "Whatever."

"Anyway, I had my fill of the butcher last night. Why don't you take *Gigi* with you for protection?"

I snorted, which earned me a glare from the cat. "Mock if you will, but I like that nickname better than Mr. Giggles," he said.

"I think you just like Brooks better," I said.

He drew back. "Now you're jealous of Brooks, too?"

I seriously didn't have enough breath in my body to argue that point. Instead, I shook my head and grabbed his warm and disconcertingly smooth body from the console.

"You might want to talk to a professional about your emotional IQ," he taunted as I jogged to the door. I shot him a glare.

"What the fuck is that?"

He wrinkled his pink nose. "If you watched Opry you'd know." For some reason, Giguhl felt he knew the fabulously wealthy talk-show host well enough to give her a nickname.

I groaned. "Gods, if you're going to start peer pressuring me to watch that crap, I might have to revoke permission to TV altogether."

He hissed. "Bite your tongue! It's bad enough Zen doesn't get the Temptation Channel. Don't take my Opry away, too!"

I breathed in through my nose as I prayed for patience. On the exhale I reminded myself that Giguhl seemed to take perverse joy in seeing steam come out of my ears. But he *was* a Mischief demon, after all. On the other hand, I was standing on a busy street arguing with a cat in a black turtleneck. "Perhaps I went too far with that threat. I see that now. But do you think you could refrain from lecturing me about my many and varied personality deficits for five minutes so I can go buy some godsdamned chicken feet?"

I hadn't known cat lips could purse before. But Giguhl rocked the martyr mask like a pro. "I suppose."

"Good. Now, please remember not to talk in there. Alodius might be okay serving vamps and mages, but I'm pretty sure he's not prepared to deal with you."

The cat muttered something under his breath but settled into my arms like a good kitty. I threw open the door and walked in. This time the Cajun Sausage Fest had a few customers waiting at the counter. I pulled a number from the machine and prepared to wait. From what I could tell, the line consisted of two mortals and a werewolf.

Alodius chatted with the mortals while he packaged up their order. Ahead of me, the were perked up and looked at me over his shoulder. His shaggy brown hair matched his eyes. As he gave me a once-over, his nostrils flared. Catching my scent, his eyes narrowed.

My mixed-blood scent—a combo of copper and sandalwood—generally confused other members of the dark races. Half-breeds were exceptionally rare, which made it hard for potential foes to decide whether I was an actual threat or merely a freak of nature.

I tilted my head in an amiable nod. He hesitated and tipped his chin in my direction. Just like that, the tension evaporated like vapor. He turned back around and tapped his cowboy boot on the linoleum.

At Alodius's urging, the humans—Germans, judging from the accents—added a pound of head cheese to their order. Not that I'm in any position to judge others' eating habits, but the idea of meat jelly made me gag. I mean, the name alone inspires images of things best not contemplated while eating.

Giguhl, however, licked his chops. As Alodius wrapped up the package, he soliloquized like a freakin' Cajun Willy Shakespeare about making the damned stuff.

"First ya brine the head—eyeballs, snoot, and all—with the hocks. Throw a couple tongues in there for some flavor. Once that's done, boil the shit out of it till the face meat's falling off..." He said more, but I was too busy trying not to vomit on the werewolf's boots. I tuned back in time to hear Aldoius declare, "Hoo-eee, that there's good eatin'."

Finally, the Germans exited with the booty. "Y'all come back now." Alodius waved the humans off and turned to the were. "Sorry for the wait."

"Give me two porterhouses," he all but growled.

Dollar signs appeared in Alodius's eyes. "You doing some grilling? We got a great sauce—"

A low growl came from the were. "Just get the fucking steaks."

Alodius nodded and scurried away to fill the request. I repressed a smile at seeing the chatty Cajun shot down. The butcher started wrapping the steaks in paper, only to receive another low rumble from the werewolf. "Don't bother."

He grabbed the meat right off the scale. He lifted the first steak directly to his mouth and chomped into it. Red juice dripped down his forearms, and he grunted like a pig at a trough as he swallowed large chunks whole.

My mouth fell open. I glanced at Alodius, whose expression was a combination of awe and disgust. Before either of us could figure out how to react, the were licked his fingers clean. That done, he dug into his back pocket for his wallet. He tossed a few bills on the counter.

"Keep the change." The were's magnanimous gesture was ruined by a loud belch. Then, without further comment, he stalked out of the store.

Alodius cleared his throat. "Well, if that wasn't the damnedest thing."

"I take it that doesn't happen often," I said.

His eyes stayed on the door, as if he expected the wolf in man's clothing to return any minute. "We get plenty of weres in here, but usually they don't get that ornery until closer to a full moon."

"Maybe his bitch left him," I said.

He shot me a quelling look. Obviously the butcher wasn't too fond of puns. A muffled groan rose from the bundle in my arms. I constricted my arms to let the cat know I didn't appreciate his opinion.

"Sooo, you're back soon. And you brought a friend." He reached to pet the cat. But Giguhl wasn't having any of it. He hissed and swiped a paw at the man. Alodius jerked his hand out of harm's way and shot an accusing glance at me.

"Sorry about that." I lifted the cat higher, playing up his indignity for all it was worth. "Apologize to the nice man, Mr. Giggles." The cat dug his claws into my arm in retaliation. I gritted my teeth and forced a smile at the frowning Cajun.

Alodius cleared his throat and said, "Anyhoo, y'all want two more pints?"

"Sure," I said. Figured I might as well since I was there anyway. "Also, Zen needs some chicken feet."

"Can do." Alodius leaned forward over the counter. "How about I throw in some nice calf brains for Kitty-No-Manners there. Might soften his disposition."

The cat groaned in my arms. For a demon who subsisted on Cheez Doodles and beer, the thought of raw brains obviously didn't sit too well. "Err, that's okay. He's on a special diet. But I'm surprised you carry brains. Is that . . . normal?"

"Darlin', us Cajuns eat everything from the rooter to the tooter." He cackled, slapping the counter at his joke.

I swallowed the bile his word picture conjured. "Oh."

Alodius laughed again. "All righty then. Let's get that blood."

He whistled tunelessly as he took the jug out of the cooler. Once he'd plopped it on the counter and pulled out a funnel he said, "So what happened to that mage friend of yours?"

I jerked a thumb toward the door. "He's waiting in the car."

Blood sloshed out of the container to land on the butcher block with a *splat*. Alodius smoothly wiped up the spill with a towel. "That's nice. Have y'all had a chance to see much of the Big Easy yet?"

I shrugged. "A bit."

"Y'all been to The Court of Two Sisters yet?"

I shook my head.

He paused, looking up from his task. "How 'bout Acme Oyster?"

"Nope."

"Brennan's?"

Another shake.

"*Cher*, please tell Alodius you been to Tipitinas?"

My eyes shifted left.

"What have y'all been doing with your time?"

"Well, I did ride a trolley and visit Jackson Square."

He clicked his tongue and shook his head, which made his jowls swing hypnotically.

"I've been busy with some personal issues." Why did I suddenly feel the need to defend myself to the man?

"Darlin', if y'all don't mind a little piece of advice?" He paused and waited for my nod.

"We all got personal—" he pronounced it "poisenal"— "issues, but that can't stop y'all from enjoying life."

I remained silent, allowing the odd man's wisdom to sink in. Was he right? I had to admit my life always seemed to have more than its share of drama. Was I using that as an excuse to avoid enjoying myself? I always thought I'd have time to pursue things I wanted once things settled down. But there was always something new to worry about, some new crisis to manage. Despite getting his point, I wasn't convinced.

After all, it felt wrong to play tourist when my sister was having the exact opposite of fun. But wasn't it Maisie who just a couple short weeks ago had encouraged me to grab some happiness for myself? Then I'd argued that as an immortal I had nothing but time ahead of me. Her response had been to point out that with so many people wanting me dead, nothing was guaranteed, especially my immortality. Of course, back then she wasn't being held against her will or on the receiving end of her psychotic grandmother's fangs. So maybe the living-it-up could wait.

Alodius handed the packages over the counter. "That'll be forty for the blood and twenty for the chicken feet." He winked. "The advice I threw in gratis."

"Okay, well, thanks for the blood and stuff."

He waved away my appreciation. "My pleasure, dar-lin'. You go enjoy this beautiful night."

I smiled. I'm not sure he'd consider casing a house for signs of vampire life romantic, but it was close enough, I guess. "Actually, we're on our way to take a stroll through the Garden District."

He smiled. "Well, now, that's good to hear. Y'all have fun!"

Ten minutes later, we parked the Gremlin next to a cemetery wall a couple of streets away from the address Mac had given us. Giguhl perched on Adam's shoulder as we walked toward Prytania Street. We approached slowly, keeping our eyes peeled for hostiles. It was after midnight, so most of the houses on the block were dark. But up ahead, a warm glow filtered through large trees shielding the houses from the street.

I checked the street number on the white Greek revival on the corner. "The next one's our target," I said, pointing. "G, think you can sneak up to one of the windows without being noticed?"

The cat looked at me with pity from atop the mage's shoulder. "That was a joke, right?"

I rolled my eyes. "Just don't get caught, okay?"

"Yes, Mom." With that, the cat hopped off Adam. His pale ass glowed in the night, making it easy to follow his trail until he disappeared behind the heavy branches shading the house.

"You picking up anything?" Adam asked.

I looked toward the mansion, using all my senses to try to search for some clue that Lavinia might be inside. Muffled rock music reached my ears from nearby. My nostrils perked up when they caught a whiff an unmistakably pungent scent. "Someone's smoking some quality Mary Jane nearby, but that's all I'm getting."

"Hmm," Adam said, keeping his eyes glued on the house. "Stay alert anyway. There's no telling what G's going to find in there."

As if on cue, the cat's moon-pale form raced out of the shadows. I bent down to catch him. Tremors shook his body. "What happened?"

He wouldn't look up as he continued to shake. A muffled whimper escaped the ball of skin in my arms. "Giguhl?" I jostled him until he looked up.

I expected fear in his eyes. Instead, the damned cat smiled like a Cheshire and a braying giggle escaped his tiny mouth.

Adam and I exchanged frowns. Either what he'd seen had been so shocking it drove him insane, or Mr. Kitty had some explainin' to do.

"Y-you guys aren't gonna believe this shit," he gasped.

Adam shifted impatiently. "Are you going to tell us, or do we have to guess?"

"Oh, you'd never guess this one." More laughter.

"Giguhl," I snapped. "Pull it together. Did you see any vamps?"

The cat made a valiant effort to get his amusement under control. Finally, he shook his head. "Nah. Mac's source was totally wrong about that. This is even better than bloodsuckers."

"Well?" Adam and I both shouted.

"C'mon, you've got to see it to believe it."

The demon jumped down and ran off, looking back over his shoulder every now and then to make sure we were coming. Adam and I exchanged a leery glance.

"Come on," the cat hissed from the darkness.

Left with no other option, Adam and I trudged after him. Even though Giguhl claimed there was nothing to worry about, I drew my gun. Adam, too, scanned every inch of the area for ambush. Finally, we pushed the creaking black gate open. When no silhouettes darkened the front windows, we crept inside. A flash of gray caught my eye as Giguhl rounded the corner of the house. I banked right and ducked under branches to reach the side of the house.

The music I'd heard earlier shook the house's foundations. It was a shock to hear the harsh electronic notes of industrial music coming from a house that could have graced the cover of *Southern Living* magazine.

When we finally reached Giguhl, he crouched on the wide stone sill of a window. "G," I whispered. "Be careful."

"Don't worry," he said in a normal speaking voice. "These douchebags wouldn't hear us if we arrived banging drums."

Frowning, I inched toward the rectangle of light in front of the window. Adam fell in next to me, his body tense. I leaned forward to peek around the edge and almost fell. Adam caught my arm. He might have shot me a curious look, but I was too busy trying not to piss myself.

Just inside the window, the room opened into a large living and dining room combo with a wide staircase rising to the second floor. But the elegant Biedermeier backdrop paled in comparison to the foreground freakiness.

The walnut dining room table served as a makeshift stage for a midget stripper. She wore a pink spangled bikini and teeny tiny Lucite stilettos. Her two fans wore artfully ripped heroin-chic ensembles. Between bong hits, their indolent hands flipped dollar bills in the air. A third guy—this one oddly Rockabilly among a gaggle of industrial scarecrows—snorted white lines from a mirror at the end of the table.

Just beyond this charming tableau, three more members of the Lollipop Guild performed many and varied sex acts with a cluster of musician types on the antique furniture. On the periphery of the off-scale orgy, a man with spiky black hair surveyed the scene from a red Empire armchair. He wore dark aviators and took frequent, methodical pulls from a bottle of Jim Beam.

I scooted in for a better look. "Am I hallucinating?"

"Depends," Adam began. "In your hallucination is the lead singer of Necrospank 5000 watching a midget give his drummer a golden shower?"

My head swiveled toward him. "Huh?"

Adam nodded toward the sunglasses guy. "That's Erron Zorn."

"Who?" Giguhl's pink nose smashed against the glass in front of his face.

"Necrospank is a shock rock band. Erron Zorn is the lead singer. He's also a mage."

I jerked in shock. "A mage? What's he doing in New Orleans? Rhea and Orpheus called all the mages to court."

Adam shrugged. "He's a recreant."

"What's that?" Giguhl asked.

"An outcast mage. They're shunned by the Hekate Council." The scorn in his voice indicated Adam's opinion on recreants in general. He paused and hit me on the arm. "Oh, shit. Is that a gimp?"

"Awesome," Giguhl breathed with reverence. "This is way better than the Temptation Channel."

"Seriously," I said. "Too bad we didn't bring snacks."

We all went silent as one of the ladies mounted the gimp. He wore assless chaps and a zippered mask. The ball gag prevented any protests as the midget slapped at his haunches with a whip, like a miniature jockey. She urged him to turn and crawl toward the couch. The second his ass swung around, we got an unobstructed view of his—

"Oh!" We all yelled in unison. I jumped away from the window, rubbing at my eyes as if I could erase the image burned into my retinas. But some things can never be unseen.

Adam blew out a breath and swung his arms around like he was trying to shake them off. Even Giguhl looked a little green around the whiskers and refused to look in the window again.

"All righty then," I said. "So I think it's safe to assume there're no vampires here."

"After that I almost wish there had been," Adam responded.

A crash reverberated inside the house. "I think that's our cue to leave," I said, turning toward the gate. The three of us skulked back to the street with postures that could only be described as penitent. I'll admit, the irony of our little trio of badasses being embarrassed by some kinky antics burned a bit.

"We must never speak of this again," Adam said.

I nodded. "Agreed."

"I never thought I'd say this," Giguhl said from Adam's arms. "But what I just saw makes me never want to speak of sex again, period."

Adam and I stopped walking to shoot him "bullshit" looks.

He sighed. "Okay maybe not *never,* but definitely not for the next five minutes." He shuddered and snuggled against Adam's chest.

For the next couple of minutes, we quietly made our way back up the street toward the car. With each step, my horrified amusement over the midget porn gave way to darker musings. Yet again, I'd hit another dead end. I'd made so little progress in finding Maisie I was tempted to put the blame on Tanith's door. It'd be so easy to just throw up my hands and believe she'd withheld some vital piece of information. Tempting, but unrealistic. Tanith had good reasons for wanting Lavinia dead, too. If she had information that would aid in that goal she would have told us, right? Which brought me right back to Sabina being a failure.

Adam fell into step beside me, with Giguhl tucked in his elbow like a football. "Uh-oh," he said. "You've got that look again."

Frowning, I looked at him. "Which one?"

"The one you get when you're blaming yourself for something."

I snorted. "I wasn't aware I had a specific look for that."

"Sure you do," Giguhl chimed in. "Your eyes get all squinty, and you get these lines between your eyebrows."

My hand flew up to the spot. Sure enough, a furrow had formed. I smoothed the skin and heaved a deep sigh. "I can't help it. I'm getting nowhere fast."

"See, that's the real problem," Adam said. "You've got pronoun issues."

The furrow reappeared as I stared at him. "What?"

"Mmm-hmm," G said. "Unlike that freaky butcher, you only speak in the first person."

I frowned at the demon. "No I don't."

"You just did," Adam said with a small smile. He nudged me with his arm. "Come on, Red. It's frustrating Mac's lead didn't pan out, but it's not the end of the world or our only lead. Whatever comes next, we'll face it together."

"Right," G said. "Go, Team Kickass!"

Adam and I shot the demon bemused looks.

"What? You like 'Team Awesome' better?"

My lips twitched. "Definitely."

"Okay," Adam said. "Now that we have that important matter out of the way, what's next?"

I took a deep breath and let the cool night air cleanse the last of the guilt. The breeze brought with it the perfume of entropy that clung to New Orleans like a tattered cape. The sharp scent of browning magnolia leaves, the dank richness of the soil, the heady musk of sex.

Just as the air started to work its magic on me, the putrid scent of dirty pennies hit my nose like a sucker punch.

I grabbed Adam's arm to still his progress. My heart hammered behind my ribs. "Do you smell that?" I whispered.

He shook his head. Not a surprise he couldn't. I owed my keen sense of smell to my vampire genes.

"Shit," Giguhl said. I wasn't sure if it was his feline

sense of smell or his innate demon instincts that alerted him, but I was too busy trying to locate the source.

"I can't tell how many, but judging from the concentration of the scent, there's several vamps nearby."

Adam tensed and searched the darkness. "Can you tell how close they are?"

I shook my head. "No, but look alive."

He nodded and we started walking again, our eyes alert for signs of attack. We crossed the street and turned left toward the Gremlin squatting in front of a lichen-covered cemetery wall. The streetlight above shone down accusingly, like it was exposing an anachronism.

One second, the path to the car was clear. The next, a wave of static was our only warning before eight vampires materialized in a circle around us. I did a quick survey. In addition to those, four more crouched on the cemetery wall. Eight males and four females total. Old, judging from the varying shades of deep red—not a strawberry among them. None held weapons in their hands, but a couple had visible blades ready to be drawn.

Blood pumped fast with adrenaline through my veins. My gun appeared in my hand as if, instead of merely relying on instinct, I'd conjured it. Luckily, I'd reloaded it with fifteen apple-cider bullets before we'd headed out.

"What the hell do you want?" I demanded. Next to me, Adam dropped Giguhl to the ground and tensed for action.

I didn't recognize any of the vamps. Not surprising, given we weren't on my turf. But judging from their confident postures, we weren't dealing with a garden-variety gang trolling for fast food.

A pale vamp, with hair so darkly auburn it was almost

black, stepped forward. "The favor of your company has been requested."

I wasn't sure which part amused me more—his outdated mode of speech, or the stupid cape he wore like Count Effing Dracula. He even had a widow's peak, for chrissakes. And the cane he leaned on was nothing more than an affectation.

"And whom, might I ask, issued such a thoughtful invitation?" I asked.

The Count tilted his head, as if I'd asked a stupid question. "Lavinia Kane."

My heart fluttered with anticipation. Now we were getting somewhere. I lifted a finger to my lip. "Hmm," I said. "If I might make another suggestion."

His lips formed a courteous smile, and one glossy eyebrow rose in question.

"How about you and your friends go fuck yourselves and we'll call it a night?"

The female who stood slightly behind him lurched forward with a snarl. She looked like something straight out of every sword-and-sorcery geek's wet dream. The sides of her long maroon hair were pulled back to create a spiky half ponytail, while the rest fell in straight sheets down her back. Instead of a cape, she wore black leather pants and a leather-and-chain-mail bustier. I could only see the hilt from where I stood, but she also had a blade strapped to her back. It wasn't one of those sleek Japanese jobbies, either. We're talking full-on broadsword action.

The Count held up a hand to stay her. Red Sonja complied immediately, but the daggers in her gaze told me she had plans for the sword that included me.

The caped wonder clucked his tongue at me in reproach.

"The Domina predicted you would scoff at her summons." He nodded to his comrades, who started closing in like a noose. The metallic slide of blade against leather echoed as the female drew her sword. The Count followed suit, pulling his own steel from within his cane. "Which is why we've been instructed to kill the mage to ensure your full cooperation."

Screw that shit, my mind screamed. My response was a squeeze of the trigger.

The Count's pale hand shot up with preternatural speed. The bullet stopped midair and fell uselessly to the cracked sidewalk.

Ignoring my shock over the unexpected magic use, I squeezed the trigger three more times in quick succession. Again with the hand wave. And again, three bullets hit the asphalt.

The vamps surrounding us didn't change expression. Not a smile or a laugh or a gloat among them. They just stood there like creepy statues, watching us with shark eyes.

Just as I considered throwing the gun at the guy to see what he'd do, a shock of energy slammed into my hand. The gun ripped from my grasp and flew to the Count. With a reptilian smile, he crumpled the weapon like an aluminum can.

Something was seriously off with these guys. And if this was a preview of what Lavinia had up her sleeve, we were in deeper shit than I realized.

Fine, I thought. He wanted to play "Who's got the biggest magic wand"? Fine. "Hey, Adam?"

"I'm on it."

Pins and needles stung the air as he called up his magic. Our opponents' black eyes glinted, but no one made a move to run or protect themselves. The sudden rise of magical power made my ears pop, and their lack of reaction made my chest tighten. But before the spell could burst out of Adam like a sonic boom, the vamps raised their hands in unison. A circle of magic rose from the street and coned over our heads like an invisible prison.

"Adam?" I said, my voice sounding more panicked than I'd intended.

"What the fuck?" he said.

Vampires aren't supposed to be able to cast circles. In fact, vampires aren't supposed to do magic at all. The only exception would be if they fed from a mage, like Lavinia had done with Maisie. And these guys worked for Lavinia. But there were too many of them to feed from one mage. Plus, Lavinia wasn't exactly known for sharing. Surely she wouldn't allow lower vampires to feed off a food source as powerful as my mixed-blood sister. She'd want all of the advantages to herself. And the Hekate Council had demanded that all mages report to the Queen's court, so they weren't feeding off local magic users. Which left me with no choice but to echo Adam's sentiment: *What the fuck?*

Adam and I fell in back-to-back, circling inside the shimmering dome of magic. "Hey, Giguhl," I said.

"Yeah?" the cat said.

"Change now, please."

A *pop* and a puff of smoke should have followed my request. But nothing happened.

"Um, Sabina?" Giguhl hissed.

"What?" I said, my eyes on Red Sonja. She smiled evilly as she stroked the hilt of her sword.

"Nothing's happening."

I glanced over my shoulder. Sure enough, Giguhl remained a cat. "Shit."

"The circle is blocking magic," Adam said. "Which means I'm useless, too."

"Okay," I gritted out. "Everyone stay calm. We'll figure this out."

During this exchange, the vampires watched and waited. Finally, the Count said, "If you're quite through, we will now kill the mage."

I jerked toward him. "Over my dead fucking body."

The Count's eyebrow rose. "That can be arranged." Then he nodded to Red Sonja. Sword in hand, she stepped through the circle. I blinked. The circle should have popped when she touched it. Instead, it stayed up. Who the hell were these guys?

Sonja swished the sword side to side like a pendulum, ticking down the seconds on Adam's life. The mage and I fell back into fighting stances. Adam might not be able to use magic, but he was one hell of a hand-to-hand fighter. Even Giguhl crouched down, ready to pounce at the bitch. Things weren't looking good for Team Awesome, but at least we'd go down fighting.

"Keep her moving," Adam whispered. "Lavinia obviously wants you alive. Use that."

I jerked a nod and kept my eyes on her blade.

Red Sonja's shoulders tensed a split second before her first swing. Time slowed. I knocked Adam to the side with my hip and rolled forward. Just as the sword began its downward arc, I swept under her legs with my own. Sonja hit the ground like a sack of potatoes.

At the same moment, I heard the Count yell something. My ears popped as the circle exploded and vampires came rushing in from all sides. As I turned to face more attackers, I noticed the vampires beyond the circle were fighting, too. I punched a male vamp and peered around his now-bloody face, trying to get a better look.

"Holy shit!" I yelled as I ducked another punch. Erron Zorn sneaked up behind a female vamp in a Victorian-era dress. He raised his hands and shot a ball of fiery magic at her. Her bustle went up in flames as he turned to zap another vamp with a spell.

Meanwhile, Sonja had risen and was going after Adam again with her sword. "Adam, watch out!"

He elbowed a female in the nose with a loud *crunch* and spun away just in time to escape the blade. I grabbed him and pushed him toward Erron and the Rockabilly dude who, despite the heavy drug and alcohol use we'd observed, were fighting like a well-trained special ops team.

Unfortunately, the vampires were well trained, too.

Erron saw us and yelled, "Get behind us!"

I grabbed Giguhl and jumped behind the line of mages. Suddenly the power rose. Goose bumps covered Giguhl's fleshy body as well as my own. Then, just as the Count and his goons turned to rush us, a mighty wind kicked up. The mages' combined powers coalesced into a typhoon of magic. Vampires scattered like dead leaves down the street.

Erron yelled. "Everyone over the wall!"

14

For most of my life I'd been a predator. But as I scampered over the cemetery wall I'd never felt more like prey. And I wasn't enjoying the role reversal.

The eight-foot-tall wall stretched the length of the street. A pair of stately black gates with a metal arch introduced the site as "St. Louis Cemetery No. 1." Naturally, the gates were chained up tight for the evening. Presumably to keep the living out rather than the dead in. But you never know.

Straddling the wall, I reached a hand back to help Adam.

The look he shot me was a comical mix of disbelief and wounded male pride. Normally he never balked at my help, but I guess the male mage audience made his ego swell. He handed up Giguhl.

"Suit yourself." I swung my other leg over and landed in a crouch on the other side. A couple of seconds later, Adam, Erron, and the other member of Necrospank 5000—the Rockabilly dude from earlier, who was the drummer, judging from the sticks jutting out of his back pocket—flashed in next to us. One of these days I really needed to have Adam teach me how to flash into places like that.

As we ran through the cemetery Giguhl whispered. "Who the fuck were those guys?" Neither Adam nor I answered. Mostly because we were too busy trying to focus on figuring that out for ourselves.

But Erron Zorn had plenty to say. "They were Caste of Nod vamps. Bad news. Members of the Caste share their powers either through blood letting or elaborate sex rituals."

Adam and I exchanged a look. How in the hell did the leader of a band know so much about a mysterious cabal? And for that matter, why was he helping us?

I started at the beginning. "How do you know that?"

Erron pointed to the left, and we all ducked between two crypts before he answered. "Twenty years ago, after my first record went platinum, the Caste approached me to join. But I wanted nothing to do with their fucked-up rituals."

I frowned. This from a man who just watched a midget riding a gimp? I also noticed he didn't bother to introduce himself. Like he assumed everyone knew his name.

"So they just accepted no as your answer?" Adam asked.

Erron smiled coldly. "Not really. No." I sensed there was a long story hidden behind that smile, but we didn't have time for the Erron Zorn story hour right then.

We ran through a side boulevard separating two rows of crypts. We bobbed and weaved, ducking between two crypts and going deeper into the bowels of the City of the

Dead. Finally, we crouched behind a crumbling structure topped with a stone cross and listened. Erron dispatched the drummer to go do a patrol, and then he plopped down on the ground next to us.

The silence here was oppressive, save for the rapid pulse pounding in my ears. Whoever these guys were, they knew better than to let an errant twig snap or heavy breathing give them away. And considering they'd already appeared out of thin air, gods only knew when or where they'd pop up.

"This place is spooky as shit," Giguhl said, breaking the tension.

Not for the first time, I wondered why fate couldn't have given me a Vengeance demon for a minion. Giguhl was a great fighter, no doubt about it, and I appreciated him having my back. But sometimes I could do without the color commentary. Like now, when we had psychotic magical vampires hunting our asses through a cemetery.

On second thought, any demon is a good demon when facing a fight with a bunch of killer vampires with wicked magic skills. "Giguhl, switch forms."

Fortunately, the resulting puff of smoke dispersed quickly on the breeze, which meant it wouldn't give away our location. Unfortunately, I didn't have any clothes for Giguhl. But given the situation, I was hardly in a place to complain. After all, a naked demon was better than no demon at all when it came to fighting.

"Gnarly," Erron said in a bored voice, his eyes on Giguhl's forked assets.

Speaking of Erron, we needed some answers. "Not to be rude or anything," I said, "but why are you helping us?"

"You set off my warded alarms earlier. I ignored the

Peeping Tom routine because I figured you were just harmless fans. But when the fight started, we felt the magic. I sent Ziggy"—he jerked his head to indicate the drummer, who'd just run off—"to check and he said a big battle was going down by the cemetery." Erron shrugged. "The other guys in the band are human. But Ziggy and me decided to pitch in."

I frowned at him. "But why help us at all? You seemed pretty content enjoying your"—I cleared my throat—"gimp."

He nodded to confirm the truth of that statement. "It's true. However, when Ziggy let me know the vamps you were fighting were using magic, I knew immediately they were Caste vamps. Easy decision then."

"What are you doing in New Orleans?" Adam asked.

"We're headlining Voodoo Fest on Halloween. My agent bought me the house as a tax shelter six months ago. The gig gave us an excuse to come christen it."

I nodded. "Well, we appreciate the help. I'm Sabina, by the way. The naked one is Giguhl." I jerked my head. "And that's Adam."

Adam and the recreant mage eyed one another for a moment. Finally, Erron said, "You're an Adherent?"

Adam tensed. "Worse than that, I'm afraid. I'm a Pythian Guard."

"Priceless," Erron laughed. "Give Orpheus my regards."

"We gonna have a problem here?" Adam asked. I watched the two men for signs of violence, ready to back up Adam if necessary.

But Erron's expression sobered. "Nah. If there's one thing I hate worse than Hekate Council ass kissers, it's Caste members."

Adam relaxed a tad and nodded. Then both males resumed their scan of the immediate area. Giguhl and I traded speculative glances. The exchange between the mages surprised me. This recreant thing was obviously a bigger deal than I thought at first.

More than the tension, something else was bothering me about the cemetery. I put a hand on Adam's arm. "Do you feel that?"

Adam shot me a worried look. "What?"

"The ground is vibrating." But that wasn't it exactly, either. It was subtle, almost like white noise, except palpable.

"Anyone picking up movement?" Adam whispered.

"Not me," Giguhl said.

I shook my head. The smell of copper was weaker here, and my gut told me the coast was clear for the moment. But I knew better than to relax.

"So what's your story, Red?" Erron asked. "Why are you fighting vamps, being one yourself?

"I'm mixed-blood, actually. The Caste vamps are working with my grandmother, who wants to wipe my mage half of the family from the planet."

Erron took that in stride. "Cool."

"Any chance one of you could whip us up some new hardware?"

Adam jumped in before Erron could offer. "I got it." He did his thing and handed over a brand-spanking-new gun. The handgrip warmed quickly in my palm. "And before you ask, yes, I remembered the apple bullets this time."

I grinned at him. On the list of things I liked best about Adam, his ability to conjure weaponry tied for third with his adorable dimples.

Erron nudged my arm. "There's Zig."

I looked up to see the Rockabilly guy walking toward us. Instead of speaking, however, his hands moved with lightning speed. Sign language? Since when are mages deaf? Or drummers, for that matter? Adam and I exchanged a look. But he looked less surprised than I felt.

"Ziggy says that there's a clear path to the wall on the other side. We could flash out, but if we do that, they'll keep coming back. They always do. I suggest we move toward the wall to draw them out. Face them down and end this now."

Erron and Ziggy looked to Adam. It rankled that they assumed he was calling the shots. But as a Pythian Guard, Adam had as much—if not more—tactical experience and training as me. Still, my pride took a bit of a ding.

"Sabina?" Adam said. "You cool with that plan?"

I smiled widely at the mancy and saluted. "Yes, sir."

His lips quirked. "Let's move."

We ducked and ran around the crypt we'd been hiding behind. Given the trick the Count had pulled earlier, I thought it best to have more than just the gun. So I reached into my boot for the knife I kept there for special occasions. I didn't think it'd do much damage against these guys, but I'd take any small advantage I could get at that point.

We forged a serpentine path through the maze of crypts and columbaria. The cemetery wasn't huge, but the height of the structures and the way they were crammed together meant lots of hiding places for enemies. Finally, I could see the wall on the opposite end of the place ahead. We rushed past a large mausoleum, dedicated to a fraternal order of some sort.

And stumbled headlong into the Count's creepy gang.

Everyone went still. The leader of the mysterious vamps tipped his chin and held out a gallant hand. "Shall we?" He held out his cane—with the blade hidden back inside—as if he actually expected me to just shrug and come along.

Adam and Erron answered the question for me with a couple of bolts of fuck-you-very-much. But this time, the vamps expected it. They scattered and rolled to avoid the strike. The magic slammed two vamps in the back and ricocheted into the caretaker's shack, which shuddered and spat bricks to the ground like broken teeth.

I delivered two bullets into the downed vamps while I had the chance. Their cinders swirled away in the breeze.

The other eight scattered. Two—the Count and a female—flanked us, and the others took to the vault roofs.

"Go up, G!" I shouted as I ran toward the Count. From the corner of my eye, I saw Adam head toward the female. Erron and Ziggy ran farther into the cemetery after the others, including Red Sonja.

The Count smiled eagerly and beckoned me with his fingers. I stuck the gun in my waistband and lunged for him. I'd use the gun only when I knew he couldn't use magic to disarm me again.

He flew to meet me. And when I say flew, I mean his feet literally left the ground. We slammed into each other. He weighed more, so when we fell I was at the disadvantage. I rolled quickly to avoid any restraining holds. As I did, I kicked out, the heel of my boot punching into his chest.

I came up into a crouch, my weight evenly distributed in case he went for the tackle. Instead he jumped up, winked at me, and disappeared. I spun in a quick circle but couldn't find him.

Still on guard for his reappearance, I palmed my gun again and did a quick scan to check on Adam. The female's body slammed back into a wall. From somewhere the mage produced an applewood stake. Before she'd recovered from her fall, he was on her. A swift downward stab and she was no more.

Magic sizzled through the air, and the Count reappeared directly behind Adam.

"No!" I dove and tackled him from behind. We rolled down the path, our limbs tangled. Behind me, I heard Adam shout something, followed by boots pounding against the packed earth. The Count came out on top, but his weight suddenly disappeared as Adam jerked him off me. The vamp's legs got tangled in his cape and he stumbled to his knees. Adam grabbed his hair back.

"The knife!" he yelled.

I tossed it and he caught it in midair. In a smooth motion, he swooped in with the blade. But before he could deliver the deathblow to the vamp's neck, the fucking guy disappeared again.

"There," I called, pointing to a crypt on the far end of the aisle. The Count had gone to higher ground.

I started to give chase, but Adam stopped me. "He's mine." With that, the mage disappeared. As I watched, he rematerialized just behind the Count and tapped him on the shoulder. The vamp spun just in time to receive a fist to the face.

Satisfied Adam had the situation under control, I looked up to see Giguhl pick up the male he was fighting. He hefted the squirming vamp over his head like a sack of potatoes. Then my demon tossed the guy down, where he landed with a *thud* at my feet.

I smiled down at him. "Ain't gravity a bitch?"

The bullet shattered his face before his body ignited.

"G, go help Adam. I'm going to find the Amazon."

As the demon leapt from roof to roof on his way to assist Adam, I ran in the opposite direction to find the female.

A streak of shadow between two buildings. I cut through the space and peeked around the corner before following. Something slammed into my back. I flew forward, the ground rising quickly to meet me. The gun skittered away upon impact. Rough hands grabbed at my arms, tried to pull them behind me. My nails found purchase on a handy patch of skin and dug in.

The female grunted and reared up, giving me enough leverage to flip over. As I came around, I bucked my hips to unseat her the rest of the way. I came up in a crouch and faced her.

I waited for her to pull the sword. Go for a body blow before taking off my head, perhaps. But she surprised me by falling back into a fighting stance. The tactic caught me off guard. Then I remembered what the Count had said about killing Adam to ensure my cooperation. Obviously, her plan was to subdue instead of kill.

That was her first mistake.

We circled each other slowly in an aisle formed between clumps of tombs. From the other side of the cluster of buildings, I heard grunts and the sounds of fists on bone. Every now and then, the fighting would be punctuated by a burst of magical energy.

The bitch's fangs flashed. "I'm trying to decide if I'm

going to impale your lover with my blade or if I'll rip out his throat. If you're nice, I'll let you watch."

That was her second mistake.

A red haze descended over my vision. My hands itched to destroy her mouth for even daring to speak those words. My fists led the way, going after her face, her torso, anything to punish her. Her foot whacked into my ribs with a painful punch to my kidneys. She followed with a chop to my throat that had me gasping for air. For her trouble, she earned a backhand. She spat a mouthful of red-tinged spit to the ground.

Apparently, the taste of her own blood flipped a switch somewhere under all that chain mail. Because the next thing I knew, she came after me in a blur of fists and kicks.

I was too busy defending against the blows to inflict much retaliatory damage. I'm not a small woman, but she had to have three inches and a good twenty pounds of muscle on me. Her assault pushed me back until we were back in the main avenue of the cemetery.

Another magical blast slammed through the air not far from where we fought. This one larger than the rest. Giguhl shouted something at Adam, followed by a high masculine scream. "Porcia!"

The blows stopped suddenly. The female had ignored the magic, but the Count's cry got her attention. *Interesting.*

She slammed past me to give aid to her comrade. Stunned by the sudden lack of pain, it took me a second to give chase. By the time I reached her, she was already climbing up a wall, trying to reach the Count.

I grabbed her by the chain mail and ripped her off the side. Above us, the Count was trading zaps with Adam while trying to ward off the blows of a severely pissed-off demon. Erron and Ziggy fended off three other vamps on the tombs across the way.

Porcia's elbow crashed into my nose. Bone crunched, followed by a warm gush of blood. I scrambled to catch her, but the haze of pain and the throbbing pain in my eyes blurred my vision. By the time I recovered enough to try again, she'd already made it to the rooftop. For a big girl, she certainly was agile.

This time, she didn't hesitate to draw her sword. Adam's back was to her as he raised a stake over the Count's chest. Giguhl held the vamp's arms from behind. Neither saw her coming.

"Adam!" I screamed.

He jerked around just in time to see the blade. He leapt to the side. Porcia flicked her wrist at the last second and the steel sliced across the mage's ribs. Adam fell hard with a pained grunt. The movement made his coat fall open, revealing a rapidly spreading red stain.

My blood went glacial. In a single leap I managed to make the roof before Porcia could deliver a deathblow. The sword hovered above her head, ready to descend. My hands clamped around her hands just as she flexed her muscles to bring it down.

"Giguhl," I grunted, struggling against Porcia's straining muscles. "Help Adam!"

I kicked with the toes of my boots against the back of Porcia's legs, trying desperately to break her grip on the sword. A blur of green in my peripheral vision told me Giguhl had gone to check on Adam.

My arms shook with the effort of pulling against Porcia's impressive strength. Instead of waiting to see who weakened first, I decided to go old-school.

I struck like a snake, aiming for her jugular. The move forced me to weaken my grip on the sword. But luckily, Giguhl was already pulling Adam out of harm's way.

The minute the sharp points broke skin, Porcia's body jerked and she screamed with rage. I clamped down harder, getting as much skin as blood. Metal clattered on stone.

My hands gripped the insides of her elbows, holding her close. Then I jerked my head back, taking a chunk of her neck with me.

She dropped to her knees. Her hand flew uselessly to the wound at her neck. Only time and blood could fix that extensive damage. Unlucky for her, she had neither at her disposal.

I spat the taste of her from my mouth and grabbed the broadsword. Gripping the leather hilt in my hand, I raised the weapon. I still had the gun tucked into my waistband. But some special moments just call for the satisfying slice of a blade.

Despite the bulkiness of the sword, I managed to bring it up easily. No hesitation or doubts stilled my hand. I brought in down hard and true. Porcia's head rolled from her shoulders.

Before it hit the roof, both it and her body burst into flames. I dropped the sword and swung around, pulling the gun as I went. Erron and Ziggy fought the Count. Their feet were on solid ground, but I had the advantage of a bird's-eye view.

"Erron, duck!"

The recreant didn't hesitate or question. He simply dropped to the ground. The Count looked up a split second after the gun's bark ripped through the night. The whites of his eyes widened and stood in stark contrast to the mottled purple of his battered face.

This bullet he caught right between the eyes.

As the inevitable sparks flared where he used to stand, I wiped a trembling hand across my forehead.

Giguhl called out. "Sabina, you need to get down here!"

I jerked back into motion. As I leapt from the building, my heart pounded.

Adam lay atop a concrete pad set into the ground. Giguhl knelt next to him, staring intently at the mage's chest. I slowed, my stomach sinking at the sight of Adam's too-white complexion and the beads of sweat gathered on his forehead.

I ran over and skidded to my knees in front of him. I felt Erron and Ziggy fall in behind me. "Tell me."

Adam swallowed. "It's just a flesh wound."

"Bullshit," I said, my concern making me default to clipped speech. I slapped Giguhl's hands away to see for myself.

So much blood. I gently lifted the edge of his shirt to get a better look at the actual wound. An angry red slash— maybe six or eight inches long—cut across his lower ribs to the muscled ridges of his abdomen. Not as bad as I'd expected, but bad enough that I wanted to kill that bitch all over again.

"Can you heal yourself?" Giguhl asked. His claws were covered in Adam's blood. My stomach clenched at the sight.

Adam swallowed and shook his head. "Too weak from all the spells."

I rounded on Erron. "You have to do it."

The musician's eyes widened. "Me?"

I leapt up to get in his face. "You'll help us fight, but you won't help him heal?"

Erron's face was placid, without a line of stress or guilt. "Can't."

I turned to Ziggy. "You, then!"

The quiet mage shook his head and held up his hands as he backed away.

"Sabina," Adam gasped behind me. I looked over my shoulder. "They can't help."

"Why the fuck not?" Giguhl demanded.

"When someone goes recreant, the Council strips them of their healing powers," Adam said in a low tone, like he was sharing a shameful secret. "It was his punishment for declaring himself outside their laws."

My mouth fell open. When he'd told me they were outcasts, I assumed he meant they just had a difference of opinion with the Council. Not that they were shunned and stripped of certain powers. But as much as I felt bad about the seeming unfairness of that situation, my priority was getting Adam healed.

"Anyway, he'll be fine. It's just a scratch," Erron said.

"You know what? If you're not going to help, you can just leave," I snapped.

"Sabina," Adam said. "They just helped us."

"Right, and now they probably just want to get back to your orgy or whatever. Don't worry about us."

Erron's eyes darkened. "Yes, we do so hate to miss out on the orgy. We apologize for intruding on your street party."

Guilt pricked behind my eyes. But I didn't have time to apologize. Adam was still bleeding. "Bye now." Dismissing the recreants from my mind, I turned to the demon. "Giguhl, go get the car," I barked.

The air popped as Erron and Ziggy left. Adam watched me with a wary expression. "Red? You need to chill."

"Just tell me what to do." It humbled me to not know what to do to help him. But since I came from a race that self-healed without trying, my knowledge of basic first aid was sorely lacking.

"Take off your shirt."

I paused. "Why?" Suspicion slowed my delivery.

He rolled his eyes. "You need to apply pressure to slow the bleeding."

Without further comment, I ripped off my jacket and tore off my tank. The way the mancy's eyes flared at the sight of me clad only in a bra told me he was far enough from death's door.

"Now what?"

"Press it to the wound. Hard."

"But won't that hurt?" He shot me an impatient glare.

I placed the wadded shirt against the cut, pressing as instructed. The fabric went from white to red almost instantly as blood soaked in.

He hissed through clenched teeth. "More."

Ignoring the voice inside shouting that hurting him more was the last thing I wanted, I did as instructed. Gods love him, he tried to hide his pain.

He swallowed hard. "Talk to me."

"About what?"

He shrugged, and the look on his face told me he immediately regretted the move.

"Okay, um, have I mentioned that if you ever scare me like this again I'm going to kill you?"

"We really need to work on your bedside manner." He paused. "But ditto."

I drew back. "Me? I'm not the one bleeding."

"Sabina, since we've known each other you've been staked twice—"

I cut in. "That first time was your fault. Or did you conveniently forget sending Giguhl to my apartment to shoot me with a crossbow?"

He winced, this time from a guilty conscience instead of the wound. "But I've had to see you in pain, too."

I held up a hand. "Okay, fine. I get into a lot of fights. Big deal. You don't have to worry about me. My body is a healing machine."

"I wasn't just talking about physical wounds, Sabina." His hand came up to rub my cheek. "Your preternatural abilities don't extend to less visible injury."

Suddenly a conversation meant to distract him from his pain had turned into a chat about my emotional wounds. Time to change the subject. "How about we discuss that after we get your very visible chest wound healed."

He tipped my chin so I was forced to look in his eyes. "Have I mentioned I'm a huge fan of that bra?"

The corner of my lip twitched. "This old thing?"

The scream of metal crashing into metal ripped a hole in the silence. Keeping one hand pressed to Adam's chest, I grabbed my gun as I swiveled on my heels. Two headlights sped toward us. I squinted and made out the shape of Giguhl's horns behind the windshield.

"Looks like the cavalry arrived," I said.

"Please tell me you're driving back to the shop. I'd hate to survive a sword attack only to die in a fiery car crash."

Giguhl slammed on the brakes. The Gremlin fishtailed and sprayed dirt and pebbles at us. I ducked over Adam to protect him from the spray. When I looked up again, Giguhl was jumping out of the car and running around the crunched fender of the Gremlin toward us.

"G, I appreciate you getting the car, but did you really have to crash through the gates?"

The demon skidded to a halt in front of me with his claws on his hips. "Well, excuse me, Miss Perfect. For your information, I've never driven a car before."

My mouth fell open. When I'd ordered him to drive, he'd had no choice but to comply. In my stress of seeing to Adam, I'd totally forgotten Giguhl had never driven a car. "Well, in that case, I'm impressed all you hit was a gate."

Giguhl's eyes shifted left. "Actually, we probably need to get moving."

"Why?"

"It's better that you don't know in case the police come calling."

Deciding I definitely didn't want to know, I began issuing orders to ensure everyone could fit comfortably in the crowded car. Once Giguhl and Adam were settled—Giguhl back in cat form in the back and Adam riding shotgun—I ran back around to the driver's side.

Just before I ducked in, a warm breeze whooshed through the avenue. A flash of something in the distance caught my eye. Almost like a lightning bug. I hesitated, hoping to catch a better look at whatever I'd seen.

But the cemetery was still again and silent as a . . . well, you know. The low hum I'd noticed when we'd come in still thrummed in my head, but otherwise, nothing.

"Sabina?" Adam's voice sounded strained from pain.

I shook off the bizarre feeling and lowered myself into the seat. "Sorry, thought I saw something. But it must have just been my imagination."

"Ooh," Giguhl said, "Maybe it was a ghost."

I laughed. "Don't be silly. Ghosts don't exist."

But just before I slammed the door, I could have sworn I heard the sound of laughter on the breeze.

15

A masculine yell echoed down the hallway, followed by a brusque, feminine, "Quit being such a baby." I rushed to the door to see what the voodooienne was doing to Adam.

The mage was laid out on Zen's worktable like a sacrifice. My eyes quickly located the source of his ire: a squirt bottle she used to flush out the wound.

"Should I bother to ask how it's going?" I asked, stepping up to the table.

Adam's jaw clenched as Zen sprayed more water. She didn't answer my question. Instead, she called, "Brooks, I'm still waiting for that yarrow!"

A faint response came from behind the closed door of the closet Zen had turned into a mini-apothecary. He emerged a couple of seconds later juggling a few glass jars and vials. "You're almost out." He held out a brown bottle to Zen, who popped the cork and looked inside.

"Should be enough." She tipped the vial, and a yellowish-green powder dusted the wound.

"What's that do?" I asked.

Her impatient gaze swiveled to mine. She shook the brown vial. "Ground yarrow. It acts as a styptic to clot the blood."

Selecting another bottle, she held it up. "Clove powder to numb pain and prevent infection." She popped off the top and liberally sprinkled the brown powder on top of the yarrow.

Adam hissed and tried to jerk away.

"Almost done," Zen said. Brooks handed her a stack of gauze. To me she said, "Make yourself useful and tear off two strips of bandage tape."

Happy to have something to do with my hands, I did as instructed. I handed Zen the first strip about the same time Giguhl sauntered in. Thankfully, he'd put on clothes—a pair of red sweatpants and a black T-shirt advertising Zen's store.

"How's the patient?"

"Ornery as hell," Zen said, smoothing the last piece of tape. "But he'll live."

"Are we done yet?" Adam asked. He made to sit up, but the woman pushed him back down with a firm hand.

"Oh, no you don't. I still have to stitch you up."

Adam grimaced. "Is that really necessary?"

Zen nodded at Brooks, who brought over a spool of thread and a long needle. My stomach flip-flopped in sympathy for Adam. "Either you let me stitch you up or it's at least a week of bed rest," she warned.

Adam's expression spoke volumes about his opinion of the second option. "Fine."

"I thought so." She smiled. "Now just lay back. This won't hurt a bit."

Giguhl coughed "Bullshit" into his claw.

Zen's head snapped up. "Don't make me kick your green ass out of here."

The demon's head ducked. "Sorry."

Zen put on a pair of bifocals so she could thread the needle. "While I'm working, y'all can fill me in on what happened."

I glanced at Adam. If talking would bother him, the discussion could wait. His eyes strayed to the needle for a moment before he finally nodded. Obviously he'd appreciate the distraction.

"We were ambushed," I began. "One second the street was empty, and the next thing we knew . . ."

I told her the whole story, from the midget orgy to the Count's threats against Adam to Erron's hasty departure. As I talked, Adam gasped from the needle's sting. His male pride wouldn't appreciate pitying glances or pauses, so I kept going. The story wrapped up about the same time Zen completed her task.

"Why did they target Adam?" she asked, snipping off the loose thread.

Leave it to Zen to focus on the part that made me most uncomfortable to talk about. "Lavinia believes Adam and I are romantically involved—"

"Because you are," Zen interrupted. Giguhl chuckled across the room. Brooks covered his mouth with his hand.

I avoided Adam's suddenly intent gaze to stare down the voodoo priestess. "Can we please focus?" Zen bit her lip to hide her smile. I continued. "It's my fault. Back in California she and I had this big fight and I told her I was carrying Adam's baby. I'd been trying to piss her off so she'd make a mistake, but I guess the mistake was mine."

"Wait," Giguhl said. "You never told me that."

I slashed a hand through the air. "By now she knows it was a lie, but she also knows Adam and I are still...partners."

Brooks cleared his throat. Zen shot Giguhl an amused look. The demon mouthed, "I told you so."

Ignoring all of them, I glanced at Adam. He winked at me, which made me more uncomfortable than the others' reactions. "Anyway, that's why she ordered him killed. She figured she'd go after someone I cared about to force my cooperation." My face began to flame about halfway through that sentence.

"That's been bugging me," Adam said. I looked up. "All along we've assumed Lavinia and the Caste wanted you dead. So why play these games?"

I shrugged. "She probably has some elaborate plan to torture me before she decapitates me."

Zen shook her head. "Girl, I hate to say this but your family is fucked up."

"Tell me about it."

But Adam wasn't done. "I don't know. I'm not convinced there isn't more to it than that."

I sighed. "Regardless, our time is best served trying to find Maisie before Lavinia can succeed in grabbing me."

"Amen," Giguhl said.

"Sounds like it might be worth talking with that Zorn fella again, too," Zen said.

As much as I hated to admit it, she was probably right. "Yeah. Maybe."

Brooks cleared his throat. "If you'll excuse me, I need to go get my stuff ready for tomorrow."

I looked up. "What's tomorrow?"

He smiled. "Our pre-Halloween party at Lagniappe.

We do it the night before because we want to hit the parade on Saturday. All us lady-boys are dressing as our favorite queens from history."

"Who are you going as?" Giguhl asked.

Brooks smiled wide. "The Queen of the Nile."

"Cleopatra?" Adam asked.

"Hellz, yeah." Brooks snapped his fingers in a Z. "I got a cornrow wig with a gold crown and everything."

"Ooh," Giguhl said. "You're gonna look fierce."

Brooks laughed. "Sing it, Gigi."

He sashayed toward the door, stopping only to deliver a playful swat to Giguhl's behind. My seven-foot-tall Mischief demon, who up until recently spent his spare time disemboweling demons in an underground fight club, blushed and giggled.

Once Brooks was out of hearing distance, I approached the demon. "What's that about?"

Giguhl flashed me a confused look. "What?"

"You're totally flirting with him."

Giguhl snorted. "So?"

"So since when did you switch teams?"

The demon frowned. "What does that mean?"

I leaned in closer and whispered in an undertone. "I thought you were straight."

Giguhl's mouth dropped open. Then he started to laugh. Great heaving guffaws.

I crossed my arms and glared at the demon. "What are you laughing at?"

"You're an idiot."

"Thanks so much."

The demon collected himself, a few stray chuckles escaping as he tried to school his features. "Sabina, I'm not gay."

"Bisexual, then?" I said.

Another snort. "Nooo. I'm a demon, silly."

I squinted at him, trying to follow that logic. "And?"

"And to demons sexuality is a fluid concept," Adam chimed in. Obviously my attempts to keep this conversation private had failed miserably.

Giguhl pointed at the mage and said, "Ding-ding-ding. Give the mage a cookie."

I held up a hand. "Wait, really?"

"Oh, sure," Giguhl said with a shrug. "We'll fuck just about anything,"

"I think that's my cue to leave," Zen said. "If you all figure out anything else about the vampires who attacked you, you let me know."

Abashed, Giguhl mumbled an apology to Zen as she passed. She patted his arm.

When she was gone, Giguhl rounded on me. "Nice going, Sabina."

My mouth fell open. "Me? I wasn't the one talking about screwing everything alive."

"Actually, it doesn't really even have to be alive—but that's beside the point. The truth is that Brooks and I are just friends."

I threw my arms up. "Then why let me think you were trying to get in his pants?"

"Ah, I was just screwing with you." He held up a claw. "Mischief demon, remember?" He paused. "But I wasn't lying. Seriously, Sabina, *anything*."

Adam heaved a weary sigh when I made gagging noises. "Guys, can we please get back to figuring out the whys of the ambush?"

I dismissed Giguhl with a shake of my head. "Okay, where were we?"

In truth, I was relieved Adam changed the subject. Where Giguhl stored his equipment wasn't really my business. I certainly had more potentially lethal issues to face.

"That we need to talk to Erron again," Giguhl said, shooting me a superior look. I rolled my eyes.

"You know what I want to know?" Adam said. "How did the Caste vamps know where we were?"

I stuck my hands in my pockets and leaned back against the table by Adam's hip. Something crunched against my hand. "Wait a sec." I removed the scrap of paper with the address of Necrospank's drug den on it. "I'll be damned." I turned so Adam could see the damning evidence for himself. When he figured it out, his face tightened into a mask of anger.

"Wait, what am I missing?" Giguhl said. I remembered then that he had been in the store with Brooks when the paper had been delivered.

"Mac's source screwed us."

"What? No way," Giguhl said. "Brooks wouldn't have hooked us up with a bad contact."

I sighed. "I'm not sure if Mac knew. But her source must have."

A frown formed between Giguhl's horns. "If you kill Mac's friend, then you're begging for problems with the were. Which might cause problems with Brooks and Zen."

I pushed away from the table. "What do want me to do, Giguhl? Ignore that Adam got sliced and diced tonight?"

"I'm not saying someone doesn't deserve to pay for selling us out." He looked me dead in the eye. "But you better be damned sure you've got the right asshole before you get physical."

Adam shifted on the table. "He's right, Red. We need a plan."

I looked at him. "Guys, it's just a conversation. And what do you mean *we*? You're not going anywhere."

"I absolutely am. You're not doing this alone."

I threw my hands up. "Adam, I hate to point this out, but you were almost disemboweled less than an hour ago. Besides, I'll take Gigi with me."

Adam pressed his lips together at my exaggeration. "First of all, considering how reluctant Mac was to introduce us to her source, this probably won't be a simple conversation." He pushed himself up on his elbows. "Second, I was nowhere near about to spill my guts." He grimaced and swung his legs over the side of the table. "And third, I might be too weak to heal myself, but I can still hold a fucking gun."

I put my hands on my hips. "Don't let your pride cause more problems than we need right now."

He drew back, stung. "Right back at ya, Red." His tone low, cutting.

I clenched my jaw. We stared each other down for a few moments.

Giguhl's head swiveled from side to side, waiting for one of us to break our stalemate. "Sabina, let him come. I'll look out for him."

My stare locked with Adam's. "No."

His biceps heaved as he slid off the table and placed his weight on his feet. One hand flew to the bandage, but he managed to step away from the table's support.

"Adam, don't be an idiot, you'll hurt yourself." My

shrewish *I know what's best for you* tone brought me up short.

Adam wasn't my minion. Hell, even Giguhl barely qualified for that title anymore. So even though it pained me to back down, I did, because Adam was a grown-ass man.

"Okay," I said finally.

Adam looked up from pulling on his shirt. "What?"

I took a deep breath. "I'd appreciate your help."

Giguhl stepped forward, his hooves clacking on the floorboards. "It's a trick, mancy!"

I shot him a look. "No, really, it's fine. Just be careful, okay?"

Adam looked at me for a moment, as if he expected me to start laughing or deliver a punch line. When I simply returned his look with my face trained into a more open expression, he pulled his shirt the rest of the way down. "Let's go have a chat with the wolf."

Lagniappe and the building that housed the club were dark by the time we arrived. The street was equally deserted as we ducked in the side entrance. We quickly made our way up to the second floor and approached the faded blue door. Despite the late—or early, depending on your race—hour, I didn't knock gently. Instead, my fist pounded the wood so hard my knuckles stung.

After five minutes of constant knocking, the door finally flew open. Mac stood across the threshold in a thin white T-shirt and a pair of ratty boxer shorts. Her only accessories were a major case of bed head and a shotgun.

When she saw the three of us standing there, she lowered the barrel with a frown. "Sabina?"

"Hey, Mac. You got a minute?"

She yawned and rubbed a hand through the nest on her head. "Do you have any idea what time it is?"

"A little after four a.m. May we come in? It's important."

She nodded over my shoulder. "Who's the demon?"

I squinted at her, confused. "That's Giguhl."

She shook her head. "I thought Giguhl was a cat." That's when I remembered the first and last time she'd seen him he was asleep in Zen's counter.

"He's both," I said. "And it's a long story. Can we come in?"

She looked more confused than ever but seemed to finally clue into the tension in my tone. "Is everything okay?"

"Actually, no. Everything is very far from okay."

She frowned and opened the door wider. "Come on in, then."

I smiled politely, but inside I was seething. The more I thought about how close Adam had come to losing his life, the more my fists itched to strangle Mac's friend.

On the way over, we'd decided Giguhl and Adam would basically hang in the back looking imposing in case Mac refused to reveal her source's identity. I'd do all the talking until and unless the time came for harsher tactics. I wasn't leaving the apartment without a name, whether Mac liked it or not.

Once we were all inside, Mac leaned the shotgun against the end of the couch. Then she walked back toward us. "Can I get you anything? All I have is beer and water."

I waved a hand.

"Okay, why don't you sit and tell me what's going on, then?" Fatigue added a slight growl to her words.

Perching on the edge of the love seat, I removed the gun from my waistband and set it within easy reach on the coffee table. If she noted the firearm, she gave no indication. She did frown when the males didn't sit. Instead they stood closer to the door, effectively blocking the exit.

Her eye movements indicated the shewolf was doing some quick thinking. "Are Brooks and Zenobia okay?" she prompted.

"They're fine," I said, keeping my tone casual. "But Adam had some trouble tonight. In fact, we all did."

She squinted. "What happened?"

"We were ambushed."

Her jaw went slack. "Oh, my gods, are you guys okay?" She looked at Adam with concern. "Adam?"

He nodded. "I'm fine. Zen's a good healer."

"Mac," I said, regaining her attention. "I need the name of your source with the vamps."

She frowned. "Why?"

I scooted to the edge of the couch. "Your source gave you that address, right? The one on Prytania Street? The ambush happened a block away from that house."

"So she was right about vampires in that house."

I shook my head. "The only thing we found at that address were a bunch of drugged-out musicians with some disturbing sexual appetites."

"I'm confused. Who attacked you, then?"

"Really? I need to spell it out for you?" I paused as her expression morphed from confusion to something harder. "Your friend sold us out."

She blinked as the implications fell into place. "You're insane! She wasn't involved."

I scoffed. "Mac, get real. Your source is a vampire, and we were attacked by vampires."

She crossed her arms and speared me with a stare. "A vampire might be responsible, but it wasn't *my* vampire."

A shadow of doubt appeared on the edges of my mind. Mac seemed too confident, too unconcerned her source might be to blame. I looked at Adam. "Mac, just give us a name so we can be sure."

Mac slammed her hands on the arms of the chair and stood. "I gave you that address because I was trying to help. And now you're accusing my friend of trying to kill you? Un-fucking-believable."

I picked up the gun. "Mac, it's not my intention to offend you, but I'm sure you can understand we can't just take your word for it."

She looked down at the weapon. "You're insane. I'm not giving you the fucking time of day now."

I glared at her. "Why don't you just call her, then? See if she agrees to meet with us."

"Get the hell out of my apartment," Mac said, pointing to the door.

Just then, a door down the hall behind Mac creaked open. A drowsy voice called, "Honey?"

Mac froze. I grabbed my gun and rose. The were threw up her hands to still me. "Everything's okay. Go back to—"

The scent of copper hit me. Well, well, well. "Come out with your hands up," I called over the rest of Mac's sentence.

"No! Stay there!" Mac shouted.

A couple of tense seconds passed before a titian head emerged from the dark hallway. It was the vampette who'd come to Mac's club a few days earlier. Her mysterious contact. And lover.

The vamp didn't raise her hands until she saw the gun pointing at Mac. The huge demon and muscular mage might have factored into her decision, too.

Her pale digits went skyward. The move raised the hem of her T-shirt to reveal a pair of white cotton underpants. "What the hell is going on?" She made sure to flash some fang.

"Tell her, Mac," I said, my gun aimed at the were's chest.

Mac looked like she'd rip my head off at the first opportunity. "This is Sabina Kane, the one I told you about."

The girlfriend's expression went all pinchy, like she was confused. "Wait, I thought we were helping her."

"We were," Mac gritted out.

"They why does she have a gun pointed at you, Mackenzie?"

"Apparently she has some trust issues."

"Where were you at two a.m.?" I demanded.

She frowned. "At Mac's club."

That didn't prove anything. She could easily have set up the ambush by phone from the bar.

"How long have you been working for the Caste?" I demanded.

Without hesitation or glancing at her lover she said, "The who?"

Mac shot me a superior look.

"What's your name?" I said, trying another tactic.

She frowned. "Georgia."

"Well, Georgia, it seems we are at an impasse. Because you gave Mac an address. And at that address, we were jumped by a group of vampires. Can you see why we might be suspicious of your motives?"

"So there *were* out-of-town vampires there?" she said, echoing Mac's earlier statement. "Are you guys okay?"

Either they were diabolical masterminds who'd planned for this eventuality and gotten their stories straight ahead of time. Or Mac was telling the truth and I was a colossal asshole.

I sighed. Adam cursed under his breath. Glancing from the corner of my eye, I caught the oh-shit look he and Giguhl exchanged.

Swallowing, I lowered my gun a fraction. "Hypothetically speaking, let's say you're telling the truth—"

"There's nothing hypothetical about it," Mac barked.

I ignored that and soldiered on. "Why did you give Mac that address?"

"You don't owe her an explanation." Mac took a step toward her girlfriend. I raised the gun, a clear warning to stay put.

"Obviously someone needs to clear this up," Georgia said. Turning to me, she said, "Mac said you needed help, so I gave her the only information I had at the time—a rumor that some vamps were moving into the Prytania house." She shrugged. "But now I have a question for you."

I titled my head. "What?"

"Did the guy who attacked you tonight wear a cape?"

My heart kicked up a notch. My fingers gripped the gun tighter in case Georgia wasn't as innocent as she claimed. "Why do you ask?"

She smiled at the tension in my voice. "Early this evening, I was in the Marigny trolling for tourists when this male vamp in a cape approached me."

"With a cane?" Adam asked.

"That's him." She rolled her eyes. "Total douche."

My mouth fell open and I lowered the gun to my side. "I'll be damned."

Now that the gun wasn't pointed at her, she lowered her hands and scooted closer to Mac before continuing. "He said his name was Rupert and he represented a group that was recruiting vampires. The guy was weird, right? So I told him I wasn't interested and started to leave. He grabbed my arm and his entire demeanor changed. Suddenly he was all veiled threats. He said there was a new power in town who was recruiting foot soldiers or some shit."

"Did he give you any names?" I asked.

She shook her head. "No, but he indicated it was a powerful female. Must be the one Mac said you're after, right? The one we need to avoid?"

I cringed inwardly. Mac had made good on her promise to warn her friends about Lavinia. I lowered my gun to my side. "Yeah, probably."

"Anyway, he says any local vampires who don't fall in line under her leadership won't live long. I acted interested and offered to spread the word for him." She shook her head, as if still surprised he'd bought her act. "He seemed happy with that, but before he could keep talking, his cell phone rang. He didn't speak, just listened. After a few seconds, he hung up. All the sudden he couldn't leave fast enough. As he ran off, he yelled back that he'd be in touch soon to check on my progress. He seemed to be in a major hurry."

By this point, Adam sat on the arm of the sofa next to me, and Giguhl leaned against the wall, listening with rapt attention. As the seconds ticked by, my stomach tightened more and more. Not only because we'd obviously accused the wrong person, but also because we were now further away from knowing who called Rupert with our location.

Figuring I might as well admit defeat, I let the gun dangle between my legs. "He was in a hurry, all right. He was on his way to attack us."

"Anyway, after that, I called in every vamp I know in the area for a powwow. Only it wasn't to recruit them."

"You were warning them to skip town?" Adam said, shooting me a look.

She nodded. "Fat lot of good it did. Only a handful decided to run."

I leaned back against the couch cushions. "And the rest? Do they plan on working for Lavinia?"

"Nope. The rest of us are staying to fight for our city."

A humorless laugh escaped my lips. "Then you're all fools."

"All right," Mac said. "That's enough. You've gotten your explanation. Now get the hell out."

"No, wait," Georgia said. When Mac made disgusted noises, she held out a hand for patience. "Why are we fools for not allowing a bully to push us around?"

I sighed from deep in my chest. The kind of sigh you take before you break bad news to a trusting soul. "Well, Georgia, the answer to your question is this: Lavinia Kane isn't just a bully, she's the godsdamned Alpha Domina. Just because you live in New Orleans instead of Los Angeles is no excuse not to understand what that title means."

Georgia shrugged. "So she's powerful."

I snorted. "Not just powerful, Georgia. Ancient. She's seen empires rise and fall. She's killed more vampires than you've met in your lifetime. Created rivers of blood in the streets of both the Old and New Worlds. And when she wants something, she won't stop until it's hers. So, yes, I believe you and your friends are fools for even considering the possibility you could defeat her."

Georgia tipped her head to the side. "Didn't Mac tell me you aim to kill Lavinia Kane?"

I licked my lips. "I do."

A slow smile spread across Georgia's lips. "Well then, darlin', I guess that makes us both fools, doesn't it?"

I liked this Georgia. She had spirit and a refreshing lack of bullshit. "You have no idea."

"Save your breath," Mac said. "She's leaving tonight."

Georgia's smile disappeared. "Like hell I am. If you're staying, I'm staying, and that's final."

Mac glanced at me before pulling Georgia aside for a whispered argument. In order to give them privacy, I turned toward Adam and waved Giguhl over. The mage blew out a long breath.

"How you holding up, mancy?"

"I'll live. If Mac doesn't turn that shotgun on us, that is."

"Oh, please, she's just mad we found out she's dating a vampire. I'll just tell her that secret's safe with us and that will be that." That earned me two incredulous looks.

The conversation across the room escalated into a full-on shouting match. "...don't let her put thoughts in your head. She's a nut job." Mac didn't even try to pretend she wasn't talking about me. In fact, she pointed a finger in my direction as she yelled, "She'll get you killed."

"I think we need to get something straight," Georgia said, her voice icy. "I only like tops in bed. When the clothes go back on, you lose the right to boss me around."

"On second thought," I said. "Maybe they need some privacy."

I stood and made my way for the door. Adam and Giguhl lagged behind, each enjoying the show too much to leave.

"I think they're about to kiss," Giguhl hissed.

I rolled my eyes and grabbed Adam by the ear. "Let's go." He yelped and rose immediately. I released his lobe and pushed him toward the door, careful not to nudge his wound.

Giguhl got less careful treatment and had to be forcibly pulled from the room. If we were lucky, the ladies would have furious makeup sex later. Then maybe Mac wouldn't come after me with that shotgun for pulling a gun on her girlfriend over a misunderstanding.

A crash sounded from inside the apartment.

Then again, maybe I should have taken the shotgun.

16

*I*n the dream, brass cuffs bound my hands to an overhead rafter. A werewolf in full-moon beast form pointed a shotgun at my face. Just beyond the light pool of a single bare bulb, the silhouette of a male paced in the shadows. Every now and then, the dim light caught the shock of red hair on his head.

"Who are you?" I demanded, yanking painfully with my wrists.

He paused. Turned. I still couldn't make out a face. "We've known each other since the beginning."

He stepped forward into the light. I gasped. He was beautiful. Too beautiful. Long cardinal-red hair, olive skin, eyes the color of wet emeralds. Tall and finely muscled. Not the bulk of a body builder, but the grace of a Greek statue. David instead of Goliath. Everything too perfect to be anything but evil.

"I don't know you."

He placed a hand over his heart and closed his eyes. Like my words wounded him. "My beloved *Lamashtu*. Soon we will be reunited. Forever."

Blood dripped down my wrist, my arms, to spill on the concrete floor. "You're a lunatic."

He looked up, his irises darker now. Crazier. "Remind her where her heart is. Who her master is."

The were stepped forward. Jabbed the cold metal into my breastbone. "I don't know you!" I yelled.

The ominous double click of the pump action.

His slimy smile evaporated. He whispered, "Where's my fucking owl?"

Boom!

I woke with a start. My breath labored, and cold sweat coated my chest. I rubbed at it, relieved to find unbroken skin. A green claw appeared in front of my face. The scent of coffee from the mug it held went a long way toward calming me.

I groped for it, but the claw moved out of range.

"You're gonna have to get out of bed first," Giguhl said, sounding amused.

Right, like that was going to happen. "Go away," I groaned, rolling over to burrow back into the pillows and blankets.

My tormentor ripped the pillow away. Unholy light and frigid air hit my face.

"Don't make me hurt you, G."

"I'd like to see you try, trampire." The covers disappeared next. "Now get up and shake a leg."

I rolled over to deliver a well-deserved glare at my minion. "What time is it?"

He stood just out of kicking range, waving the mug in the air like bait. "Four."

No wonder Adam sent Giguhl in to wake me. Four in

the afternoon to me is like four a.m. to humans. Though my room had heavy quilts over the windows, I squinted against the ambient light streaming through the door Giguhl had left open.

"Why?" I barked.

Giguhl sighed and stomped across the room to retrieve a pair of sunglasses from the bedside table. "Gods, you're such a diva," Giguhl complained as he handed them over.

"Bite me, demon." With great effort, I swung my legs over the edge of the bed and sat up with a groan. Pushed the echo of panic from the dream away like a bad memory. Not surprising I'd have a stress dream, given everything going on. "Where's the mancy?"

"He went to go buy some more blood for you. Said when he gets back we're all having a meeting before we head out to do the ritual with Zen."

I'd forgotten all about Zen's suggestion that we try to contact the spirit world that night. I ran a hand over my face and yawned. "What's the meeting about?"

Giguhl shot me a look. The disastrous conversation with Mac rushed back to me, along with Georgia's revelations. "Oh, right." I held out my hand for the coffee.

He crossed his arms and glared at me. My feet slammed into the floorboards and I pushed my butt off the bed. I stalked over the demon and glared up at him. "Happy now?" The sunglasses probably ruined the effect, but he seemed to sense failure to comply would result in pain.

He handed the cup over with a sneer. "Jesus, you're bitchy today."

I took a couple of bracing gulps, not caring that the brew had gone lukewarm. "Didn't sleep well," I said between chugs.

"Tell me about it, sister. The mancy's got toenails like a fucking sloth. Scratched my calves up to be damned. Not to mention, the hell-owl started screeching like a banshee two hours ago."

I stopped mid-sip. "Oh, shit." With everything else going on, the owl in the fridge had totally slipped my mind.

"Don't worry. Apparently Zen and Brooks hadn't forgotten about him like the rest of us. Zen said she fed him some rats yesterday while we were out."

I blew out a breath. "I can't believe we forgot about him."

"You know what you need?" Giguhl said. I raised a brow, bracing myself for a punch line. "A to-do list. Might help you keep track of all the beings who want you dead and the satanic birdlife you've kidnapped."

I imagined the list in my head:

1. *Perform voodoo ritual on evil owl.*
2. *Find out who sold us out to the anachronistic Caste vampires.*
3. *Make amends with lesbian werewolf.*
4. *Rescue twin.*
5. *Murder grandmother.*

I wasn't sure whether to laugh or cry. "Yeah, I'll get right on that."

Giguhl heard the sarcasm. "Suit yourself, but don't come crying to me if you forget who you're supposed to kill when."

I rolled my eyes and went to get clothes from the dresser. "I need to grab a shower."

That was his cue to leave, but Giguhl lingered, looking unsure of himself. I shot a meaningful look to the door. "Hello?"

He kneaded his claws together. "Um, there's something I need to tell you."

My stomach clenched. That kind of talk from a Mischief demon was never good. "What now?"

His goat-slit eyes looked at the floor. "I kind of, well—and it totally wasn't my fault since I was asleep," he said. "But I kind of sort of made a move on Adam last night."

I choked on my coffee. "You tried to sleep-sex Adam?"

"I didn't sleep-sex him. Just kind of, well, humped his leg a little." A bark of laughter escaped me before I could stop it. The demon's head drooped. "I guess my subconscious thought he was you-know-who."

Despite my horrified amusement, I tried to remember Giguhl was still recovering from being dumped. Mostly he seemed unaffected, but I guess the demon had more layers than I gave him credit for. I swallowed the remaining giggles and pasted an empathetic expression on my face. With my free hand, I patted him awkwardly on the arm. "I'm sorry."

He looked up, his gaze narrowed suspiciously. "What, no jokes?"

I shook my head. "Don't get me wrong. I would have paid good money to see the look on Adam's face—" Giguhl pulled away. I grabbed his arm. "Look, I'm sure Adam understands you didn't really mean to—" I bit my lip to stop the giggle threatening to break free. "Get frisky with him."

Luckily Giguhl didn't notice my struggle and went to plop down on the bed. "I miss her sometimes."

By *her*, I assumed he meant Valva. I set my clothes on

the bedside table and sat next to him. Seeing him look so downtrodden made me uncomfortable. I felt totally ill-suited to be handing out love advice. Patting his knee awkwardly, I said, "That's understandable, I guess."

He looked up then. Uncertainty shadowed his expression. "Really?"

I shrugged. "Sure. I mean, until she revealed her true colors"—*by stripping in front of a room full of horny vampires before causing a full-on stripper brawl and getting my friend's bar burned to the ground*—"you guys seemed to really be into each other."

His lips turned down into a demonic facsimile of a pout. "I just don't get it."

"Me, either. You're a great catch, and if she couldn't see that it's her loss."

"You think?" He looked up from under his eyelids.

"I know it. You deserve a demon who understands how lucky she is to have you."

"I guess so."

I gave his shoulder a friendly bump. "In the meantime, maybe we should put a divider between you and the mancy in bed."

The demon's lip twitched. He looked up with a sparkle in his eyes. "Or he could sleep with you." His black eyebrows waggled suggestively.

Now it was my turn to sigh heavily. "I don't know, G."

His nostrils flared as if smelling drama. "Ooh!" He shifted to face me. "Tell Gigi all about it."

I shrugged. "Not much to tell, really. We've definitely grown close and all, but I keep holding back."

"Oh, Sabina," Giguhl said, shaking his head sadly. "What are you doing?"

I drew away. "What do you mean?"

He tilted his head and shot me a get-real look. "Don't play dumb with me, trampire. We both know you're hot for the mancy." I opened my mouth to argue, but he steamed ahead. "Don't even bother to deny it. The question is, why do you keep sabotaging something that could be really great for both of you?"

I rolled my eyes. Just my luck to have a minion who considered himself the Dr. Phil of the demon world. "I'm not sabotaging anything." I looked away, unable to bear the knowing look in his eyes.

"Whatever. I think you need to go find that boy and tell him how you feel about him. Then you need to ride him like a tilt-o-whirl."

"I can't."

"And why not?"

"You mean besides the numerous attempts on our lives, the sister to save, and the grandmother to kill?" He shot me a look that clearly indicated those were bullshit excuses. "Fine, how about the fact that we'd basically be recreating my parents' Greek tragedy?"

His expression didn't change except for a raised eyebrow. I looked up to the ceiling, knowing what I was about to do might be a horrible mistake. On the other hand, maybe sharing the burden of my secret might lessen its power. I hesitated for a second and then went for broke. "There's something I haven't told you."

"You're frigid? I knew it!"

I slapped his arm. "No, I'm not frigid."

"VD?"

"Shut up and listen before I lose my nerve."

He mimed locking his lips.

I let out a rush of breath. "Okay, remember in New York when Maisie helped me escape so I could go hide out with Slade until things blew over after the Banethsheh incident?" When the demon nodded, I rushed forward. "Well, the thing is I kind of sort of *hadsexwithSlade*."

The demon's eyes widened into saucers. "What the fuck were you thinking, Sabina?"

I shushed him and looked around to make sure no one heard him. Then I remembered we were alone. "Clearly, I wasn't thinking. I could make excuses about thinking the mages had turned their backs on me and finding comfort in the arms of an old friend, but that doesn't really matter right now."

He waved a claw. "Oh, I don't care about all that. I meant what were you thinking keeping this dirt from me? You know I loves me some gossip." He leaned in eagerly. "Was it good?"

I blinked. "Aren't you going to give me shit for betraying Adam?"

The demon shrugged. "If I recall correctly, you and Adam weren't—and still aren't, I might add—an official item."

I frowned. While he was technically right, the excuse didn't sit well with me. "No, but we'd discussed exploring that option when he returned from Queen Maeve's court."

Giguhl placed a talon over my lips. "Hush! You need to listen to Gigi now." I squinted at him until he removed it. He turned fully toward me and placed his claws on my shoulders. "Are you listening? Because I'm about to lay some serious insight on your ass."

My first instinct was to tell him I didn't want to talk

about it anymore. But in the end, curiosity got the better of me, so I nodded.

"Your guilt is just an excuse to avoid facing your fear of intimacy."

I opened my mouth to argue, but the knowing look the demon shot me then told me I'd be wasting my breath. Because, really, who was I kidding? "Let's say you're right," I said slowly. "What do I do about it?"

"Well, first of all, you're going to have to make the first move. Adam knows you're skittish and doesn't want to scare you off."

"When exactly am I supposed to stage this seduction?" I leaned forward. "Tonight in the cemetery during the voodoo ritual, or right before I kill my grandmother?"

Giguhl rolled his eyes. "You'll know the right time. Trust that shit. The trick is not sabotaging the moment because you're too chicken to let yourself be happy."

"Okay, so let's say for the sake of argument I make a move and everything works out." My stomach did a little flip-flop at the idea of seducing Adam. "What about the Slade thing?"

He looked me right in the eye and said, "You don't tell him."

"But—"

"No, you can't tell him. If what you say is true and the thing with Slade didn't mean anything, then I say what Adam doesn't know won't hurt him. Besides, how do we know Adam didn't get himself a little piece of faery ass while he was in North Carolina?"

That stopped me. A red haze dripped down over my vision at the mere thought of Adam cavorting with another female. "He wouldn't do that."

"Sabina, he's a male," Giguhl said. "He'd totally do that, especially when you've been so quick to deny any interest in him every time it comes up."

My fists clenched in response. Giguhl must have sensed my competitive streak rising to the surface, because he soldiered on. "Are you really gonna let some trampy faery steal your man?"

My eyes narrowed. "No!"

Giguhl clapped a claw on my back. "That's my girl."

My resolve sputtered. "But what do I do until the right moment presents itself?"

The demon patted me on the arm. "Just act natural. Be yourself."

Oh, right, sure. Most days when I looked in the mirror I felt like I was looking at a stranger. How the hell was I supposed to be myself when the mere thought of being that emotionally vulnerable made me want to cut my losses and run the hell away?

Right then, the apartment door opened in the living room, announcing Adam's arrival. Giguhl shot me a meaningful look as he rose from the bed.

A second later, Adam's sandy head poked around the doorframe. "What's up?"

I froze. Normally I would have used the opportunity to embarrass both males about the aborted sleep sex. But now all I could do was stare at Adam, feeling completely self-conscious.

"Sabina?" he said, coming farther into the room. Next to me, Giguhl cleared his throat, a not-so-subtle reminder. "Everything okay?" Adam continued.

My eyes darted wildly about the room as I searched for something to say. When my gaze landed on the clothes I left on the bedside table, I jumped up. "I need a shower."

I grabbed the clothes and brushed past a very confused mage before seeking refuge in the bathroom. Through the door, I heard Adam call, "Make it quick." Then, in a lower tone to Giguhl: "What's her deal?"

"You know, Red. She's never *quite herself*"—he raised his volume to make sure I got the message—"when she first wakes up."

Thirty minutes—and a strident lecture with myself—later, I descended the steps to find everyone gathered at the store's counter again. It stuck me as odd that Zen's store always seemed empty, but then I remembered my nocturnal nature meant I missed out on her key business hours.

Adam and Zen's heads were bent over a book when I walked up. The mage glanced up. "Hey. Your blood's over there." He tilted his head to indicate the far corner of the desk.

"Thanks." I tamped down the hangover of self-consciousness from earlier. Like Giguhl said, until an opportunity presented itself, I needed to keep my head in the game. Allowing this Adam thing to distract me like I was some angsty teenager with a crush would be a colossal mistake.

While I broke open the container of blood, I tried to look over Adam's shoulder at the book. "What's that?"

Adam looked up and wrinkled his nose at the pot of blood that was about four inches from his face. I pulled it away immediately with a mumbled apology.

As I took my first sip he said, "We were just going over the ritual for tonight to make sure we didn't forget anything."

I nodded and looked around for Giguhl but didn't find him. "Where's Mr. Giggles?"

Adam jerked a thumb toward the stairs. "He's helping Brooks with his costume for tonight."

Zen closed the book and made a final note on the list she'd been making. "Adam said you guys had some trouble with Mac last night."

I quickly swallowed the mouthful of blood. "She was pretty pissed."

She clucked her tongue. "I wouldn't bet on her forgiving you anytime soon, either. Werewolves love to hold grudges."

I looked at Adam. "It's unfortunate, but we have bigger issues to deal with. Like the fact we're still no closer to finding Maisie, or who Lavinia's informant is, or what she's planning." Frustration made my chest feel full and heavy. I set the blood on the counter. "It seems like we've been feeling our way through this, reacting to everything Lavinia's thrown at us instead of being proactive."

"The ritual should help," Zen said. "The spirits will tell us where to find your twin."

I wished I shared her optimism. But honestly? I didn't put much stock in voodoo as a problem solver. Sure, mage magic was powerful and effective for a variety of problems. Mages were created by the goddess Hekate—their very birthright was the ability to harness magic. But humans? I knew a lot of mortals dabbled in arcane arts, but to me that seemed more superstition and elaborate ceremony than real magic. And of course there were also those like the palm readers in Jackson Square who preyed on the superstitions of naive mortals to make money. The fact that Zen was part mage didn't mean much to me, either. Generations of genetic dilution had to have stunted her ability to tap into the same sources of power as a full mage.

However, Adam had read the ritual and seemed to believe it would help, so I was willing to go along with it. What other options did I have at that point, anyway? "What could it hurt?" I said with a shrug.

Zen gathered her book and notes. "With that resounding endorsement, I'm off to ready the last few supplies. Be ready to head out in an hour."

Zen disappeared into the back office. Adam continued going over the spell while I polished off the blood. A knock at the front door had me setting down my mug and reaching for my gun.

Adam and I exchanged alert, cautious glances. He got my back while I made my way toward the front. I stayed to the side of the door just in case someone decided to take a cheap shot through the shaded window. But when I pulled back the shade, Georgia smiled and waved back.

Releasing the breath I'd been holding, I flipped the deadbolts and threw open the door. Georgia strolled right in wearing a pair of skinny black jeans, a green chiffon tank covered with a black cardigan, and ballet flats. For a woman who presumably spent the better part of the night embroiled in a lovers' spat, her demeanor seemed downright cheery.

"Hey, y'all."

I glanced behind her, fully expecting the sullen face of a certain wcrewolf to follow her in. Georgia saw the look and said, "Don't worry. I'm alone."

I closed and locked the door before turning back to her. Adam joined us, nodding a greeting to the vamp. "What's up?"

"I've come to offer my help," she said, raising her hands in a magnanimous gesture.

I squinted at her. "Help with what, exactly?"

"Defeating your grandmother, obviously."

"But I thought Mac didn't want you to—" Adam began.

Georgia slashed a hand through the air, cutting him off. "That's between Mac and me. All I'll say on that matter is it would mean a lot to me if you'd keep our relationship under your hats. What with mating between the races being forbidden and all. Especially when one of the lovers involved is the niece of the Alpha of New York."

"I'd imagine Michael Romulus wouldn't be so keen on the lesbian thing, either," Adam said. "He'd want an advantageous male match for Mac to strengthen the pack."

Georgia nodded solemnly. "That, too."

I sighed and crossed my arms. "Look, Georgia, I'm the last person to be scandalized by your relationship. I'm a mixed-blood myself, remember?"

"That exactly what I told Mac," Georgia sighed. "But she can be a tad . . . unreasonable when it comes to protecting our privacy."

I shrugged. "Like I said, if Michael Romulus finds out about you two, it won't be from Adam or me."

Adam nodded his agreement. "Is that what really brought you here?"

Georgia shook her head. "No I came here to offer you the assistance of eight able-bodied vamps."

"How exactly do you think you can help us?" Adam asked.

Georgia strolled over to a shelf containing a collection of candles. She lifted a black one with a skull painted on the glass. "You guys want to find Sabina's grandmother, right?"

I crossed my arms and bobbed my head. "Technically, we're trying to find my sister, but they'll be in the same place."

"Well who better to help you find someone in New Orleans than a group of local vampires? We know every nook and cranny and feeding ground in the city."

Adam and I traded a look. *Hmm*.

Georgia rushed ahead. "We form search teams and canvass different areas for signs of your grandmother, sister, or any Caste members." She set down the candle and pulled a piece of paper from her back pocket. Spreading it out on the counter, she motioned Adam and me to join her.

Curious, we approached to find the sheet was a map of New Orleans. "What I propose is we divide up into two teams, each responsible for canvassing a specific zone. Since all known confrontations have occurred in the Garden District and the French Quarter, we'll start there."

Adam had gone into tactical mode. "How many per team?"

"Each section will get five people. I figure that way, no one stands a chance of being caught alone if they stumble onto more of your grandmother's goons or the bitch herself. Plus with that number we should be able to cover each zone tonight."

"Wait," I said. "You said you only had eight vamps total. Who are the other two?"

"That's where you guys come in. We need the two of

you to each go with a team, since you have more experience with Lavinia and her henchmen."

Adam glanced up at me from where he bent over the map. I stood straighter with a sigh. "I guess we could postpone the ritual with Zen..." I said, thinking aloud.

"Not possible. Zen said it needs to happen tonight since tomorrow's Halloween. We can't afford to put it off any longer."

"Shit," I said.

"But there's another option," he said, standing straighter. "You can go with Zen. Giguhl and I can handle the patrol."

I grabbed the mage's sleeve. "Excuse us for a minute," I said over my shoulder at Georgia. In the corner, I rounded on Adam. "No fucking way."

He frowned at me like I was being unreasonable. "It makes sense, Red. In cat form, Giguhl can get places vampires and mages can't."

"No, not that. You're not sticking me with voodoo duty to go have all the fun. Besides, you're the mage, it makes more sense for you to help Zen with the spell."

Adam cocked an eyebrow. "Since you've conveniently forgotten, you're a mage, too. A Chthonic one, at that. Your powers are far better suited than mine for spirit work."

I slammed my hands on my hips. "Need I remind you that my Chthonic training was cut short because I incinerated someone? I don't know the first thing about using those powers and you know it."

He crossed his arms. "Still, I have the ability to flash my team out of a jam if shit goes down. Besides, you'll only be assisting Zen. You probably won't even need to use magic."

His expression had a mulish slant that I'd come to associate with me losing arguments. I sucked my teeth while I considered the situation. If I was being honest, while Georgia's plan had merit, the chance of them finding and killing Lavinia was slim. Sure, they might find a lead on her, but Lavinia was far too wily to allow herself to be cornered. But they might find Maisie. And Adam had already said he wouldn't make a move on that front without Orpheus's leave. That meant I wouldn't miss the rescue.

On the other hand, Zen and Adam both seemed convinced that these spirits could help us get info from Stryx that would lead us to Maisie. Combining the approaches increased our chances of finishing all this much sooner than if we did them separately.

Finally, I poked Adam's chest. "Watch your ass out there."

He grabbed my finger. Spread my hand open and placed a kiss on my palm. I felt it way down in my toes. "Ditto."

Commotion on the stairs had all three of us looking up. Brooks—or rather Cleopatra Pussy Willow—was a vision in white chiffon and gold lamé floating down the steps. The gold beads at the bottom of each braid clicked in time with his steps. The light glinted off the head of a gilt cobra sitting proudly atop a golden crown perched on his head. A rubber snake wrapped around his wrist like a poisonous bracelet. Behind Cleopatra, Giguhl followed like a devoted manservant with the train of the gown held gently in the tips of his claws.

Adam whistled. Georgia and I clapped wildly. Even Zen came out of the office to cheer for the queen. When he reached the bottom step, the queen regally lowered his chin and executed a little curtsy. "Thank you, darlings."

Giguhl joined the group, looking as eager and nervous as a stage mom. "What do you guys think?"

"Super hot," Georgia said.

"Totally," I agreed.

Adam nodded enthusiastically by my side. "Nice asp you've got there."

Cleopatra stroked the rubber snake suggestively and winked. "Likewise."

"I wish we could be there for your big performance," Zen said.

"Me, too. But Mac said she'd record the whole thing."

At the mention of Mac's name, Georgia's face fell. It wasn't Brooks's fault for bringing up the werewolf's name. As far as I knew he wasn't privy to any of the previous night's drama.

"What song are you singing tonight?" I said quickly.

Brooks twirled, flaring out the white panels of his dress. "Dancing Queen!"

I snorted. "Of course. It's perfect."

Zen cleared her throat. "Sabina."

I looked up. The voodoo priestess tapped her wrist to indicate it was time to go. "Right." I squeezed Brooks's arm, careful not to muss his ensemble. "You're gonna kill 'em dead."

Behind me, Adam and Georgia were talking in low tones. The mage called Giguhl away to fill him in on the plan. Zen went to join them, and I trusted Adam to let her know about the changes in the agenda. Brooks noticed the sudden change in mood. "What's going on?"

"Oh, nothing. They're just discussing tonight's plan. When do you head out?"

The fae glanced at the clock behind the counter. "Mac's

picking me up in half an hour. I'm not walking to the club in these heels, honey."

I hesitated. "Do you want us to wait with you?" Obviously, we needed Georgia out of there before the werewolf arrived and put the kibosh on the plans, but Zen and I could probably wait.

But Pussy Willow wouldn't hear of it. "That's okay. I'll just use the wait to run through my routine again."

"Okay," I said. "But be sure to keep the door locked. Don't open it unless you know for sure it's Mac."

An elegant hand shooed away my concerns. "Sweetie, ain't nobody gonna mess with the Queen of the Nile."

*A*n hour later, I found out the hard way that digging graves was far preferable to exhuming them. When Zenobia led me into the cemetery, I'd been expecting another one of New Orleans's famous cities of the dead with stately mausoleums and tombs. Instead, Holt Cemetery was a collection of graves dug into the soggy Louisiana earth. Dilapidated wooden and pitted marble headstones jutted from the ground at odd angles like rotten teeth. Our footsteps crunched on seashell-and-gravel walkways overgrown with weeds.

As I trudged along, I mentally cursed Adam. Talk about pulling the short straw. He and Giguhl got to have all the fun while I was stuck on grave-robbing duty.

I tripped on a grave marker. The movement jostled Stryx's cage, which sent the owl into another tizzy of rage. I held the cage as far from my torso as possible to avoid the swiping talons and beak.

"What's the deal with this place?" I called over the owl's racket. His annoying ass combined with the buzzing in my head did nothing to improve my mood.

Just like at the cemetery Adam and I chased Stryx into the other night, a low-level vibration hummed here. I popped my jaw to release the pressure building up in my head. I considered asking Zen if she felt it, too, but she didn't show any signs of being affected by the pressure. She just marched ahead like a woman on a mission.

"Not all of New Orleans's residents can afford fancy mausoleums like those found in the St. Louis or Lafayette cemeteries," she said, following some invisible path through the place. "So the poor get buried in potter's fields like this."

I listened and followed her toward a row of graves near the back. Drooping oaks weighed down by Spanish moss slumped over the pitiful mementos left by mourners. Everything from matted teddy bears to Mardi Gras beads and plastic flowers to whiskey bottles decorated the pitiful mounds.

"Families get one plot," she continued. "They have to pile the coffins on top of each other. And when the water table rises, bones pop up from the soil." She kicked at something on the ground. I blinked at the femur that rolled from the overgrown brush.

She finally stopped at an unmarked mound under a low-hanging oak branch. She pointed to a spot under the tree. As I set the cage down in the shadows, I surveyed the grave.

Unlike most of the other plots we'd passed, this one wasn't covered in weeds or mementos. For some reason the sight of bare soil seemed even more depressing. Maybe it was because the freshly turned earth indicated a recent death—or maybe it was the lack of anything signifying that someone cared enough about the grave's resident to leave flowers or even a plank of wood indicating his or her identity.

Zen set down her leather satchel and withdrew a small shovel with a retractable handle.

"What the hell are you going to do with that?" I demanded.

She smiled. "*I'm* not doing anything." I caught the spade easily and then almost immediately dropped it.

"Like hell. I'm not a grave robber."

She sighed. "We're not robbing anything. I told you, we just need to have access to the body to make a complete connection with the spirit."

I frowned. "Can't they just speak through you or something?"

She frowned. "I'm not a TV psychic, Sabina."

I gritted my teeth and tried to remember she didn't have to help me. At least Stryx had shut the hell up. The only sounds coming from the cage now were an occasional hoot or the scratch of claw against the newspaper we'd laid in the bottom.

"Well, what are you waiting for? The grave isn't going to dig itself." She withdrew a thin cigar from her coat pocket and clamped it between her dazzling white teeth. Once she'd lit the thing, she looked up and raised her eyebrows. Zenobia's face glowed red from the tip of the cigarillo, and for a second I wondered if the voodoo priestess had some demon blood in her.

"If it makes you feel any better, the graves are only about four feet deep. Any more than that and the soil gets too soggy."

Yeah, that made me feel tons better. Instead of arguing more, I speared the ground with the shovel, taking out my indignation on the soil.

As I worked, Zen was generous with the advice but

stingy with the offers of help. It occurred to me that if she was as good at magic as everyone seemed to think, she'd have been able to remove the dirt without a shovel, but then I guess that would have deprived her of the pleasure of bossing me around.

Zen hadn't been kidding about the families stacking bodies on top of each other. On my way down, I encountered two jawbones, a handful of phalanges, and a partial spinal column. The other problem was the lower I went, the wetter the dirt became. By the time my shovel hit something solid, I was smeared with mud and gods knew what else.

I used my hands to find the edges of the coffin and clear off the top to open it. She peered into the pit where I crouched. "Be careful when you open the lid. We need to preserve the body as best we can."

I wiped my brow with a dirty hand, no doubt leaving a muddy streak on my forehead. "That's what I don't get. Won't the embalming process make reanimation a problem?"

She smiled in an overly patient way that set my teeth on edge. "We're just providing a temporary vessel for a spirit. The plumbing doesn't need to work."

"If you say so." I brushed dirt from the coffin, clearing space around the edges. Finally, I worked my fingers along the lip and lifted. A sickly sweet vapor rose from the box. I covered my nose with my hand and peered in.

Now, I'm no expert on decomposition, so I had no idea how long the guy had been in there. But judging from the smell, he'd passed his expiration date by a long shot. Of course, since we're talking about a corpse here, *freshness* is a relative term, I guess.

The powder blue suit and ruffled shirt implied a disco-era burial, but for all I knew the choice could have been motivated by lack of money or taste. As for the state of the corpse, well, it wasn't pretty. If the mortuary had bothered to apply funeral putty to this dude it was long gone. Instead, greenish veins webbed across bloated gray skin. which created a gruesome marbling effect.

"How long has he been dead?" I asked.

She shrugged. "According to the obit I found online, Kevin Johnson was buried four days ago. That's perfect for our uses since *nanm* resides in the soil near the body for nine days before it ascends." At my look she explained, "*Nanm* is his animating spirit."

I nodded that I understood. "Well, he smells pretty rank for only four days in the ground."

"Sabina," she intoned. "A little respect please."

Gritting my teeth, I hefted his stiff bulk over my shoulder. Something squished ominously. "I swear to the gods, if his dead guy juices get on my jacket you're buying me a new one."

She rolled her eyes and held her hands out. "Hand him up to me so you can climb out."

I shook my head. "That's okay, I got it."

She raised an eyebrow, the only clue I'd nicked her pride. But she backed away, allowing me room to shove the body onto the lip of the grave. Easy work given my head and shoulder loomed above the ground.

Once I climbed out and brushed the worst of the funk off my jeans, she pointed. "Set him by the bird."

I complied, laying him out on his back under a branch draped with lacy Spanish moss. Zen grabbed her bag and came to join us. From it, she withdrew a glass vial and

pulled the cork lid. She poured brittle herbs from the tube
into a clay pot of sorts. It kind of looked like one of those
incense burners hippies buy at head shops.

"What are you doing?" I asked.

"This," Zen explained in a business-like tone, "is an
incense made from sage, juniper, and rosemary." She bent
down to light the incense with a thin shaft of wood she'd
lit with a match. From the scent, I guessed cedar, but I
wasn't sure. A few seconds later a thin tendril of smoke
wafted up from the cone of herbs.

She moved to the body. This time she removed a larger
jar—the kind southern women use to preserve rhubarb
in—and the lid opened with a *pop*. The liquid inside was
clear, but the astringent scent rose like vapor, making my
eyes water.

"This is witch hazel. Helps focus the spell so the spirit
we want shows up instead of someone else."

I nodded like an idiot even though she wasn't looking
at me. She was too busy sprinkling the liquid all around
the body. I had a fleeting moment of pity for the dead man.
I'd imagine few people anticipate that their bodies will
end up half naked under a tree while a voodoo lady sprin-
kles them with astringent toner. Despite my dislike of
humans in general, the whole thing felt disrespectful. And
I began to wonder if there might be a better way to find
the answers I was seeking.

"And this…" She pulled another cigar from her pocket—
this one was thicker than the last. Like a huge brown phal-
lus. "…is a Macanudo." She raised another lit cedar scrap to
the stogie. She sucked at it so hard her cheeks went concave
and a cloud of tobacco-scented smoke swirled around us.

I waved a hand in front of my face to clear the smoke.

Just when I was trying to figure out how the cigar fit into this whole thing, she knelt next to the body.

"Hey, help me pry open his lips," she said over her shoulder. "Just be gentle, we need the jaw intact."

"What are you going to do?" I said, eyeing the cigar with suspicion.

She sighed and glared back at me over her shoulder. "The smoke is a conduit for the spirit. We have to make sure it enters his body and reaches his center."

"Wait, you're not seriously about to put your mouth on the cold, dead lips of that man, are you?"

"It's either his lips or his anus."

"Lips it is, then."

"We're going to have to snip the threads the mortician used to sew the jaw shut. There's a pair of scissors in my bag." She nodded to the head. "And make it quick."

I dug through the bag until I found a small pair of nail scissors. What I didn't find in the bag was a pair of rubber gloves. Awesome.

I crouched next to Zen, who held out her hand for the scissors. Of course. That meant I had the fun job of spreading the corpse's lips. They perched on his face like two frozen grubworms. Working quickly, I spread them so Zen could do the snipping thing. A couple of seconds later, the jaw went slack. I thought the outside of the corpse smelled horrible, but that was nothing compared to the noxious odor of grave breath that escaped his mouth. I reared back and covered my mouth and nose with my hand, cursing my vampirically heightened sense of smell.

"Good," Zen said, dropping the scissors. "As I blow the smoke in there, I need you to call on helpful spirits to guide the *nanm* back into his body."

I looked at her for a moment. All this spiritual stuff was over my head. "How do I do that, exactly?"

Her sigh seemed to say *Do I have to do everything around here?* She picked up a gourd covered in colorful strands of beads. "Simple. Take the bottle of rum from my bag. Sprinkle it in a circle around the body. As you do so, say the following three times: 'Generous Spirits of the Loa, I summon and evoke thee to aid us in our quest for information.' When that's done, prick your finger and let the blood drop to the dirt."

I grabbed the bottle of rum, resisting the urge to take a couple of shots from it. Didn't want to piss off the Loa. I did as Zen instructed, repeating the incantation as I formed a wide circle around the body. Just in case, I added Hekate and Lilith's names to the chant. I didn't want the goddess and the Great Mother to think I'd switched teams or anything.

As I did so, Zenobia leaned over the man's face and blew a steady stream of smoke between his gaping lips. While she did this, she shook the gourd rattle over his chest. Meanwhile, I focused all my energy on calling the spirits like she'd said. After a few moments, a tingle started in my midsection and a warm breeze swooped through the graveyard. Taking the blade I'd grabbed from her bag, I pricked the tip of my finger and milked two drops from the wound.

The second the blood hit the ground, Kevin's body jerked once. Twice. At the same moment, Stryx screeched like a banshee.

My eyes widened and I took a step closer, careful to stay outside the rum-soaked circle. Sure enough, the guy's eyelids spasmed like he was trying to open them but couldn't. Zen placed a gentle hand on his shoulder. "May your spirit be at ease, Mr. Johnson. We seek information. Will you aid us?"

The moan that escaped the man's lips then sent goose bumps rippling across my arms. Stryx's sudden frantic wing flaps told me I wasn't the only one spooked.

Zen looked up with a worried expression. Then she spoke to Kevin Johnson's spirit again. "Mr. Johnson? We seek to communicate with the owl called Stryx. Will you aid us?"

The corpse's eyelids popped open then. Two flesh-colored domes popped off the pupils and slid to the ground. My gorge rose at the sight of his sunken eyes with their cloudy white irises. Zen scooted back on her butt. "That's not supposed to happen."

I stilled. "What do you mean? I thought we were trying to wake him."

She shook her head. "His mouth should be the only thing moving."

Stryx's screeches started up again. And this time, the zombie spoke, as well.

Need fly! Kevin growled from where he lay. *Escape mixed-blood. Find master.*

I paused as his words sunk in. "Hey, it's working. Kevin, can you ask Stryx where they're keeping Maisie, please?"

Stryx screeched.

A second later, the corpse yelled. *Help!*

"No, Kevin, we need to know where Maisie is. Maisie," I enunciated, stepping to the very edge of the circle.

Big box! Cat piss. Master come! Kane! HELP!

I frowned. "What?"

Stryx's frenzied movements continued so hard that the cage fell over. The crash shocked Kevin out of stillness. His gray hands clawed at the dirt until he had enough momentum to rise into a sitting position. I stumbled back, wondering if this was normal. I had my answer when Zen freaked the fuck out and ran out of the circle screaming.

I grabbed her as she darted past. "Whoa! Hold on. Where are you going?"

Her eyes were wild. "The spell went wrong. He shouldn't be moving."

I frowned at her, my heart thumping. "What?"

"We accidentally reanimated him. He's a revenant!"

My brow hurt from frowning at her so hard. I'd heard the term *revenant* before but couldn't quite put my finger on an exact definition. Before I could ask Zen, however, a terrible moan to my right grabbed my attention. Kevin Johnson was on his feet. His coordination was off, so he didn't so much walk as *shamble*.

"Wait. Are you telling me that"—I pointed an accusing finger at Kevin—"is a godsdamned *zombie*?"

Before she could answer, Stryx started squawking louder and pushing against the edge of the cage. His frantic movements rattled the cage so hard it rolled. Fortunately, the ruckus distracted the zombie and he stopped moving toward us like a drunken toddler. Kevin was still tuned into the owl's thoughts, so he provided a running commentary. *Fly! Must fly! Need master!*

Unfortunately, he also started lumbering toward Stryx's cage.

"Shit," I whispered. "I don't suppose you have any zombie-be-gone in that bag of yours?"

Zen's rapidly retreating voice reached me from half-way across the cemetery. "Screw the owl. It's every man for himself."

"Some voodoo priestess you are!" I yelled after her. I wanted to drag her back and make her deal with this, but I didn't have time. Because at that moment, Kevin the Zombie was grabbing at Stryx's cage. The owl's shrieks of alarm only seemed to egg the revenant on. He also continued to scream Stryx's thoughts. *Danger! Fly! Master, help!*

In between screams, Kevin smacked his lips like a fat man at an all-you-can-eat buffet.

"Okay, Sabina." I gave myself a pep talk. "Pull yourself together. It's just the reanimated corpse of a human." Louder, I yelled. "Hey, Zombie Boy!"

"Gargh?" the zombie groaned, and his stiff neck swiveled so he could gaze at me with his dead, dead eyes.

I rubbed my head in what I hoped the zombie would find an appetizing manner. "Come and get it!"

He waved an arm as stiff as a tree branch in my direction. Then he started groping at the cage with rigored fingers. I probably shouldn't have been offended that a zombie just shooed off an opportunity to eat my brains, but I had to admit it stung.

By this time, Stryx's cries must have had no meaning, because Kevin had stopped his translations in favor of moans.

"Fine. Have it your way." I grabbed my gun from my waistband.

"It won't work." Zen's voice came from far away. I looked over my shoulder and saw her crouching behind a bush near the entrance.

Ignoring her, I turned back around and squeezed off five rounds in quick succession. The zombie's body jerked with each impact, but he didn't fall or even drop the cage.

"Told you!" a faint feminine voice called.

Mmmoooaaannn. Kevin had finally gotten the door of the cage open and was fishing around inside for the frantic owl.

"You gotta cut his head off," Zen yelled.

Of course I did. As I ran to look for something to use in the weeds, the zombie let loose an eerie victory cry. A second later, my hand closed around the handle of a garden spade. Not ideal, but better than the portable shovel I'd used to dig the grave.

I turned in time to see the zombie's maw open wide. Despite his stiff limbs, the revenant's strength was impressive as he managed to grip the struggling owl and lift it toward his gaping mouth.

"No!" I drew the spade back and started running. It happened in slow motion. My legs burning. The head of the tool swinging through the air. Kevin's jaw crashing down on Stryx's head. The jolt of impact slamming up my arm.

The zombie fell to the side, spewing a mouthful of feathers as he went. But I'd been too late. The owl's ravaged carcass dropped to the dirt at my feet.

The zombie moaned and rolled. Before he could work up enough momentum to rise, though, I slammed my boot heel into his chest. A grunt escaped his chest. His hands clawed at my shins.

I looked down on him like an avenging angel, raising the spade handle up with the metal end pointing down. Beneath me, the zombie went still. His grotesque face morphing into a pitiful mask of fear.

"Mother?"

I slammed the spade down with all my might. It stopped partway through the neck. Putting my heel on the shoulder of the metal, I stomped down until the spade broke through with a *crunch* and lodged in the soil beneath the zombie's severed neck.

Panting, I wiped the back of my shaking hand across my forehead. A twig snapped behind me. My heart kicked back into gear as I spun.

"Shit!" I yelled when I saw it was just Zen. "You shouldn't sneak up on people like that." My heart down-shifted, but my ire was still up. I glared at the human. "Thanks for all your help, by the way."

She crossed her arm. "Forgive me, but some of us aren't immortal."

"Whatever." I sighed and looked down at the Stryx's lifeless body. "Now what the hell am I supposed to do?"

"I think you're missing the bigger issue here."

"What?"

She pointed to the headless zombie.

"Oh. You must have done something wrong."

She shot me a look. "I did everything right. The only variable was you." Her eyes narrowed. "You're half-mage, right?"

I nodded. A bad feeling crept through my midsection all the sudden.

"But you don't use your powers?"

I looked down at my boots. "Not really."

"What did he say to you before you killed him?"

I looked up quickly. "You heard that?"

She raised an eyebrow.

"He said 'Mother,' " I mumbled.

She pursed her lips and crossed her arms. "Sabina, why would a zombie think you're his mother?"

I had a really bad feeling I knew the answer, but I didn't like it at all. "*Hypothetically*, does it matter who the blood comes from in the spell?"

She pursed her lips. "Sometimes. But you'd have to be a very powerful mage for this"—she pointed at Kevin's corpse—"to happen." Her tone clearly communicated that Zen believed I was a run-of-the-mill mage with sub-par skills. I agreed on the skills part, but—

I swallowed. "You mean like a Chthonic mage?"

Her eyes flared. "You're a Chthonic?" she roared. "Why the hell didn't you tell me that sooner?"

I shrugged. "I didn't know it mattered!"

"Of course it matters! Chthonic magic amplifies necromancy spells tenfold! Especially if there's blood involved!" She shook her head at me. "Unbelievable! I sensed darkness in you when we met, but I figured it was just the vampire thing."

"Well, excuse me," I said. "It's not like I've ever done something like this before. Rhea should have told you."

She threw up her hands. "Gods of the Loa, you're unbelievable. This isn't Rhea's fault. At the very least Adam should have mentioned it."

"Hey! At least I took care of it. Which is more than I can say for some people, who ran and hid."

She started talking under her breath. I only caught a few words, but I stopped listening when I heard "misbegotten daughter of Satan."

"Okay, so I think we can both chalk this up to a lesson learned," I said. "Can we go now?"

She stopped pacing and shot me a glare so hot my

cheeks burned. "Not so fast there. You've got a body to rebury."

My mouth fell open. "You've got to be joking."

She looked pointedly at the spade. "Don't forget the owl."

18

An hour later, I slammed out of Zen's car. My first priority was a shower. Between the mud and the bits o' Kevin coating my clothes, I felt like a walking hazmat disaster.

Zen followed more slowly. Smart of her. I'd found her merely annoying before, but after the confrontation in the cemetery and her judgy attitude over my honest mistake, I couldn't stand the woman. The whole thing had me seriously regretting my promise to have a kinder, gentler attitude toward the mortally challenged.

Of course, part of my foul mood might have stemmed from the fact I'd rammed headfirst into another dead end. As I stomped up the back steps of the store, I prayed Adam and Giguhl's recon had been more successful than my clusterfuck of a night.

I threw open the door and prepared to go inside, but something stopped me. It took me a second to realize what was off. For a Friday night, the store was abnormally quiet. I held a hand up to Zen. "Wait here."

She frowned but was smart enough not to argue.

I pulled my gun and entered the office at the back of the building. I stopped to listen, but the place was silent except for the echoes of the crowds of Bourbon Street. I made my way to the thick curtain separating the office from the store.

I blew out a breath and silently parted the panels. The store looked like a bomb had gone off. I cursed. A quick scan revealed overturned tables, broken glass, and color- ful debris littering the floor. Then my eyes landed on something sparkly by the stairs that made my blood go cold—a golden cobra atop a black wig. Luckily the corn- rows weren't still attached to a head, but since Cleopatra was supposed to have vacated the premises hours earlier, the sight sent me into full-on crisis mode.

The old me would have charged in with guns blazing. But I held myself back. The intruders could still be in there. Given the recent run-in with a group of crazy-strong magic-wielding vamps, it wasn't prudent to proceed with- out backup. I forced myself to back away from the curtain and go outside.

Zen's face was tense with worry. "What's going on?" she demanded.

"I'm not sure yet." I didn't mention the wig. No reason to scare Zen until I could get inside and assess the true extent of the damage. Instead, I pulled the cell phone from my pocket and punched the preprogrammed button. Adam answered on the second ring.

"What's wrong?"

"I need you. How far away—"

The hair on my arms prickled a split second before Adam materialized not three feet from where Zen and I stood. I punched the "end" button. His eyes did a quick scan of the pair of us. Then, rushing up the steps, he said, "What's the situation?"

I glanced at Zen, not wanting to scare her but needing to be honest. "Someone broke into the shop."

Zen sucked in a breath. "Thieves?"

I shook my head. "Not sure. But they definitely did some damage in the store. Couldn't tell if anything"—or *anyone,* I silently amended—"was taken."

Adam turned to Zen, in full crisis-management mode. "You got any weapons inside they could find?"

"Upstairs in my apartment. A shotgun."

"Shit," I said. "Okay, I need you to listen—"

Zen made a worried noise. "What about Brooks?"

I schooled my features to hide my suspicions. "He's probably at Lagniappe. Besides, Mac would have called if she got here to pick up Brooks and found this."

"Zen, you stay out here and call Georgia. She's with Giguhl. Tell them to get here as soon as they can. In the meantime, do not come in there until we give you the all-clear. Got it?"

Zen's mouth worked and her eyes were a little wild. I grabbed her by the shoulders. "Adam and I need to go figure out what's happening. Will you be okay here for a few minutes?"

She swallowed and seemed to come back to herself. "Be careful."

I looked at Adam. "Let's go."

Leaving the human in the courtyard, Adam and I reentered through the office. When he saw the disaster area that used to be the store, his jaw went hard. Through the drawn shades on the front windows of the store, the silhouettes of passersby, totally unaware of the drama unfolding a few feet away, paraded past at intervals. As my adrenaline surged, I found myself envying their ignorance.

I motioned toward the stairs and the discarded wig. Adam saw it and jerked his gaze to mine. A brief flare of anger crossed his face before his expression returned to mission-ready. He pointed up, indicating I should take the lead.

As quietly as possible, I climbed the stairs, careful not to put too much weight on the risers. An inconvenient creak might warn any remaining intruders. At the top, I pointed down the hall. While he moved to check out this floor, I continued up to the third story.

My heart pounded in my ears. Underneath the fragrant herbs kicked up by the destruction downstairs and the musty odor of old building, the scent of fresh blood and lavender reached my nose.

I prayed it didn't belong to Brooks. That Mac had picked him up before all this happened. That maybe there was a logical explanation for him leaving behind the wig. But something in my gut told me my prayers were wasted. Because barring one of the intruders being fae, there was no other explanation for that telltale lavender scent. Not in the concentration I was detecting. As this realization hit me, I started praying death had come quickly for the faery.

I'd just reached the top of the stairs when a creak sounded behind me. I swung around with my gun raised. Adam held up his hands on the landing below. I relaxed a fraction. As he climbed the rest of the way, he shook his head solemnly.

I acknowledged this with a jerk of my head. Then I turned to approach the closed door to the attic apartment.

The collision of boot heel against wood sent shock waves up my leg. The door exploded inward. I rushed in with gun ready for action.

The living room was empty except for more signs of intrusion—bashed TV, ripped couch cushions, overturned coffee table.

"Clear," I whispered.

Adam rushed in and went to check the kitchen. I covered him as my eyes scanned the room for anyone who might be hiding. A couple of seconds later, he came back shaking his head.

My eyes moved to door number two. Something told me I didn't want to see what waited on the other side. The scent of blood was stronger here. I glanced at Adam. His expression was determined but wary. He tipped his chin down and angled his gaze toward the panel.

I blew out a slow breath as Adam's hand gripped the knob. Twisted. I raised my gun. A squeak of hinges. The panel receded, revealing the darkness beyond.

My better night vision meant I went in first. Blood saturated the air. I scanned the corners first, finding nothing but strewn clothes and toiletries. When no one jumped out at me, my eyes moved to the bed.

A large body-shaped lump huddled under the bedspread.

"Don't you fucking move," I said in a low, ominous voice. Adrenaline surged through me. I sidestepped to the side of the bed, my gun trained on the lump.

"Get the light."

A second later, light flared. My sensitive eyes stung from the sudden brightness, but I gritted my teeth and kept the gun steady.

The first thing I noticed was the stain set against the

cabbage roses on the gaudy damask spread. The red blotch bloomed like a wound among the floral tragedy.

My hand started shaking. I didn't want to pull the cover back. The lump hadn't moved through all the commotion. Dread pooled in my stomach. Adam stepped up on the other side of the bed. Our eyes met over the bloodstain. Resignation tightened Adam's features. He grabbed the edge of the coverlet and whipped it back.

The world tilted on its axis. A chill passed through me like someone had walked over my grave. "Goddess protect us."

The damage rendered the face unrecognizable. Bloated eyelids stained purple. Distended cheekbones split and bleeding. Nose bent and crushed. A gag smeared with streaks of red stretched the swollen lips into a grotesque facsimile of a smile.

I wanted to pretend that battered body before me belonged to a stranger. But the inevitability of the truth mocked my hope.

Adam ducked in and placed two fingers at Brooks's neck. "There's a pulse."

I was too busy trying to control my rage to feel relieved. My hands shook as I fumbled with the knots of the gag. Adam worked on the ropes binding the fae's hands and feet.

As I worked, I tried not to focus on the blood pooling on the white sheets. The metallic-lavender scent of his blood and the lingering stink of violence made my throat fill with bile.

When I finally pulled the gag away, a thin whimper escaped his lips. I clung to the unsettling sound as further evidence he lived. But judging from the extent of his wounds, just barely.

"Brooks?" I shook him gently, careful not to touch the lacerations on his arms. My voice sounded abnormally loud and panicked to my own ears. "Can you hear me?"

His tongue darted out, probing the corner where the gag had burned the skin. "'Bina?"

I put a hand on his brow. He cried out and tried to pull away. My heart clenched. I couldn't imagine the terrors Lavinia's goons perpetrated on his fragile body. "Shh. It's okay. You're safe now."

Because of the swelling, his eyes were sealed shut. But with a trembling hand, he reached out and grabbed my arm. I sat carefully on the edge of the bed and held his hand. The tips of his golden fingernails were jagged and bloody. His grip was so weak I tried to share some of my strength through our connected palms.

I looked up at Adam. His eyes glowed with suppressed rage. My own insides felt like a cauldron of acid. But we had to make sure Brooks stayed alive before we released the valve on our anger.

"Brooks," he whispered, lowering to his haunches. "It's Adam. I need to check your wounds, okay?"

Brooks's head moved restlessly on the pillow as he struggled to talk. Worried he might hurt himself more, I squeezed his hand. "Try to be still, okay?"

He seemed to settle then—whether by choice or simply weakness, I didn't know. It didn't really matter, I guess. The important thing was Adam had a chance to look him over.

After a few minutes, he pulled me away with a promise to Brooks we weren't going far. "He's lost a lot of blood," he said. "I can try to help with the pain, but his injuries are too extensive for my healing abilities."

Biting my lip, I looked back at the bed. The faery's complexion had the gray pallor of impending death. I clenched my fists until my nails cut half-moons into my palms. "We have to do something."

"Go get Zen."

"Okay," I said and rushed toward the door. A heavy calm had settled over me. The ability to detach was a survival mechanism that had served me well many times in my life. Later, it would catch up with me and I'd use the rage to my advantage. "Anything else?"

His gaze crept back to the bed. "You can pray."

19

An hour later, I sat on a picnic table in the courtyard behind the store, praying to every god and goddess from every pantheon I knew. Giguhl sat in a nearby chair, his claws clasped between his legs as he joined me in silent vigil.

Acidic guilt added fuel to my cosmic pleas. I'd been so wrapped up in the mission and my own drama I never considered the risk Zen and Brooks were taking helping us. But now Zen's shop was destroyed and Brooks's life hung in the balance. I clenched my fist against the dark stew of emotions simmering in my gut.

Inevitably, my thoughts drifted back to another fae— my old roommate Vinca. Her funeral had been the first I ever attended. Not because I hadn't known anyone else who'd died. But because all the others had died by my hand. Vinca was also the first female friend I'd ever had. And she'd paid for that friendship with her life.

In the time that had passed since her death, I'd reached a stalemate with my guilt. My logical side maintained that Vinca knew the dangers when she'd insisted she be

included in the raid on the vineyard where my first showdown with Lavinia had occurred. But my conscience con-
stantly reminded me that if I'd only been smarter, faster,
better, I could have prevented her death.

Just as earlier tonight, I could have stayed with Brooks
instead of leaving him alone and vulnerable while I pur-
sued my own goals. Unlike Vinca, he hadn't been fully
briefed about the real dangers we all faced. Also, while
Vinca died fighting in a battle she'd adopted as her own,
Brooks had been ambushed and punished to send me a
message. Hadn't Lavinia promised as much? That those
around me would suffer until I surrendered?

I glanced over at Giguhl, whose head hung in his claws.
When he'd stormed into the courtyard shortly after I left
Adam and Zen to work on Brooks, he'd gone ballistic with
worry. It took both Georgia and me to restrain him from
going to Brooks. Once he'd calmed down enough to collapse where he sat now, Georgia left to go find Mac. The
were hadn't answered her cell when we tried to call her,
which obviously was a cause for alarm. Georgia promised
to get in touch once she had news.

On the other side of Zen's building, Bourbon Street's
Friday-night pre-Halloween party raged on. Tinny notes
from brass instruments meshed with the pounding rhyth-
mic basslines. Laughter and shouts punctuated the music.

Part of me longed to prowl through that street like the
predator I was raised to be. The scent of fresh human
blood was strong even where I sat, so removed from the
action. But another part of me, one I didn't quite recognize, longed to just observe the humans. To try and understand how they could forget their mortality long enough
to dance in the streets.

Brooks was mortal, too. All fae were. That was the rub. They could heal themselves, and some fae species naturally lived longer than others. But when it came down to it, there was only so much damage magic could heal.

The rusty hinges on the back door squeaked to announce Adam's arrival. His stoic expression gave nothing away. I stood slowly, wiped my damp palms on my jeans, and waited for him to share his news. Giguhl came to join us, his face tight with worry.

Worry lines creased Adam's face, aging him. His white T-shirt was spattered with blood, like some sort of morbid Jackson Pollock painting. "The good news is he's still alive," he began.

I blew out a relieved breath. "Thank the gods."

He held up a hand. "The bad is he might not make it through the night. He's got extensive internal bleeding, and one of his lungs collapsed."

Blood drained from my head in a rush. I bit my lip with my fangs, hoping the physical pain would override the emotions enough to help me stay focused.

"We have to take him to the hospital," Giguhl said.

Adam shook his head sadly. "Not an option. Brooks's fae heritage might present itself in bloodwork. And even if it doesn't, they'll ask too many questions about how he got hurt. Maybe bring in the cops."

"How can you say that?" Giguhl demanded. "He needs help!"

"I know. But there's another option."

"Magic," I said.

Adam nodded. "But not what you think. My healing powers are too rudimentary for this sort of work."

"Voodoo?" Giguhl offered.

"Nope. Voodoo remedies are a lot like homeopathy. For big healing magic, you need a mage."

I blinked. "But you said—"

"I said *I* couldn't do it. But Aunt Rhea can." He jerked a thumb toward the building. "Just called Orpheus before I came out. Rhea's in Chicago, trying to convince the mages there to join the others at the Queen's court. It took some fast talking, but I convinced him to send her here."

"How soon?" I asked.

Just then the air shifted. A window on the second floor lit up with a sudden flash. Without another word, the three of us hauled ass inside.

Adam's silver-haired aunt wasted no time in getting down to business. No warm greetings or demands for explanations. By the time we made our way into the room, she'd already taken the situation in hand.

"I need dried sage, fresh sprigs of lavender, a bag of salt—sea salt, not iodized—and a pair of blue and purple candles—pillars, not tapers."

Zen nodded. "Got it."

"Adam, tell me what you've tried so far."

While he relayed the herbs and spells they'd tried, I stood beside Giguhl, holding his claw.

A groan came from the table as Brooks drifted back into consciousness.

Rhea stopped midsentence and bent over him. She placed a hand on his forehead and whispered something too low for me to hear. He settled immediately.

Turning back to Adam, she said, "We have to hurry. You and Sabina will assist."

My mouth fell open. "What? I—"

"None of that. Get over here and help us heal your friend."

One thing about Rhea, she may have looked like an earth mother, but when it came to giving orders she'd have given Patton a run for his money. I released Giguhl's claw with a wan smile and went to stand next to Adam.

Zen rushed back in with her arms full. "I found everything you needed."

With an economy of movements, Rhea made quick work of placing the candles at the four corners of the table.

"I'll be in the hall if you need me," Zen said quietly. Obviously, she didn't want to be in the way. Rhea didn't argue. Instead, she shot her friend a distracted but appreciative glance as she sprinkled Brooks's body with lavender. "Take the demon with you, please."

Giguhl obviously heard her, but instead of leaving, he crossed his arms and glared at us with a mulish expression.

"Giguhl, it's okay," I said. "We'll call you back in as soon as it's done."

He crossed his arms. "No way."

Rhea spoke up then. "Okay, but you stay out of the way and don't make a sound. And whatever you do, don't break the circle."

He zipped his fingers across his lips and tried to be as invisible as possible. Naturally, it didn't work at all, given it's hard to miss a seven-foot-tall demon in sweatpants and a hot pink shirt that read *Laissez les bons temps rouler.*

I shot my minion an encouraging smile before giving Rhea my full attention. "Now what?"

"Pour the salt to make the circle. Make it wide enough

so we can both move around the table." She turned to Adam. "The second the circle is poured, light the candles. Blue first and then purple."

While I cast the circle and Adam prepared to light the wicks, Rhea gathered the bundle of dried sage. She whispered something. The tip of the bundle sparked, and then tendrils of smoke curled up toward the ceiling. She walked clockwise around the table before turning and going the opposite direction.

"Sage clears out the bad energy and purifies the ritual space." Her tone was the same one she'd used when she gave me my lessons in New York.

The circle was finished, so I set the bag under the table, careful not to inadvertently smudge the line. Adam quickly lit the candles as instructed. Then he took a spot across the table from me.

Rhea stepped up to stand over Brooks's head. "We're going to invoke a cone of power. If you're ever alone you can do this by yourself, but we're going to combine our energies for more potency."

Adam closed his eyes and breathed deeply of the sage-scented air. His hands rose, and his left hand grasped my right. Rhea took my left and joined her left with Adam's right. Together we formed a triangle inside the circle, which I remembered from my lessons lent even more power to the circle.

"Now," Rhea whispered, "do you remember how I taught you to call on your powers?"

I did, of course, but I had a question. "Yeah, but aren't my talents the exact opposite of what we need here?"

Frown lines formed on her forehead. "What do you mean?"

"Chthonic powers are mostly about death and destruction."

Adam's eyes popped open. I felt his gaze on me even as I continued to look at his aunt for explanation.

She shook her head emphatically. "On the contrary, my dear. Your Chthonic powers also give you an immense capacity for healing."

"But how do I access that? Before I had to tap into the pit of rage inside me to use them."

She smiled. "For healing, you tap into the deep well of love you try to keep hidden."

I shifted on my feet, suddenly uncomfortable with the turn in conversation. Adam's hand tightened on mine. I cleared my throat. "Okay."

"You ready?" Rhea asked.

"No."

They knew I was lying, so they closed their eyes. I followed suit and tried to locate a part of myself I barely knew. I spent so much of my life denying that I had any emotions at all. Then I'd allowed myself to be fueled only by red-hot anger and a need for revenge. But now I searched the far corners of myself for anything resembling what I assumed love might look like.

Rhea began to speak in a low tone. The words were in Hekatian—the ancient magical language used in spell work and rituals by mages. Despite my limited knowledge of the language, I somehow understood their meaning. "Goddess Hekate, Mother of Magic and Night Queen, raise your torch, that your light may illuminate the path toward healing. Goddess Diana, Moon Maiden and Mother of the fae open our vision and protect your humble servant so he may live to carry out your will."

Inside, I pushed below the black cloud of anger, vengeance, and fear hovering in my midsection. Farther down, I found a deep pool. With a trembling touch, I brushed the surface, causing a ripple. When the waters calmed again, I recognized faces just below the surface. Adam and Rhea were there, but so were Giguhl and Vinca. Brooks, too.

Something shifted and the waters rose up over me like a tide. Instead of the fiery power I called upon to destroy, this surge swelled gently. Warm instead of hot. The emotions here were deep purple instead of angry red. My chest filled—diaphragm swelling and ribs expanding. Pushed outward and up. Through my limbs and into my fingers. Rose in my throat like a primal call.

My eyes flew open as the power surged from me. My skin tingled where it touched Adam and Rhea. Their eyes were open, too, and glowing with their own energies. Our powers met and mingled, rising up in a swirling vortex of color shot through with sparks of light.

Rhea's voice sounded far away, echoed. "We three unite to pour healing into this broken vessel. We three unite to absorb his pain. We three—"

Adam caught on first, his deep voice joining in. "...to pour healing into this broken vessel. We three—"

My own voice picked up the chant. "...unite to absorb his pain."

The cone of power at the center of our triangle condensed and began to stream into Brooks's body. His shoulders lifted from the table as his body rose to receive the healing energy. At the same time, a second ribbon of energy—darker, thicker, and tinged greenish-black—rose from him and split into three streams.

Now I finally understand why Rhea needed Adam and me to assist. I only received one-third of the negative energy, but it was so intense my teeth gritted and cold sweat covered my skin. My stomach roiled with nausea as the borrowed pain tried to dig its claws into me. Breathing deeply through my nose, I struggling to balance the two opposing flows of energy.

Adam's pupils were now full black. Rhea's hand tightened on mine. I expanded my focus until I could see all of us through my third eye. Three sets of hands joined in common purpose. Three pairs of lips chanting the same invocation. Dark and light energy flowcd through us, around us, between us. Until finally, a single clean stream of energy ran through Brooks. Then three streams of power rushed back into their sources and were absorbed. But only one mage collapsed to the ground.

20

$\mathcal{M}$y head pounded like hellfire. My limbs felt weighed down with lead. I opened my eyes and immediately regretted the decision. The room spun like a drunken dervish. I slammed my lids shut again until my stomach quieted its protests. Breathing through my nose, I chanced another peek. The world had stilled while my eyes were closed. Even better, Adam's face came into focus above me. Dark smudges under his eyes and worry lines aged his handsome face. "Welcome back."

"Hi," I croaked.

His lips spread into a slow, relieved smile. "Hi."

I swallowed again to wet my dry throat. "What happened?" Now that the world had stilled, I realized we were on the living room couch. My head rested on Adam's lap and his hand stroked my hair, helping restore my equilibrium.

"You passed out." His finger brushed a spot on my forehead, making me flinch. "Hit the table on your way down."

That certainly explained the headache. I jerked as memory of the healing ritual returned. "Brooks?"

I struggled to sit up, but Adam pushed me back down with a firm hand. "Is sleeping. But you need to take it easy. Your body needs time to recover."

"Why are you fine? You did the ritual, too."

"Actually, you and Rhea did most of the heavy lifting energy-wise. Besides, she and I have more experience controlling the power surges. In time you'll learn how to harness it without sapping your strength."

That made sense, but I didn't like lying there like an infant. "Well, I'm fine now."

The look he gave me would have withered lesser women. "You're fine when I say you are. In the meantime, it's rest for you. Doctor's orders."

My eyes narrowed. "Are you trying to play doctor with me, mancy?"

The corner of his mouth lifted. "Absolutely."

"Bael's balls," a grumpy voice said from somewhere nearby. "Will you two get a room already?"

I lifted my head and found a grinning Giguhl sitting in a floral armchair. "Hey, G."

"Hey yourself. I'd ask how you're feeling, but I know your stubborn self will just lie."

I grinned at the demon. "You're probably right."

"But if you ever scare me like that again, I'm going to kick your ass."

I laughed. "Even unconscious, I could still take you, demon."

Giguhl's black lips spread into a smile. "I'm glad you're okay, Red."

"That makes two of us," Adam said.

Warmth in my midsection burned away the lingering fog. I laughed uneasily. "Jeez, you guys make it sound like I was on the brink of death or something. I just fainted."

Adam shot me a fierce frown. Obviously my flippant attitude toward their concern hadn't gone over well with either male. "Sorry. But I'm good." Two dubious glares greeted my declaration. "Really."

"Yeah, yeah," Giguhl said. "Regardless, you're going to relax even if we have to tie you down."

He rose and walked to the bedroom, presumably to check on Brooks. With him gone, the room felt emptier of more than just his big body. I sighed and looked up at Adam. He rubbed a thumb across my cheek. "He wasn't lying, you know."

I frowned. "What do you mean?"

His head tilted toward the door. "We're allowed to care about you."

My stomach flip-flopped. "I know," I said uneasily.

"Do you really? Because whether you like it or not, you're stuck with us." When he said "us," I got the distinct impression he really meant to say "me." "Can you handle that?"

I licked my lips and tried to tamp down the sizzle of awareness. My throat suddenly felt dry again, so instead of responding, I just nodded.

His hand moved down to caress my arm. "Actually, now that I think about it, I don't think the word 'care' covers it."

"You don't?" I whispered. Oh, shit, was this "the moment" Giguhl had predicted?

His eyes glistened curiously as he shook his head. When he didn't continue, I raised a hand and cupped his face. He lowered his forehead to mine. Swallowing hard, he whispered, "You scared me, Red. You dropped like a boulder and I couldn't get to you fast enough."

I didn't think about what I was doing. Didn't try to rationalize it. Didn't second-guess. I just raised my lips to his and allowed my kiss to tell him what I was feeling. And when his hands gripped my arms and he returned the kiss with a fierceness that should have scared me, I didn't pull away.

Adam and I had kissed before. Passionate kisses that left both of us wanting more. But this kiss wasn't a lusty tangle of tongues and lips like the others. Instead, it was an unfurling of emotions denied for too long. And for the first time, being in Adam's arms didn't spark the fear that normally made me want to run from what he offered.

After I don't know how long, Adam pulled away a fraction. My lips spread into a self-conscious smile. "Wow," I said, brilliant as always.

He chuckled. "Understatement of the millennium."

I raised my face for another kiss. He hesitated. "What?" I asked.

"Not that I'm complaining, but isn't this the part where you usually try to convince me how bad of an idea this is? About how we can't afford distractions?"

I cringed inwardly, remembering the last time we'd discussed the distraction issue. "Let's just say I could use a little more distraction in my life."

He laughed out loud then and rewarded me with another kiss. "Would it be presumptuous of me to say that I look forward to repeatedly distracting you as soon as possible?"

"Um, guys?" Giguhl's voice came from the doorway.

"Sorry to interrupt your special moment, but you need to see this."

Adam pulled away with a groan. "Speaking of distractions," he said under his breath. To Giguhl he said, "This better be good."

I wasn't too thrilled by the interruption, either, but something in Giguhl's voice cut through the pleasant haze. "What's wrong?"

"A severely pissed-off werebitch is calling you out downstairs."

Ten minutes later—five of which were spent arguing with the mage and demon—I made my way out into the courtyard. Before my doting caretakers allowed me to leave the living room, they made me chug two pints of blood. Now they flanked me like bodyguards. As much as I appreciated their support, it annoyed me, too. Even weak, the day I couldn't defeat a stinking werewolf was the day I handed in my fangs.

Mac prowled through the courtyard like a caged animal. Nearby, Georgia paced and bit her nails. When I exited, the vamp looked up and rushed over before my feet hit the cobblestones. "Sabina, I'm sorry. I tried to explain—"

"No, Georgia," Mac snapped. "This is between the trampire and me."

I stepped down into the courtyard and crossed my arms. "That's Miss Trampire to you, werepuppy."

"Sabina." Adam's voice held a clear rebuke, but I ignored it. Mac was a werewolf. Her instinctive need for hierarchy meant I needed to establish dominance early or things would get out of control.

"What's going on, Mac?" I said, keeping my voice casual.

Her eyes narrowed. "This is your fault."

I didn't bother dragging it out or playing coy. She blamed me for what happened to Brooks, and sarcasm would only add fuel to this potential fire. "I know."

She faltered. Tilted her head and flared her nostrils as if trying to smell a trick.

"However," I continued, "I'm not the only guilty party here."

She cocked her chin. "What does that mean?"

"Where were *you* last night?"

Mac's eyes skittered to the left. "Something came up. Had to cancel the show. I called Brooks to tell him."

"When?"

"Around eight-thirty."

About ten minutes after we left. But that didn't let her off the hook by a long shot. "Why did you cancel?"

She puffed up. "That's none of your fucking business."

"Mac," Georgia said quietly. "Tell her."

Mac glared at the vamp like she wanted to throttle her. Georgia received it with a placid expression. Finally, the were sighed deeply. "One of my employees was found dead last night."

"Who and how?"

"A vamp queen who went by the name Elvira Bathory." Mac's voice cracked. "Last night was going to be her final show."

Georgia walked up to put an arm around Mac's shoulders. "Elvira was one of the locals who decided they didn't want trouble with the Caste or your grandmother. But I guess trouble found her first."

"Wait a second," Adam said. "How do you know she was killed? Vamps burn to ash when they die."

Georgia rubbed Mac's back when the were shook her head like she couldn't speak. "Elvira always wore a necklace."

Mac dug into her pocket and removed a simple gold chain with a fleur-de-lis pendant—a symbol sacred to both New Orleans and vampires due to its association with the goddess Lilith—and a crumpled piece of paper. "We found them stabbed into Elvira's door with a dagger." She held out the paper to Adam but wouldn't surrender the necklace. Adam cursed under his breath.

He held up the paper for me. "The first of many if the vampires of New Orleans do not cooperate."

"Good gods," Giguhl said, reading over my shoulder. "Lavinia sure knows how to drive a point home, doesn't she?"

I jerked to glare at the demon. A blur of motion in my peripheral vision and a low growl were my only warning. Mac slammed into my back. "It's all your fault!"

My face smashed into the cobblestones. Before she could pin me down, I flipped and bucked her weight off me. Adam moved as if to restrain her, but I called out, "No!" I rose quickly and assumed my fighting stance. I met Mac's feral eyes. "Come on."

Mac crouched low, snarling with anger. Adam backed away slowly. Judging from his expression, he'd intervene if things got too serious. But I was too busy suddenly fending off another attack to worry about Adam.

An upper hook caught me under the chin, forcing my teeth together with a painful *snap*. I returned the favor with a jab to the ribs, followed quickly by a left hook to

Mac's liver. That really pissed her off. Her fingers bent into claws—not literal claws, since it wasn't a full moon—and swiped across my cheek. Skin split open with a cold sensation before warm blood oozed down my face.

That really pissed me off.

My spinning back-kick knocked Mac off balance. Her arms windmilled as her body teetered on the edge between equilibrium and flat-on-her-ass. I threw my upper body back and lifted my bent leg, but before I could deliver the blow that would teach Mac a lesson, the back door of the shop burst open.

"Stop!" Rhea's voice cracked through the air like a gunshot.

I glanced toward her with my leg still raised. That split second of distraction was all Mac needed to tip the scales. She shot forward, ramming her shoulder into my midsection. My feet flew off the ground. Mac screamed with exertion, slamming my back down onto the top of the patio table. The wooden frame cracked and collapsed under the force of the collision.

Stunned, I lay with my eyes focused on the early morning sky. The sun still hadn't cracked the horizon, but I could feel its fledgling rays pulling on my diaphragm. Rough hands grabbed the lapels of my jacket, but before Mac could haul me up, an ear-piercing shriek ripped through the courtyard. Mac and I stilled, our heads swiveling in unison toward the horrible sound.

Zen scowled at us from the bottom step, a white air horn clutched in her hand. Behind her, Rhea crossed her arms, her eyes crinkled with judgment.

"Hasn't there been enough violence for one night?"

I pushed myself off the ground, my joints aching and

my ass smarting from the impact with the table. Mac paced nearby, tensed for another round.

Zen's hand went to her hips. "Look at ya. Both so full of piss and vinegar." She shook her head at us. "Well, guess what? You're both directing your anger at the wrong enemy."

I didn't bother even looking at Mac, but I pretty much assumed her expression matched my own. We might not be trying to maim each other anymore, but we sure as hell weren't going to duck our heads like abashed children.

Seeing our hesitation, Zen turned to Rhea. "Youth," she complained.

My hands shot to my hips. "I'm older than you."

"Me, too," Mac added.

The human's eyes widened with irony. "Could have fooled me."

My mouth snapped shut.

Zen rounded on Mac. "And you! Carrying on when one of your friends is dead and other nearly dead. It's shameful and disrespectful. You should know better."

Mac toed the cobblestones with her Doc Marten. "Sorry, Zen."

"Don't sorry me, go apologize to Brooks."

Mac's head snapped up from its formerly submissive posture. "He's awake?"

"No," Rhea said. "But only because I gave him a potion to make him sleep so his body could regain its strength."

Mac frowned at Rhea. "Who the fuck are you?"

Adam, who had been hanging back by Giguhl until now, puffed up. "Hey! Show some respect."

Rhea held up a hand and shook her head at her nephew. "My name is Rhea Lazarus. In addition to being that one's aunt"—she nodded toward Adam—"I'm the High Priest-ess of the Elder Moon and spiritual advisor to the Hekate Council. I'm also the one who helped Adam and Sabina save your friend's life last night. Who the hell are you?"

Mac didn't like that little dose of her own attitude. "I'm Mac Romulus."

"She's Michael's niece," Adam added. Rhea's eyes widened in recognition of the name of an ally.

"Now that we've established we're all on the same side," Rhea said pointedly, "I'll let you go check on your friend as long as you understand I will not hesitate to zap your ass if you cause that fae any unnecessary stress."

Mac didn't need to be told twice. She ran off, brushing between the elder mage and the voodoo priestess. Georgia followed at a more sedate pace, muttering apologies for Mac's rudeness.

The werewolf's departure dispelled some of the heavy vapor of tension hanging over our group. Adam and Giguhl reached the ladies before I did, but we all formed a loose circle. Rhea looked at me. "Shall I assume you don't need any healing?"

I touched the back of my hand to the wounds on my cheek. When I pulled it away, only a few small drops of blood smeared my skin. Luckily, the blood I'd chugged on my way down made fast work of the minor injuries I'd sustained from the scuffle.

"Yeah, I'm fine."

"Good," Zen said, picking up the conversation. "Because we have something to show you."

I frowned at the females. To say I didn't like Zen's tone would be an understatement. More like it sent warning bells off in my head. "What is it?"

Adam stood next to me, and his palm slipped through mine in a sort of preemptive comforting maneuver.

"You're going to want to sit down," Rhea said.

My stomach sank like an anvil in a pool. "I'll stand, thanks."

Zen and Rhea exchanged a worried glance, then the voodooienne grimaced at me. She reached into the pocket of her work apron. It looked like a wrinkled piece of paper at first. "I found this on the shrine in my parlor."

She placed what turned out to be a crumpled Polaroid in my hand. My heart stuttered and a gasp escaped my lips. On automatic pilot, I lifted the picture closer with a shaky hand. Adam leaned toward me to get a better look himself. He cursed under his breath and his hand fisted around mine.

Smears of blood—Maisie's?—marred the image. Using my thumb, I rubbed at the stain but only managed to spread it like a red varnish across Maisie's face. The blood turned her skin and the gag obscuring her mouth pink. Her eyes were narrowed like she was trying to shoot lasers at the photographer. In front of her, she white-knuckled a newspaper bearing Thursday's date. Under the picture, Lavinia had written in thick black marker, "The clock is ticking."

Adam took the picture from me and showed it to Giguhl, who for once didn't have a witty comment or joke. Smart of him.

Two emotions battled for dominance inside me. The first was relief. We finally had confirmation Maisie was alive. But it was cold comfort, given the realization we were no closer to knowing her location than we'd been back in Los Angeles.

The second emotion was more toxic. A combination of anger and guilt that made my stomach cramp and my vision go blurry red. My hands shook with it. I squeezed my eyes shut to block the truth out.

"Sabina?" Adam said quietly.

My eyes stung when I opened them. "She's fucking toying with me."

He nodded. "She's trying to throw you off your game. Don't give her the satisfaction. Focus on the fact Maisie's alive."

"Call me crazy, but I'm having a hard time focusing on the bright side right now." I ripped the picture from Giguhl's claw and shoved it toward Adam's face. "Look at her! She's gagged and bound with brass chains, Adam."

He took the picture from my fingers and held it up in my face. "No, you look. Does she look like she's in pain or scared?" I pulled my glare from him and looked again.

"No," I admitted. "She looks pissed."

"Exactly. That anger will help her survive." He grabbed my shoulders and turned me to face him. "But if you let yours get the best of you, it won't help anyone."

Rhea placed a hand on my arm. "Adam's right. This is upsetting for all of us. But we can't allow Lavinia's psychological warfare to distract us."

I took a deep breath, both pushing down the anger and tightening my mental defenses at once. Rhea was right—I wasn't the only one here who cared about Maisie. Rhea and Adam had known her longer than I had, yet here they were comforting me. Shame at my selfishness coated my insides.

Giguhl held up a single talon. "Guys, I hate to add fuel

to this fire, but we've got a more immediate issue to deal with. Lavinia knows where we're staying."

Zen nodded resolutely and stepped forward. "Actually, that's not the worst of it." We all looked at her, bracing ourselves for whatever her verdict was going to be. "Until we figure out who's been spying on us, finding a safer place to stay will be impossible."

Adam crossed his arms over his chest and stroked his chin. "The first thing we need to do is set up a watch. Sabina and I will take turns—obviously Sabina gets the night shifts."

"Adam, that's crazy. How are we going to make any progress if we're on opposite schedules and spending all our time waiting to be attacked?"

"She has a point, Adam," Rhea said. "We can ward the entrances and exits as a precaution."

"I still say we need someone on watch, at least at night when the attack is more likely."

Giguhl raised a claw. "What about me?"

I shot the demon a grateful look. He really was the perfect candidate for the job. He didn't have my pesky day/night issues and, even though I rarely admitted it, he was probably the most powerful being of our little trio. Demons are notoriously hard to kill, and Giguhl's mischievous personality also made him pretty wily in a fight.

"That would be a big help, Giguhl. Thanks."

His horizontal pupils flickered in surprise. "Really?"

I frowned. "Yeah. Is that a problem?"

He tilted his head. "No, it's just you usually argue when I volunteer for jobs."

My conscience prickled. He was totally right. "Well,

your little talk the other night helped me realize I need to start treating you like a real member of this team. So, yes, I'd like you to take point of the perimeter. Please," I added for good measure.

Giguhl stood up with a satisfied smile on his black lips. "You won't be sorry, Red. I'll keep the perimeter tighter than a nun's cooch." With that charming metaphor, he ran off to begin securing the building. The four of us remaining watched him go for a moment before Adam cleared his throat.

"Now that that's settled, what are we going to do about this spy situation?"

Rhea looked around. "Do you all really believe Lavinia has someone watching you?"

Zen, Adam, and I formed an arc of nodding heads. "Someone close enough to know our plans. Otherwise, how did they know when to attack last night when none of us were here?"

"And the two Garden District incidents," Adam said, referring to the dearly departed Stryx and the Count's vamp gang.

"Speaking of," Zen said, "how did the patrols go tonight?"

Adam grimaced. "Nada. Not one sign of Lavinia in the French Quarter tonight. Of course, you called before we made it over this way. But I haven't had a chance to ask Giguhl—"

Zen spoke up then. "While you two were inside checking the place out, he told me they didn't find anything, either."

"Any word from the spirit world?" Adam asked Zen and me.

The voodooienne and I exchanged a look. "Not as such, no," I said finally.

Rhea's eyes went all squinty and suspicious. "What?"

I quickly filled Rhea in on the ritual we'd planned on doing, stopping just short of the unanticipated outcome.

"So what happened?" Adam asked. His expression matched his aunt's. They knew we were hiding something.

"Wait a second," Rhea said. "You did warn Zen about your Chthonic powers first, right?"

My eyes shifted left. "Um." Zen crossed her arms and tapped her toe on the ground, shooting accusing looks between Adam and me.

"No," she said. "And neither did you, old friend."

"What am I missing?" Adam said.

I continued to avoid everyone's gaze, so Zen took over. "What you missed was Miss Thang over here summoning a revenant."

"Rev—you mean a *zombie?*" Adam shouted.

Rhea's mouth dropped open. "Good gods. What were you thinking, Sabina?"

The combined force of their judgment brought my hackles up. "I made a mistake, okay? But I also cleaned up the mess."

Zen nodded reluctantly. "It's true. She did manage to kill it. Eventually."

I crossed my arms and shot the mages an I-told-you-so look. But Zen wasn't done. "It's just a shame the owl had to die before she could get the answers she needed."

"Owl?" Rhea said. "You mean Stryx?"

"It's a long story," I said. "But the ritual wasn't a total loss. Kevin"—at their blank stares, I explained—"that's the zombie, did manage to translate the owl's screeches for a few seconds. Mostly it was a lot of calling for his master. But he did say a couple of strange things."

Everyone looked at me expectantly. I sighed, knowing what I was about to say would make them question my sanity. "He said 'big box' and," I paused, " 'cat piss.' "

Adam's head tilted and his eyes narrowed. "What does that mean?"

"No idea. But I'd just asked where Maisie was when he said it. After the box and the cat thing, he said 'Master come' and 'Kane.' " I shrugged. "Maybe they're clues."

"So basically other than knowing you can summon zombies, which is kind of awesome by the way," Adam said, shooting me an admiring glance, "all we have to go on is a picture of Maisie and vague references to boxes and cat urine?"

Rhea sighed heavily. "This is not good at all. The Council anticipated far more progress by now," she said. "I'm wondering if we should consult with Orpheus."

"What?" Adam said. "No. What if he tells us to pull out of the city to regroup? We can't leave Maisie here."

"Orpheus wouldn't do that to Maisie. Most likely he'd want to send in reinforcements."

I frowned. "But I thought warm bodies were in short supply."

"I've been having some success with my recruiting efforts. Just before I came here I convinced several Chicago-area mages to join the cause. Maybe we can persuade Orpheus to bring the war to Lavinia before she can succeed in her plans with the Caste."

"No," I said. "We're close. I can feel it. As much as I hate what happened to Brooks, Adam was right. Lavinia is trying to unsettle us. That tells me she's worried we'll figure out her scheme. Plus, we're not totally dead in the water. We still need to talk to Brooks."

Rhea opened her mouth to continue, but a loud squeak got our attention. On the second floor, Georgia leaned out of the window she'd forced open.

"Brooks is awake."

21

Rhea and Zen entered first, leaving Adam and me to linger in the doorway of the crowded room. Apparently, Giguhl had heard Mac's call, too, because he already sat by Brooks's hip.

"Hey, guys!" the faery called from the bed, his voice surprisingly chipper. Hard to tell how genuine the reaction was, given his appearance.

Mac and Georgia obviously waited a few minutes to call us up. The tattered, blood-smeared dress he'd had on earlier was gone. His new wig, a simple black bob, and large Jackie O sunglasses accessorized a pink housecoat. Only the lower portion of his face was visible around the huge shades. The pink gloss shining on his lips accentuated his unblemished complexion.

Zen and Rhea approached the bed, leaning in to consult with the fae. Giguhl rose to give them a moment and approached us. I whispered to him and Adam, "I'm surprised they put him back in drag."

Giguhl responded in an equally quiet tone. "After the

violence he endured, he probably feels safer behind the costume. More able to dissociate from the reality of it."

I didn't even try to act surprised at such an insight coming from the demon. Mostly because I suspected he was right.

I certainly wasn't a stranger to hiding behind a facade to deal with things. Ironic, though that Brooks's reaction to feeling vulnerable was to sink further into a persona many considered weak. While my own reaction was to deny any vulnerability whatsoever. Regardless of our differing methods, my heart went out to him. Yet another reason to find out what the hell had happened so I could make Lavinia and her goons pay.

I excused myself from Adam and Giguhl and went to talk to Brooks. "Hey," I said, approaching the bed.

His head angled toward me, but I couldn't see his eyes through the dark lenses. "How are you feeling?"

"Never better, honey." He flashed his pearly whites, but tension shadowed the smile.

Mac stepped up. She turned her back to me and addressed everyone else. "He was just about to tell us what happened."

"She," the drag queen corrected. A knife's edge of tension made his tone higher than usual

Several tense looks zinged among the rest of us. Zen recovered first and patted Brooks's shoulder. "Are you sure you're ready? It can wait."

"Actually, I feel amazing. If *someone*"—he jerked his head toward Mac—"hadn't threatened me, I'd already be out of this bed."

"You're gonna stay put, and that's that," the were said, crossing her arms. Brooks looked around for an ally in his bid to rise but found none. Instead of arguing further, he lay back against the pillows with a huffy breath.

"Fine," he said. "The truth is I don't remember much."

Giguhl patted his arm. "Just tell us what you do remember. Start with what happened right after we left."

"Mac called about ten minutes later and told me she was calling off the show. I was worried because she wouldn't give me any details, but her voice sounded real strained and angry." He looked up at Mac. "What happened?"

I'll give Mac this—she's got a convincing poker face. "It's not important right now. Keep talking."

Brooks's lips puckered up. "Fine, be that way." Obviously he thought Mac was hiding some juicy gossip. "Anyway, I'm ashamed to admit I threw a bit of a diva fit after I got off the phone. There I was all dressed up and no place to go. So I decided to fix myself a martini and call some of my girls to see if they were free to go out."

Up until that point, his tone was breezy and bitchy— like Pussy Willow—but when he continued, the snark was gone. "I was on the second step when I heard the crash at the back door." He swallowed hard. "At first I thought it might be you guys, but then I saw the hoods."

I stepped forward. "What do you mean?"

"I mean some KKK shit." He mimicked pulling a hood over his face. "Only these were red—except for one dude who wore black. Before I could figure out what the hell was going on, about a dozen of the assholes swarmed me. I tried to run, but my Cleopatra costume was designed for lounging on a settee, not running from robed madmen. Anyway, I tripped. Lost my wig." His voice cracked. I imagined if he'd removed the glasses, his pupils would be dilated with remembered fear. "A few split off and started tearing shit up in the store while the rest carried my livid ass up to the third floor. I fought them as hard as I could, but..." He trailed off.

"Was there a female vampire with them? Lavinia?" I asked.

Brooks shook his head. "No, just the dudes. At least I think they were all dudes—hard to tell with the hoods and the no-talking thing."

I frowned. "No talking?"

"Yeah. From the minute they came in until they finally stopped hurting me, none of the bastards said anything. The guy in the black robe, he seemed to be in charge. But he just stood to the side chanting something, never spoke to the others. The ones who... beat me, they didn't look at him, either. Just moved real methodical. Like they were programmed or something." Brooks shivered. "Creepy."

"I hate to ask this," I said, trying to keep my tone even, "but did any of them bite you?"

Another shake. "They weren't vamps, I don't think. No magic, either."

"You said the one guy chanted. Were they doing some sort of ritual?" Adam asked.

The fae hesitated, swallowing hard. Paler than when we'd come in. I wasn't sure if it was the emotional stress of rehashing things, or the physical toll of everything catching up, but I knew pretty soon Zen and Rhea would kick us out. Before that happened, I needed to know whose ass I needed to go medieval on.

I grabbed his clammy hand and gave him a reassuring smile. "I know this is hard, but it's important. What exactly did they do to you?"

Mac lurched forward, her expression confrontational. But Rhea grabbed the were's arm and shook her head.

Brooks missed the exchange because his gaze was on me. At least I think it was. Hard to tell with the sunglasses. "After they hit me for a while," he began, pausing to collect himself, "they tied me to the bed. I couldn't see much because of the blindfold." He swallowed hard as the first tears spilled from under the glasses and onto his cheeks. "They cut me. Deliberate shallow slashes. It was the black-hood guy. I recognized the voice. And each time he cut, he'd say, 'Master Mahan, accept this sacrifice.' "

The tears flowed freely now. I placed my other hand on his, trying to lend some of my strength.

"Who is Master Mahan?" Georgia asked.

"He's the leader of the Caste of Nod," Adam said. "Did they say anything else?"

Brooks sniffed and managed to get a hold of himself. "Just after they tied me up, one of the others came in and told the leader he couldn't find the owl."

I blinked. "They were trying to find Stryx?"

He nodded. "Black Hood seemed pretty pissed the owl wasn't here. Knocked me around some more until I admitted you'd taken him with you. Then he seemed almost scared, like he was going to be in big trouble."

My stomach clenched. If the robed terrorists were that worried about losing the owl, I couldn't imagine Master Mahan would be too thrilled to learn I'd gotten his owl eaten by a zombie.

But something else bothered me, too. Despite the ritualized cutting, nothing in his story implied his attackers were members of any of the dark races. Vamps would have enjoyed the blood play more. Mages would have used magic to accomplish their aims. Weres or faeries didn't fit, either. A new suspicion started forming in my mind.

"I know you said you didn't get a good look at them, but is it possible these guys were human?"

Everyone in the room reacted physically to the question. Mac was the most vocal, with a loud snort.

Brooks crossed his arms and leaned back. "I didn't think of that before now, but you might be on to something. It took four of them to hold me down, which seemed weird at the time. I mean, I'm not exactly muscular, you know?"

"Yeah, but you're a fae. That means you're still stronger than an average human male," Giguhl observed.

"Here's what I don't get: Lavinia has access to magical vampires," Georgia said. "Why would she bother with humans?"

Zen cleared her throat. The vamp cringed. "No offense." The voodoo queen nodded and turned her attention back to the conversation.

"Maybe they're humans who serve the Caste," Mac offered. "What with the robes and chanting, they sure sound like a secret society to me."

Adam's eyes widened. "Wait a second. Were they wearing any symbols?"

"Oh, yeah," Brooks said. "There was an eye symbol on the hood—right here"—he pointed to the middle of his forehead—"above a pyramid, you know like on a dollar bill?" Everyone nodded. "And then on the right breast of their robes was a kind of crest thingie. I didn't get a good look before they blindfolded me, though."

"Do you remember any details about it?" Rhea asked.

"There was a fleur de lis, I think. Maybe a moon, too."

Something tickled the back of my mind, a smoky tendril of memory. "Was there a key?"

His shoulders drooped as he shook his head. "I should have paid better attention, but..."

I shot the fae a sympathetic smile. "Not your fault."

Adam's solemn gaze met mine. I knew he was recalling the same thing I'd remembered. But I wasn't ready to voice my suspicion yet. Not until I had more proof. I grabbed a piece of paper from the desk and scribbled the symbol from memory. I'd only had a couple of brief glances at it, but I think I managed to get the gist. "Like this?"

He took the sheet and lowered the sunglasses just enough to peek at it. What I could see of his eyes made my heart clench. Capillaries crossed the white of his eyes like tiny red webs. He lowered the glasses more for a better look. "That's it, I think. You've seen it before?"

My teeth clenched so hard my jaw cramped. "Unfuckingbelievable."

Adam took the picture from Zen. "How'd we miss this?"

Giguhl grabbed it from Zen. "Oh, shit!"

"Guys?" Rhea said. "Talk to us."

"We know who's been feeding Lavinia our locations," Adam said tightly.

I crossed my arms and shook my head as my brain went back over my theory to check for holes.

"Well?" Mac said, her voice dripping with impatience. "Who?"

Adam raised his eyebrows, I nodded, perfectly happy to let him take lead on this. Maybe they'd believe it more coming from him. "Alodius wears a tie pin with this symbol."

Zen let out a frustrated breath and leaned forward. Her

expression said she wasn't buying it. "You're jumping to conclusions. New Orleans has a long tradition of fraternal orders and benevolent societies. A fleur de lis and crescent moon? Name one building or sign or T-shirt in this city that doesn't feature one of those symbols. Hell, even keys are everywhere."

"How about the fact that two major incidents happened right after we visited his shop?" I counted them off on my fingers. "First Stryx shows up right after our first trip to buy blood. Then the vamp attack after Giguhl and I went in."

Adam piped up. "And I went there last night to get Sabina some blood."

I nodded. "Did Alodius say or do anything strange while you were there?"

"He was pretty curious about what you were up to. Even asked specifically what we were doing last night. I lied and told him we were taking in the show at Lagniappe. I didn't think anything of it at the time, since he's always so damned chatty. But what if he was trying out if the coast would be clear for the attack?"

Mac snorted. "Jesus, you guys are unbelievable. Alodius is a nice old man. Why would he do something like that? He's friends with these two." She nodded toward Zen and Brooks.

I turned on the werewolf. My conscience nagged at me that she might be right. We were going on assumptions, not real proof of treachery. But I couldn't just let the coincidences slide without investigating. "Adam told him we were all going to see the show last night. They didn't expect him to be here."

"Her," Brooks whispered so low I barely heard it. I shot him a look, but Zen jumped in.

"Tread carefully here, Sabina. I overlooked your accusations about Georgia because I knew she and Mac could handle you. But Alodius is a human, and until you have real proof, I won't allow you to harm him."

"Look, we're not saying he's directly responsible," Adam said. "But the evidence so far dictates we at least have a conversation with him."

"Right," Mac sorted. "I've been on the receiving end of one of your 'conversations,' and I'd put cash money on your chat with Alodius getting physical real fast."

I speared her with my gaze. "What do you want us to do, Mac? Ignore this? Overlook what happened to Brooks and Elvira? Both attacks were ordered by the same person—Lavinia Kane. How long do you think it'll be before she sends someone after Georgia? Or you, for that matter?"

"What?" Brooks shouted. "What happened to Elvira?"

Mac shot me a glare that promised a slow, painful death. "She was attacked, too, honey. She"—Mac swallowed hard—"she didn't make it."

Brooks's head fell into his hands as the dam broke. Mac's chin raised and her eyes hardened as she looked at me. "I take care of my own."

My conscience prickled for upsetting Brooks, but now wasn't the time to go soft. I crossed my arms and nodded toward Brooks. "You can't be everywhere, Mac. They were attacked at the same time."

She tensed to lunge at me. "Maybe I should save your grandbitch the trouble—"

Her body froze midspring. "Oh, hell no!" Giguhl's voice cracked like a whip. Mac dangled from one of his claws like a puppy from his mother's teeth. "Someone needs to teach you some manners, werebitch."

"Giguhl," I snapped. "Put her down. Now."

The demon sighed and released her. Back on her feet, the were stared me down for a moment. "Fuck all of you."

She jumped into motion, grabbing Georgia by the arm before storming toward the door. Brooks called after them, but Mac stomped out with Georgia in her wake without another word.

"I'll just show them out and do another perimeter check," Giguhl said. I nodded and dismissed Mac from my mind.

"Look," I said to Zen. "I'm not looking to hurt the guy if he's innocent. But human or not, we can't take the chance he's working against us."

Zen sighed heavily, looking torn. Rhea placed a hand on her arm. "There's an easy way to find out if he was involved without beating it out of him."

I perked up, hoping Rhea's solution might offer a compromise to end the stalemate. Rhea nodded toward Brooks. "Take Brooks with you. If Alodius was involved, he'll be surprised to see the fae healthy."

"Absolutely not," Zen all but shouted.

The drag queen perked up in the bed. "Actually, I'd love to see the expression on his face when he sees me looking fabulous again. If he's guilty, that is," he amended.

"Are you sure? I know you're feeling physically better, but I don't want to upset you any more than necessary."

In response, Brooks threw back the covers. "Just give me five to fix my face and throw on something a little less comfortable."

"No," Zen said, moving toward the determined fae. "It's too risky."

Brooks stood and took Zen's hand. "I appreciate your concern, darling, but I'm not going to spend the rest of my life hiding because some assholes decided to send a message. If my presence will help Sabina and Adam get answers, then I'm all in."

I added, "We'll be safe."

Zen's eyes jumped from Brooks to me as she weighed whether to keep arguing. I think we all suspected this wouldn't end well for the Cajun, but I couldn't blame her for trying to protect Brooks from further distress. Finally, Zen nodded and forced a smile for her friend. "What are you going to wear?"

Brooks laughed and took the woman by the arm, leading her out of the room to discuss wardrobe choices.

I blew out a breath and turned toward Rhea. "Giguhl's on watch. If you need anything or if anything odd happens while we're gone, make sure he knows."

Rhea nodded but clearly had something else on her mind. "While you're gone I'm going to call Orpheus and fill him in. I think it might be a good idea to have a couple Pythian Guards here to back you up."

"Not yet," Adam said. When she opened her mouth to argue, he held up a hand. "Until we have a chance to sort out this human angle, we don't need the complication. Plus if the building is being watched, someone's bound to notice them arriving."

"I agree," I said. "Right now the situation is too volatile to involve any other lives."

Rhea sighed and thought about it for a moment. "All right, but I'm still going to check in and tell him I'm staying for the time being."

Adam paused. "I'm not sure that's a good idea, either."

"Why not?"

I jumped in to add my two cents. "Because everyone has a target on their head now. Adam and Brooks have already been injured."

Adam stepped forward. "If something happened to you—" His voice cracked. I shifted and swallowed against the unexpected emotion that tightened my throat.

Rhea grabbed Adam's hand and shot me an affectionate but determined smile. "I'm well aware of the risks. And I might be old, but I'm stubborn. No one's taking me down without a fight."

Next to me, Adam smiled proudly at his aunt. "It's true. She's kicked my ass more than once."

If Adam could put aside his concerns for Rhea's safety, then so could I. Besides, I liked having the old bat around.

"Okay," I said. "But from now on no one is alone—not here and definitely not on the streets."

Adam and Rhea nodded, but before either could say anything a femme fatale appeared at the door. Obviously getting into the spirit of the impending interrogation, Brooks had opted for black leather pants, six-inch-high platform boots, and a hot pink bustier under a leather bolero. "It's time to show that butcher this kitty's got claws."

Adam whistled low. I smiled approvingly at her choice of attire. "Lookin' fierce, Brooks. You ready?"

"Brooks is dead, honey. From now on I'm Pussy Willow."

*I*nstead of taking Zen's voodoomobile again, Adam opted for just flashing us to the neighborhood near Alodius's shop. Pussy Willow—who insisted we use that name as well as feminine pronouns for *her* from now on—seemed so eager for our mission that she didn't balk at the unconventional mode of travel. As for me, the magical transportation limited my exposure to the bright morning sun, so I was all for it.

Therefore, a couple of minutes after walking out of Zen's shop, we stood on the front stoop of Cajun Sausage Fest. Luckily, the hour was so early that no tourists or locals saw our arrival. Unluckily, it also meant Alodius's shop was closed.

In deference to Halloween's arrival—shit, how had it already gotten to be Saturday?—he'd pasted cardboard decorations of cackling witches with striped socks and vampires with big, fangy smiles in the darkened windows. "Cute," I said, leaning to the window for a peek inside. "I can't tell if he's in there. What are the chances he's in the back?"

Adam peered up to the second floor of the building. "I say we give him a call and find out." He pulled his knapsack around and dug in it, finally coming up with the magnet Alodius had given me the other night. I'd totally forgotten about passing it to the mancy then. Luckily, Adam never seemed to throw anything away from his trusty portable magic kit.

"Thanks." I smiled at him and took the phone he offered. Alodius answered on the third ring.

"Yell-oh?"

"Hey Alodius, it's Sabina. I hate to call so early, but—" I cut off dramatically, hoping he'd take the bait.

After a pause, he bit. "Is everything okay, *cher*?"

I put a little wobble in my voice. "No. I need some blood really bad. Is there any way you could meet me at the store? I'm already here. Normally I wouldn't ask, but it's an emergency."

"Now, now, darlin', don't you worry your pretty self. Alodius lives right upstairs. Be down in jiff."

"Really? Thank you so much."

"However—"

"Yes?"

"Seeing how it's after business hours, we're going to have to charge a tad extry."

I pursed my lips. I'd like to show him a "tad extry" myself, the opportunistic ass. "That's fine. Please hurry."

I clicked off the phone and turned to Adam and Pussy Willow. "You guys stand around the corner. Follow me in two minutes later."

Adam nodded. "Got it. Be careful." Then he took Pussy's arm and the two jogged past the next store to wait out of sight.

I reached back to touch my gun, more to reassure myself than out of any real fear I'd forgotten it. The light came on then in the store, signaling Alodius's arrival. He must have used a back staircase from his living quarters. I attempted to look defeated as he waved and came to unlock the door.

"Sabina? Darlin', you look like death warmed over. Come on in and tell Old Alodius what's wrong."

I hesitated. Despite his welcoming smile and concerned demeanor, it'd be a mistake to underestimate Alodius. Gods only knew what nasty surprises he could have waiting in the shop. Casting a quick glance to my right, I didn't see Adam or Pussy Willow, but I felt their presence and knew they'd have my back if the crazy Cajun tried anything. Besides, he might be a traitor, but he was still a human, and the day I couldn't hold my own against a mortal was the day I took up sunbathing as a hobby.

I swallowed and lowered my head meekly—at least I assumed that was the vibe I was giving off. I didn't have a lot of experience with meekness. "Oh, Alodius, it was horrible."

I brushed past him. Inside, I moved the counter and leaned against it forlornly. This position was chosen strategically so he had his back to the front door. It also meant my back wasn't exposed in case any of his robed buddies were hiding in the storeroom. "I don't know where to begin."

"Start at the beginning, *cher.*" Impatience crept into his tone now.

"My friend Brooks was...he was murdered last night."

"What?" Alodius shouted.

I paused. "Did you know him? He worked for Madam Zenobia."

Alodius's face had turned an interesting shade of red. He sputtered for a moment. I couldn't tell if he'd realized he'd given something away or if it was genuine shock. "He came here a time or two for Madam Z. Are you sure he's dead?"

I nodded sadly. "But that's not all. Whoever killed him also destroyed Zen's shop."

This seemed to shock him less than hearing about Brooks's pretend death. "That's a shame." He paused. "But back to the fae. You're absolutely positive he died?"

"I'm afraid so." I shook my head, keeping my eyes on the Cajun. "Who would do such a terrible thing, Alodius?"

Alodius punched a fist into his palm. "Those sons-a-bitches!"

I moved in closer. "Which sons of bitches?"

He choked and kicked his feet. "What? I just meant whoever's responsible should pay." He looked away with wild eyes.

I got in his face. Grabbed his collars. "Who?"

His mouth worked like a hungry carp's. "I—they were just going to scare y'all a little."

I tightened my fists on his ring-around-the-collar and lifted. His doughy body struggled against the reverse of gravity. Exposing my fangs, I hissed, "Names. Now!"

The bell over the door announced the arrival of Adam and Pussy Willow. "He better have confessed to something, Red," Adam said by way of greeting. "Because we agreed no violence until we had proof."

I dropped Alodius. His ass hit linoleum with a *crack*. Probably broke his tailbone, judging from the moans of pain. "We were getting to that. Alodius was just about to tell me everything he knows." I nudged him with my boot. "Right?"

Alodius cringed and looked up at the six-foot-tall diva in heels towering over him. "Brooks!" His voice cracked. "You're alive!" Then he paused and swiveled his gaze to me. "Wait a second. What the hell's going on here? Why did you say he died?"

Pussy Willow crossed her arms and glared down at the man. "Brooks did die, darlin'. I'm his better, bitchier half."

Alodius shook himself, clearly lost. "What the sam hell's going on?"

Adam knelt down and looked into the human's eyes. "Here's a clue. Next time you want to hide your involvement in attempted murder, make sure to take off the tacky tie pin that links you to the crime." Adam flicked the pin in question with his fingernail.

The man blanched but raised his chin. "You're grasping at straws. A tie pin don't prove nothin'."

"Bullshit," I barked. "Are you telling me if I go upstairs I won't find a red hood in your closet?"

He swallowed so hard his Adam's apple bobbed frantically among his jowls. "Alodius wasn't there! The shop was open. You can ask anyone."

"Fine. Maybe you weren't there," I said. "But you're involved. And you're going to tell us everything you know."

He shook his head and tightened his fat lips.

Maybe a professional interrogator would have kept trying to get the man to admit his involvement. Me? I preferred a more direct route. I hauled the Cajun up by his armpits. "Adam, get the butcher knife. I'm gonna cut the truth out of him."

The Cajun's eyes went wide with fear. "No!" Spittle flew from his fat lips and landed on my face. I'd had no real intention of cutting the sad little man, but if he kept spitting on me I might change my mind.

"Start talking, then." I carried him over to a chair and tossed him down in the seat. He groaned and rubbed his backside.

"Ouch! No need to be violent."

I got in his face. "On the contrary, there is every need to get violent. This isn't a game, Alodius. It's as fucking serious as it gets." I grabbed the picture of Maisie from my pocket. "This shit here makes me want to inflict some major pain on someone. Unless you start giving us something we can use to find my sister, that someone will be you."

The space between us filled with the tang of urine. I glanced down at the rapidly spreading wet spot on the front of Alodius's trousers. A shudder wracked the human's body as he tried to collect himself. His eye welled with tears and his face went red.

I dropped him to escape the body fluids. He slumped on the floor and openly wept. "I'll give you something to cry about you miserable piece of shit."

"Sabina," Adam said quietly.

Snot bubbled from his nose. "They'll never induct me now," he wailed.

I stepped back with a sigh and crossed my arms. "*Who* won't?"

"The Benevolent Brotherhood of the Eastern Mystery."

Frowning, I looked at Adam, who shrugged and shook his head. Pussy Willow looked equally lost. "Who the hell are they?"

Alodius snorted and swiped at his tears. "They're only the most powerful secret society in human history."

I pressed my lips together. "If they're so powerful, why haven't we heard of them?"

Alodius looked up at me like I'd said something ridiculous. "You hard of hearing, *cher*? It's called a *secret* society for a reason."

Adam crossed his arms. "Please. Most people have heard the names of lots of secret societies—the Rosicrucians, the Illuminati—"

The mortal made a rude noise. "Those guys are pussies. The Brotherhood has the true power."

"Such as?" I prompted.

He pressed his lips together and twisted his fingers in front. Then he crossed his arms and leaned back.

"Well, now, look who's suddenly rediscovered his sac." I placed the ball of my foot on the edge of his chair and pushed. The chair fell back with a clatter and a flurry of curses from the sprawled Cajun.

"You no-good bloodsucker. See if the Brotherhood don't teach you a thing or two."

"You're testing my patience." I stood over him with my boot heel on his fat belly. "Why did the Brotherhood attack Zenobia's store?"

The spiked point of my heel ground into his midsection. "Jesus, watch the pancreas, will ya?" he groaned. "I'll talk."

The sudden shift to first person told me I'd won. With a smile, I delivered one more jab of my spiked heel before jerking my head at Adam. The mage rolled his eyes and righted the chair before helping the man back into it.

"Now," I said, putting an extra dose of menace into my voice. "Start at the beginning."

Alodius ran a hand over his sweaty forehead, smoothing

the flap of hair back over his pate. "It all started a week ago. At the monthly meeting, the Big Brothers informed us initiates that we needed to keep our eyes out for a magepire and—"

I held up a hand. "Hold up—*magepire*?"

Adam snickered behind me. I shot him a glare before turning it on the mortal.

"Yeah, that's what you are, right? Half and half?" I pursed my lips together and rolled a hand for him to continue. "Anyways, they said you'd have a mage and maybe a demon with you. If we saw any of you, we were to call in immediately. Imagine Alodius's delight when you strolled right into the shop a few days later."

"Why did they want to know about our movements?" Adam asked.

He shrugged. "Dunno."

"You didn't ask?" I said, my voice heavy with disbelief.

"Are you kidding? Initiates don't ask questions. We follow orders."

"So you called them each time after we left the shop," Adam said. "That still doesn't explain how that information got back to Lavinia."

"Who?"

I rolled my eyes. This guy was a bigger idiot than I'd given him credit for. "Lavinia Kane? The leader of the vampire race? The one who's been sending her goons after us based on the information you've been giving your stupid secret society."

"Hey! The Benevolent Brotherhood of the Eastern Mystery isn't stupid. We raise lots of money for literacy at our annual crawfish boil."

I threw up my hands and turned to Adam. "You better take over before I kill him."

The mage moved in, pulling a chair up next to the frustrating butcher. "Alodius, I need you to focus, okay? We understand you were just following orders."

I snorted and rolled my eyes. As I did so, I looked at Pussy Willow. Every muscle in her body tensed, including her fists, which clenched and unclenched like they wanted to get busy. As Alodius waxed poetic to the mage about honor and patriotic duty and a bunch of other bullshit, I sidled up to the faery.

"Hey," I whispered. "You doing okay?"

A muscle worked in her jaw. Her eyes never left the butcher. "Mmm-hmm."

"Don't worry. Adam will get to the bottom of this. He gives great good cop."

Pussy Willow's head nodded slowly to acknowledge my statement, but I had the feeling she wasn't all there. I couldn't blame her for her anger over Alodius's involvement. Now wasn't the time for a heart-to-heart, though, so I patted her stiff arm and focused on Adam's progress—or lack thereof.

"No, I didn't know that Nostradamus was a member of the Brotherhood. But I really need you to focus. Did you see anything odd when you went to the temple recently?"

"Like what?"

Adam gritted his teeth. "Like vampires?"

Alodius waved a wave. "Oh, them. Yeah. This one fella was at our last meetin'. Big Brother Devereaux introduced him as 'Rupert.' Seemed kind of sissy with the cane and cape and all."

Adam looked up at me. "The Count?"

I nodded. "Did you speak to him?"

The butcher shook his head. "Nope. He just kind of sat

in the back, listening. Seemed odd, since only members of the Brotherhood are allowed in the ceremonial room. But," he shrugged, "B. B. Devereaux explained the vamp belonged to a group that funded a lot of our activities."

"Did he mention the name Caste of Nod?" Adam asked.

Alodius pursed his lips. "Don't think so, but it was kind of hard to hear what with being in the back of the room and the goat's constant bleating."

Adam made a face at the goat comment and then leaned back in the chair. "Why did the Brotherhood go after Brooks?"

Alodius's face went hard. "You told me about the drag show, remember? They expected the store to be empty. Must have improvised when they found him there."

"Her," Pussy Willow whispered fiercely.

"Did the Brotherhood let you in on their original plan?" Adam asked.

The man sat up straighter in his chair. "Yessiree. After the first two calls, the Big Brothers themselves call Old Alodius into their high chamber. Said they were planning something big for All Souls' Day and they needed you there." He looked at me when he said this. "Only they had to be real careful about it, because you couldn't know you were being set up. They said next time you showed up we had to ask you about your plans. They needed to know when you'd be gone so they could set the plan in motion."

"What was this plan exactly?" Adam said.

"They was gonna bust up the shop and leave some clues to get you where they wanted you."

"Where do they want me?"

"They didn't tell me. All they'd say is they were gonna

summon Master Mahan at just after midnight on All Souls' Day."

"Summon him?" My eyebrows slammed down. "Who exactly is Master Mahan?"

"He's the almighty power behind the Brotherhood."

I craned my neck, waiting for more. But he was done. "That's it?"

He raised his palms. "They don't tell the pledges details. Supposedly all the secrets are revealed at initiation." He paused. "And thanks to you, that'll never happen now."

"You have no one to blame but yourself for that, moron. Did they mention anything about a mage? Maisie Graecus?"

He shook his head. "Nah. Although," he paused. "Now that you mention it, they said something about once you were there they could finally kill the 'the other one.'"

My heart kicked up a notch. "And that didn't concern you? Knowing they planned on murdering someone?"

He pulled his gaze south and shrugged. I stepped toward him, intent on shaking some conscience into him.

"Okay." Adam stepped in, grabbed my arm. He shot me a meaningful look that clearly commanded me to chill. I forced myself to relax and crossed my arms. "So to review: Alodius knows jack shit about what's happening except that the Brotherhood's goal was to plant evidence at the shop to make sure you show up to a ritual to summon the leader of the Caste."

"If he's the leader of the Caste, why does he have to be summoned?" I asked.

"And why do they need you there?" Adam asked. "After all, back in New York they couldn't wait to kill you, because they thought you'd stop the war and prevent Lilith's second coming. Now they need you alive for some purpose."

My head ached as I tried to follow the serpentine paths of fact versus prophecy. Basically, the Caste believed that a war between the dark races would result in Lilith returning to earth from the underworld. The Caste believed their role in assisting the goddess in her return would earn them a special place with her. In addition, they—and a few others—believed I was a prophesied Chosen who'd stop the war and usher in a period of peace between the races. That's why the Caste tried to kill me in New York, but just like Adam, I couldn't figure out why they suddenly decided I would be useful.

"I don't have a fucking clue what's going on," I said. "But I do know one thing: We're going to find out where this ritual's going down and ambush the shit out of them."

"Not that I disagree with that plan, but I really don't like the idea of strolling in there without knowing more about this summoning," Adam said. "And how are we supposed to find out where it's happening?"

"Weren't you listening?" Alodius said. "They left the clues in the shop."

My head swiveled in his direction. "Shut. Up. I've already seen what passes for clues to your Brotherhood, and they suck."

"Just trying to help."

My mouth fell open and I sputtered at him for a second before Adam spoke for me. "Why in the hell would you try to help us? You're the one who told them when to attack the shop."

He shrugged. "Figure helping might convince y'all not to kill Old Alodius."

"Unbelievable," I breathed.

"We're not going to kill you," Adam said. I hit his arm. "What? He didn't do anything but give them information."

As I reeled from that, the mage turned back to Alodius. "But I do have one question. How could you help the Brotherhood when you knew they planned on destroying your friend's business?"

The man shrugged. "Weren't no skin off this nose. They promised Big Poppa would finally be initiated as a reward. Plus, Zen ain't exactly family, and her mumbo jumbo goes against all of God's commandments."

Adam frowned at the man. "That's interesting coming from a member of a secret society that ignores that whole 'Thou shalt not kill' thing."

"Already told you the fae wasn't supposed to get hurt! They said they was just gonna knock over a few things. Besides, that boy don't look like he got one scratch on hisself."

Pussy Willow exploded forward. "*Girl, she,* and *herself!*"

I twisted around to stare at her in shock. "Easy now."

Pussy Willow pointed a long red nail at the man. "Not until he says it."

Alodius's expression became bullish. "Darlin', you got a nice rack, but dollars to donuts you're packing some meat in your drawers." He leaned back and crossed his arms. "That makes you a *he.*"

It happened fast then. Pussy Willow drew, aimed, and

cocked the gun before I could wrap my mind around what was happening.

"No!" Adam shouted, lunging. But it was too late. The gun exploded. The recoil sent Pussy Willow stumbling back, her heels squeaking against the slick linoleum. The bullet hit Alodius in the forehead. A single line of blood dripped from the blackened hole. The Cajun gasped just before his body went slack and slid to the floor.

In the aftermath, the shop was silent, but my heart hammered in my ears. Adam grabbed the weapon from Pussy. Her hands shook, and rage made her eyes glow with hatred as she stared down at the body.

"What the hell were you thinking?" Adam shouted.

"He disrespected me." She said the words like they were a simple statement of fact.

"Brooks—" I began.

"Pussy Willow!" she screamed. The dam broke. Hot, angry tears ran down her face, smearing her makeup. She swiped at her eyes, leaving black streaks of mascara behind. She looked so brittle that I immediately swallowed the lecture I'd been about to deliver.

"Hey," I said, approaching her slowly. "I'm sorry. It's just, well, I thought we weren't going to kill him."

"The mage decided that. No one asked me."

I put an arm around her shoulders. She trembled uncontrollably now.

"I've never k-killed anyone before."

Adam's anger seemed to have vanished about the time the tears started falling. He shifted uneasily on his feet and cleared his throat. Men never could handle tears from females. I guess the mage was no exception. "Adam," I said quietly. "I need you to take care of the body. Get some bleach—he probably has some in the back room—and wipe everything down. We can't have the Caste or the Brotherhood knowing we got to him first."

The mage looked so relieved to be excused that he rushed off without an argument. As I led Pussy toward the front of the store, Adam made quick work of wrapping the body in a tarp. Making sure her back was to the crime scene, I rubbed her arms. "Listen, no one blames you for what just happened. I've killed people for far lesser offenses."

She sniffed. "Really?"

I nodded. "I used to be an assassin for the Dominae. I can't even count how many people I've killed." I was lying. I knew the exact figure, but that wasn't what she needed to hear.

Her eyes widened. "Does it get any easier?"

This time I told the truth. "Yes. But there's a cost. In order to cope, you end up shutting down a part of yourself that makes you capable of empathy and connection to other people. I hope that never happens to you."

She tilted her head. "I'm not buying that."

I frowned. "What do you mean?"

"Sabina, I just killed someone you needed for information, but instead of yelling at me, you're going out of your way to make me feel better about it."

My cheeks heated at the truth of her words. I was saved from having to respond by the *clank* of a bucket hitting the ground, followed by a masculine curse. "Anyway, I think I need to go help the mancy before he bleaches his clothes. Are you going to be okay?"

She took a deep, shuddering breath. "Yeah."

I patted her arm and went to help Adam hunt down

blood splatter. The scent of bleach assaulted my nose. Grabbing a sponge from Adam, I began to scrub away bits of Alodius. As I worked, I decided Pussy Willow's assessment wasn't exactly accurate. After all, if I was so able to connect with people, why did bonding with her make me so uncomfortable I preferred to clean up a crime scene instead?

23

*A*fter dumping Alodius's body in the back of his walk-in freezer, we flashed back to Zen's courtyard. We trudged up the stairs silently, each lost in our own thoughts. At the top, Pussy Willow quietly excused herself, claiming she needed to go fix her face. I suspected she really just needed some time alone to process everything. Probably, she also couldn't face the idea of telling Zen and the others what she'd done.

When her door closed with a *click,* Adam turned to me. "What should we tell them?"

I thought over it for a moment, weighing the options. "We'll tell them I did it." When he opened his mouth to protest, I shook my head. "It'll be easier. They won't be surprised if I claim responsibility, and it'll avoid the additional drama being thrown at PW."

He smirked. "PW?"

I shrugged. "I'm cool switching to 'she' and all, but that name is a mouthful. Besides, every one needs a nickname. Right, mancy?"

He blew out a breath. "Okay, let's get this over with so we can focus on coming up with a plan."

I nodded and led the way toward the sound of voices coming from Zen's workroom. As we got closer, Giguhl's animated voice drifted through the door. "...then the Incubus said, 'Rectum? I damned near killed him!' "

I paused just outside the door, turning to Adam. "What if we don't find her in time?" The idea of facing everyone down and admitting we failed to get Maisie's location again made my stomach cramp. At least now we knew when. We just needed to figure out *where*.

Adam grabbed my hand. "Hey," he said quietly. I looked up into his familiar warm eyes. "We're close. Don't lose your nerve now."

I squared my shoulders. "You're right. Let's go."

Opening the door, I pasted a smile on my face. "Hey, guys."

Zen, Rhea, and Giguhl looked up. From the looks of things, they'd been busy trying to clean up. Zen looked up from lighting a candle on her restored altar, which featured a few new items, including 151-proof rum, iron nails, and a machete.

"How did your errand go?" Zen blew out the match.

I sighed. "Not so good, actually."

Giguhl narrowed his eyes. "What happened?"

I ran a hand over my face. "Unfortunately, we were right. Alodius was involved in the attack. He wasn't here, but he was the one feeding intel to the attackers."

"Where is he?" Zen asked, but her eyes told me she already knew the truth.

"Dead."

She crossed herself and closed her eyes.

Rhea stepped up. "Did you get any information out of him first?"

Adam filled them in on everything we knew. When he finished, Zen dropped into a chair, looking a little shell-shocked. "I still can't believe he was wrapped up in this, this Brotherhood. I've known him for years. He always seemed so friendly."

Part of me envied her ability to have faith in people. On the other hand, I couldn't believe she wasn't cursing the man's name. Because of him, her business was ruined and her friend was experiencing some major emotional trauma in the aftermath of a brutal beating.

"Regardless, we have some information to go on now. It's not much, but it's more than we had three hours ago," Rhea said.

"We should pay Erron Zorn another visit," Adam said. "Now that we know Lavinia and the Brotherhood are planning on summoning Master Mahan, any info he can give us about the Caste might help."

I sighed deeply. Once again, time was working against us.

Zen looked up. "We didn't find any other clues while we were cleaning. That must mean the picture of Maisie is the key to finding the location."

I reached into my jacket and held up the photo. Zen took it from me and we all gathered around her. "Okay, here's the plan," she said. "You and Adam pay the recreant a visit and find out what you can about the Caste. Rhea and I will scan the photo into my computer and analyze it for clues."

I felt torn, wanting to be both places at once. "You'll call the minute you find something?"

Zen and Rhea nodded. "Absolutely."

"What about Pussy Willow?" I asked. "She's pretty shaken up after everything."

Giguhl stepped forward. "I'll go check on her before I do my rounds."

I smiled at the demon. "Thanks, G." I turned to Adam. "Let's go."

The demon sun was high in the sky by the time we finally found Erron. The delay in locating him was due to a brief detour to his house. A surly little person, who it turns out wasn't a hooker at all but Erron's hairdresser, greeted us at the front door and informed us—after five minutes of arguing—that we'd find him at City Park doing his sound check. With everything else going on, I'd almost forgotten it was already Halloween and that Erron was playing Voodoo Fest.

When we finally found him in the huge park, Erron stood at the foot of a large stage overlooking an empty grassy area. Rows of oak trees flanked the green space, which, come nightfall, would be filled with thousands of Necrospank 5000 fans. In the meantime, the sun beat down on us like a drunken stepfather. Luckily, in addition to the pints I'd chugged at Alodius's shop, I'd had the forethought to toss a couple extra in Adam's backpack, because otherwise I'd have been useless for the rest of the day.

In contrast to the idyllic park setting, the air filled with the metallic, thrusting beat of industrial music. Erron stood at the foot of the stage hugging a microphone like a security blanket, rocking back and forth in a trance. Then, suddenly, his voice rose over the music like a rusty nail down a chalkboard. Other than a few "fucks," he might as well have been screaming in tongues.

I leaned toward Adam. "Someone's got some anger issues."

A smile lifted the corner of Adam's mouth, but he kept his eyes on the recreant. "Let's hope he's gotten it out of his system enough to chat."

We moved forward then to climb the stage's steps. That move gained us the attention of festival workers in yellow windbreakers who wielded walkie-talkies like weapons.

The commotion with the workers was loud enough to distract the keyboardist, who missed a couple of notes. I know that because a beat later, Erron Zorn, who until that time had been lost in his song, stopped screaming and spoke in a deadly calm voice. "Nicodemus." He didn't turn around to address his bandmate. "Do we have a problem?"

"Erron," Adam called. The lead singer's head tilted up and slowly turned. His eyes narrowed into an icy stare.

"I'm in the middle of a sound check." He said it like he fully expected us to apologize and back away slowly.

"We need your help," Adam said.

Erron smiled humorlessly. "The last time I helped you, that one"—he jerked his head toward me—"thanked me for my efforts with insults. And now you interrupt my sound check and expect me to drop everything because you have a problem? Not bloody likely." He nodded to the band. A split second later, the stage filled with the ear-splitting music again. Erron turned his back to us and started singing again as if nothing happened.

Adam nudged me with an elbow. I shot him a glare. His eyebrows rose and he pointed toward the recreant's back. I set my jaw and looked to the sky for patience, only to find the sun's cornea-searing light instead. I blinked back the tears of pain and sighed. Time to grovel. Again.

"Erron!" I yelled. My voice evaporated into the wall of sound. Gods, I did not have time for this shit. So I pulled my gun from my waistband, pointed it to the sun, and pulled the trigger five times. The music cut off abruptly as band members dove to the stage. Only Ziggy, the deaf mage drummer, remained at his station behind the drum kit. He shook his head and rolled his eyes in judgment. Meanwhile, Adam cast a freeze spell on the bouncers, who were about to tackle me from behind.

Erron's scream trailed off as he turned slowly. I'd expected another glare, but apparently gunplay amused the mage, because he smiled wryly. "You could have just tapped me on the shoulder."

I ignored his sarcasm and forged ahead with the apology to get things moving. "Look, I'm sorry if I insulted you the other night. I wasn't aware of your . . . limitations. Someone I care about was injured, and you refused to help him. But perhaps I could have been a tad more . . . diplomatic with my delivery." I paused for a breath. "Now, since your band is already distracted, would you please take a break and speak to us for a few moments?"

Erron watched me, as if pondering whether saying no would result in more gunfire. I raised an eyebrow and tapped the gun on my thigh to let him know it would.

Finally, he nodded. "Take five," he said to the band. To me he said, "Let's go to my dressing room."

Two minutes later, Adam, Erron, and I sat on stained couches in the recreant's dressing room. Serving trays on the coffee table offered an assortment of deli meats, cheeses, and Quaaludes. After Adam and I each refused his offer of drinks, he opened a bottle of top-shelf vodka he pulled from an ice bucket.

"So what's up?" Erron propped his booted feet up on the coffee table. His raven hair was expertly mussed, and he wore his trademark aviators.

"We need you to tell us everything you know about the Caste of Nod."

Erron slowly swallowed his mouthful of liquor. "How much time you got?"

"Not much," Adam said. "How about the Cliff's Notes version."

The recreant leaned forward and set the bottle on the table. "I think you two better tell me what the hell you've got yourselves mixed up in first."

"We don't have time for all that," I said. "We have it on good authority that some members of the Caste, a secret society of humans, and the leader of the vampire race are trying to summon Master Mahan here tomorrow night. So anything you can tell us that will help us defeat them and him would be great."

Erron threw back his head and laughed. Then he raised the bottle of vodka in a mocking salute. "If that's the case, I suggest you two have a drink, after all."

I frowned at him. "Why?"

"Because you might as well get drunk until it's time to kiss your asses good-bye."

"You know who he is?" Adam asked.

Erron took another sip and nodded.

Recalling my dream with the beautiful male with the bright red hair and the werewolf with the shotgun, I said, "He's a vampire, right?"

"No," the recreant said. "Not exactly."

Adam crossed his arms. Obviously the mancy was as tired of the runaround as me. "Are you going to tell us or not?"

"Master Mahan isn't a vampire." Erron leaned forward like a man about to divulge a bombshell. "But he is the father of all vampires."

My mouth fell open. I turned slowly to look at Adam. He spoke first. "Are you telling us that the leader of the Caste of Nod is Cain? As in Mark of Cain, Cain and Abel, Lilith's lover Cain, Cain?"

I started laughing before I could help myself. How gullible did this dude think we were?

Erron nodded, his expression serious. "Yes. And I could tell you all sorts of stories about him. But the only thing you need to know right now is that you cannot and will not beat him. So you either need to figure out a way to make sure the Caste doesn't summon him to New Orleans or you get the hell out of town."

"And you better stick to songwriting, mage, because fiction isn't your forte," I said. "Of anyone in the history of the dark races who I'd believe as the leader of the Caste of Nod, Cain would be the last."

"Why do you say that?"

"Because Lilith dumped his ass for a chance to marry Asmodeus and become the Queen of Irkalla. Why would Cain start a secret group who worships Lilith so much they want to bring about her second coming?"

Erron slammed his bottle on the table. "You're assuming the rumors you've heard about the prophecies are true. You're also assuming that Cain has told the truth to his followers about why he wants Lilith to return. Sabina, Cain was the first murderer in history. Do you really think he's trustworthy?"

"*If* he is the leader of the Caste, then why do so many dark-race members trust him?" Adam said. "Surely someone else would have asked those same questions by now."

Erron shrugged. "Charismatic cult leaders have convinced otherwise intelligent beings into all sorts of irrational action throughout history."

Adam ran a hand through his hair. "Okay, I think we need to back up. How do you know all of this in the first place?"

Erron leaned back in his chair. "I told you before that the Caste tried to recruit me?" We nodded. "*Recruit* might have been an understatement. Stalked me was more like it. The harassment went on for a while and I kept resisting. They escalated by beating Ziggy within an inch of his life. He recovered eventually, slowly, but his hearing never returned. And when that didn't convince me, the Caste killed the rest of the band."

Adam gasped. "Oh, my gods. The plane crash. That's what really happened?" Erron's face remained impassive, but he didn't argue. I frowned at them until Adam explained. "It was big news when it happened. The plane got caught in a storm and went down over the Atlantic."

"They were meeting me in Europe to start a tour. Ziggy was still in the hospital, and I'd gone ahead to spend some quality time with a Parisian model. The thing the news didn't report was that the entire band was made up of mages back then. No way that plane would go down with their magical abilities to save them. Something else happened."

"You believe it was the Caste's doing?"

"You have to understand, I was pretty fucked up after that," he said, lighting a cigarette. "Even though Ziggy and I had gone recreant in our youth, I tried to ask the

Hekate Council for help. Of course they denied me. Not surprising. I had already lost half my mind. The newspapers said it was 'exhaustion,' but I had a complete nervous breakdown. Anyway, long story short, once I got my mind back, I made it my mission to make the Caste pay for what it had done. Used every resource at my disposal." He exhaled a long stream of gray smoke. "Eventually, I found a group in Europe that had been documenting the Caste's supposed activities. With their help, I spent years trying to find out who their leader was.

"Eventually I found him—Cain. Back then his base of operations was a penthouse in Tokyo's Roppongi district. As I stood over his bed with a gun to his temple, he calmly said he was impressed with my dedication. Said killing my band was regrettable, but it was my own fault for being so stubborn. That did it." He paused, rubbing at his forehead. "I just snapped. Put a gun to his head and pulled the trigger."

When he paused for another drag, I realized I hadn't taken a breath since he began his story. I swallowed in some air and breathed, "What happened?"

"Nothing." Erron laughed, the sound filled with acid. He lifted a finger to his forehead like a gun. "Apple-cider bullet to the brain and the fucker just laughed at me. After that, I was so scared I flashed the fuck out of there before he could retaliate or kidnap me or whatever."

Erron took another long swig of vodka, as if the alcohol could cleanse away the lingering bitterness of the memories.

"I didn't sleep for six months after that, worried he'd show up and kill me. But eventually I realized he was done with me. It took a couple more years to get my shit together enough for a comeback tour with a new all-human band—except for Ziggy, of course."

"So Cain is immortal," Adam said.

"I don't accept that," I said. "Vampires are immortal, too, but we can still be killed. The forbidden fruit might not weaken him, but he wouldn't get very far without his head."

"But that's the rub," Erron said. "Have you read the legends about Cain?"

I scoffed. "My grandmother is the head of the vampire race. Of course I know the Cain legends."

"Not the vampire legends, Sabina. The human ones. From the Bible."

I laughed. "Of course not."

"When God punished Cain, he marked him with red hair, a symbol of his immortality. But then God took it a step further and said that anyone who managed to kill Cain would be punished sevenfold."

"What the hell does that mean?" I demanded. "You can't die seven times."

"No," Erron said. "But you and six of the people you love most can be killed and your souls doomed to eternal punishment."

I crossed my arms. "This is bullshit. We came to you for fact, not human fucking folklore."

"Sabina," Erron said, "Cain killed everyone I cared about because I turned down an invitation to his club. I don't know what you've done to gain his interest, but you need to take this threat seriously. And if I were you, I'd spend less time doubting his power and more time trying to figure out how to stop the Caste from summoning him tomorrow."

"Why would Lavinia and the Caste need to summon him?" Adam asked. Obviously the mancy bought Erron's story—or was much better at humoring psychos than me.

Erron shrugged. "Beats me." He tossed the cigarette into a half-empty beer bottle and rose. "Now your five minutes are up."

At that moment Adam's cell rang, bursting into the shocked silence like an alarm. Adam jerked to grab it, walking a few steps away to listen.

I jumped up to intercede Erron. "Just hold on a second."

Adam flipped the phone shut. "Zen said they need us to come back."

"Did they figure out where Maisie is?"

He shook his head. "She didn't elaborate, but she sounded excited. We need to go. Now."

With my adrenaline surging with hope, I turned to convince Erron to help us. "Listen, we need your hel—"

He cut me off. "No. Don't waste your breath trying to convince me to join your cause. I've faced this foe before and got my ass kicked. It's taken me too long to rebuild my life to throw it away again on a suicide mission."

"That didn't stop you the other night," Adam said, his voice low and angry.

Erron looked at him. "A fist fight with a few Caste vamps is a schoolyard rumble compared to the massacre you're courting if you don't stop this summoning. Now, I wish you the best of luck, but I have a sound check to do."

With that, Erron Zorn walked away.

"Fucking recreants," Adam muttered. Then he flashed us out of the dressing room and back to Zen's office.

Zen punched a couple of buttons and clicked the mouse until the picture of Maisie appeared on the large monitor. I took a deep breath and tried to focus on the periphery instead of at my sister's ravaged body.

Rhea pointed to a sliver of stone in the upper corner of the shot. "At first we thought that might be nothing, but then we realized it's the bottom of a stone wing."

My eyes started to sting from squinting, but the shape was indeed vaguely wingish. I pulled back a bit to get a new perspective. "And there's a foot, I think. A statue, maybe?"

"An angel," Rhea said.

I looked at Zen. "Do you recognize it?"

She shook her head. "This is a Catholic city. Angel statues are everywhere."

I made a frustrated sound, but Rhea said, "Wait for it."

Zen zoomed again. Adam grabbed my hands and squeezed. I glanced at him in time for him to breathe, "Oh, my gods."

My eyes jumped back to the screen. Beside me, Adam let out a curse that would make even Giguhl blush.

The writing said: *Requiescat in pace.*

"When we saw that, we realized that Sabina's conversation with the zombie wasn't totally wasted," Zen said.

I frowned at her. "What are you talking about?"

"You told us Kevin said 'cat piss.' " Rhea pointed to the plaque. "*Requiescat in pace.* And the other part, about the big box—maybe Stryx meant a tomb."

Adam bumped my arm. "Oh, gods, Sabina. What was the other part Kevin said?"

I was too distracted to answer. My sister was being held in a fucking tomb. In a sick way, it made perfect sense that Lavinia had Maisie hidden in one of New Orleans's Cities of the Dead. Lavinia no doubt found it amusing and somewhat inevitable that our final battle would take place among so many symbols of mortality.

"Sabina?" Adam prodded.

I shook myself out of my morbid thoughts to answer. "Something about 'Master, come,' and then"—I paused, my eyes shooting to his knowing gaze—"Oh, my gods. All this time I thought he was saying my last name. But he was really telling us Master Mahan's true name."

Rhea and Zen exchanged a confused look. "I think you two better start talking." Rhea said. "What exactly did the recreant tell you?"

I was so busy cussing at myself that Adam filled them in on Erron's revelations about the leader of the Caste.

"Gods," Rhea said when he finished. "Orpheus is going to have a stroke when he hears this."

"But before we figure out how to stop the summoning," Zen said, "we have to figure out which cemetery they're keeping Maisie in."

"Well," Adam began slowly. "At least we know she's in

a cemetery, right? That should narrow things down." As much as I appreciated him trying to put a positive spin on things, I couldn't muster even a forced smile.

Zen clicked the mouse and the image zoomed out again. "I wish I shared your optimism," she began. "Do you have any idea how many cemeteries there are in greater New Orleans?"

Adam shrugged. "A dozen?"

Zen shook her head. "More like forty." As that sunk in with the weight of lead, she continued. "Some we can rule out immediately—like Holt Cemetery, the one Sabina and I were at the other night—but that's maybe a handful. There's no way we could search the remaining thirty or so by tomorrow night. And even if we could, we don't have any way of knowing which crypt she's in."

Hearing the odds laid out in such intimidating numbers made my heart sink.

"There has to be a way. Lavinia wants Sabina to find this place." Rhea tapped the screen. "It would take all the fun out of it for her if she failed. We must have missed something."

Zen leaned back in her seat. "I'm inclined to agree with you, but I'm not seeing anything else in this photo that could point us to the exact place."

She looked at Adam for confirmation. He hesitated and then shook his head. "I don't see anything else, either."

My fist slammed into the desktop, making the monitor jump. "I don't accept that!"

Three pairs of solemn eyes looked at me with something bordering on pity. Rhea touched my shoulder. "Sabina—"

I shook her off. "No. Don't tell me to calm down. We're too close to getting her back to give up."

"No one's saying we should give up," Rhea said, ever the voice of reason. "We just need to come at this from another angle."

"Right. Maybe Rhea and Zen missed something when they cleaned the shop," Adam said. "We can split up and scour the whole building."

I ran a hand through my hair. "For what, Adam? It's not like they left a brochure for the cemetery lying around. Lavinia wouldn't want it to be that easy."

"But you said it yourself, she wants you to find this place. There has to be another clue, and right now all we have is this picture to go on."

I took a deep breath. "You're right. I'm sorry."

"You know what?" Rhea said. "Enough with this guesswork. I say we try to find Maisie using the best tools at our disposal." When Adam and I stared at her blankly, she smiled. "Magic."

"I already thought of that," Adam said. He pointed to the picture and the cuffs binding Maisie's hands. "The brass makes it impossible to trace her, because it blocks her energy."

Rhea shook her head. "Not a tracking spell."

"Are you saying there's some voodoo spell that might work?" I asked, glancing at Zen.

"Nope. Voodoo isn't good for this kind of thing. I think Rhea's talking about something Hekatian," Zen said.

"Not precisely." The silver-haired mage squinted at me as she chewed at her lip. "More like something Chthonic."

I shook my head before she finished the word. "No way. Zen, you saw what happened with the zombie. Tell her she's crazy."

Zen rose from her chair and went to a bookshelf against

the wall. "The revenant rose because I didn't know I needed to adjust the spell. If someone had told me in advance that you were a Chthonic, the whole thing could have been avoided." She paused to shoot a pointed look at us before she continued searching the shelves.

"What exactly do you have in mind?" Adam asked.

Rhea joined Zen at the bookshelves. Together they scanned the rows. A couple of seconds later, both made little "Aha" sounds and reached for the same book.

"Here it is," Zen said, taking the book from Rhea's hands. She blew across the surface of the leather binding. Dust plumed up like smoke. She coughed and waved away the cloud. "This book belonged to my grandfather. He was an energy manipulator like Adam, but he had an extensive library of magical texts."

Rhea went to look over her shoulder while Zen flipped through the pages. Finally, she stopped and opened the book wider. She pointed to something on the page and Rhea's eyes lit up. "Hmm."

"Yeah?" Zen said. The two females seemed to forget Adam and I were in the room. "I'd need to get some friends here to help, but I think it'll work."

"She'll need a focus," Rhea said slowly. "Something to tether her to this plane."

"Hello?" I said. "I'm right here?"

"How about Adam?" Zen offered. "He's powerful enough to handle the magical output, and their connection is strong."

Adam cleared his throat and shifted uneasily beside me. I avoided his eyes but began tapping my foot.

Still, they ignored us. "It'd be nice if we had something of Maisie's, too," Rhea said.

"Guys!" I raised my voice. "Not that you bothered to ask me, but I do have something of Maisie's."

They both looked up as if suddenly remembering they had company. "Oh?" Rhea said.

I held up my sister's amulet by its chain. "Now will you please tell us what the hell's going on?"

Later, there'd be plenty of time to regret this. But for the moment, I didn't care about the inevitability of penance owed. Zen and Rhea promised this would work, and I trusted them.

Adam leaned in close, setting off a flurry of flapping wings in my stomach. A halo of candlelight glowed around his head. I swallowed and tried to focus on the soothing drums from outside the circle. The beat braided through the small room, surrounding us with its own kind of magic.

Zen's friends had arrived half an hour earlier. Four black women varying in ages from late twenties to an octogenarian with milky eyes riddled with cataracts. They'd brought with them two young males, who drummed in the corner. Zen and Adam quickly filled them in on the plan while Rhea tried to soothe my worries by explaining exactly what was going to happen. I was surprised anyone had been able to reach the store with the sea of Halloween revelers clogging up all the French Quarter's avenues. This ritual must be something special for all of them to miss one of the biggest holidays New Orleans had to offer.

The plan was for me to astral project, using Maisie's necklace as a homing beacon to track down her location, or more specifically, the smear of her blood on the box in the picture. Rhea explained it wasn't so different from interspatial travel, except my physical body would remain fixed while my soul made the trek. I didn't exactly love the idea of my soul leaving my body, but she assured me every precaution would be taken to ensure my safe return. Which was why Adam sat inside the circle with me. He was to act as my anchor, a lifeline should I have trouble finding my body again.

"Relax," he whispered. His breath tickled my ear, sending a shiver down my spine.

I blew out a long, slow exhale and willed my shoulders to relax. Hard to do when my heart insisted on pounding a staccato beat in my chest. He took my clammy hand in his warm palm. His eyes met mine, and a small smile flirted with his lips. "Do you trust me?"

I swallowed, my throat clicking from dryness and nerves. "Yeah." The word was so quiet, I wondered if he heard me. When the smile widened, I knew he had. He moved closer, so close I could feel the heat of him on my face. My lips parted—

"We must hurry," Zen said. "Once the portal is open, you will only have a few minutes. If we can't hold it long enough for you to return, Adam will pull you back."

Adam winked at me before pulling away. He mirrored my posture—a half-lotus position—and placed his hands over my upturned palms. Just beyond his shoulder, I saw Rhea watching silently, ready to lend aid if magical intervention was needed.

For a moment, I regretted Giguhl's absence. But I felt better knowing we had a demon keeping watch in case Lavinia or the Brotherhood decided to make another house call. Adam squeezed my hand, refocusing my attention on the present.

"Good," Rhea said. "The physical connection between you and Adam must not waver or the tether could be broken."

I swallowed, my eyes not leaving Adam's as I spoke to Zen. "Won't my body go slack once my spirit leaves?"

"No," she said. "Your body will enter a trancelike state. You'll remain in that pose until your soul returns."

I nodded slightly, careful not to let my gaze wander from Adam's. The intimacy of staring into his eyes for such an extended period should have made me want to squirm. Instead, I felt grounded, safe.

"All right, let's begin," Zen said.

The women in the circle began swaying, chanting. Candlelight flickered in my peripheral vision. The drums picked up tempo, the rhythm pulsing through the floor and up through me, into my chest.

"Close your eyes and breathe deeply," Zen said.

With one last look at Adam, I allowed my lids to drift closed. My breath came in on long, slow inhales. The scent of herb-infused smoke spiced the air. It filled my belly, rounding it, before I pushed it back up and out to the count of five.

The hair on the back of my neck tingled, signaling a rise of power. Unlike a magical circle cast to protect or bind those inside it, this one felt more like a door had opened. Air rushed through the room, bringing with it the scents of rich soil, black iron, fresh blood—the perfume of the underworld.

"Keep breathing. Focus. See Maisie's face, call to her." Zen's voice rose above the increasingly frenetic chants of her comrades.

I blocked out everything but the whoosh of air into my

nose. The deep, vibrating rush of exhalation. Maisie's image appeared in my mind. She wore ceremonial robes: the traditional Greek chiton she wore for Hekate Council meetings and rituals. Her red-and-black hair was pulled back into an elegant chignon at the nape of her neck.

Maisie? Can you hear me?

A few more breaths. The vision in my head smiled and beckoned me with a raised hand. A faint sensation tickled the edge of my brain. My pulse quickened, but I kept my breathing even.

Maisie, show me where you are. Help me find you.

My body swayed in circles, like a compass trying to find true north. In my head, the image of Maisie shifted, morphed. Now her hair stuck out wildly around her head. Smudges of dirt and blood marred her face, her chiton. I knew on some level I was now seeing Maisie as she was the night Lavinia took her. The specter in my head raised a hand, beckoning me to follow.

A deep hum pulsed through me, tugged gently at my cells. The image in my head wavered. I knew if I surrendered I'd lose her for good. My breaths were incredibly deep now, and after the next exhalation, I released my soul to the air. A faint *pop*, a contraction. And then, like mist, I rose from my body.

I looked around, through the iridescent shimmer of the portal, and saw my body surrounded by a deep red aura. Adam still sat across from me, his eyes open and staring intently at my absolutely still form. His aura glowed dark blue shot through with tendrils of gold. Where our hands met, our energies combined and rose in sparkling ribbons of deep purple and gold.

All around us, bodies undulated in hypnotic movements, their mouths moving in sync as they chanted and their auras flashing every color of the rainbow. Zen's energy ring stood out among the hues, a flashy silver. And in the corner, a halo of golden saffron hugged Rhea's body.

Sound was different now. The chants and drums reached my ears slowly, distorted as if filtered through water.

Sabina.

The weak call gained my full attention. I lifted my face and flew upward until the ceiling gave way to starry night sky.

When I was young, I always wished I could fly. I dreamt of taking wing over cities and fields and oceans. I prayed to the Great Mother Lilith to help me soar away from the life I'd been born into. Eventually, time passed and I grew resigned to never knowing that kind of liberation.

But right then, as my spirit rose high above Bourbon Street, yearning for the thin sliver of moon, I knew real freedom. Far below, miniature costumed humans cele-brated and danced alongside colorful floats. Tiny orange lights dotted the cityscape—pumpkins set out for mortal trick-or-treat rituals. Beyond the city lights, the dark waters of the Mississippi beckoned me with their secrets. Something niggled at the back of my consciousness. Some preoccupation I couldn't quite recall.

Pushing the urge to remember aside, I flew. Flew so fast the world ceased to be more than streaks of color. I spun and weaved through the air, separated from mun-dane sensation by a whisper-thin sheet of shimmering magic. Unlike the times I traveled magically in my body, no cold wind froze me now. No vertigo unsettled me.

Instead, the air was calm and warm. I felt centered and at peace. No pain could reach me here.

I'm not sure how long I simply indulged my desire to soar, but soon a deep, nagging awareness caught my attention. Like a muted pounding on a thick door. Or drums pulsating in my chest.

To the northwest, a pixel of light throbbed in time to the sound. Drew me to it like a magnet. Almost as soon as I set my thoughts on discovering the source of the light, I flew toward it, as if thought alone had willed me toward the destination. And when I saw the patch of green punctuated with rectangles of gray, my purpose rushed back to me.

Maisie.

I looked around, trying to recognize landmarks or signposts that might clue me in to the location. Just beyond the cemetery was a large expense of green space—a park? Spotlights swung wildly through a canyon formed between tall oaks. Thousands of tiny human shapes undulated far below to music I couldn't hear. But if I had to guess, the song sounded a lot like rusty nails and bitterness. Ironic that we'd been so close to this cemetery just a few short hours earlier.

Pulling my thoughts from Erron Zorn and missed opportunities, I focused on taking note of landmarks. At the far end of the cemetery, a large stone building capped with a colorful dome loomed. A major road ran in front of the building, while residential streets bordered the three remaining sides of the cemetery.

The light below tugged at me, drawing me down toward the earth. My spectral feet touched grass, but the sheet of magic kept me from registering any sensation. Now the vaults I'd viewed from above rose above me. And straight ahead, as if someone had held a black light to a splotch of white paint, my sister's blood glowed brightly on a slab of stone.

More a box than a tomb, the structure rose only to hip height. Just large enough to accommodate a single coffin.

Until that moment, I'd held out hope that we'd been wrong. That even Lavinia wasn't sadistic enough to imprison Maisie in a crypt. But now I understood my grandmother's cruelty knew no bounds.

Instead of running, my feet swished just above the ground as I moved swiftly toward the light's source. Finally, I stood before the tomb and reached out with my transparent hands. Only instead of grasping the stone, they passed through it. I tried again, focusing this time. Still useless.

I cried out. "Maisie!"

I bent over the tomb and listened. Called out again. No response. Then I realized that if my hands had passed through the solid form, then maybe my voice also passed through visceral reality. Like a ghost.

If I'd been in my corporeal from, my chest would have tightened with pain. To be so close to Maisie yet unable to free her was torture. Since I couldn't cry from the pain of it, my spirit contracted, grew heavier.

"Maisie," I said, my face bent over the lid. "We're coming for you. Please be strong."

"She can't hear you."

I reared up and spun. Out of instinct, my hand reached for a weapon that wasn't there. An orb floated several feet away, pulsating hotly. Every instinct in my body told me to turn and get as far away from it as quickly as possible. I tensed for flight when it spoke again.

"You've never been a coward. Why start now?"

My heart turned to ice, and my feet suddenly felt encased in concrete. Slowly, knowing beyond reason I hadn't imagined the familiar voice, I turned. Instead of the radiant orb, the silhouette of a man materialized.

He leaned against the wall of a crypt. I say leaned, but he was far from solid. His body shimmered with translucence, but I would have recognized that frown anywhere.

"David?" I breathed.

"What's wrong, Sabina? Aren't you happy to see me again?"

I've seen lots of fucked-up shit in my life. Hard not to when one spent the majority of their life killing for a living. Of course, since my family tree is filled with vampires and mages, and one of my best friends is a demon, one might also imagine running into a ghost wouldn't be a big deal. But considering this particular specter was the ghost of a friend I'd murdered, I was having some trouble not pissing myself, metaphorically speaking.

"David?" I repeated stupidly.

He spread his arms wide. "In the flesh, so to speak."

Thinking was like wading through oatmeal. I looked around for some sort of clue about what I was supposed to say or do. But the silent crypts weren't offering up any etiquette tips. "How? Why?"

The apparition crossed his arms. "The how doesn't matter. Not really."

"And the why?" My voice sounded thick.

A smile quirked the corner of his lips—an odd sight on a nearly transparent man. "Before I tell you why I'm here, we need to get a few things straight."

"I'm listening."

He moved closer. His legs didn't move, though. His body just kind of glided above the grass. I clenched my jaw against the instinct to run again. Then I remembered I wasn't in my body and my astral form probably looked a lot like his right then. He finally stopped a couple of feet away.

"First, you need to know I am not here because I want to be. You're the last person I'd be helping if I had a choice."

Not a surprise, really. I swallowed the fear clogging my throat and nodded.

"And don't ask who sent me. You wouldn't believe me anyway."

I might be confused and shocked, but I wasn't an idiot. "Tell me anyway. Just for kicks."

The corner of his mouth twitched. "She said you'd demand to know." He shrugged in a suit-yourself gesture. "Lilith sends her regards."

My mouth fell open, but he continued on as if he hadn't just dropped an epic bombshell on my ass.

"Second, this is really happening. Your sister is inside that box."

"Wait a second," I interrupted. "*Lilith* sent you?"

He nodded impatiently in a yes-we've-covered-this way. "Why?"

He rolled his eyes. "Sabina, she's the Queen of Irkalla. We don't question her motives without serious repercussions."

"No, I mean why send you?"

He crossed his arms. "Instead of Vinca, you mean?"

That stopped me. David died before I'd ever met Vinca. If they'd met in Irkalla I highly doubted it was just a coincidence.

"Lilith thought you'd spend too much time blubbering to the nymph about being sorry you got her killed to listen."

I tried to sort through the flurry of questions scrambling to get out. But before I could choose one, he interrupted. "Look, we don't really have time to play twenty questions right now. Soon that mage of yours is going to panic and pull you back."

"I'm so confused right now."

He shot me a look. "All you have to do is listen. Can you handle that?" He paused until I nodded. Then he smiled at me, like he was going to enjoy sharing his message. "Lavinia is really going to summon Cain here tomorrow."

I squinted at him. "That's your news?"

He grimaced. "Let me finish. You're going to have to make some tough choices tomorrow night. Choose unwisely and all will be lost."

My stomach cramped. "What are the right choices?"

He shrugged. "That's the wrong question."

I clenched my fists in frustration. "What's the right one?"

"The correct question is: Can you have it both ways?"

"Godsdammit, David. Enough with this cryptic bullshit."

"There's something else," he said, ignoring my growing agitation. "The human told you the summoning would happen at midnight?"

I didn't bother questioning how he knew what Alodius told me. "Yeah."

"He was wrong. That's what they told him to tell you. Lavinia knew you were smart enough to figure out his involvement. If you show up at midnight, Cain will already be here and all will be lost."

I sighed from so deep in my chest that it took a good five seconds to clear all the air. "What exactly is Cain's plan for me?"

"Sorry, babe. I can't tell you that. There's rules about these things. But I can tell you that there will be repercussions for years from your choices tomorrow night. And more battles to come before this all plays out. That is, if you survive, which, let's face it, would take a miracle at this point."

Pushed past the limits of patience, I threw my fist at his nose. Only instead of making contact, it passed through his face with a sickening frigid sensation. His mocking laughter was one insult too many. "You're an asshole."

"Nice. You killed me, but *I'm* the asshole."

I sighed. "Look, David, you have to know if I had it all to do over again—"

A slow smile spread across his lips. "You'd have done the same thing." I frowned and opened my mouth to argue, but he held up a hand. "Let's not bullshit each other, Sabina. There's powerful forces at play right now. Things bigger than the both of us. Whether you'd killed me or not, you'd still be in the middle of it."

I shook my head. I didn't deserve to be let off the hook. "You don't know that."

He tilted his head and regarded me with a mixture of pity and regret. "Actually, I know it for a fact. Like it or not, we're all just fate's pawns." He looked up at the sky for a moment. Wind rushed through the clearing, too chill even for October. A tunnel of shimmering magic formed over us. "It's time to go."

"Wait, I have more questions."

He shook his head. "I'm all out of answers. Bye, Sabina."

I opened my mouth to call out, but suddenly the wind reversed direction, creating a vacuum. The force sucked my soul up and into the tunnel. I screamed, struggling to stay. To demand David give me more answers. But the pull was too strong.

Colors swirled and danced around me in fast-forward. Warped sound assaulted my ears. Then, before I knew it, my soul crashed back into my body like a comet. The impact forced a gasp from my lungs. My eyes flew open. A scream ripped from my chest, "David!"

25

Cool liquid splashed over my raw vocal cords, soothing the heat left from my impression of a B-grade horror actress. With each breath, the herbal-fresh-purple scent of the lavender oil Rhea applied to my temples slowed my pulse. But as much as I appreciated the aromatherapy and the water, what I really wanted was to be alone. To have some time to gather my thoughts and weigh options. To collect myself before I had to talk. But judging from the eager stares pressing in on me and the tension thickening the air, privacy was a luxury I couldn't afford.

When the final drop of water hit my tongue, Rhea took the glass away. Before the meager mouthful worked its way to the back of my throat, the questions had begun. I tried to keep my tone even and relay everything I remembered with cool detachment. It wasn't easy, though, and before long the strain of little sleep, exposure to the sun earlier that day, astral projection, emotional upheaval, and good old-fashioned stress caught up with me. By the time I finished, my throat was hoarse and clogged with unshed tears.

Adam took my palm and squeezed it. "She's going to be all right, Sabina. We'll get her back."

Giguhl patted my back. He'd come in after Zen asked her voodoo pals to give us some privacy. "You did good, Red."

Pussy Willow walked in with the map Zen asked her to fetch. She handed it to me with a small smile. Shadows under her eyes hinted at fatigue, but I was glad to see she'd emerged from her rooms.

I unfolded the map with clumsy, shaking hands. Finally, I managed to spread it across the floor between Adam and me.

"The cemetery is right next to City Park." I ran my finger over the map, trying to retrace my path in two dimensions. I circled an area. "Somewhere in here."

Zen lifted the map to get a closer look. "There are six cemeteries within a mile of the park." She pointed to a spot on the map. "We can rule out Metairie Cemetery, because that's across the interstate. And this here," she moved her finger, "is Holt Cemetery."

Remembering the name from our visit there, I shook my head. "Definitely wasn't that place. All the tombs were aboveground." Then I remembered the detail I'd forgotten to mention. "There's a large building set at one end, like it's connected somehow. Looked kind of like a government building."

PW frowned. "Did it have a dome?"

"Yes."

"I'll be damned," Zen breathed.

"What is it?" Rhea asked. Everyone leaned in, eager to hear Zen's answer.

She waved the map in the air triumphantly. "They've got her in the Guild Society Cemetery."

On the heels of that announcement, several different reactions filtered through the room. Giguhl and PW high-fived each other, Zen crossed herself, and Adam and I shared a confused look.

"I hate to be a downer, but are you sure?" Adam asked.

Zen nodded eagerly. "Yes, the Guild Temple of Philosophy and Art has a cemetery behind it for members and their families."

"Why would the Brotherhood use a cemetery owned by another secret society to hide a prisoner?" he continued. "Alodius acted like they didn't think too highly of other fraternal orders."

"Unless," Giguhl said, "The BBEM and this Guild Society are one and the same?"

The room fell silent as we all pondered the possibility. "But I know some of the members of that lodge," Zen said finally. "They do all sorts of charity work. After Katrina hit, they raised a ton of money for displaced families."

"Yeah, and Alodius seemed like a great guy on the surface," I said. "Face it, Zen, people have all sorts of secrets. Especially, I would imagine, people who join secret societies."

"Look," Zen said, "that might be true, but does it really matter? We know where Maisie is now."

"Actually, it matters a lot if Guild Society sects throughout the world are all working with the Caste," Adam replied.

"You sound like one of those wacko conspiracy theorists," Zen said.

"Zenobia, a secret Brotherhood trashed your property and almost killed your friend. Do you really deny that some serious conspiracy is afoot here?"

She pursed her lips. "You have a point."

"Okay, I think it's time to table the theories for now and focus on next steps," Rhea said. "We need to take all of this information to Orpheus and the Queen."

I'd known this moment would come, but that didn't make it any easier to swallow. "There's no time. We need to go in tonight."

Adam's gaze shot toward me. "Why tonight?"

"David said that Lavinia wanted us to show up after she'd summoned Cain. If we wait too long, he'll already be here when we go in."

Rhea shook her head. "Not possible. Too many logistics need to be sorted out first. And as much as I know you hate asking for permission, Orpheus and the Queen deserve to have a say in the decision."

"Besides," Giguhl said. "No offense, Red, but you look like warmed-over death."

I frowned at my minion. "Thanks, G."

"Just sayin'." He shrugged.

The stubborn set to Zen's chin told me that arguing would only make her dig in more. So I switched tactics. "Is there any way to talk to them without going back to court? Some sort of magical conference call that would speed this up?"

PW spoke up. "Or we could, you know, use computers like the good Lord intended."

Adam stood and helped me up. "Rhea, call Orpheus and tell him to get himself and the Queen in front of a computer STAT."

*   *   *

Thirty minutes later, Rhea wrapped up her debriefing of the situation to Orpheus and the Queen. Adam sat next to his aunt, occasionally clarifying points or answering questions. I stood behind Adam like a spectator. We'd agreed, given the Queen's dislike of me, that it would be best for the mages to take point on the discussion.

"Judging from the evidence you've presented," Orpheus began. He stood next to the Queen, who sat in a throne at the head of a conference table made from burled wood. Apparently the treehouse court had state-of-the-art conferencing and computer systems, because it took no time for them to pop up on Zen's computer. "The best course of action would be for you to sit tight tonight. We will send a contingent of Pythian Guards and Fae Knights to assist you in the attack tomorrow at midnight."

I tensed but kept my mouth shut. Adam shifted uneasily. "Sir, with all due respect, I feel that any delay on our part would not be advisable. Lavinia is expecting us at midnight. Why not attack tomorrow afternoon or at sundown at the latest?"

Zen spoke up from her position next to me. "Actually, during the day won't work, either. Tomorrow is November 1—the Day of the Dead. The cemeteries will be full of families leaving flowers on the graves of their relatives. Some cemeteries even host masses completed with brass band parades, second lines, and picnics. If you try to attack before the cemetery closes at sundown, you'll risk human casualties and/or police intervention."

"Which means Orpheus's plan is still the best option," Queen Maeve said. "Draw up a list of supplies you'll need and we'll send them with the team tomorrow."

Almost as soon as she stopped talking, Adam was ready with a rebuttal. "While I agree that waiting until dark is probably the best option, I really think we—"

"Who asked you to think?" the Queen snapped. "We have made our decision."

My gut clenched for Adam. How dare that bitch belittle him like that? I jumped in. "It's the wrong decision," I said in a loud, clear voice.

The Queen's eyes widened. "You dare?"

"Sabina," Adam said.

"No, this is bullshit. We told you what David said—"

"David? You mean the ghost you supposedly saw who claimed he was sent by the goddess Lilith?" the Queen snorted. "Surely you don't expect us to make battle plans based on a hallucination."

My mouth fell open. "You'd rather make plans based on the lies of a human who conspired against us, then?"

"Sabina," Orpheus said. "Stand down."

"No, I—"

"Sabina," Adam gritted out. The tension in his tone told me I was only making things worse. Onscreen, the Queen's expression went permafrost.

With a tight jaw, Adam spoke quickly. "She meant no offense, Your Magnificence. We're all a little tense."

"Yes, well, I'm sorely tempted to demand she be taken off the mission altogether for her insolence," the Queen said.

I tensed to speak again, but Zen grabbed my hand in warning. I looked up at her and she shook her head hard. "Trust Adam," she whispered so low I barely heard it.

"I'll keep her in line," Adam said. My stomach tightened at his words. But then my ears registered his tone of voice. Was it me, or did I detect some trademark Lazarus irony?

"Fine," Maeve said. "Now, I'm sending the captain of my guard, Ilan. He will lead the attack."

"What?" Adam barked. The Queen's eyes narrowed. "Your Magnificence," he said, recovering smoothly. "Ilan is a proud and capable warrior, but I'm concerned his lack of involvement in the mission thus far might not make him the best choice of lead."

"I suppose you feel you should have the honor?" The Queen said. "Doubtful you can handle both that and keeping the mixed-blood in line. She seems quite a handful."

Orpheus spoke up. "Adam is one of my most trusted Pythian Guards. His knowledge of the complexity of the situation makes him the obvious choice."

The Queen waved an insolent hand indicating her agreement. "Fine. Now that that's settled, we have some news." Maeve shifted in her throne with excitement. "Ever since we discovered Tanith was telling the truth about Maisie's whereabouts, we've been in talks. In fact, we're quite close to finalizing a peace accord. The only roadblock we face is that Lavinia is still alive. As long as she remains so, she is still the de facto leader of the vampire race."

The Queen let that hang in the air for a couple of seconds. "Therefore we will need you to ensure Lavinia Kane dies tomorrow night."

I let out the breath I didn't know I'd been holding. On some level, I'd been expecting her to say we couldn't kill Lavinia, after all.

Adam nodded. "Not a problem. That's on our list of things to do."

"You misunderstand," she said. "Killing Lavinia will be your sole priority."

Adam's head snapped up. "I don't follow." His tone clearly implied he followed perfectly well but rejected the implications. Couldn't blame him, since I felt like she'd just sucker-punched us.

In a bored tone Queen Maeve said, "Let me spell it out for you: If it comes down to a choice, you will sacrifice Maisie Graecus to kill Lavinia Kane."

"What?" Orpheus gasped. "We didn't discuss this!"

My fists clenched so hard the skin of my palms split open. At the desk, Adam's shoulders went rock hard and the muscles of his neck corded into knots.

Maeve's response to Orpheus dripped with ice. "I do not need your leave to make orders."

"You do when your decisions doom my people to death. I demand you rescind your order."

The Queen speared the High Councilman with an icy stare. "You forget yourself, mage. At present you are little more than a beggar at my door. I have tolerated your opinions as far as I am willing." She rose. "Lavinia dies. It is the only way to ensure the war you couldn't prevent yourself doesn't come to fruition. I hope the girl makes it, but not as much as I want to end the threat Lavinia poses to all members of the dark races."

Orpheus was red-faced and panting. A parade of strong emotions marched across his face as he struggled to find an appropriate response. Watching the drama unfold onscreen, I felt like a voyeur to his shame.

The air in the office was so thick with tension it was hard to breathe. I stepped forward and put a hand on Adam's shoulder. His hand came up to grab mine, his grip so tight I winced. We might all have a stake in this, but Adam was watching his boss and mentor get emasculated in public. And Orpheus's next move could well dictate all our fates.

"What say you, mage?" the Queen said finally. "Will we remain allies, or will you let your conscience deprive you of both sense and shelter?"

Finally, Orpheus cleared his throat. Only instead of puffing up like a man about to tell someone to go fuck themselves, his shoulders sagged with surrender. "We remain allies," he whispered finally.

"A wise choice," the Queen said. "Lazarus, you have your ord—"

It happened fast. Adam leapt from the chair with a roar. By the time I pulled him away, his fist was a bloody mess and the computer screen lay smoking and mangled on the floor. Along with his illusions.

26

The Halloween party on Bourbon Street raged late into the night. I stood at the attic window, watching people dressed as vampires, demons, wizards, faeries, and were-wolves stagger around on the street below. To them Halloween was a time for make-believe. For tricks and treats. For costumes and party decorations.

Little did they know the beings they pretended to be weren't just the stuff of myths, folklore, or fiction. And the reality of our world was a far cry from silly masquerades and street parties.

In fact, this Halloween in particular marked either the dawn of our salvation or the eve of our destruction.

I snorted at my maudlin thoughts and turned away from the window. Staring out windows was no way to make life decisions. So I went to clean my guns instead.

After Adam's freakout, I'd allowed Rhea to take him away for a chat. Part me of me wanted to fight her for that role, but given my own brittle state of mind at the time, I was in no position to help Adam calm down.

I scrubbed a hand over my face and pulled out my cleaning supplies. I laid out my weapons on the table: my specially made handgun with a handful of vampire-killing apple bullets, two mundane Glocks, a couple of daggers with applewood handles. Not nearly enough for the battle tomorrow. But the same bitch who'd just casually discarded my sister's life as unimportant was also sending enough weapons and manpower to ensure we had a fighting chance of saving it.

How did things get so fucking complicated? On one hand, my gut told me I should ignore my disgust over the leaders' priorities and focus on using their resources to achieve my own goals. I'd just have to use every resource at my disposal to save my sister and ensure Lavinia Kane died before she could summon Cain. Not an easy agenda, but it beat facing off with Lavinia armed with nothing but a few weapons and a bad attitude.

On the other hand, I'd be a fool not to face reality. Even with the Fae Knights and Pythian Guard as backup, Lavinia had the advantage. No doubt about it. So my other option was to go tonight to save my sister. Lavinia wasn't expecting us until tomorrow, and from what I'd seen in my astral projection, the tomb was totally unguarded. If I left now, I could be in and out in less than an hour. Then we could go in with guns blazing tomorrow and not have to worry about Maisie getting caught in any actual or political crossfire.

But, if I had a third hand, I'd remind myself that that kind of thinking was totally Old Sabina. The angry one who worked alone. The rebellious one who ignored potential consequences to do what suited her own purposes. The lonely one who didn't trust anyone. Hadn't I learned yet that I was at my best when I allowed myself to depend on those who'd proven themselves trustworthy?

Adam and Giguhl had saved my ass more than once. They'd supported me through some pretty low times and high-fived me after victories. They were more than my friends. They'd become just as much my family as Maisie, maybe more in some ways.

I smiled as memories of our exploits played like a highlight reel through my head. As I did, the tang of cleaning solvent tightened my nostrils. With methodical strokes, I wiped down all the components. I guess Giguhl and Adam were a lot like my weapons now. I wouldn't enter a fight without some firepower. And now I couldn't imagine sneaking out without letting them in on the plan.

The door opened and the mancy strolled in as if my thoughts had summoned him. When he saw me, he stopped abruptly, as if he hadn't been expecting to see me. His high color hinted at embarrassment, too. After all, the last time I saw him he was murdering a computer.

"Hey," I said softly. I shoved the gun back into the bag. My stomach dropped the minute he walked in. Seeing the lines of tension on his face made my protective instincts go into hyperdrive. "How are you?"

"Fine." He walked forward and grabbed his backpack from the armchair. He seemed to dismiss me completely as he rummaged through it.

"Want to talk about it?"

"Not really." He didn't look up.

I sighed. "Adam, please just talk to me."

When he looked up, the heat in eyes was so intense I had to look away. I'd seen Adam angry before, but nothing like the rage rolling off him in hot waves. "Why? So you can tell me you were right?"

I frowned. "Right about what?"

"When we started this mission, you questioned the leaders' motives. But I, being the good little Pythian Guard, chanted the party line like it was our fucking salvation." He laughed bitterly. "Guess the joke was on me all along."

I walked to him and squatted next to the chair. "You listen to me," I said, forcing him to look at me. "This isn't about who's right or wrong. It's beyond that now. The truth is Orpheus did what he had to do as the leader of the mage race."

Adam jumped up so fast I fell back on my ass. Towering over me, he yelled, "How can you defend him? You, of all people?" He jabbed a finger in the air. "Maisie is your sister."

I clenched my teeth and rose to face the mancy. "Look, Adam, I know I'm not always the most level-headed person around. I've certainly done my share of yelling and bitching about the unfairness of this situation. But you know what? That shit won't save Maisie." I poked at his chest with a finger. "It fucking sucks that Orpheus didn't stand up to that bitch. But what choice did he have? Fuck up his alliance with her on the off chance we might have to make a choice between Lavinia and Maisie? She'd turn every mage out on the streets if he did that."

"Whatever," Adam said. He raised his chin. "I won't be a pawn for the Queen like Orpheus. Maybe Erron was right to go recreant."

I crossed my arms. "So what are you gonna do, mancy? Walk away to prove a point? Leave Maisie behind and let Lavinia win because Orpheus made a shitty decision?"

His gaze shifted guiltily.

I forged ahead. "You're the one always telling me to use my head. So when are you going to start using yours?"

His eyes narrowed. "So what? I'm supposed to sit around and take orders from the Queen's fucking captain? Because don't fool yourself. The minute Orpheus bent over for Maeve tonight, Ilan earned the right to call the shots tomorrow."

I got in his space. "No, you ass, I expect you to remember that you're not alone in all this. We're a godsdamned team, remember?"

He stared me down for a moment. Then his lip twitched. "You really need to work on your pep-talk skills, Red."

"Yeah, well, you need to remember your place. Where's the calm, level-headed Adam I've come to depend on? I'm supposed to be the surly nihilistic one, remember?"

Before I knew what hit me, he'd wrapped his big arms around me for a hug. I embraced him back for a few moments, savoring the feel of him. Offering him the comfort he needed but wouldn't ask for outright. Finally, he whispered, "I don't know how we're going to win this one, Red."

My mind chose that moment to offer up the image of Adam lying still and pale as he bled in the cemetery after the Caste vamp attack. The cold fist of remembered panic clenching my throat, I swallowed hard. "Me neither."

It was one thing to talk about logic and bravery and spout trite motivational speeches. It was something else to have Adam touching me and know these might be our last moments alone. Ever.

There was time to discuss plans tomorrow, but now I

had something more important to discuss with him. "Adam," I began, my voice hoarse. "I need you to promise me something."

He held my gaze, his thumb stroking my cheek. "Anything."

"No matter what happens tomorrow, we won't lose Maisie. Even if it means..." I swallowed hard. "Even if it means you have to leave me to do it."

He tensed and pulled back to look at me. "Sabina—"

I placed a hand on his chest to quiet his protests. "Stop. I need to say this. If something happens to me, you have to promise me you'll be sure she's okay. I've fucked up a lot in my life. Made a lot of stupid, selfish choices. But I need this to be right. You're able to flash out of the battle, which means you have the best chance of saving her. So if things go south, I want you to leave me and get her to safety."

His eyes burned into mine as his other hand came up to cup my face. He leaned in and placed the softest of kisses on my lips. Then he pulled away a fraction and whispered, "If you think I'm the kind of guy who'll run away when the woman I love is in trouble, you don't know me very well."

The bottom fell out from under me. The L word destroyed my equilibrium. Up until he said it, I'd barely managed to hang on to my composure, but now my throat ached and tears stung my eyes. "Dammit, mancy," I said, my voice thick.

His gaze was dead serious. "I'm just stating facts. I'll do everything in my power to ensure Maisie is safe, but I'm not leaving you behind. Ever."

A tear splashed on my cheek. I swiped it away with a

shaking hand. I wanted to scream at him that he didn't understand. This wasn't just about saving Maisie. I needed to know he'd be safe, too. I wasn't sure if I could handle the biggest fight of my life, saving my sister, *and* worrying about his safety. If I went down, if Lavinia gained the upper hand, if she succeeded in summoning Cain, I needed to know he wouldn't try to play the hero.

His green eyes held mine, his warm hand a pleasant weight on my arm, his lips so close. His sandalwood-and-warm-male scent mixed with the comforting aroma of gun oil.

That's when it hit me. I couldn't control what might happen tomorrow, but I could decide what happened tonight. And I could think of nothing more important at that moment than showing Adam how much I cared about him.

Cared? That wasn't exactly the right word, was it? The problem was I'd never loved anyone before. Not really. But I knew the feelings I had for the mancy were stronger and deeper than anything I'd felt for anyone. If that's what love is, then so be it. I guess it took facing death to finally strip away my excuses for not fully living. For not fully embracing my feelings for the male who looked at me now with his own feelings so nakedly displayed in his eyes.

We stared at each other for a few moments, like we were waiting for some new catastrophe to interrupt. As I looked into his green eyes—emotion making them the color of leaves after a rainstorm—I remembered what Giguhl said about the right moment presenting itself. And I knew without any doubt this was it.

I stepped away from Adam and moved toward the door.

His eyes widened and his face fell as he watched me retreat. But instead of walking out the door, I closed it and flipped the lock with a definitive *click*.

When I turned back toward him, my back against the door, I was shaking whether out of nerves or anticipation—or both—I didn't know. But I did know that seeing the hesitant smile spread across his lips made my heart thump in my chest. He took a step toward me, but I shook my head. "Stay there."

His smile faded. Obviously expecting more games, he crossed his arms and watched me with a wary expression. I held his gaze steadily as I slipped the jacket from my shoulders and let it fall to the floor.

Slowly, with deliberate movements, I raised the hem of my shirt and tossed it aside. Under his appreciative gaze, I removed my boots and jeans until, finally, I stood before him clad only in a black lace bra and panties.

His gaze forged a lazy path down my body before reversing direction. When his eyes met mine again, he arched an eyebrow in approval.

After weeks of foreplay, part of me wanted to shred his clothes off and mount him without preamble. Instead, I slowly walked toward him. Taking my time, savoring the anticipation.

When I finally stood before him, he reached for me, his hot hands sliding against my hips. But when he went in for a kiss, I shook my head. Grabbed the hem of his shirt. The movement forced his hands to release me so he could raise his arms.

My gaze dipped to the muscled expanse of his chest, down the ridges of his stomach to the Hekate's Wheel peeking from the waistband of his jeans. I traced the labyrinthine design with the tip of my finger. His muscles danced at my touch.

I bit my lip and looked up at him from beneath my lashes as I used two fingers to release the button at the top of his fly. His breath quickened to match my own. Our eyes met and the air shifted as need dug in its claws.

The game was over. No more seduction required. Our mouths met, wet and hot. Twining. Busy hands made quick work of my bra. Every sense filled with Adam—his sandalwood scent, the hot feel of his skin, the taste of his tongue. The combination left me punch-drunk and greedy for more.

We fell back onto the bed in a tangle of limbs. I tore my mouth away and rose up to straddle him. His hand found my breasts and worshipped them with the reverence of the converted. He sat up, his mouth replacing his hands. His tongue soft and teasing. His teeth sharp and hard as he pushed me past the threshold between pleasure and pain. My hands dug into his hair, urging him on.

Delicious friction built lower down where two scraps of thin fabric were all that separated us. But just when I was about to push aside the lace and cotton, Adam flipped me over. The muscles in his chest and arms bulged as he leaned over me. Kissing down my chest, my stomach, my thighs. A magical tingle danced across my skin. I blinked, surprised to find myself completely naked. I looked down and realized I wasn't the only one.

The mancy shot me an impish grin. Then I forgot what I was going to say because his hot breath teased the sensitive skin of my thigh. Without further warning, he dove in and delivered a long, slow lick that made my eyes cross.

Soon, my nails dug into his scalp and my hips rocked. Fangs scraping against my bottom lip, I searched for the orgasm he offered.

I didn't have to look far.

The next moment, every muscle in my body stiffened. Adam rose up and absorbed my yell into his mouth. I tangled my tongue with his, enjoying the flavor of myself on him. Before the last spasm passed, I flipped him over, keeping our mouths connected.

Unable to wait any longer, I impaled myself on him. He obliged with a thrust of his hips. I stilled his movement with my hands on his shoulders. He seemed to understand my need to lead without hearing the words. I rode him hard, my knees digging into the mattress.

His hands threaded into my hair. I enjoyed the pain and rewarded him with a kiss made of tongue and fang. I nipped at his lip, drawing his sweet blood into my mouth. Adam moaned his approval. He pulled my head up and tried to meet my gaze. I closed my eyes against the wave of emotion building in my throat.

"Look at me, Sabina." His hand caressed my face. "Open your eyes."

I released my clenched lids. His pupils were dilated, and I almost believed I could see his soul hovering just behind them.

Our panting breaths mingled between our lips. Our hands glided over sweat-slicked skin. Our bodies yearned toward shared pleasure.

The visual connection, the physical one, the taste of his blood on my tongue morphed into a powerful yearning for his blood and something else—something even more primal. It snaked up through me and, judging from the light in Adam's eyes, through him, too. Sparks of light rose around us, like frenzied fireflies.

"Do you feel it?" he whispered.

I swallowed and nodded, intrigued and not a little afraid of the power we created. The magic we made, literally and figuratively. Together.

I pulled away before I could give in to my baser temptation. But Adam's hands wrapped around my neck and pulled me down. In his eyes, I saw the permission I sought but wasn't sure I was ready to accept.

"Do it," he whispered. His head tilted to the side, exposing the corded column of his throat with its seductive vein throbbing beneath golden skin.

I'd like to say I overcame my instincts and refused. That I was too strong to indulge that particular desire. In the light of day, it's easy to say you'd never do something. But when the moon rises and passions are high, well, that's another matter.

I hesitated, giving him a chance to change his mind. But he urged me on with his hands. To ease the way, I licked the salt from his skin. Suckling it until he was moaning and his thrusts picked up speed. Then, when I was sure he was distracted, I bit down.

Adam gasped and went totally still. I pulled away instantly, afraid I'd hurt him or that he might push me away. Instead, his hands pushed my face back to his neck. His blood flowed into my mouth freely. Tentatively at first, I lapped at the spot.

Only when he began thrusting again did I allow myself to fully indulge. I'm not sure if it was his mage genes—or just something about Adam in particular—but his blood tasted both sweet and spicy, like cinnamon and sugar and cardamom and every good thing ever. The infusion made the blood in my own veins dance, like a shot of effervescence to my system.

Right then, with Adam's blood in my mouth and his cock deep inside me, I experienced my second true moment of freedom. The spasms sent me higher, bringing him with me. Our bodies didn't literally levitate, but it sure as hell felt like we were flying. The French may call it "the little death," but I'd never felt more alive.

I collapsed on Adam's chest, letting him support my weight. My body felt both hollow and completely filled. I closed my eyes and surrendered myself to the aftershocks. Behind closed lids, flashes of red told me the sparks continued to flash around us. Adam's chest heaved beneath me, and his hands roamed over the slick planes of my back.

When he slid from me, I felt the loss keenly. I opened my eyes in time to see the tiny lights fade around us.

My breathing slowed and he shifted beneath me. I lifted my cheek from his chest, fully expecting awkwardness to ruin the moment. But when I looked in Adam's green eyes, I felt…confident. No, more than that. I felt powerful. Whole. Full of the mysterious and sacred feminine knowledge passed down from the Great Mother herself.

His lips lifted. "What are you thinking? You're smiling like the Mona Lisa."

I kissed him once, twice, three times. "Nothing."

He eyed me suspiciously through droopy lids. "One of these days, you're going to tell me all your secrets."

I ducked my head to hide the fade of my smile and the lie in my eyes. "I don't have any secrets."

My conscience raised its head. After everything we'd just shared, I knew I had to make a choice tomorrow. I told myself it was for his own good. Sure, he might hate me after it was done. But better angry and alive than aware but doomed.

His hand tipped up my chin. I schooled my features but couldn't quite meet his eyes. "Hey," he whispered. "Don't go chasing dark thoughts. Just enjoy the fact we're here together, finally."

I forced a wobbly smile and kissed him softly. My eyes stung, so I squeezed them shut and tried to show him everything I felt without saying the words I knew he wanted to hear. It seemed wrong somehow to give voice to them now. As if speaking them would sharpen the betrayal.

Finally, I pulled away and looked him in the eyes. "You're absolutely right. By this time tomorrow, everything will finally be as it should."

The steady pings of rain on the roof woke me. Of course, *woke* was a relative term given how poorly I slept. Every time I closed my eyes, my mind filled with images of everything that could go wrong.

Adam's body pressed against my back. A muscled arm snaked around my waist and his hand cupped my breast. I closed my eyes and savored the feel of him. A risky indulgence, but one I justified because it might be my last moment with him alone.

Too soon, the pressure in my gut from the sun's descent forced me to move. Judging from the pressure, it was about four o'clock. Just an hour or so before night's shadow spread over the Big Easy.

After the day spent making love, Adam slept soundly. His eyes didn't flutter when I carefully removed his hand and slipped from the bed. I dressed quickly, my eyes on him for any sign of waking. Finally, I grabbed my gun from the nightstand and shoved it into my waistband. Just as the weapon slid home, Adam murmured my name and rolled away. I stilled, expecting him to jump up and demand an explanation. But he settled down and soon his slow, even breaths were the only sound in the room.

As I watched him, I realized that David had been right that a tough choice would have to be made. After the Queen's order, I'd assumed the Maisie-versus-Lavinia issue would be that choice. But now I knew the choice was between saving those I loved and pursuing my own goals.

Too many lives had already been disrupted. Too many bodies injured. And in the early morning hours, wrapped in Adam's arms, I asked myself the question that sealed my fate: Could I live with myself if anyone died? Not just Maisie, but Adam, Giguhl, Rhea, Zen, Georgia, or, hell, even Mac.

I'd been through it before. With Vinca. Her loss was still a hot, sore spot on my heart. Losing her hadn't killed me, but it still haunted me. But Vinca died when I was the old Sabina. The one who didn't understand the meaning of loss. The one who didn't think about the consequences of actions.

This was the new me. The one who had more friends than she ever imagined. The one who had it in her power to protect those friends. This me understood that losing any of them would destroy me. So, in reality, this sacrifice I was about to make was totally selfish.

Maybe I hadn't changed so much, after all.

I mentally shook myself. I knew one thing: The mere thought of Adam dying made me want to scream. Plus, one small sacrifice on my part meant he wouldn't have to choose between duty to the Council and his conscience. I might not be able to offer him pretty words, but I could at least give him this much.

Besides, the more I thought about it, the more I realized going it alone seemed some sort of inevitable poetic justice. This whole drama had started with my parents and their star-crossed love affair. And now it would end with their daughter. I'd do everything in my power to save my sister, and then I'd do whatever it took to kill my grandmother before she could summon the master.

Fuck fate and David's fatalism. I was going to make destiny my bitch.

With one last, longing look at Adam's smooth, muscled back, I grabbed my boots and tiptoed from the room. Like a thief in the night, I crept down the hall. When I reached the door to the workroom, I heard the muffled sounds of Zen and Rhea making plans. Holding my breath, I made it by the door without any creaks of the floorboards to give me away. Farther down the hall, the fae's door was also shut. But instead of hushed voices, I heard the telltale sounds of a snoring demon. Apparently, Giguhl had crashed in PW's room. I paused, placing my hand on the door.

Not being able to say good-bye to Giguhl was one of my biggest regrets with this plan. Once I was dead, Giguhl would immediately return to Irkalla. Demons were always tethered to the mage who summoned them. If the mage died, the demon went back to the underworld. Adam would be able to bring him back, though, and I prayed they'd at least keep in touch. But if that wasn't possible, I prayed my friend would eventually be able to forgive me.

Downstairs, I rushed through the empty shop, grabbing Zen's keys from the back office as I went. I threw on my boots and opened the back door. With my hand on the knob, I stopped and looked over my shoulder. Behind me, the dark shop, with its musty, mysterious smells, sat in quiet judgment. Ahead, the rain had stopped, leaving the courtyard heavy with the scent of wet cobblestones and the sharp green scent of plants. A few rogue rays of late-afternoon sun broke through the cloud cover.

Oddly, I didn't fear death. Not if it was on my own terms. And not if it meant that everyone in the building above me stayed safe.

I paused as Pussy Willow's words from the day before came back to me. Guess she was right, after all. I was capable of connection. Maybe even love.

Yeah, I decided, *love*.

Because even though I didn't have a lot of history with that particular emotion, what else could explain this sudden unfamiliar but fierce need to protect?

Ironic that I finally figured that out right before I left them for good. Would Adam forgive me? Giguhl? Eventually, I decided. After they got past their anger.

Behind me, the concussion of a large expenditure of magical energy exploded through the building. My heart contracted from the pressure and the curtains in the office fluttered. The Queen's knights and the Pythian Guard had arrived. Which was my cue to exit. With any luck, Adam would be so busy dealing with them he wouldn't be able to come looking for me until it was too late.

As the sounds of male voices and the pounding of boot heels filled the store, I took a deep breath and stepped out into the light. Then, without another backward glance, I ran toward the street. But I couldn't help feeling like I'd left something important behind.

I checked the clock as I sped through the French Quarter. Four-twenty p.m. Since Lavinia couldn't handle the sunlight, she'd be forced to wait until true night to perform the ritual to summon Cain. That meant I have about forty minutes to get to the cemetery, get Maisie out of harm's way, and kill Lavinia.

At the last minute, I'd forgone Zen's Gremlin in favor of a black Kawasaki motorcycle I'd found parked off Bourbon. I revved the engine and sped up, enjoying the familiar power of 180 horses between my thighs. My own bike—a cherry-red Ducati—had met an untimely end on a highway outside Boisie several weeks earlier thanks to Lavinia's assassins. I still hadn't finished mourning its demise. But now I leaned into the power and allowed myself to enjoy the breeze on my face, the dip of my stomach, the brief moment of freedom.

Ten minutes after I left Zen's shop, the brakes squealed to a halt in front of the Cajun Sausage Fest. I hated the time this would waste, but I knew better than to go into a confrontation with Lavinia without ample reserves of blood. Even though I'd recently fed from Adam and his blood still tingled in my veins, I wasn't taking any chances.

The sign we'd hung on the door read "Closed for religious observances." Few in a Catholic-rich city like New Orleans would question the Cajun closing down for All Saints' Day. That meant I didn't have to worry about anyone snooping around looking for Alodius while I was inside. I pulled his keys from my pocket and clicked the lock open.

In the shop, the reek of bleach assaulted my nose. I kept my eyes averted from the spot where the Cajun's body landed the day before. There was nothing left to see there anyway after our thorough clean-up job.

I went straight to the counter for some blood. Only when I pushed back the sliding lid of the fridge, I found nothing but a few steaks and a rump roast. Cursing, I ran toward the back and through the plastic curtains.

Inside the walk-in freezer, slabs of meat hung from hooks like gruesome party decorations. I pushed past them toward the back, where tall shelves held hams, sausage links, and a few jugs of blood. Lifting the nearest one, I popped open the plastic lid and tossed it back.

Cold blood coated my tongue, leaving behind a gamey flavor. Knowing Alodius, it was probably raccoon or opossum or some other roadkill cuisine. I cringed and had to force myself to swallow. Blood is blood, and this beggar definitely couldn't be a chooser.

I also kept my eyes averted from the pile of meat in the corner, covering the body of the Cajun. When you kill vampires, their bodies exploded. The ultimate in self-cleaning. But humans? Always a mess. Luckily, no one would find the Cajun's body until long after I was gone, and there was nothing to tie Pussy Willow to the crime.

I grabbed an extra jug of blood from another shelf, just in case. If Lavinia had really been feeding from Maisie, she'd need a hefty infusion. My stomach cramped at the thought. I speeded up so I could get to her sooner.

When I turned to leave, I spied a shotgun propped up in the corner. A box of shells sat on a shelf nearby. I grabbed both before exiting the freezer. Regular bullets can't kill vampires, but a well-aimed shotgun blast sure as shit can take one's head off, leaving them very, very dead. Since all I'd brought was the three guns and two daggers, I added the shotgun to my pitiful arsenal.

I rushed back through the plastic curtain, juggling my supplies while I took another swig of blood from the open jug.

"Let me guess." The masculine voice was deceptively quiet and so cold a chill passed over me. "You had a sudden craving for boudin?"

My heart stuttered in my chest. Blood sputtered from my lips. My hands jerked. Shotgun shells scattered, and blood puddled across the floor between us like a crime scene.

Adam leaned against the glass meat case with his arms crossed. A black duffel bulged at his feet. His expression wasn't giving away anything, but his tense shoulders hinted at barely leashed anger.

I opened my mouth to speak without any idea what to say. Luckily—or unluckily, as the case may be—Adam saved me from formulating an appropriate response. He held up a hand. "Don't." He breathed deep and closed his eyes. "Don't speak if you're just going to lie."

My stomach clenched. Visceral pain tightened my chest. "How did you find me?"

"Does it really matter?" He opened his eyes and speared me with a look. "And save your breath. I know exactly what's happening here. But I've got news for you, Red. Sacrificing yourself doesn't make you a hero. It makes you a godsdamned idiot."

My mouth fell open as indignation flooded out the guilt. "Excuse me? How does wanting to protect you make me an idiot?"

"Wanting to protect me doesn't make you stupid. What makes you stupid is that you honestly believe it's your job to protect me. Have you thought about what will happen if Lavinia gets to you before you save Maisie?"

"That won't—"

He bulldozed on like I hadn't spoken. "You'll both be

dead, and then Lavinia, the Brotherhood, and the Caste will kill the rest of us. Not just me, Sabina. Giguhl, too. PW, Zen, Rhea, Orpheus. And once we're dead, nothing will stop the war. Then, if what we know about the Caste's prophecies are true, when mages are finally wiped off the face of this earth, Lilith will return and kill all the dark races. So, forgive me if I'm not in awe over your noble martyrdom act, but when it means the potential annihilation of everyone *I* know and love, it's real hard to work up any admiration for you or your idiotic plan."

His words hit me like a punch in the gut. It was bad enough he was looking at me like I'd betrayed him. But the truth of his words cut deep. If I failed, all that and probably worse might happen.

But he wasn't done. "Last night you reminded me that we were a team. What happened to that, Sabina?"

"Don't you see? I'm doing this for the team!" I hefted the shotgun barrel to my shoulder. "Besides, I'm not going to fight the entire Caste. I'm just taking out Lavinia. One way or another."

He went totally still as the implications sunk in. Then, like someone flipped a switch inside him, his fist shattered the glass case. When he finally spoke, icy rage lowered his voice. "I can stop you. You know it."

My chin came even as tears stung my eyes. "Why don't you try?" Part of me wanted it. Wanted to fight him. But not magic to magic. Fist to fist. Then, maybe, I could turn my anger outward instead of this searing pain tearing me apart from the inside. "Why don't you hit me?"

"If you don't know the answer to that question, then everything we shared last night was a lie." He laughed bitterly. "But maybe that was your goal all along."

My stomach cramped at the coldness in his gaze. "What the hell is that supposed to mean?"

He snorted and shook his head. "I can't believe I didn't put it together earlier. Kill two birds with one stone, right? Get your rocks off one last time before you kick the bucket and distract me so I didn't see this coming. So I couldn't prevent you from pursuing your sick fucking death wish."

"You sonofabitch! You know that's not what that was about!"

The caustic humor drained from his face. "You know what? You want to get yourself killed? Fine. But I'm not going to let you take Maisie down with you. You said it yourself, of the two of us, I'm the only one who can flash her out."

When I'd made this decision, I knew Adam would be angry. It's just I'd hoped he wouldn't find out until after I was gone. That part of the plan had just gone to shit, but in the end the result was destined to be the same. So I sucked down the pain and pushed it into the shadowy corner of myself. Added it to the reserves I'd draw from later if I needed to use my Chthonic magic to take out Lavinia.

"You want to help me? Fine." I forced the corners of my mouth up in a mocking smile. "But the minute Maisie's free, you get the hell out of my way."

"Don't misunderstand. I'm not helping you. You might have been fooling yourself all along, but your goal is and always has been taking out Lavinia Kane. By getting Maisie to safety, I'm just clearing an inconvenient to-do off your list. But rest assured, the minute I have Maisie, I'm gone. I won't stay around to watch you and your grandmother act out your fucking Greek tragedy."

I gritted my teeth. Part of me wanted to argue with

him. To tell him to go to hell for implying Maisie wasn't my priority. But in the end, I let it pass. After all, having Adam focused on saving my sister would make it easier for me to concentrate on ensuring Lavinia wasn't a threat to either of them in the future. And if Lavinia showed up before we were ready, Adam could just zap both of them out of there. So why didn't any of this make me feel better?

"Suit yourself. But just you. The others need to stay out of this."

"I told Giguhl if he didn't hear from me to call everyone off. Good thing, too. If they knew what you were planning they might get in your way. And we both know how much you hate distractions." He bent to pick up the duffel and tossed it at me. "The reinforcements arrived loaded for war. You might want to avail yourself of some party favors. Until you're ready to surrender your life, that is."

His words slammed into me like shrapnel. Instead of responding to his dig, I slammed out the front door and into the street. The faster I could get to the temple, the sooner Adam would be rid of me. And the sooner I'd find an end to the pain of knowing I'd hurt him so badly he was now looking forward to that moment.

28

After a tense drive in which Adam refused to touch me despite sitting behind me on the bike, I parked just outside the cemetery gates behind the temple. The building sat dark and appeared deserted. But I knew better than to not expect company pretty damned quickly. Knowing Lavinia, she had the place under surveillance or magical wards rigged up around Maisie's prison. That meant, as much as I hated to admit it, having Adam with me might be a blessing.

Of course, judging from the scorn on his face or the fact he didn't spare me even a glance as he dismounted the bike, he didn't necessarily agree with my assessment. But dwelling wouldn't do me any favors. So I shoved it all away—the pain, the regret, the fear. Emotions had no place here. Any one of those feelings could get me killed before I was ready to go. And combined, they all but guaranteed it.

I forced steel into my spine and resolve into my gut. Adam didn't wait for me to say anything. Just took off toward the gate in long, purposeful strides. Removing a gun from my waistband, I covered his back.

The gate swung open without a sound. Adam held out a hand, indicating he wanted me to lead the way to Maisie's tomb. Without a word, I pushed ahead, ducking as I ran through the avenues of tombs. Behind me, the only indication he followed was the occasional muted crunch of boots on gravel. I kept my eyes out for other shifting shadows that might foretell an impending ambush.

In the lengthening shadows of deep dusk, nothing moved save the occasional breeze. The rain had stopped, leaving mist to rise from the damp earth like hazy spirits. As in the other cemeteries I'd visited since arriving in New Orleans, a low hum buzzed in my ears. But now I knew it was a result of my Chthonic powers reacting to the death energy there, and I was able to push it aside and focus on my task.

When Zen said people left flowers on tombs for All Saints' Day, I expected a couple of sad carnations. Instead, elaborate wreaths and bouquets leaned against the monuments. Some people had even left offerings of food and bottles of liquor. Debris and candles littered the grounds, like we'd just missed a huge party.

Soon, we reached the tomb I'd seen in my astral projection. Adam and I ducked nearby, next to another, smaller mausoleum. Even as I looked for traps or guards, my eyes sought out some sign of David's ghost among the marble slabs. I still hadn't figured out why he'd come or who sent him, but I guessed I wouldn't now. Unless he showed up again or until I met him again in Irkalla. And by then it'd be too late.

"Cover me," Adam said, his body tensed to dart across

the open space separating us from the tomb. I grabbed his arm.

"Be careful. It might be booby-trapped."

He nodded curtly. Paused. His gaze met mine. I held my breath, wondering if he'd relent enough to say a final farewell. But just when I expected him to say something, he bolted away like a sprinter.

A lump formed in my throat at his easy rejection. The lack of emotion in his gaze. The loss of connection. The loss of Adam, period. Gritting my teeth, I scanned the area for unfriendlies.

Behind me, I heard Adam grunt followed by the gravelly slide of stone against stone. I turned in time to see the lid to the sarcophagus crash to the ground. It split apart into several pieces.

Adam began chanting under his breath. The breeze carried tendrils of magic toward me. The hair on my arms stood but soon relaxed as the magic fizzled abruptly. He cursed under his breath. Again, nothing.

I raised the gun and did another sweep, but the cemetery remained quiet except for the sound of Adam struggling against something heavy. His muscles strained as he tried to lift something from the box.

"Sabina," he whispered.

"What?" I called quietly over my shoulder, my eyes scanning the perimeter.

"Come help me with the lid."

I did one last sweep as I backed toward him. My boots sunk into the muddy ground. When I reached him, I saw sweat beaded on his forehead from exertion. He jerked his head toward the foot of the metal box inside. "Grab that end."

I looked down to see some sort of metal sarcophagus resting inside the marble crate. No wonder Adam's magic didn't work. The entire body-shaped box was covered in intricate brass scrollwork. Still, I didn't understand why Adam couldn't use his muscles to pry the thing open until I hooked my fingers under the edges and pulled. "Holy crap," I grunted. "Brass shouldn't be this heavy."

Veins stood on his neck as he gritted out a response. "It's cast iron. Now lift!"

Our feet dug in for leverage and we put our backs into it. And with that, we still only managed to lift the lid a fraction. Even cast iron shouldn't have been that heavy. They must have warded it or something to make it harder to get into. Or get out of.

My muscles shook with the effort, but spurred on by being so close to seeing Maisie, I ignored the strain and redoubled my efforts. Then, finally, with one last heave, Adam and I managed to flip the heavy top up and over the edge of the marble box. It hit the ground with a loud thud.

We leaned forward to peer inside. At first, my heart dropped, thinking we'd opened the wrong vault. The pale, gaunt figure inside resembled something out of a horror movie. A tattered gray gown with bone-thin flesh poking through. Face covered in a black muslin shroud. Then the smell hit me. Unwashed flesh and excrement. Fear and rage. I covered my nose and mouth with my hand as nausea threatened.

I glanced up at Adam, whose eyes were wide with shock. "What the—"

A spine-jarring wail cut off my question. I jerked my gaze back to the box, where blood-caked fingers clawed at the shroud. Out of instinct, I jerked back and pointed the gun at the body. Adam held up a hand and reached in to pluck the fabric from the face.

I gasped. "Maisie?" The name came out in the form of a question, because the being inside the box looked a hell of a lot more like the Crypt Keeper than my identical twin. Cheekbones jutted from skin so desiccated her fangs and teeth protruded from almost nonexistent lips. Unfocused blue eyes rolled wildy in their sockets. Black-and-red hair matted down with dried blood in places and sticking up like porcupine quills in others.

"Maisie, honey? Can you hear us?" Adam whispered.

Her head twisted toward the sound of his voice. But instead of calming her, it seemed to enrage her. A high, thin growl, not unlike a wounded animal's, echoed through the cemetery. Her twig arms jutted toward the mage, her fingers bent into talons. Adam pulled back just in time to avoid being grabbed. Fear lit his eyes as he met my shocked gaze across her thrashing form. "Help me!"

I grabbed her flailing wrists as gently as I could. But even wasted away as she was, I had trouble subduing her. A major problem, since we were trying to sneak her out. "Maisie, it's Sabina. You need to calm down and be quiet."

But Maisie was beyond understanding. Blood-starved and terrified and enraged. Adam helped me try to hold her down. Our efforts only made things worse. She fought harder, alternating between rabid snarls and snapping her fangs at any available flesh.

"Ouch, dammit!" Adam yelped. A rivulet of blood ran down his forearm and splashed Maisie's face. She snorted and tried to frantically reach the drops with her pale tongue.

The pitiful sight sent a shard of ice through my heart. "Bind your wound. I've got her," I barked, taking her other wrist from Adam.

"I'm fine," he said, his voice tight.

I looked up and glared at him. "The scent of your blood isn't helping. Bind it. Now."

A muscle in his jaw worked, but he finally pulled away to rip a strip of fabric from his shirt. Satisfied he'd take care of it, I focused on trying to restrain Maisie without hurting her. But the scent and taste of Adam's blood made her jackknife up in the box in pursuit of more. She managed to pry a hand loose. Talon nails swiped a painful trail across my face. My skin throbbed hotly along the shallow slashes.

"Maisie, stop!" I pulled my face out of range of her snapping teeth.

I briefly considered trying to help her with my own blood. But I discarded the thought immediately. Allowing her to feed from my own vein was too dangerous. She was too ravenous. Besides, it was only a matter of time before Lavinia showed up to see my reaction to her little gift. Depleting my reserves now wasn't an option.

"Adam, there's a jug of blood in the bike's storage compartment."

He didn't argue. One second he was beside me and the next he disappeared. Maisie had risen up above me, bearing down. It took everything I had to hold her off.

I felt rather than saw Adam's reappearance. "Maisie!"

The scent of animal blood reached my nose the same instant Maisie's body went stiff. Her head jerked around with a growl. She leapt at Adam, ripping the jug from his hands. She threw back her head and poured the red liquid into her mouth. It splashed her cheeks, ran down her chin, splattered the shredded remains of the chiton. She snorted and slurped at the plastic like a dog intent on licking every last drop from a bowl. Finally, she tossed it aside and proceeded to run her tongue over her fingers, her chin.

Meanwhile, I'd made my way slowly back around the vault to stand next to Adam. I wasn't foolish enough to believe one measly container of blood would be enough to satisfy her. Especially when, in her haste, she'd managed to spill half its contents all over herself. She'd been without for more than a week and endured Lavinia and gods only knew who else draining her. So the desperation made sense. And if my suspicions were correct, the physical and psychological trauma of her captivity would demand twice or three time as much blood as she'd normally need. What worried me most, though, was that the blood she'd just consumed might give her just enough strength to make a real go at either Adam's or my jugular.

Looking up at her red-streaked, skeletal face as she sucked blood from the fabric of her dress, I felt real fear. Palpable, bone-chilling fear. The kind that comes when you think you've seen it all but something comes along that far exceeds your worst nightmare. Because when the blood-crazed female finally opened her eyes, I didn't see my sister in there. The earthy, generous, kind-hearted Maisie had checked out, and this blood-starved beast had taken up residence in her body.

"More." The gravelly voice hinted at destroyed vocal cords. From starvation or from days spent screaming for help that never came, I didn't know.

Adam held up his hands. "We'll get you more soon. But first we need to get out of here."

"More!" the wraith that used to be my sister screamed.

I stepped forward, slowly. "Maisie, sweetheart, Adam needs to take you home now. He'll get you blood as soon as you get there, okay?"

Maisie threw back her head and howled. "Blood!"

"Maisie, stop!" I jumped at her, grabbing the frayed hem of her chiton and yanking. "We have to get you to out of here."

Her body swayed and she cackled. Her knees creaked as she lowered herself to look into my face. "Shh." A single dirty finger ran down my cheek. "The black dog howls at the crossroads." She threw back her head and howled like a wolf at the moon.

Every hair on my body stood at attention. I grabbed her arms with suddenly frigid hands. Keeping my voice steady, I said, "Time to go."

She cocked her head like a bird. "The skeleton clock is ticking, ticking, ticking."

A chill ran down my spine, like someone walked over my grave. The words she'd spoken? They were straight out of the vision quest I had back in New York. I had no idea what they meant, but hearing them come from my sister's mouth felt like a seriously bad omen. "Adam, grab her. You two have to get out of here."

"But—"

I jerked my head around to glare at him over my shoulder. "Now!"

He jumped into motion then, wrapping his arms around Maisie. She cackled again as he held her tight to his chest like a baby. "What about you?"

I pulled a second gun from my belt, my eyes already searching for whatever was coming. "Dammit, mancy, just go!"

He hesitated. And in that split second, Maisie's screeching laughter cut off abruptly. The sudden silence was heavy. In the next instant, my sister, looking like Carrie after the prom, whispered, "Too late."

Before I could react to the downright creepiness of her hushed words, a gate on a nearby crypt slammed open. Red-hooded figures swarmed into the clearing. An instant later, magic crackled through the clearing as several Caste members flashed in.

Driven by instinct and adrenaline, I spun and started shooting. "Go!" I shouted over my shoulder at the mage.

Bullets flew thick through the air. I tried to pick off as many of the enemy as possible. My goal was to distract them long enough for Adam to get the hell out of Dodge. But when no signs of magic tightened the air, I chanced a look over my shoulder.

My heart stuttered and my breath whooshed out like I'd been sucker punched.

My grandmother tilted her head and smiled at me. She wore a low-cut scarlet silk number—like this was a fucking formal ball instead of an ambush. Standing next to her was a familiar Avenger demon whose presence chilled my bones. But it was the brass garrote wrapped around Adam's throat that made my heart stop.

"We are so thrilled you decided to join us for the party," Granny Dearest said. "Now, why don't you drop those weapons before my friend here removes the mancy's head. You remember Eurynome, don't you, dear?"

29

I gripped the guns tighter in my clammy palms. "I'm the one you want. Let them go."

Lavinia smirked and crossed her arms. The entire audience of her flunkies had gone silent, waiting for her command. "You still believe this is all just about you? I suppose that's to be expected from an only child."

"I'm not an only child." I nodded toward Maisie, who struggled against the hold of two Caste vamps. "But if I tend to act like one, you have no one else to blame but yourself."

Her eyes narrowed. "Actually, if it'd been up to me, neither of you would have existed at all." She waved a ringed hand through the air. "But that mistake will be rectified soon enough. Now do as Grandmother asked and drop the weapons."

My heart galloped and cold sweat bloomed on my back. Funny thing about playing the hero—no one ever tells you how hard it is to be brave when you're scared shitless. But if I dropped my weapons, I'd lose my chance to end this. I knew that as sure as I knew this was the only way to save Adam and Maisie.

Instead of lowering the guns, I raised them—one filled with vampire-killing bullets and the other mundane. Time slowed. Adam shouted something. Movement from my left. The hair on my neck prickled, warning of an impending magic attack. No more time to hesitate.

Exhale.
Squeeze.
Explosion.
Chaos.

The spell slammed into me like a freight train. Vertigo as it knocked me off my feet. Crushing pain as my body slammed into stone. An inevitable slide followed by the crunch of bone against earth. On some level, I knew the spell came from Eurynome. I'd been subjected to his particular form of magical torture before on a New York subway platform. Luckily, Giguhl had been there that night to intervene while the spell ravaged my body. Now, however, familiarity didn't lessen the spell's impact. The magic spread beneath my skin like thousands of fire ants trying to consume me from the inside.

Lost in a haze of pain, I was only vaguely aware of scattering bodies and frantic shouts. A flash of light illuminated the red capillaries in my eyelids. Somehow I managed to pry one lid open. Sure enough, a plume of smoke rose from the area where Lavinia had stood only moments earlier. Frantic bodies swarmed the spot, blocking a better view.

Eurynome bore down on me like an avenging angel. And just behind, Adam struggled to remove the brass wire from his neck. The mouth that kissed me just hours ago now opened wide in agonized shouts I couldn't hear.

"Go!" I tried to yell, but the words came out in a weak croak. Tears sprang to my eyes. Bittersweet. Pain, yes. Regret. But also, relief. Finally, my bullet found its target. Two months too late. But finally.

A shadow fell across me. Blocking my view of Adam. Not long now. I closed my eyes and accepted my fate.

"Bring her to me!"

My eyes popped back open. The screech cut through the pain like a knife. Made my heart lock up in my chest. I couldn't see past Eurynome's hooves, but I'd know that banshee cry anywhere. After all, I'd grown up hearing it every time I displeased the Alpha Domina.

"No!" My tongue felt too large for my mouth. Rough claws grabbed at my arms. Weak and dizzy, I fought the demon as best I could. Which was not nearly good enough. Never good enough.

The Avenger demon dragged my limp body toward the clump of Brotherhood robes. Tears stung my eyes, blurring my vision. The Brothers parted to reveal the enraged countenance of Lavinia Kane bearing down on me.

Pain from Eurynome's attack dampened the heat of her palm against my face. But my head whipped back from the impact. The severe planes of Lavinia's pale face came back into focus. As did the harsh red circle that spat blood from her chest.

The wrong bullet had hit the right target.

My eyes shifted to the charred, smoking remains of the Caste vampire who'd taken the right bullet. And fate whispered in my ear, "Who's the bitch now?"

Lavinia leaned in as the icy realization of failure spread

through my limbs. "You're going to scream before I send you to Irkalla."

Her threat didn't touch me. The moment I realized she survived, I detached. Retreated into myself, totally removed from the promise of future pain. Nothing could hurt more than the knowledge that my mistake had signed both Adam and Maisie's death warrants. That it signed my own didn't matter.

"Do your best," I slurred.

Sharp fingers dug into my jaw, forcing me to meet eyes glittering with a mixture of rage and madness. "But first, I'm going to make you watch me drain that mongrel lover of yours dry."

That did it. As much as I struggled to remain separate from this horrible reality, the tears started to run freely.

What is it they say? Pride goeth before the fall? Well, mine went the second I realized the cider bullet missed her. "Let him go."

Lavinia scooted closer, squeezed my chin tighter. "What was that?"

I swallowed the bile and taste of copper coating my tongue. "Spare him."

"Ah-ah-ah, ask nicely."

"Please."

"If you're going to beg, do it properly. Please, who?"

I closed my eyes. "Please spare him, Domina."

She released me as if she couldn't stand to touch me. "Pathetic." She spat on the ground at my feet. "No blood of mine begs for the life of a mage!" She turned her back to me, dismissing me like an abomination.

Just beyond her, I finally spied Adam again. Despite the new gashes on his lip and forehead and the hands bound in front of him in brass shackles, he looked so brave with his shoulders thrown back and his head held high. His eyes burned at me with strong emotion. I knew better than to hope love made his eyes shine. Everything he'd predicted—and worse—had come to pass. Shame and regret washed over me like acid. That I begged for his life wouldn't matter. If it weren't for my stupidity, his life wouldn't be in danger at all.

Near the vampires holding Adam, a burly male with a copper-colored buzz cut backhanded Maisie. Her body slumped instantly, and the vamp hefted her easily over his shoulder. Eurynome wrenched me from the ground. My feet struggled to hold my weight and I stumbled. My clumsiness earned me a cuff to the back of the head.

The same claw that hit me grabbed a handful of hair to lift me off the ground. Eurynome's gravelly voice sounded next to my ear. "Where's your pet now, bitch?" He raised a claw to hit me again, but Lavinia's voice stilled his hand.

"Enough! We want to be sure there's enough left of her for the Master." To the rest of the bad guys she called, "Take them all inside. It's time to begin the summoning rites."

The stained-glass dome depicted scenes from the Garden of Eden. Not the story mortals know from their Bible, but the story of Lilith and Adam, the Great Mother's exodus to the Red Sea and her eventual union with the outcast Cain.

Hundreds of candles lit the rotunda. Set in niches and along the floor, their light cast menacing shadows on the faces of statues standing guard along the perimeter.

Brass chains scraped my wrists and ankles. A linen gag choked my throat and abraded the sensitive corners of my mouth. Cold air raised gooseflesh on my arms and legs, which were exposed thanks to the flimsy ankle-length tunic they'd forced on me.

Turning my head on the black marble slab, I looked across an expanse of polished stone floor to the slab holding the prone body of my sister. The Caste members had dressed her in the twin to my gown, but the fabric nearly engulfed her emaciated frame. She looked too still lying there, too brittle. She hadn't made a sound since passing out after the vamp struck her. Part of me hoped she remained unconscious during whatever horrors our grandmother had planned for us.

Lavinia entered leading a procession of her flunkies. Eurynome and the Caste members came first with their golden eight-point-star pendants flashing in the light. Behind them, the robed and hooded Brotherhood silently followed, chanting low over the candles they each carried.

At the end of the dark procession, I spied a flash of golden hair and bare flesh. My chest ached. Lavinia probably got some sick glee out of stripping Adam and forcing him to wear nothing but a scrap of fabric around his waist. Hoped to degrade him. But the truth was, he'd never looked stronger than with his head raised high as the Brothers led him to his death. The Hekate's Wheel on his lower stomach stood out in sharp contrast to the stark white of the cloth over his hips.

His eyes flicked to mine. For a brief instant, I swore I saw a trace of longing and regret in the green depths. But the Brother leading him shoved at his back, forcing him to stumble. He regained his balance quickly, but he moved out of my line of sight. I craned my neck, trying to see him again, but Lavinia moved in, filling my vision.

An icy finger ran down my cheek. She leaned over me with a swish of silk and the scent of dirty pennies. "I've changed my mind," she said. My eyes flared, but inside I knew better than to hope her next words would be our salvation. "Even though I'd love to make you watch as I drain your mancy lover, I'll admit I detest the flavor of mage blood. It has its benefits, naturally, but the taste is just," she shuddered, "vile."

She pulled away. "But this opportunity is too good to waste. Luckily, the perfect solution presented itself." She snapped her fingers. Three Brothers rushed forward and begun loosening Maisie's bonds.

I shouted against the gag and jerked against my own chains.

"Having your sister feed from your lover is just good sense. Because you took so long to find her, she's weak and in desperate need of blood. A good feeding will restore her enough for the rites. And, well, the poetic justice is just delicious."

I fought harder. The fabric muffled my screams into impotent moans and the metal dug into me until blood ran freely. Lavinia patted my shoulder. "I'm thrilled to see you agree." Turning to the Brothers, she called, "Begin."

The men slapped Maisie's face until she woke with a start. Her body had already used up the little bit of blood she'd consumed and now yearned for more. Three more Brothers came forward to help restrain her. She fought against them like a berserker, all claws and fangs.

Lavinia groaned, clearly annoyed by the complication. "Eurynome, please assist the mortals."

The Avenger demon emerged from the clump of beings. His hooves stomped against the stone, and his ram's horns lowered with purpose. He pushed the mortals out of the way. He subdued Maisie easily, wrapping his arms around her like steel. Then he lifted, carrying her toward Adam.

Two vampires grabbed Adam's arms and pushed him forward. Now that he could see what was happening, his composure fled. His hands were bound, so he used his shoulders and head to fight. For his insolence, he received a fist to the gut. As he fell to his knees, I strained against my bonds. Tears streamed down my face, and my throat burned from muffled screams.

Lavinia clapped and nodded to the vamp to Adam's right. He unsheathed a knife. Adam saw the glint of metal and shied away. The blade slashed across the skin just above his heart. Blood bloomed and spilled down his chest and his abdomen to stain the white fabric.

The scent of blood hit Maisie like an electric shock. She strained and hissed in Eurynome's grasp, eager to feast.

"Release her," Lavinia said. The second the demon loosened his grip, Maisie flew at Adam. I squeezed my eyes shut as bile and tears choked me. It was bad enough to hear what was happening, to hear Maisie's greedy sucking and Adam's agonized groans. But Lavinia was determined to milk every possible ounce of pain from this moment. She pried my lids open, holding my head captive with her arms. Forced me to watch my twin bent over the neck of the male I loved.

"Look at what you've done to them," Lavinia whispered. I jerked my head, desperate to block out the sight of Maisie's red-and-black head bobbing against his chest.

So much blood. Too much. A grimace of pain contorted his pale, dear face.

Her fingernails dug into the soft skin around my eyes, drawing blood. But I was too crazed with guilt and horror to register the pain. If anything, the red blurring my vision was a blessing. "Oh, no, you must watch and understand. Your existence brings pain to all unfortunate enough to meet you. Witness how you destroyed them. Just as you killed my beloved Phoebe."

I stilled. I'd always known I served as a painful reminder to Lavinia of my mother's death. But I never understood until that moment the depth of her depraved hatred. The unfairness of laying blame at my door. My mother's choices had been her own. My birth was neither my choice nor my fault. Her death was not my doing, but her own.

The simple truth hit me like a bolt of electric clarity.

I remembered Adam's accusations earlier about me having a death wish. And I realized he'd been right. Just like Lavinia, on some level, I, too, had blamed myself for the horrible circumstances and ensuing drama of my birth. Believed I didn't deserve to be alive because of my shameful heritage. Didn't deserve love or understanding, affection or empathy.

Lavinia orchestrated these horrors. She'd kindled the self-hatred for decades. Manipulated me from the start. And I'd bought into all of it because I didn't know another way to live. But I knew better now. I knew because of the mage who offered his love, the sister who'd taught me about family, and the loyal demon who showed me the meaning of friendship. They'd stood beside me despite my protestations that I didn't need anyone. I'd been a godsdamned fool to allow Lavinia's poison to cloud my judgment. She was the worthless one. The selfish one. The one who allowed hatred and vengeance to fuel her actions. Not me. Not anymore.

But even as these realizations dawned, so did the knowledge it was too late. My eyes burned as I watched Adam grow paler by the second. Already the fight had fled his muscles and he slumped into Maisie's eager grasp.

Then, like someone flipped a switch, his entire body stiffened. The whites of his eyes overwhelmed his pupils. A final gasp signaled his surrender. And then the mage I loved slumped to the floor.

Dead.

The scream that rose in my throat came not from my vocal cords but from the very root of my soul. My body filled with a rage so strong it could crumble mountains.

Maisie stumbled back, her limbs trembling as she stared down at Adam's bloodied body. The infusion had restored some of her awareness and the realization of what she'd just done. With wide, haunted eyes, she threw back her head. "No!" Her haunted scream echoed off the dome.

Lavinia released me and went to go inspect his body. I slammed my stinging eyes shut and gathered my strength for another primal scream. Only instead of air rushing from my lungs, something shifted. The raw emotions gave way to power building in my diaphragm. This time the rage and love combined, twisting together like DNA to create a force more powerful than any I'd called upon before. I embraced the burning ache of it. Stoked the fire. Called out to Hekate and Lilith to aid me.

Lilith, Great Dark Mother and Goddess of the Night.

Hekate, Goddess of the Crossroads and Bringer of Light, hear my pleas. Lend me your great and terrible power to balance the scales. Break my bonds and fill me with your dark energy. Help me avenge this blasphemy.

A loud *crack* echoed through the chamber. A tidal wave of dark power washed over me. I threw back my head as it slammed into me. Filled me. The force of this primal magic jerked my body upright. Sent a shock wave of power through the room.

The dome overhead shattered. The colorful glass fractured into a million fragments and rained down on the rotunda. Shouts and cries filled the room as humans and Caste members ducked and ran for cover.

All around, the walls cracked like eggshells. Falling plaster and stone joined the glass. The building creaked and moaned with the promise of collapse.

Black and red auras danced on the edges of my vision. I blinked and realized my chains had shattered along with the glass. The release of energy and the sharp shards had sent several of my enemy to the ground. But my focus zeroed in on the bitch in red. She sat on the ground near Adam's body, looking dazed.

My burning gaze locked on Lavinia like a heat-seeking missile. With deliberate movements, I removed the gag and tossed it to the floor.

"Lavinia Kane." My voice was different. Deeper, echoed, as if I spoke with three voices now: mine, Lilith's, and Hekate's.

Lavinia's eyes flared. She rose quickly, backing away before stumbling over Adam's body, kicking at Brothers and Caste members who got in her way. I rose slowly. There was no fear now. Only power and purpose.

My senses buzzed, taking in every sound, shape, and smell in the room and beyond. The air vibrated against my skin. My tongue tasted her fear and confusion. And it pleased me.

Eurynome stepped between the Domina and me. I tilted my head to look up at him. Sounds in the distance registered in my expanded consciousness. A smile spread across my lips. The demon's black eyes flickered to a chunk of plaster that fell just to my right, barely missing my shoulder. I didn't flinch.

The air shimmered, signaling the demon's intent to deliver another of his signature pain spells. The aura around him flared up a split second before the doors to the temple burst open. Eurynome's spell shot toward me like flame. The spell licked up and over the cone of Chthonic power the goddesses wrapped around me. The demon's black lips fell open in shock as cavalry rushed in the door.

"Eurynome!" a familiar voice shouted.

His head swiveled to the right to see a flash of green rushing toward him like a freight train. Giguhl tackled Eurynome, and the two demons slid across the stone floor before slamming into the wall.

I didn't have time to watch Giguhl finally get his chance to finish the Avenger once and for all. Nor did I stop to see who else my minion had brought to the party. I could feel each of them—Rhea, Pussy Willow, Mac, Georgia, and about twenty other mage, werewolf, vampire, and fae allies both inside and outside the building.

As much as I appreciated their assistance, my sole focus was pursuing the Domina. "Lavinia!" Her head whipped around, her eyes finding me through the haze of dust and the bodies littering the path between us.

"Quickly!" she screamed. "Summon the Master!"

To her right, two Caste members—a vampire and a mage—huddled together with an ancient tome. A third Caste vamp held a knife to Maisie's neck in front of the two with the book. She stood limply in his grasp as he used her body to shield his comrades. Her wide, haunted eyes met mine across the space. Her pale face, the bodice of her chiton, and her hands were coated in Adam's blood. She looked up, and for a nanosecond I could have sworn that behind the broken gaze I saw a spark of the old Maisie. The one I knew before Lavinia conspired to rip us apart and break our spirits.

Decision time. I could take the Caste members out now. End the chance of Cain joining the party. But Maisie stood directly in the line of fire.

An ear-splitting *crack* echoed through the rotunda. One of the beams that held up the dome crashed to the floor, crushing the bodies of two human Brothers. Lavinia sprinted toward the door, pushing the chanting Caste members and Maisie ahead of her. Bodies scattered as the other combatants rushed to follow her example. The urge to give chase was strong, but I wouldn't leave Adam and Giguhl behind. Dead or alive, I'd never abandon my team again.

I raced through the room, leaping over bodies of the falling, fighting against stragglers running toward the exit. I skidded to a halt several feet from where Giguhl still battled Eurynome.

"Giguhl," I said. "Finish him!"

As if spurred on by my command, Giguhl seemed to expand and harden. Eurynome raised his claws to deliver a spell. As the white-hot flash of magic zinged through the air, Giguhl ducked and rolled. He came up hard and fast at the Avenger. Claws slashed Eurynome's face. Black blood oozed from the wound. Before the ram-horned demon could retaliate, Giguhl delivered swift jabs to Eurynome's midsection, pushing him back toward the curved wall. The impact forced a new, thick crack up the already unstable wall.

I rushed toward them, determined to help Giguhl finish this quickly. My minion didn't have access to the kind of magic that could send the Avenger back to Irkalla. But I couldn't get a clear shot with Giguhl in the way.

I grabbed an iron spear from the hands of one of the statues. "G, catch!"

His uppercut slammed into the Avenger's chin. Turning his head slightly, Giguhl saw the spear flying toward him and caught it. In a smooth motion, he spun around and slammed the metal through Eurynome's chest. The iron impaled the demon and pinned him to the wall.

"Move!" I yelled.

Giguhl didn't stop to argue or question. He simply lunged to his right, clearing a path for me.

My hands thrust forward. *"Iddumu bara nadzu!"* A bolt of black energy sizzled from my fingertips. The spear acted like a lightning rod and delivered the spell directly to Eurynome's chest. One second the Avenger squirmed and screamed to avoid the spell, and the next he was a pillar of black coal and ash.

My mouth fell open in shock as Giguhl jumped off the ground to run toward me. "Holy shit! You just incinerated him!"

I swallowed the bile that rose at the scent of burning flesh and brimstone. "We need to get the fuck out of here!" I jerked my gaze to Adam's body.

Beside me Giguhl stilled. "What happened?" he whispered brokenly.

Another loud *pop* echoed through the crumbling chamber. No time for post mortems or mourning.

"Lavinia happened." I pulled Giguhl with me. "C'mon, we've got to go."

Crisis mode kept me insulated from the horrific reality that I was staring at the lifeless form of the male I loved. That reality would hit me like an atom bomb once the crisis was over. If I survived.

Giguhl gently lifted and cradled Adam's body. With a hand on the demon's back, I ran for the door, keeping my eyes averted from the mancy's closed eyes and the blood covering his chest.

Together we reached the opened doors a split second before the rest of the shattered dome's steel frame broke free. We lunged into the night as the impact boomed and a cloud of dust exploded behind us.

We stumbled out onto the stone balcony. Leaning my back on the stone railing for support, I looked back at the imploded room. I blew out a breath. "That was too close."

A magical percussion burst through the night. In its aftermath, I finally heard the sounds of fighting far below in the cemetery. I turned slowly. "Oh, my gods," I breathed.

While I'd been busy inside, Lavinia's goons had run straight into the waiting arms of my own personal cavalry. And they'd brought reinforcements in the form of several Pythian Guards and Queen Maeve's knights, judging from the uniforms. Plus, on the periphery of the fighting, Zen and PW gyrated and twirled among the tombs.

As I watched, a cyclone swept through the cemetery. A

clump of Brothers flew through the air like so much con-
fetti. I'd seen that maneuver before. My eyes sought out
Erron Zorn, who stood on the roof of a tomb with Ziggy
by his side. I don't know who or what convinced him to
change his mind, but I didn't have time to do anything but
be grateful for their presence. I had to find Lavinia before
she could summon Cain.

"Giguhl, take Adam to Rhea. Then go look for Lavinia.
We have to stop her."

Giguhl nodded solemnly. "Watch your back, Red."

I met my friend's eyes. "You, too, G."

With a final nod, he shifted Adam's limp body in his
arms and ran toward the stairs.

I turned and climbed up on the railing. On the far side
of the battle I spotted Lavinia, the three Caste members,
and Maisie. The Domina attacked a faery from behind.
Her fangs ripped out his neck so fast he didn't know what
hit him. As his body fell, she relieved him of his sword.
She looked up then and saw me. She wrapped an arm
around Maisie's neck and raised the sword in salute. The
iridescent faery steel glinted wickedly in the moonlight.

I'd felt the sting of such a blade before. Specially designed
by the fae for killing vampires, the magical blade was made
even more deadly in the hands of my grandmother.

But not as deadly as me. The powers of Lilith and Hekate still thrummed through my veins like lightning. A fact
Lavinia Kane would soon discover.

I raised my arms up toward the sky, turning my face
toward the waning moon. The dark energy pulsed through
me. I dove, somersaulting through the air. My war cry
burst through the night.

Time to end this.

30

My feet barely hit the ground before a Caste vampire lunged with fangs bared. Without slowing, I heaved a bolt of underworld magic his way. Heat licked my back as his body exploded.

Legs pumped faster. I dispatched a clump of Brotherhood humans. A flash of red between two crypts caught my attention. I started after Lavinia.

"Sabina!" Rhea's shout made me stop short.

I turned to see the silver-haired mage cornered. She stood in front of Adam's prone body, fending off attacks from three Caste mages. I ran up behind one of them and jerked his neck to the left. I didn't stop to watch him fall as I went after the second. This one saw me coming and turned to blast me with a flaming orb. Again, the cone of power protected me. I stood fully and shot a cocky smile at the shocked mage.

Lifting my hands, I threw some magic of my own at him. He grunted as the spell hit him in the midsection. He ignited instantly. Screaming and flailing, he was burned alive.

The remaining mage turned tail and ran away. My bolt hit her in the back and threw her forward into a group of three Caste vampires. Their clothes caught fire, and the four bodies created a writhing funeral pyre.

Breathing heavily, I turned back to Rhea. Instead of looking relieved, her face was a mask of worry. "Where's Maisie?" she demanded.

"Lavinia." Her face hardened. She glanced down at Adam's body before looking up with tears in her eyes. Before she could speak, I held up a hand. I couldn't handle it now. "Get the hell out of here."

She wrapped her arms around me for a quick, hard hug. "Goddess protect you." Her voice lowered to a fierce whisper. "Now go kill that bitch."

I pulled away and turned my back to her before emotion could get its claws in me. Running, I beelined for the crypts I'd seen Lavinia disappear between earlier. Spurring my legs faster, I burst out of the narrow aisle ready for action. Only instead of finding Lavinia, I discovered the males who'd been chanting inside. The vampire still held a knife against Maisie's throat, but she appeared to be unconscious again. The book they'd been chanting from earlier lay on the edge of the slab. Their voices mingled with words I couldn't translate.

I ran right toward them, tossing aside the vampire with the knife. A bolt of Chthonic magic slammed into his body, frying him on the spot. The other vamp left the mage and sprang at me. He slammed into me before I could shoot him with a spell. We rolled and tumbled across the grass, slashing at each other with fists and fangs. He landed on top, pinning my legs down. With one hand, I gripped his wrists to prevent the knife's downward motion.

His gold Caste medallion batted around between us, hitting my face as we struggled. I freed a hand and grabbed the symbol, twisted. It broke free from his neck easily. Gripping it between my fingers, I jabbed at his eyes with one of the star's points. His hand flew to the ruined eye as he screamed. I bucked my hips to unseat him. Rising above his writhing body, I lifted my hands and gathered the power, ready to slam him with a spell.

The attack came from behind. A soft *swish* of metal through the air. A grunt. The sharp sting of blade through skin. I lurched back, my shoulders pulling together and my head thrown back. Despite the tingling pain, instinct forced me to bend and duck away from the inevitable follow-up swing. I fell and rolled away just as the blade sliced the air again.

The faery steel worked quickly, its magic immobilizing the muscles on the left side of my back. With effort, I rose to face Lavinia. She raised the sword again, her eyes glittering with deadly intent. Grimacing against the spreading numbness, I crouched into my fighting stance.

The vampire on the ground had recovered enough to sit up. Lavinia looked at him from the corner of her eye. "Summon the Master. Quickly."

The Caste mage resumed his monotone chanting. With each word, I felt the clock ticking down.

The vampire pulled himself from the ground and limped away to assist the mage. As he went, he grabbed the ceremonial knife from the grass. I started to lunge after him, but Lavinia slashed the blade through the air, capturing my full attention.

"You're not going to ruin my plans this time, you little bitch." She slashed and parried, pushing me away from my sister. "Once the Master arrives, he'll make you regret ever being born."

Behind Lavinia, Zen and PW appeared from between the crypts surrounding us. I was surprised the voodooienne allowed PW to come along. But when I saw the satchel strapped to the fae's back, I realized Zen relied on her trusted assistant just as much as I relied on Giguhl. Plus, PW might be brittle after the attack, but she was still a faery. That meant she could easily take out human opponents. Hell, if properly armed and motivated, she could even take out vamps or mages. Especially with her hair-trigger temper and mad voodoo skills.

Hoping to distract Lavinia from their arrival, I said, "Doesn't it bother you that you have to rely on someone more powerful to meet your goals?"

She smiled and flicked the blade. "You won't be taunting me once Cain makes you his slave. Ironic, isn't it, that the Chthonic magic the mages taught you will be the weapon he uses to destroy them?"

I stilled as pieces of the puzzle clicked together. All the chances Lavinia had to kill me. Her demanding my surrender instead of fighting in Jackson Square. The vague threats. The rites. Cain wanted me alive. Needed me alive so he could use my Chthonic magic for some nefarious purpose. "Well, that certainly changes things," I said, half to myself. Lavinia frowned. I smiled. "You're scared of Cain. And I bet he'd be pretty pissed if you killed me before he could use me."

"I fear no one," she said, but her eyes exposed the lie.

The voodoo practitioners worked quietly behind the vampire bent over Maisie. Zen sprinkled amber liquor all over the ground. PW lit a cigar and handed it to Zen. The sweet, smoky scent drifted toward me. My lips quirked as I realized what Zen wanted me to do. But first I had to keep Lavinia distracted until the time was right.

"Man, I never thought I'd see the day when the Alpha Domina lowered her neck in submission to a male."

Instead of answering my taunt, she struck. I raised my left hand to fend off the attack. The blade sliced across the muscles above my wrist. Blood sprayed from the wound, dripping down my arm. I screamed as acidic pain ripped through my flesh. Fell back, my ass hitting the dirt.

As Lavinia advanced for another hit, the Caste mage shouted. "He's coming!"

My grandmother paused, jerked her gaze over her shoulder. I looked past her and blinked. The air next to the vampire was shimmering.

"Sabina, now!" Zen shouted.

The air more solid now. A male human form.

I slammed my wrist to the dirt and ground it in. As I did, I yelled, "Spirits of the Loa, Hekate, Great Mother Lilith, I summon and evoke thee to guide these spirits to strike down my enemies!"

A male. Translucent. A shock of red hair—the same hair I'd seen in my dream with the werewolf and the shotgun. Master Mahan. Cain.

The combination of Zen's spell and my blood forced the earth to shift and buckle. Horrible groaning and pounding began inside the nearby tombs. The vamp cringed and looked around. The loss of concentration made the transparent form of the Master waver and go static.

Lavinia had gone still, her eyes alert but worried. "What is that noise?" she yelled.

I didn't have to answer, because in the next instant the first revenant broke through. It—the level of decay prevented me from guessing a gender—exploded from a vault near the spot where the vamp and mage had almost succeeded in summoning Cain.

Pushing its way through the humans, the zombie went straight for the vampire. Judging from the screams of the vamp, he'd never seen a zombie before. The mage dropped the tome and tried to run. Two revenants broke off to catch the mage, who screamed as their rotted bones dug into his neck. Couldn't blame him for his fear—no one ever expects zombies.

When the mage released his death rattle, Cain's shimmering form *popped* and disappeared as the aborted summoning spell wore off.

Skeletal hands clawed at the vamp's head, tearing clumps of red hair, the pale skin left in ribbons. A loud, wet crunch as the skull gave way. I averted my eyes as the zombie fell to the ground to feast on the vampire's twitching body.

"No!" Lavinia watched the display in horror. "By the gods, what blasphemy is this?"

I rose on shaky legs. "I figured since you and Cain are so interested in my Chthonic magic, I'd arrange a little demonstration."

More revenants burst free from their tombs. Four broke off from the pack and headed for Lavinia. Instead of running or screaming, she flashed her fangs and fell into a fighting stance. If I hadn't hated her with the white-hot passion of a thousand suns, I might have admired the way she faced them down.

"Wait," I called.

Hollow eye sockets set in gray skulls turned toward me. "She's mine."

The revenants backed away, some even bowing on creaking bones. Lavinia regarded me with wary eyes as I approached. In the distance, the sounds of fighting were dying down. A muted cheer rose. But as long as Lavinia breathed, this battle would never be over.

I picked up the sword. The hilt felt warm in my hand. The heat from Lavinia's hand hadn't dissipated. My grandmother's chin rose. "You're a fool."

I paused, swinging the sword in front of me. "I know."

Behind Lavinia, the third member of our fucked-up family stumbled in our direction—a pale, blood-streaked specter. Seeing the murder darkening Maisie's eyes, I realized she had every right to crave Lavinia's death, too. In fact, she had more. Lavinia had used me and manipulated me my whole life. But the tragedies Maisie had endured in just a few days overshadowed anything I'd endured at our grandmother's hands.

Lavinia cocked her head, obviously confused by my easy agreement. Slower, she said, "You didn't stop him tonight. He'll find you."

I was done with vague threats and archaic prophecies. Instead of responding to her dire prediction, I said, "I have one question for you."

"No, I never loved you," she barked.

I laughed. "Seriously? You think I haven't figured that out by now?" I spread my hands wide and nodded to my blood-spattered body and the carnage surrounding us.

Her eyes narrowed into slits. "Then why do you hesitate? Do the deed, or admit your fear."

She was right, I was stalling. Not because I was afraid.

But because doing so would allow the scales to balance once and for all. "My question is this: Weren't you the one who always told me to never turn my back on an enemy?"

She frowned. "Yes. Why?"

Maisie struck then. Her fangs cut deep into Lavinia's neck. Caught off guard, the Domina froze in shock. Maisie's arms clamped around our grandmother as she bit deeper and drank greedily from the jugular. Lavinia reanimated with a vengeance, struggling and screaming for help. But no one was left to help her. Soon, her pale complexion took on the powdery blue cast of impending death.

Passing through the bowing revenants, I limped toward the slab where the Caste guys had held Maisie. I reached it just as Lavinia screamed my name. Picked up the book and shoved it into my waistband, when the screams cut off abruptly. I released the Chthonic goddess powers back into the ground where they belonged. As the dark, shadowy energy swirled out of me, a wet ripping sound reached my ears. Closed my eyes when a flash of heat scorched my back.

Ding dong, the bitch was dead.

The knowledge should have filled me with joy. Instead, I felt hollow. Totally empty.

I looked up to see Zen, PW, and Giguhl watching the display with somber expressions. "Go help her," I said quietly. Despite the fact I knew I'd done the right thing letting Maisie kill Lavinia, I couldn't face her right then.

"Um, Sabina?" Giguhl said. I looked up. "What about them?" He nodded to the revenants.

I sighed and turned toward the rotting crowd. I didn't worry I'd have to kill them all like I did Kevin. This time, by instinct, I knew the revenants merely waited for my command. "Your work here is done. I release you. May you rest in peace."

The zombies obeyed immediately. As they shambled slowly toward their crypts and tombs, Giguhl and Zen went to Maisie's kneeling form. Soft keening sounds rose from her huddled body as she rocked next to the scorch mark that had once been our grandmother. My conscience told me I should go to her.

But I couldn't. The image of Maisie feeding from Adam was too fresh. Besides, I wasn't sure I could be anyone's cheerleader right then. Adam was dead, Maisie was broken, and I felt...nothing. No hope for the future. No confidence everything would work out. Hell, I wasn't even sure I'd actually won, given Lavinia's prediction that Cain wouldn't stop coming after me.

But as I turned away, I knew one thing: Letting Maisie kill Lavinia had been the right choice. Instead of feeling robbed of the opportunity for revenge, I felt like justice had been done. Maisie had just served our grandmother a heaping spoonful of her own bitter medicine.

I just hoped for two things. One, that Maisie would recover quickly from her wounds—both physical and emotional. And two, that eventually I could look at my sister's face and not see the feral monster who killed the male I loved.

*B*ack in the main boulevard, the green expanse lay in ruins from pools of blood and blackened circles from dead vamps. Scorch marks marred the white stone tombs. The air stank of spent magic and death. Several mages and fae bent over the bodies of fallen comrades, tending to wounds or whispering blessings for the departed.

The protective instinct that had insulated me from reality was already receding. My nerve endings sizzled like live, exposed wires. My arm and back screamed from injuries. But the wounds on my heart caused the greatest pain. Because even though Lavinia was finally dead, achieving that goal—even indirectly—had come at too high a cost.

I paused as the truth slammed into me like a battering ram. David had predicted tough choices with long-range consequences. Had he known I'd choose to go it alone and fail, thus setting off this chain of events? Or would any choice have netted the same outcome?

And how would the choices I made tonight impact all of us going forward? Obviously, my choice to allow

Maisie to kill Lavinia would be a factor. On the other hand, Lavinia's death would allow the peace accord among the fae, mages, and vampires to go forward. But could Tanith really be trusted as an ally? And would the Queen or Orpheus listen to me when I told them any peace was tenuous as long as Cain still lived? The weight of those big questions was almost too much to bear in the wake of such personal loss.

I looked up at the moon and allowed the heaviness to settle deep into my bones. Closing my eyes, I imagined Adam's face in my mind. I realized the image was a memory of the first time I'd seen him in that smoky vampire bar in Los Angeles. He'd been trying hard not to be noticed, but a male like Adam was hard to miss.

A tear ran down my cheek. Hard to miss in a lot of ways.

May the Great Mother wrap you in her arms and keep you safe until I can join you.

Footsteps crunched on the grass. I looked up and saw a familiar silver-haired mage emerge from between two crypts. "Rhea?"

She wiped a bloody hand across her brow. "Sabina. Thank the goddess you're okay."

"What are you still doing here? Why would you risk staying?" Pain and worry added an acidic edge to my words. When I thought about how she could have been injured...or worse, my chest tightened.

"Sabina, I might be an old woman, but I'm not a coward. Besides, I had healing to do here."

"But—"

She slashed a hand through the air. "What's done is done."

The dam broke and I threw my arms around her. "I'm so sorry."

Her silver brows slammed together. "What in the world are you apologizing for? I told you Maisie's prophecy was right."

I pulled back, my face wet with tears. "What?"

She smiled at me. "The prophecy. About how you were going to unite the dark races and stop the war? Look around you." She motioned in a circle, "You brought together fae, mages, demons, weres, vamps, and, hell, even a human. Lavinia is dead. The war is no longer a threat."

I boggled at her. Had grief over Adam's death made her come unhinged? "What? I don't care about that—"

"Well, you should, because you lost the bet." The bet she referred to was one we made back when Maisie told me about the prophecy. I'd told the mage I didn't believe in fate or in my ability to unite anyone. She told me she reserved the right to rub my nose in it when I was proved wrong. "And because you lost, consider yourself officially I-told-you-so'd."

Considering the Cain factor, I felt her words were a tad premature. But what bothered me more was the lack of emotion she displayed. "Rhea, are you feeling all right?" I asked, putting a hand to her forehead. "I was trying to tell you I'm sorry about Adam."

She frowned. "That wasn't your fault. Besides, it all worked out in the end."

"What?" I whispered. How could she say that?

"I will say, though, it took just about every resource I had at my disposal to revive him."

My stomach somersaulted. I grabbed her arms. "What!"

She shot me a look. "Sabina? What—"

Movement behind Rhea captured my attention. A familiar silhouette emerged from behind the tombs like an apparition. My knees went weak. Reaching blindly toward a vault wall for support, I both cursed and thanked the goddesses for the Chthonic powers that allowed me to see Adam's ghost one final time.

A low keening cry rose from my diaphragm. "Oh, gods, Adam!" The pain was literally too much to contain.

Seemingly oblivious to my agony, Rhea turned and put her hand on her hips. "Adam? I told you to stay put."

The ghost looked up and stilled, one hand pressed against his chest and the other against the solid wall of the tomb. A white bandage marred with a splotch of bright red wrapped his chest.

Rhea's voice sounded far away. "You're going to reopen your wound stumbling around like that."

That's when it clicked that, unlike David's ghostly form, I couldn't see through Adam.

"I needed to..." He paused. "Sabina?"

At the sound of his voice, my knees finally buckled. "Adam?" I whispered brokenly.

He took a step toward me. The move forced his handsome face into a grimace of pain. Something about that expression—so real and unghostly—finally convinced me that he was real.

Alive.

Oh, my gods. He's alive!

I moved without conscious thought. Moved so fast I'm not sure my feet actually touched the ground. Finally—miraculously—my arms clamped around his solid form until I clung to him like a vine. Hesitantly, his own arms slid around me as great, heaving sobs wracked my chest.

"Hey," he said. "It's okay."

I wanted to explain, but I couldn't speak. Just a few seconds ago I was convinced I'd never be okay again. But now, the hope I'd abandoned reignited in my chest.

From far away I heard Rhea mumble something about giving us some privacy. My head rubbed back and forth on his shoulder. I wanted to explain, but I couldn't speak. His hands found my face, gently urging me to look at him. "Did someone not make it?" His voice cracked. "Maisie—"

A whole new round of sobbing began, robbing me of speech. Unable to control myself, I launched at him again, pressing my lips to his. He returned the kiss slowly at first and then relaxed into it, deepening it with his tongue.

I squeezed with my arms, my hands grabbing at his back. He jerked back abruptly, hissing in pain. I stilled, finally noticing the bright white bandage strapped across his chest. "Oh, gods!" I cried. "I can't believe it."

He looked up from his chest. "It's okay. Just a little tender." He smiled and leaned in for another kiss.

Realizing he misunderstood my meaning, I put a hand to the left of the bandage, stilling his progress. "No."

His expression fell, tightened. "Hey, you kissed me first."

I shook my head. "No, you fool, I don't mean no more kissing. I meant, I thought you were dead."

Light dawned in his eyes. "Oh, gods, Sabina."

"I saw you f-fall and . . . and then you were so still . . . I thought it was too late and I never got a chance to tell you—" My voice cracked as a fresh round of tears began.

He pulled me to him, his arms wrapping around me

again. Surrounding me with his sandalwood scent. I breathed in deeply as he rocked me, placing soft kisses on my hair, whispering, "It's okay. I'm here."

The storm of emotion passed quickly, leaving me exhausted. I lifted my head from his shoulder. Placed my hands on either side of his dear, handsome face. Looked him in his eyes, which were red and glistening with his own emotions. "I love you," I said. "I'm sorry I hurt you by sneaking out. I was trying to protect you. All of you. But I only ended up making things worse. Can you forgive me?"

His expression was serious, too serious for my comfort. "You love me?"

I tilted my head. Was that a trick question? "Of course."

"Then I should probably tell you I forgave you for your decision five minutes after I realized you'd left."

My mouth dropped open. "What? But those things you said—"

He rested his forehead against mine. "Were said out of fear." He swallowed hard. When he spoke again, his voice was thick with emotion. "The thought of you facing all that by yourself—the idea of you dying alone—made me more terrified than I'd ever been in my life."

I kissed his lips softly. "I was scared, too," I whispered against his lips. Memory of watching my sister feed from him reared in my mind. I pulled back. "Oh, gods—Maisie."

He stilled. "Did Lavinia—" His voice cut off as if he couldn't bear to voice his worry that Maisie might be dead.

I shook my head. "No, she's alive. But she still thinks she killed you."

He grabbed my hand and pulled. "Let's go."

His injuries slowed our progress, but before we made it halfway back across the main avenue of the cemetery, Giguhl entered the area. When the demon saw Adam he went statue-still. Then he was nothing but a blur of green. Adam didn't have time to brace himself before Giguhl was on him. "Mancy, you're alive!"

Adam groaned. "Not for long if you don't stop squeezing."

Chastened, Giguhl gently lowered Adam back to the ground. The demon's claw came to rest heavily on the mancy's shoulder. With a huge grin Giguhl said, "Godsdamn it's good to see you."

Adam smiled up to the demon. "You, too." He reached for my hand and squeezed it. "Looks like Team Awesome lives to fight another day."

"Damn straight," Giguhl said. "Although if it's all the same to you, I'd prefer it if another day doesn't come ever."

I smiled at my demon and my mancy. "Amen."

The demon rounded on me. "And you, no more of this running-off-by-yourself nonsense."

My joy dulled. Time to pay the piper—or the Mischief demon, as it were. "I'm sorry, G. I thought I was protecting you guys."

The demon crossed his arms and puckered his black lips. "Magepire, please. You think I don't know you by now? I appreciate the sentiment, but next time you decide to go off half-cocked, come talk to Gigi first, okay?"

I smiled up at him. "You're the best minion a girl could ask for, Giguhl."

"Yeah, well, when we get back to New York you and

me are gonna have a nice long chat about our roles in this relationship."

I opened my mouth to retort, but movement near the tombs grabbed all our attention. The rest of our ragtag army emerged from between two mausoleums. Zen and Rhea stood on either side of Maisie, supporting her weight. My sister's head hung so low her limp red-and-black hair curtained her face. The infusions of blood from Adam and Lavinia had filled out her body a bit, but her skin still looked too pale.

"Maisie!" Adam called, half running, half limping toward her.

Her face came up slowly. But instead of jerking in surprise or blinking in shock, she regarded him with dead eyes. Seeing her lack of reaction, he stumbled to an awkward halt a couple of feet away. "Maisie?" he whispered.

With a shaking hand, he reached for her. My stomach clenched as she shied away.

"Don't touch me," she said in a venomous tone. "I'm tainted!"

I moved forward to intervene. But Rhea shook her head. Feeling helpless and hurting for both of them, I clenched my fists.

"No you're not, Maze. It's okay." He tried again, and this time she allowed him to place a gentle hand on her arm. "It's not your fault."

Her body began to tremble uncontrollably. "I killed her, Adam."

He pulled her toward him as sobs wracked her body. "Shh. It's going to be okay."

Beside me, Giguhl's claw found my hand. I looked up at the demon with tears blurring my vision. For the first time since I let Maisie step in and kill our grandmother, I wondered if I'd made the right decision. Of the two of us, Maisie was less experienced with violence. She'd already been through so much. And even though her actions were just to my way of thinking, I knew Maisie never would have done the deed if she hadn't believed Adam was dead. And even if she'd been able to muster the rage to kill Lavinia, she would never have chosen to feed from the Domina as the means. As far as I knew, Maisie had never drunk directly from a living being until tonight. She was the one who got me started on bagged blood as the more humane option. And to return the favor, I'd just introduced her to the more violent side of vampire life. The blood she'd consumed—both Adam's and Lavinia's—and the killing would likely haunt her for a long time to come.

While Adam continued to comfort Maisie, the other mages and fae joined us. Everyone fell into a loose circle, and many of the faces looked to me as if for guidance. If they'd been expecting a speech, they were disappointed. I had no energy or desire to wax poetic about great victory over our foes. Instead, I sighed deeply. "Zen, I think it's best if you and PW come with us to the fae court. The heat's going to be on once the mortal authorities discover what happened here."

As if conjured, the sound of sirens carried to my ears. We had to get out of there.

Zen looked around at the ruined building, the evidence of battle. Finally, she said, "That's probably best. As long as we can return eventually if we choose."

I looked around, performing a quick head count. "Where are Mac and Georgia? Erron, Ziggy?"

Giguhl spoke up. "They all left once the fighting was done."

I mentally added not being able to say good-bye to them to my long list of regrets. Mac and I had our conflicts, sure, but she'd come through in the end. As had Erron. Maybe one day I'd be able to thank all of them in person.

But for now I had to get everyone to else to safety and then deal with the questions waiting for me back at faery central. No doubt the three leaders of the dark races were eagerly awaiting news of Lavinia's death so they could claim victory and move on with their plans.

One of the faeries stepped forward, a tall, muscular male with the bearing of one used to leading. Ilan, I presumed. "The Queen instructed us to cover up any signs of battle. It's too risky to leave evidence behind."

The sirens grew closer.

Giguhl squinted at him. "How exactly are you going to cover this up?" He gestured around. "Look at this place."

Red flashing lights reflecting off the walls of the building and screeching tires signaled the arrival of the cops. A Pythian Guard, a black-haired mage I'd met in New York named Wallace, looked at Adam for a decision.

"Too late," Adam said. "Everyone circle up."

"But the Queen—" Ilan protested.

"Would be even more pissed if she had to bail the captain of her guard out of jail," Adam barked. "Circle. Up."

Everyone jumped into action, grabbing the hands of those closest. No time to stop and look around. No time to reflect on what happened here. No time to worry about what tomorrow would bring.

Adam grabbed my right hand and Giguhl my left.

Static crawled across my skin. I looked from my best friend to my lover to the dark, haunted eyes of my twin.

Rising power made my chest tighten. And then, as I looked up at the sky to thank the goddesses for sparing everyone I cared about in the world, a voice called out, "Stop and put your hands up!"

The air *popped* and we were gone.

Acknowledgments

The word *thanks* seems so...inadequate sometimes. Especially when you're acknowledging people who support and ensure you get to pursue your life's dream every day. Ply me with enough wine and I'd blubber about the following people for hours.

Devi Pillai, editrix extraordinaire, who makes sure I look like I know what I'm doing with this whole writing thing.

Jonathan Lyons, my amazing, very patient agent. Thanks for being so cool and for reminding me to focus on what's important.

The geniuses at Orbit: Lauren Panepinto, Alex Lencicki, Jack Womack, Jennifer Flax, and the sales and marketing gurus, who make Sabina and her author look so good and make sure that people know about the books in the first place.

Suzanne McLeod, my kickass critique partner and an amazing writer in her own right.

The readers, who preach the gospel of Giguhl to everyone they know. You guys humble and amaze me.

Booksellers, the world's most passionate book lovers. You guys rock!

The League of Reluctant Adults and Leah Hodge, whose support and snark are essential to this writer's sanity.

The Migues, Wells, and Hughes families, who inspire and support me in all sorts of remarkable ways.

Zivy and Emily, my best sister-friends and members of my own Team Awesome.

Mr. Jaye and Spawn, who were dragged along for this ride but endure it with patience and humor. ILY. NTB.

And finally, thank you, New Orleans, for being the best muse ever. Please pardon any creative licenses I took with you. I hope, at least, I did your spirit justice.

extras

about the author

Raised in Texas, **Jaye Wells** grew up reading everything she could get her hands on. Her penchant for daydreaming was often noted by frustrated teachers. Later, she embarked on a series of random career paths before taking a job as a magazine editor. Jaye eventually realized that while she loved writing, she found reporting facts boring. So she left all that behind to indulge her overactive imagination and make stuff up for a living. Besides writing, she enjoys travel, art, history, and researching weird and arcane subjects. She lives in Texas with her saintly husband and devilish son. Jaye Wells has her own website at www.jayewells.com.

Find out more about Jaye Wells and other Orbit authors by registering for the free monthly newsletter at www.orbitbooks.net

if you enjoyed
GREEN-EYED DEMON

look out for

SILVER-TONGUED DEVIL

Sabina Kane: Book Three

also by

JAYE WELLS

All around the track, the crowd of vampires, werewolves, fae, and mages—mostly males—went apeshit. Males leaned in over the banked side to pound on the planks and scream for blood. They'd come to the right place. The Hell on Wheels Roller Derby was a carnival of fists, fangs, and cat-fights.

The pack rounded the second corner when the ref blew the whistle to put the jammers into play. Soon they'd attempt to skate their way through the cluster of blockers to try and score. In the meantime, we blockers were trying to incapaci-tate each other as quickly as possible.

I delivered an elbow to Scarlet O'Scara's nose. The satis-fying crunch and spray of blood distracted me from the werewolf coming up on my rear. The fist slammed into my back with the force of a sledgehammer. Two ribs snapped. A split second later, spine-bending pain almost sent me to my knees. My skates scrambled for purchase, but I somehow managed to dig in and right myself.

"Oops," Bitch N. Heat said, shooting an evil smile over her shoulder. The wolf on wheels wore boy shorts, fishnets, and a tank top with a skull bedazzled on the back. Lucky for me it wasn't a full moon, or that elbow would have thrown me across the room.

I welcomed the pain like an old friend, my legs pumping

harder, faster. I finally caught up with her at the next bend. Delivered a stabbing jab to kidneys as I passed. I considered following it up with a leg-sweep, but I needed to buy some time for my ribs to finish healing.

Rounding the corner, I skated ahead of Bitch. Giguhl screamed from the sidelines, "Look alive, Red! Jammer's coming!"

I looked over my shoulder and spied my real prey. The black star on her helmet looked like a bull's-eye.

The jammer for the Jersey Devils went by the name Ima Cutchoo. She was tough for a mage but lacked my vampire stamina and speed. In a real battle, her magic skills might have made her a contender, but the brass armbands we were required to wear put the kibosh on that option.

I slowed so she could catch up, dug in, and bent my knees. Muscles bunched, waiting to strike. Ima fought off bumps from my teammates but passed them easily, earning two more points. On her left, our own jammer, a fae named Stankerbell, struggled to make it through the gang of Jersey Devils defenders.

Decision time: Should I help my own jammer score, or take out Ima so she couldn't?

The scent of blood filled the arena. Heightened my predatory instincts, made my fangs throb. Made answering my own question easier. But also raised a new one.

How long's it been?

I turned to glare at Ima. She made eye contact, her eyes sparkling with confidence. My own eyes narrowed with deadly determination.

Three months? Four?

All around me, my teammates were taking out Jersey Devils to clear a path for Stankerbell. A faery slammed to the floor and rolled into my path. My leg muscles screaming, I jumped her writhing form. The crowd went insane. Hands and fists slammed into the wood to urge us on. In the chaos, some fingers might have been rolled over, but it was hard to tell screams of pain from screams for blood.

She was gaining on me. Almost there.

Not quite four—next week it'll be March.

Ima's panting breaths reached my ears as she rode my ass. I could feel her indecision, her brain working to decide the safest path around me. I held myself in check, luring her into a false sense of security. Then, just as she drew up on my right, I threw out my arm like a snake's strike. Clotheslined. Ulna to windpipe—a satisfying crunch. The force of the blow knocked her feet into the air. She hovered there for a moment like someone had hit the pause button for a better view of the action. Then gravity kicked in, and *bam*! Her back slammed into the wooden floor with a loud crack as her spine broke.

Whistles screamed. Boos and cheers from the audience. Gurgles from Ima as she curled up on the hard ground and spat blood. A mage healer rushed out onto the track to help the fallen Devil.

I skated away. The crowd apparently didn't approve of my strong-arm tactics, because their cheers quickly turned to boos. Even in dark-race roller derby, there were some lines one didn't cross, apparently. I raised a fist and extended the universal salute finger to share my opinion of their rules.

Ignoring the threats coming from the Devils' bench, I aimed for the center of the round track and Giguhl. He wore green shorts with knee-high tube socks and a T-shirt that advertised the name of our team, the Manhattan Marauders. A clipboard and a scowl accessorized his coach's uniform.

"Seriously, Red?" he demanded. "This isn't Thunderdome. You can't maim the other team."

Considering some of the maneuvers he'd pulled off during Demon Fight Club, I found his judgment hypocritical. I ignored him and bent over with my hands on my knees. I wasn't really winded. But the adrenaline was already evaporating, and, in its wake, lethargy pulled at my shoulders. Shutting out the jeers and glares surrounding me, I went back to my mental calculations.

If March is a week away, that means it's been 113 days.

I glanced up to see the ref point at me and jerk a thumb. Apparently, my hit earned me time in the penalty box—the big-girl version of a time-out. Heaving a sigh, I stood and put my hands on my hips. I should have been pissed. Put on a show for the audience. But I was too bored to care.

"Nice going, Betty Bloodshed!" This from one of my own teammates, a werewolf named Merry Machete. I cringed at my ridiculous moniker. When Giguhl told me about the roller-derby team he was putting together, I thought it'd be a fun way to work off some aggression. Instead, I was forced to adopt a ridiculous handle and wear fishnets that rode up my ass. And now they expected me to follow stupid rules about not disfiguring opponents? Where's the fun in that?

I looked past Merry to the crowd surrounding the ring. The makeshift amphitheater had been built in the basement of Slade's club, Vein. The room used to be used for Demon Fight Club, but after an unfortunate incident involving a Lust demon and a mage with ADHD, Slade had been forced to close down the fight club. That's when he and Giguhl came up with the idea for Hell on Wheels Roller Derby Night. The mostly male crowd for the fights adapted easily to the change. In fact, if anything, they seemed to enjoy the spectacle of violent, scantily clad women on wheels even more. Go figure.

Speaking of the audience, they seemed to have recovered from their disgust over my actions and were now demanding more thrown elbows, more tripping, more fighting. I was overcome with disgust. These mages, vampires, and faeries were nothing more than armchair warriors. They wanted controlled violence they could experience vicariously. But put them in a dark alley with a Vengeance demon and they'd all crap their pants.

Giguhl stood watching me with his arms crossed. Guess I wasn't moving as fast to the penalty box as he'd like. I raised an eyebrow and tried to tamp down the black fog gathering behind my eyes. This wasn't Giguhl's fault.

I took off my helmet and shook out my hair. Sweat drenched the red-and-black strands, plastering them to my face and neck. The electronic scoreboard caught my eye. In addition to the score—24 to 16, advantage Devils—it also flashed the time. One a.m.

Wait, that makes it 114 days, doesn't it?

I looked away from the clock and my gaze landed on a familiar, handsome face in the crowd. Adam sat three rows up. Seeing me look at him, he raised his chin slightly.

For a moment, the easy intimacy of the simple gesture warmed me. One of my favorite things about being part of a couple was that we barely needed to speak anymore to have an entire conversation. One raised eyebrow, a nod, a simple touch could convey more than an hour's worth of conversation.

Of course, it was also one of the worst things about being in a couple. The same mundane magic that allowed us to communicate so effortlessly also gave Adam the power to read me at will. I couldn't hide anything from him anymore. No more privacy, even in my thoughts.

Of course, I could read him, too. And judging from the frown on his face, I knew that before the night was over we'd argue about what I'd just done.

That's got to be a record—114 days. Time flies when you're not having fun.

I looked away from the weight of his stare. Suddenly the idea of sitting on a bench like a punished child was too much. I needed air. I needed solitude. I needed blood.

"I'm out of here." I wasn't sure if those words were for Giguhl's benefit or my own.

The Mischief demon shot me a look. "Why do I get the impression this isn't just about the penalty?"

"This is lame, G. I'm not cut out for roller derby." And by "roller derby," I really meant roller derby *and* everything else my life had become. Predictable, settled. Safe.

"Well, excuse me, Miss Thang. I thought you'd enjoy a new hobby. You're the one always bitching about being bored."

"Skating in a circle wearing fishnets and a helmet isn't exactly my idea of a good time, G."

The demon's eyes narrowed. "You and Adam been having problems?"

My stomach dropped. I crossed my arms and glared at my best friend. "No." It wasn't a lie, exactly, since the problem in that equation was me, not the mancy.

The demon pursed his lips. "Is it already that time of the season, then?"

Unlike mortal women, most vampire females ovulate only once a quarter, usually corresponding to the solstice and equinox schedule. As it happened, we were still a few weeks out from the vernal equinox. "Jesus, can't a girl want to inflict a little pain without being sexually frustrated or on the rag?"

We both paused to watch the healers carry Ima Cutchoo off the rink on a stretcher. She was alive but probably had a pretty intense round of healing spells in her near future to repair the broken spine. As they carried her off, her eyes found me. It'd been so long since I made a new enemy, I almost enjoyed seeing the hatred burning in her eyes.

Once she was gone, Giguhl turned back to me. "Then what's your deal, Red?"

It's been 114 days since I killed anyone. And I don't know who I am anymore.